A Penny Parcel

A PENNY PARCEL

Avery E. Hitch

Cover models: Sterling Hitch, Matthias Wissmann, Stephen Wissmann, Austin Wubbels, Hannah Wissmann, Havilah Hitch, Sarah Howat, Joshua Howat, Bristol Hitch, Tanner Wubbels, Susanna Wissmann & Alaythia Wissmann.

WinePress Publishing (PO Box 428, Enumclaw, WA 98022) functions only as book publisher. As such, the ultimate design, content, editorial accuracy, and views expressed or implied in this work are those of the author.

Unless otherwise noted, all Scriptures are taken from the 1905 Workman's Edition King James Bible.

ISBN 13: 978-1-57921-840-9
ISBN 10: 1-57921-840-7
Library of Congress Catalog Card Number: 2006900374

To Jesus,
because He chose me when
I was an orphan and
taught me truth.

Thank you, Lacey

Table of Contents

1. Wounded 13
2. The Upper Crust 43
3. The Orphanage 49
4. Mr. Bowtie and the Baby 57
5. A Baby Doll Family 63
6. Decision & Dread 77
7. "Forever?" 89
8. A New House 99
9. The Apothecary 121
10. Gray Skies 131
11. The Reputation 141
12. Crossfire 159
13. Discipline & Disaster 169
14. Six Sundays Spent 181
15. Ruth's Family 197
16. OPEN 209
17. The Trophy 217
18. A Visit from Mrs. Harms 225
19. The Pitiful Party 231
20. Chickens 245
21. Escape 255
22. The Tanners 263
23. Of Social Situations 271

24. Consequences 279
25. Pain 289
26. Being Free 297
27. Truth 303
28. Visitors 311
29. Changes 325
30. Going Home 333
31. Christian Men 347
32. Courage & Resolution 363
33. Miracle 369
34. Wesley's Reservations 381
35. A Game 391
36. Mama's Little Angels 399
37. Company 409
38. To Choose Love 421
39. Holiday Traditions 433
40. A Christmas Present 439
41. Luke's Promise 449
42. Violated 469
43. Mr. Bowtie's Secret Ties 477

ONE

Wounded

Ashley stared up at the grisly man and wondered why he kept asking her age. "Six years old," she repeated for the third time. This time he smiled, and she smiled back.

"Six years old, 'ey?" His voice was kind, and he touched her arm gently. "What a nice little girl. Well, Martha, you did good on this one. Real fine." He tipped Ashley's chin and looked at her. "Just the right age too. Have you shown her around the place?"

The chubby woman shook her head and banged a spoon against the pot she was holding. The porch looked ready to fall down on top of her, and the floor sagged beneath. "Haven't had a spare minute since I got home. The children are out and about, and my back hurts like the devil. Give her a tour; supper ain't ready yet anyway."

The man took Ashley's little white hand in his and started off on a walk. She followed him willingly. Finally it was her turn to have a family.

"Have you ever lived on a farm?" Mr. Berk asked, and Ashley shook her blonde head. "We'll teach you how to do it. Have you met the other children?" She shook her head again. "There are three of them. You'll get along well enough. I expect you'll be accustomed to our style of living in just a couple weeks."

He strolled on a grassy path toward a large red barn and pointed out the pasture and the privy on the way. Ashley felt safe standing beside such a big, protective man. She sidled close to him and rubbed his hand with her thumb. So this was what it was like to have a daddy.

"I work at the factory," Mr. Berk said. "The children and Miss Martha take care of the farm during the day, and I do the rest of the work at night. You'll have chores while you're staying with us. Everyone has to carry their own load. Mind you get your work done, so we can all be happy. This is the barn, where we keep our horse and two chickens. Miss Martha will have you doing work in the house mostly. The boys do the barn chores. What's your name again, sweetheart?"

Ashley told him, melting like butter when he talked so gently.

"That's a lovely name. You have a sister now; her name's Bonnie, and she's—what is she?—I think she's about nine now. She's a sweet thing. You'll share a bedroom with her; how's that?"

Ashley nodded and smiled.

Mr. Berk briefly showed her the stench-filled barn, and then they returned to the house. Mr. Berk introduced Ashley to his children, Jack, Henry and Bonnie. The boys had full heads of dark hair and they were brawny and tall. Bonnie, a cold-faced girl, stared at Ashley and made her squirm. Ashley held tightly to Mr. Berk's hand and relaxed. She sat next to him during supper and kissed him good night at bedtime.

The other children ignored their father as if he didn't exist. They didn't talk to him during supper and they went to bed without acknowledging him. In the attic bedroom that night, Bonnie bounced onto the bed, saying with a cock of her head, "You talk to Pop too much."

Ashley said boldly, "You're ungrateful. You have a daddy and you don't even talk to him."

"Not ungrateful," Bonnie said as she stripped off her clothes. She stared at the new girl and her dark eyes sneered. "Father is perfectly wonderful when he's at work. Haven't you ever had a father before?"

"No." Ashley took off her old, brown shoes and wondered if she'd ever get a pair as nice as Bonnie's. They were shiny and black, and the laces were brand new.

"Oh. Well, Mother says that men are all the same. You can marry for love, but you'll die for loneliness."

Ashley quietly put on her nightdress and slipped between the cold sheets. The mattress was poky and lumpy, and the bed squeaked when Bonnie lay down beside her.

"I get most of the bed 'cause I'm older and bigger than you," Bonnie said. She shoved Ashley toward the outside and Ashley grabbed the headboard to keep from falling off.

"Leave me enough room to sleep, at least," Ashley retorted, scooting back. Bonnie turned over and pressed against Ashley until the six-year-old yielded and slept on her side on the very edge of the bed.

In the darkness, Ashley heard crickets, and frogs sang a song somewhere outside. This was her first night ever outside the orphanage walls, and she felt strangely lonely. She had dreamed of having a real family ever since the other orphans had put the idea into her head, and she had finally arrived at her destination. Even though the attic was dusty and smelled of mold and sweat, it could be home. At least she had a family.

The next morning, Bonnie woke Ashley early. The girls dressed and scurried downstairs, where Mrs. Berk was making breakfast. Ashley was disappointed to be told that Mr. Berk had already gone to work. Mrs. Berk frigidly told the girls that Jack and Henry were in the barn and would soon be going to school. Bonnie and Ashley were to get water from the creek.

"You can't go to school 'cause you're too young," Bonnie explained as they made their way to the cold creek in the middle of the pasture. "Father doesn't send us till we're at least eight 'cause he wants us to help Mother. I didn't go till this year."

"What will I do here?" asked Ashley in a squeaky voice.

"Stay with Mother. She'll cook and clean, and you'll watch the chickens. We have to watch them during the day because sometimes they get out of their cage and wander from home. Father straps Jack and Henry if the chickens get away."

"Oh." Ashley didn't know what "strapping" was. The boys at the orphanage had talked about being strapped by their fathers before they were orphans.

"You must watch the chickens very carefully," Bonnie said, getting very close to Ashley's face. She dipped a bucket into the creek and brought it up dripping. "Else you get strapped with the boys."

"I can watch two silly chickens," Ashley said.

Bonnie gave her a warning glare as they returned to the house.

Sitting on a log stool in front of the chicken pen, Ashley rested her chin in her hands. Mrs. Berk hummed loudly and off-key from where she was cooking a pot of stew over a fire in the yard. Ashley plugged her ears. The orphan girls had told her she couldn't sing, but Ashley was sure she could sing better than Mrs. Berk.

The two hens squawked in the pen, and Ashley glued her eyes on them. One was jet black and the other was red and white. They had glassy eyes and short beaks that pecked at the ground and the remainder of the corn that Jack had thrown that morning. The red one was bigger than the black one and Ashley wondered if the red one was a boy. It reminded her of the orphanage boys as it pecked at the black one's back and screeched every time the black one came near. The boys at the orphanage were bullies, just like that red chicken. They were always playing tricks on the girls and using their strength to conquer.

The red chicken jumped at the fence and flapped its wings as it tried to fly. Ashley laughed at it. What a stupid bird. There was no way it could get over the tall fence. Not even a six-year-old girl could get out of that fence if she were locked in.

Ashley became bored very quickly and she wandered into the barn. The sun was hot and the dusty cool of the barn made her sigh. Mrs. Berk had told her to watch the chickens, but she hadn't said that she couldn't play while she was doing it. Occasionally, Ashley looked back at the pen and the two birds. She saw the red hen eat a fat grasshopper and squealed out loud. Mrs. Berk yelled at her from the porch, and Ashley fell silent. She hadn't realized that chicken-watching was such a tedious job.

Mr. Berk returned from work after the children were in their beds.

"I'm going to see Daddy," Ashley announced when she heard the parents talking downstairs.

"I wouldn't," warned Bonnie. "He just got home from work. It's late. Leave him alone."

"Why? I'm sure he wants to see me."

"No, he doesn't. He's tired."

"Doesn't he say good night?"

"No." Bonnie dropped onto her pillow and lay on her back with her hands crossed under her head.

"Do you like school?" Ashley asked.

"Yes."

"Why?"

"'Cause I have friends there. Besides, why would I want to stay here with you all day? You're a baby."

"I am?"

"Yes. Only babies have to stay home. Important people go to school and become something."

"You stayed home when you were my age."

"Yes, well, I wasn't as stupid as you when I was your age."

"What do you mean?" Ashley's lip quivered.

"Just be quiet and go to sleep. I'm tired and I have a test tomorrow."

"What do you think I'll have to do tomorrow?" asked Ashley.

Bonnie rolled over and Ashley felt a spring in her back. "Watch the chickens."

"Again?"

"Why do you think we adopted you?"

"That's all I'm going to do?"

"Yup. Father and Mother didn't have a baby after me, so they needed another kid to watch chickens. Labor. That's all you're good for."

Ashley didn't know what labor was, but she supposed it was watching chickens. "Don't I ever get to cook?"

"Nope. After we get home from school and do chores, Mother lets us play until supper. If Father's home, I go to bed right after."

"Why don't you stay up and talk to him?"

"Why should I?" Bonnie looked at Ashley over her shoulder.

"'Cause he's your daddy! Bonnie, you don't know what it's like not to have a daddy. You should be more thankful."

Bonnie closed her eyes. "Thank you, God, for Father," she said in a mocking voice. "What a nice man You gave to be my daddy. Amen. There. Happy?"

"That wasn't very long."

"Make up for me. Pray your little heart out. Pray that you don't lose any chickens tomorrow."

Ashley grew to despise chickens. She complained every day until Mrs. Berk threatened to send her back to the orphanage. Then she busied herself in the smelly barn and around the coop and half-heartedly watched them. She named the red chicken Ronny because it was a persistent bully like the Ronny at the orphanage. The black hen was named Katie after KatieAnne, Ashley's shy orphan friend. No matter how many times Bonnie told Ashley that Ronny was a girl, the six-year-old still called her Ronny. She scolded Ronny through the fence every time the old hen attacked Katie, and during the long hours she spent alone, Ashley searched for bugs to feed Katie. She drew pictures in the dirt and built a tipsy tower out of the logs that were piled by the chicken coop.

She told herself stories, sang songs that she used to sing with the orphan girls, and found pictures in the clouds.

Ronny and Katie squawked and fought, but they never tried to get out. There were at least ten holes in the flimsy wire fence, but Ronny and Katie steered clear of them. They stayed in the middle of the pen and picked at dead weeds and oblivious bugs and the corn that Jack threw.

One afternoon, Ashley had the grand idea that she would repair the chicken coop for Mr. Berk. She took down her tower and placed one log over every hole in the fence. When Ashley finished patching, she sat down and watched Ronny and Katie. Mrs. Berk was inside the house, and the farm was quiet. A single bird sang in the tree by the porch, and as Ashley listened to it, she studied Ronny. The grouchy hen pecked on every chunk of wood Ashley had rested against the fence. After several pushes against the barrier, the weary chicken finally gave in.

Ashley smiled to herself. "All fixed," she whispered. "The chickens will never get out again."

Ashley stood from her stool and clapped her hands together. She looked toward the house. When she didn't see Mrs. Berk, Ashley slipped away under the pasture fence. She needed a drink from the creek, and then she would play in the forest and check on the hens every once in a while. Not that she had to; not even cunning Ronny had any chance of making it through her patches.

Ashley skipped down to the creek and dipped her hands in the ice-cold water. The summer sun was hot, and she washed her face and blinked her eyes in surprise. The water at the orphanage was always slightly warm. Ashley took off her old, brown shoes and stuck her feet into the water. She lay back on the grass and sighed in contentment. So this was what it was like to be free. Free from the orphanage. Free from Mrs. Harms and Miss Elizabeth. Free from school, where she had spent the past two years toiling over words and sums. Freedom was just as wonderful as the other orphans told her it would be.

The little girl closed her eyes against the blinding sun and rested her arm on her forehead. Her feet were soon numb from the cold water, and the sun beat down on her and made her toasty warm. Soon, little Ashley fell asleep.

Darkness was creeping up on the Vermont countryside when she awoke. She sat up with a start and pulled her aching feet out of the water. She crawled for her shoes, which were scattered on the bank a little distance away, and when she pulled her stockings on, her eyes smarted in pain. Not even the thick shoes could take away the stiffness of her feet.

Ashley painfully limped toward the farm. She saw Mr. Berk's horse tied at the hitching post, and she heard loud noises coming from inside the house. The boys and Bonnie would be home by now. It was probably already suppertime.

Ashley hurried through the tall pasture grass and slipped under the fence. She rubbed her arms with the evening chill and trotted toward the house. Mr. Berk would be waiting to give her a hug, and kiss her and tell her what a good girl she was. She had patched the chicken fence for good; there would be no more labor. Now Ashley could help with cooking and sweeping, and she could play while Bonnie was at school.

The shouting got louder, and Ashley hesitated. She heard Jack yelling, and then Mr. Berk's deep voice interrupted him. The front door swung open and Jack stumbled onto the porch. Henry followed, and he tripped and fell. Mr. Berk yelled a foul name. Ashley froze in her tracks. She ducked behind a tree, her heart racing. Mr. Berk came out the door and kicked Henry until the boy stood and obeyed the command to go to the woodshed. Jack tried to fight, but Mr. Berk slapped him and the boy ran ahead.

"Both my chickens—gone!" Mr. Berk screamed. Ashley gasped. She glanced back at the chicken coop and wildly searched for the feathery hens. There was no trace of them.

"We didn't do it!" Jack screamed.

Mr. Berk leapt off the porch and the boys ran toward the woodshed.

"Don't talk back to me," Mr. Berk yelled. Ashley cowered and trembled behind the tree. "What an idiot of a boy! You know full well that you're in charge of my hens, and you purposefully let them out to provoke me. You know you shouldn't cross me. Stupid boy," he muttered under his breath.

Mr. Berk passed Ashley's tree, and the little girl cowered behind it. The woodshed door slammed when the boys entered it. Ashley saw Mr. Berk unbuckle his belt.

Bonnie was quiet in bed that night. She gave Ashley most of the covers and all but one foot of the mattress. Ashley snuggled under the covers and pulled them up to her chin. She remembered the talk Mr. Berk had had when she confessed that she had neglected the chickens. He had sat her on his knee and told her she must repair the fence better next time. And she must watch the chickens. If they got away again, she would get in trouble.

Mr. Berk said that Jack and Henry deserved to be strapped. They were impertinent and rude, and Mr. Berk must make them into good men. Ashley was sweet and gentle, and Mr. Berk would deal kindly with her. But she must watch the chickens. They were rare, precious animals.

The screen door slammed downstairs, and Ashley jumped. Bonnie sighed when two sets of footsteps came up the stairs.

"Did you find them?" Bonnie called when the boys passed by their room.

Henry kicked the door open, then stomped by. Jack entered and approached Ashley's side of the bed. She saw his big form move carefully, as if he hurt. He bent over her. Ashley's eyes grew wide. She could sense his strength as he rested his hands on the bed on either side of her. She felt his breath on her face.

"If you ever leave that chicken coop again, I'll lock you up in it," Jack seethed. She pushed him away in panic. He caught her arm and shoved it down on the bed. "Do you understand me?"

Ashley saw his eyes in the darkness, and she cringed. One was swelled.

He pressed her wrists down on the bed. "I'll lock you in that coop and build a log house around it, and you can eat corn with the chickens. Don't you ever leave your log seat again—never. Not even if you're wasting away with hunger or dying of thirst. If you ever let those chickens out of your sight, even for one second, I'll kill you. I'll grind your poor little soul into the dirt. Then I'll feed you to the wolves." Jack's hand trembled and it made Ashley's whole body break out in a cold sweat. He tried to straighten, but groaned in pain.

"They were roosted in the forest," Jack told his sister as he moved toward the door. "Not a feather harmed. Not a single feather."

As he left, Ashley heard Bonnie sniffle.

Ashley watched the chickens better the next day. She spent two hours patching the fence. Even though she was sure that Ronny and Katie couldn't get out this time, she didn't leave the area. She didn't want to find out what it would be like to be fed to a pack of hungry wolves. No wonder Mr. Berk strapped Jack. He was a naughty boy.

When the boys came home, Jack immediately went to the chicken coop. He passed Ashley as she sat on her log stool and she noticed that the swelling around his eye had gone down, but he winced as he walked. Jack gathered the chickens in his arms and locked them in the barn for the night. Then he retreated to the house without praising Ashley or inviting her to supper.

When Mr. Berk came home he sat Ashley on his lap and asked, "Did you watch my chickens today, sugar?"

She smiled. "Yes. They're safe."

"Good girl." He patted her head. He was holding a bottle in his hand. Ashley had seen bottles like that on the street, and Miss Elizabeth had told her not to touch them. She said they were vile and nasty. Miss Elizabeth must have been wrong. Mr. Berk would never touch something vile and nasty.

Supper was quiet. Jack and Henry stared at their plates the entire time, then went to bed immediately after. Bonnie helped her mother clean the kitchen while Ashley sat on Mr. Berk's lap. He told her a silly story and stopped midway through to laugh until his big belly jostled.

When Mr. Berk retired to bed, Ashley saw Bonnie take his bottle and dump it out the back door.

"We don't have school tomorrow," Bonnie told Ashley that night. "Jack and Henry have to weed the garden. I'm going to my friend's house in town."

"What will I do?" asked Ashley.

"My chores."

"Your chores?"

"Well, someone has to do them." Bonnie glanced at Ashley. "Just because you were an orphan doesn't mean you get special privileges. I've been waiting a long time to have a little sister. I'm older, so it's only fair that I get to spend some time with my friends while you stay home. You must do everything Mother tells you to do, and make sure you get all the chores done well. Father will be home early tomorrow. I don't want him to think I slacked off with my work."

"But I have my own chores. I have to watch the chickens."

"Father goes to work early tomorrow, so Jack won't let the chickens out into the pen until right before Father gets home. You mustn't tell Father they weren't out all day. Do you understand? If you tell Father, Jack will get strapped again. And I'll make sure you get strapped too."

"Daddy won't hurt me."

Bonnie's eyes narrowed. "I'm warning you, Ashley: be good. Don't argue or backtalk or try to blame anyone else. When Father brings his bottle home, you must be especially good. Go to bed as soon as you can."

"I don't want to go to bed. Daddy tells me stories. I like sitting up with him."

"You just don't get it, do you?" Bonnie shook her head. "Well, if you're too stupid to take my advice, fine. Learn the hard way. But don't say I didn't warn you."

Ashley turned over angrily, and Bonnie finally left her alone.

Ashley did all of Bonnie's chores the next day. She swept the floor, washed the dishes, scrubbed Mrs. Berk's enormous kettle, and filled the wood box to overflowing. Then she went to check on Ronny and Katie. Jack and Henry were in the garden, and Ashley snuck past them to the barn. There, the chickens were locked up in a tiny cage against the wall. Corn was scattered under the cage, and Katie was pecking at it through the wire. Ronny had her head tucked in her wing when Ashley arrived, but as soon as she heard the barn door slam, she began cackling loudly. Ashley tried to pet Katie through the cage, but Ronny pecked her finger.

"You're a naughty bird," Ashley said, sucking on her finger. Ronny jumped on Katie's back and began pecking her head. Ashley shrieked at her. She found a stick and poked it at Ronny, but the hen kept pecking. Katie fought and complained. When Katie fell slack and silent, Ashley thought Ronny must have killed her.

"You're a bad, bad bird!" Ashley screamed, violently poking at Ronny. She unlatched the cage door. Ronny jumped out and flapped her wings in Ashley's face. When Ronnie flew away, Ashley touched Katie. The bird revived and followed her friend.

Just then Jack came running into the barn.

"You let them out," Jack yelled. "Henry! Come quick! The chickens are out!" The boy ran after Katie, but she followed Ronny through a hole in the wall and into the forest. Jack ran out the barn door and nearly collided with Henry. Henry called Ashley a foul name and ran after the hens.

Ashley heard the boys pounding through the forest. She poked her head out the barn door and saw them winding through the trees. Ronny and Katie cackled and screeched, and Ronny flew to a short branch in a pine tree. Katie tried to follow, but Henry came down on her back and squeezed her in his hands. Jack got a stick and knocked Ronny out of the tree, then dove after her. He caught her by the foot and dragged her into his arms. Ronny pecked and fought until Jack squeezed her head in his hand. Then she was silent.

"Why'd you let them out?" Jack yelled as he and Henry marched toward Ashley.

"The cage is too small. Ronny was hurting Katie."

"Ronny and Katie?" Henry laughed.

Jack gave her an angry frown. "What were you planning to do with them? Let them run loose?"

"I was going to put them in their pen," said Ashley.

Jack grabbed her arm in a painful grip. She squealed and tried to get away, but he jerked and dragged her behind him.

"You want to put them in their pen?" Jack fumed. "Fine. You can watch them, then. You can make sure they don't get out of that holey cage. You can sit in there with them and make sure Ronny doesn't hurt Katie."

As they neared the chicken coop, Jack opened the door and shoved Ashley through it. She stumbled and almost fell, but caught herself on the fence. Henry threw Katie in after her, and Jack dropped Ronny just inside the coop. Jack slammed the door and locked it. "If you let one of those hens so much as peck outside this pen, you'll regret it, twerp. I'll be watching you from the garden."

Ashley tried for the entire afternoon to get out of the chicken coop. She tried to crawl through the holes, but the logs she had used to repair the fence were too heavy for her to move from the inside. She tried to crawl up the fence, but it bent beneath her weight. She jumped, dug, and tore. The lock was strong and out of her reach. The fence was tall, and there was no way she could escape.

Through all her struggle, Ashley didn't make a single peep. She knew Jack and Henry were watching her from the garden. She wasn't going to give them the satisfaction of hearing her cry.

When darkness fell, Ashley collapsed beside the fence. The ground was covered in chicken manure, but she didn't care. Ronny and Katie found a corner and nestled into it. Ashley wanted to cry, but she held off until Mr. Berk could see how much Jack and Henry had traumatized her. Those naughty boys would get strapped, and they would deserve it.

Jack and Henry went into the house, and Ashley wondered if Mrs. Berk would miss her. Bonnie came home, but she didn't look for Ashley. Finally, Ashley saw a horse coming down the lane, and she jumped to her feet. Just before she called for Daddy, Ashley saw that Mr. Berk was not the only man on the horse. There was another one; he was incredibly tall. The man stopped the horse at the hitching post and Mrs. Berk came out the door. Then the man pulled Mr. Berk off the horse and dragged him inside. Ashley wondered if Daddy was hurt. Surely not. He was singing.

The man came out of the house after a few minutes. He mounted the horse and rode away, and Ashley wilted in desperation. She screamed for Mr. Berk. Eventually, she succumbed to bawling, and then to sobs. The nighttime air was thick, and the hens scolded her for not letting them sleep. At last, when the moon was the only light in the sky, Ashley lay down beside the fence and fell asleep.

When she awoke in the morning, Ashley was stiff, and she got up slowly. When she saw where she was her heart dropped to her toes. The countryside was still. Mrs. Berk wasn't outside. Jack and Henry weren't in the garden. Bonnie wasn't sweeping the porch.

Ashley hollered for help. She looked in every direction, but didn't see any sign of life. She looked for the chickens. Ronny and Katie were gone.

Frantically, her eyes darted around the chicken coop. To her great mortification she found a large hole, apparently made by some animal during the night. One of Katie's black feathers was caught on the poky wire.

Ashley pulled at the fence and eventually made the hole bigger. She crawled out of it, and the wire scratched her arms and her face. Once she was free, Ashley ran to the house. She swung open the screen door. When she heard Mrs. Berk humming, she collapsed in a chair.

"My lands, child, what are you doing?" Mrs. Berk scolded from the kitchen.

"The chickens got out," Ashley said.

"Go find them!" Mrs. Berk exclaimed.

"I can't. I don't know how. They're probably far away in the forest."

"Get out of this house and find those chickens, missy. I don't care if you don't come back till next week; don't come back without them."

Mrs. Berk stomped toward Ashley with the broom, and the little girl flew out the door. Weak with hunger and trembling from fear and exhaustion, she collapsed on the porch for one second, but Mrs. Berk was on her heels. She ran toward the forest, refusing to allow fear to cripple her.

Ashley searched until she thought the other children would be home from school. She was just coming out of the forest when she sighted Bonnie and tears sprung to her eyes.

"You didn't find them?" Bonnie hollered.

Ashley's shoulders drooped.

"You can't come home without them."

"But they're not in there." Ashley's voice faltered. "I looked everywhere. They must've gone to the pasture."

Bonnie shook her head and Ashley heard her swear under her breath. "They never go to the pasture; they're probably roosting in a tree somewhere. Father's going to be home soon. You have to find them."

"He'll understand. I'm going to tell him what Jack did to me. He locked me in the chicken coop, Bonnie! I spent the whole night in there!"

"You deserved it. You let the chickens out when you knew you shouldn't have. Now you've lost them. Jack's going to get in just as much trouble as you are if you don't find those hens. Go back and look!"

"I'm not going to!" Ashley stomped her foot and then wearily sat on a log. Her stomach was a tight knot of hunger, and her head pounded mercilessly. Just thinking of returning to the forest made her ache worse.

"You are going back." Bonnie grabbed Ashley's wrist and yanked her to her feet. Ashley pulled back and fell to the ground. When she started crying, Bonnie shouted at her and pulled her up again. She shoved her into the forest and followed, scolding the entire way. Ashley tried to fight back, but she was too weak.

Mr. Berk came home before Jack and Henry. The girls were still hunting near the edge of the forest, and when Bonnie saw him, she shrunk back and hid Ashley behind a tree. The way Bonnie gripped her shoulders to hide her from Mr. Berk made Ashley nervous. She didn't think Mr. Berk would hurt her, but Bonnie was obviously afraid of him.

Mr. Berk went to the chicken coop first. When he saw the hole in the fence and the missing hens, his face turned red.

"Martha!" Mr. Berk screamed, and Ashley cowered behind the tree. "Where are my chickens?"

Mrs. Berk came out the front door and put her hands on her hips. "Cool your temper. They've run away, but the children will find them. Just come inside and stop fretting."

"Who lost my chickens?" Mr. Berk yelled.

"What does it matter?" Mrs. Berk turned around.

"It matters to me. Answer me, woman!"

"The new girl lost them. They escaped through a hole in the fence. She'll find them." Mrs. Berk entered the house and slammed the screen door, but Mr. Berk didn't follow. He sat on Ashley's stool and waited.

"He's going to stay there until we come back," Bonnie whispered. "If the chickens aren't with us, we're done for."

"Maybe he can help us find them," Ashley said as she took a step away from the tree.

"Don't!" Bonnie grabbed her shoulder. "Leave him alone, Ashley. Please. Just look for the chickens."

Ashley was too weak and hungry to look anymore. She ran away from Bonnie and the forest, and straight to Mr. Berk. When the man laid eyes on her, she expected tenderness, but she saw anger.

"Where are my chickens?" Mr. Berk demanded.

"Jack locked me in the chicken coop," Ashley said. "I was there all night, and when I woke up they were gone. I'm so hungry. I've been searching all day."

Ashley fell into his arms. His stiff hands gripped her arms. Ashley tried to pull away, but he didn't let go. "I told you that you would get in trouble if you lost my chickens. I told you to watch them. You knew what would happen if you lost them! You're a miserable, irresponsible child. Ungrateful! You're a naughty little devil who will never make a good woman."

Mr. Berk stood and his grip made Ashley shriek in pain. She shrunk back in terror but was too weak to fight. Mr. Berk dragged her to the woodshed and her feet left the ground. Ashley heard Bonnie scream from the edge of the forest when he reached for his belt.

Ashley understood now. It was a very bad thing to be naughty, and saying sorry was no use. It was Daddy's responsibility to make good men and women out of his children. It was very easy to be good. You just had to watch the chickens.

Jack and Henry found Ronny and Katie when they got home from school. They were in their little cage in the barn when Ashley fell into bed. Ashley was still sobbing when Jack and Henry came upstairs. Jack entered and approached her.

"You all right?" he asked with surprising warmth in his voice. He touched her arm, and she winced and pulled away. "I'm sorry."

"Don't touch me." Ashley wanted to be embraced and held and comforted, but it hurt too much.

"It's not in your head or your face, is it?"

"No."

"Good." Jack stroked her hair and Ashley saw pity on his face. "He usually leaves that alone. Did you get something to eat?"

"No. Go away."

"I'm trying to help."

"You locked me in the chicken coop."

"I was trying to teach you a lesson so he wouldn't have to. Spending a night in the chicken coop isn't half as painful as this."

Ashley closed her eyes and breathed through the ache. She hadn't had food in a full day, but she wasn't hungry. She wanted to throw up.

"It'll be better tomorrow," Jack said. "I'll fix the coop before I go to school in the morning. All you have to do is watch the chickens. I'll put them away before Father comes home."

"I don't want to watch them." Ashley's voice broke. "What if they get out?"

"They won't. I'll make sure the coop is safe. Henry and I will come home early tomorrow, just in case you've lost them. We can find them before Father gets back." Jack touched Ashley's hair again. "Are you sure you're all right?"

"I don't know."

"Can you breathe OK?"

"Yeah."

"Good. You'll heal. Don't worry; it's not permanent. Just be good, Ashley. Be really, really good. Stay away from him. We'll try to help you."

Jack touched her hair once more, nodded at Bonnie, and left. Ashley tried to roll over but the sting in her legs was too painful. Bonnie had given her cool cloths, but they didn't help much. They were hot now, and the weight of them made the pain even worse.

"Don't worry, Ashley," Bonnie whispered. She stroked the little girl's back and squeezed her shoulder. "It'll be better in the morning. You don't even have to see Father tomorrow. We'll go to bed early."

"Why does he care so much about the chickens?" Ashley squeaked.

Bonnie continued to rub Ashley's back. She was silent for a long time. "He drinks too much," she said. "He's been drinking since he was Jack's age. Sometimes, even when he's not drinking, he kind of goes insane."

"What does that mean?"

"It means he doesn't know what's going on and he makes us do stuff that's stupid 'cause he thinks it's important. Mother says that a long time ago, Father raised chickens and won lots of money for them in contests. These two chickens are the last ones he has, and he thinks he's going to win a ribbon with them and get enough money that he won't ever have to work again. He thinks that if he loses the chickens, he'll be poor the rest of his life."

Ashley nodded. All she could think about was going back to the orphanage. Mrs. Harms and Miss Elizabeth would comfort her. They might even get Mr. Berk in trouble. She just had to find a way back to the orphanage.

Ashley watched the chickens with powerful determination from that day on. Jack and Henry came home early as often as possible, and Ashley learned how to lock up the chickens before Mr. Berk arrived. She lived in constant fear that something would happen. Often she awoke with dreams of the chickens escaping. Once she snuck through the dark, eerie night to make sure they were still in their cage.

The bruises healed quickly enough, but the belt left permanent marks on Ashley's legs. When the bruises finally disappeared, many of the wounds turned into scars.

Mr. Berk was very kind to Ashley as long as the chickens were safe. He brought her candy and told her stories at night. He read her books and stroked her hair and called her pet names that made her melt inside. Ashley tried to keep up her defenses, but she was starved for love and accepted it in any form.

"We're having company today," Bonnie told Ashley one sunny morning in late summer. "Father has friends from town who are coming to supper. When I get home from school, we'll help Mother make supper, and then we can play. Father might make us sit a little while, but he doesn't like us around much. Jack said we can go swimming."

Ashley's eyes shone. "In the creek?"

"Yeah. It's cold at night, but we like to go, anyway. Sometimes Mother lets us sleep in the barn after we swim. If we get too wet, she makes us dry our clothes before we come inside."

"Can I leave the chickens in their cage today?" asked Ashley.

Bonnie's eyes narrowed. "Father probably already put them in the coop. If he comes home early and finds them in the cage, you'll be sorry."

Ashley shuddered. She wasn't willing to take chances.

"Just watch them, like usual. You can use my slate and pen to draw if you want."

When the company arrived in mid-afternoon, Mr. Berk was already home.

The boys put the hens away the minute they returned from school, and Ashley checked the cage lock three times. Then she and Bonnie went to help with supper.

"This is our new little girl," Mr. Berk said when Ashley stepped through the door. "Her name is Ashley."

A kind-looking woman sat in Mrs. Berk's broken rocker holding a baby. She smiled at Ashley. The man nodded in approval, and Ashley stared at him. He seemed to be looking right through her.

"She's a true gem," Mr. Berk said. He put his hand on Ashley's shoulder and she cuddled next to him.

Mr. Berk and the man began talking, and Bonnie and Ashley helped Mrs. Berk finish supper. When it was on the table, the boys came in, and everyone sat down. Jack and Henry talked with the man, and Ashley heard them laugh. She had never heard either boy laugh.

Mrs. Berk told Ashley to get the jelly from the kitchen. She obeyed, and just as she grabbed the jar off the counter, the woman with the baby came into the kitchen.

"How are you, darlin'?" she asked tenderly.

Ashley spun around and stared, wide-eyed. "Fine," she muttered.

"I need to ask you a question. You don't have to tell me everything, but I want to help. Just answer me this one question?"

Ashley nodded. She twisted the jelly jar in her hand.

"Does your new father ever . . . hurt you?"

Ashley stared at the woman. She wanted to cry. She wanted to tell her what had happened. She wanted to explain about the chickens and Jack and Henry and the hole in the fence. She stood frozen for a moment, and mumbled, "Kind of."

"Might I help you, madam?" Mr. Berk's voice boomed. Ashley's heart sank. The man stood in the doorway of the kitchen, watching.

"I was just talking to Ashley about her new home," the lady said. "She's glad to be away from the orphanage. Aren't you, sweetheart?"

Ashley nodded with a baffled stare.

"Yes, well, come along, Ashley; Mother needs the jelly. No more loitering, sugar."

Ashley walked past the lady and into the dining room. Mr. Berk followed. When Ashley took her seat, she saw Bonnie's eyes on her, and she read warning. She had done something wrong.

The children were dismissed shortly after supper, and they scurried to the creek. Bonnie told Ashley to walk with Henry, and she hung behind with Jack and whispered all the way. Ashley wondered what she had to say.

When they reached the creek and plunged into the cold water, Jack watched Ashley like a buck protecting his doe. Every time the house door slammed, Jack stood and looked toward the porch. Ashley felt the tension in the air, but she didn't know what it meant. Maybe the company was bad. Maybe the children wanted them to leave.

"Let's go to bed. I'm plumb tuckered out and it's cold out here," Henry said as he dropped onto the creek bed and spread his arms.

"Baby," Bonnie snickered, splashing him. Henry kicked back at her and she plopped into the creek with a shriek.

Jack stood and looked toward the porch, and everyone froze.

"Why do you keep doing that?" Henry asked. "It's just the company leaving. The chickens are in their pen."

"I know." Jack looked at him critically. "I'm not worried about the chickens." He glanced at Ashley, and she began trembling.

The children abandoned the creek and fled to the barn. Bonnie and Henry made a big bed out of the straw pile while Jack sat on the edge of the loft and wrung out his shirt. His jaw clenched over and over, and the muscles in his arms bulged every time he squeezed.

"He's fretting over nothing," Henry told Ashley. "Jack's always been a worrier. He probably has a spelling bee tomorrow, and he knows he's gonna fail." Henry laughed, but Bonnie didn't.

All the children jumped when the barn door opened.

"Where's that girl?" Mr. Berk hollered. Ashley dove into the straw pile.

"We just got home from swimming. She's asleep," Jack lied.

"I don't care. Get her down here. She spilled her guts to that good-for-nothing woman, and she's got consequences to face."

"She didn't spill her guts," Jack said. He looked down on the brawny form of his father. "That good-for-nothing woman tried to squeak something out of her, but she wouldn't tell."

"She did too! I heard her. Give her to me now, Jack, or you're going to regret it."

Jack stiffened. "Deal with it in the morning, Pop. She's asleep."

Mr. Berk made it up the ladder before Jack could shove it away from the loft. He hit Jack, then yanked Ashley from the straw and belted her. Bonnie shrieked. Henry tried to grab the belt, but Mr. Berk hit him too.

Jack scrambled to his feet. He received several lashes before he pulled the belt from his father's hand and then pushed Ashley away. She fell back into the straw, hot tears streaking down her cheeks.

"Leave her alone!" Jack screamed. Henry and Bonnie retreated behind the straw.

"She's gotta learn her own lessons!" Mr. Berk grabbed at the belt, but Jack threw it to the barn floor. "Step out of my way, Jackson. Let her take her lumps without getting in the middle of it."

Jack stepped between his father and Ashley. "She's just a little girl. Talk to her. Let me belt her. I'll do just as good a job as you will, I promise. I'll teach her her lessons. I'll make her watch the chickens. I'll teach her not to talk. Go to bed. I'll take care of her."

"You don't have the guts to make anything cry," Mr. Berk sneered. "You're as soft as a woman. There's not a nerve in your body, Jack Berk. You couldn't belt a grown man if he were killing you."

"I'll do it." Jack stood tall and reached for his own belt. "I'll make her cry. I guarantee you she'll change. You'll never lose another chicken in your life."

Mr. Berk spit on Jack's shoe. "If you won't let me give her her lumps, you'll have to take them yourself. Be a martyr. Somebody's gotta pay."

Silence ruled the loft, and Ashley breathed deeply, trying not to whimper. She saw Jack's shoulders slump slightly. Then he looked his father straight in the eye. "Fine. I'll take it."

"Jack, no!" Bonnie shrieked, but the boy was already climbing down the ladder.

"Give it to me, Pop!" he yelled. Mr. Berk stared at Ashley and spit again before following his son out of the loft.

The next day Ashley took the rags Bonnie had given her and pressed them against her legs as she sat on her stool. There weren't a lot of wounds this time, but they constantly stung. Ashley watched Ronny and Katie peck at their corn, thinking what stupid things chickens were.

Around noon, Ashley heard the screen door slam. She looked toward the house and saw Jack walking toward her, holding a tin plate in his hand.

"Here. Eat." He set it on a log and turned back.

"Are you all right?" Ashley asked. She saw the marks that the belt had made on his arms when he had tried to pull it away last night.

"Fine." He looked back at her, and she wilted at the sight of him. He had a bruise on his cheek and a swollen lip. "Don't worry about me. I can take anything he gives. He would have killed you."

Ashley began to cry. "I didn't mean to tell that lady anything. She asked me if he ever hurt me, and all I said was 'kind of.' I didn't want to lie."

"You can't ever tell anyone." Jack clenched his jaw. "Not even if they threaten to kill you, don't ever say a single word. What goes on in that woodshed is nobody else's business, do you understand? If you ever squeak again, I'm not going to rescue you. You have warning enough."

Before Ashley could answer, Jack walked away.

Six months passed and Ashley grew up. Her body stayed the same size; she was thin and frail for lack of good food, but she was smart. The belt was making her into a good woman. She learned to hate men.

Ashley finally gave up hope of going back to the orphanage. Bonnie told her that it was at least ten miles away, and that was much too far to walk before Father found her. Ashley thought of trying to find a neighbor's house, but when Henry drew a map of the area for her, she understood how alone she was. Even Jack didn't try to escape.

Ashley was given chores to do along with her chicken-watching duty, and she did everything perfectly. Ronny and Katie had no chance of escape when Ashley was in charge.

The only time Ashley saw the belt was when she sassed to Mr. or Mrs. Berk, or when she put the chickens in their cage early. Jack sometimes tried to defend her; once he even told Mr. Berk that he had already strapped Ashley, but it didn't do any good. She still got the belt. Mr. Berk had to do it with his own hands.

"There's coyotes in the area, Ashley," Jack said one winter morning. He dropped the chickens into the coop and locked the door. "They love to eat chickens. Make sure you watch them."

"Do they come out during the day?"

"Not usually, but I won't be home until late tonight. I have to stay at school till six. Father will be home around four."

Ashley forced herself not to bite her lip. "He doesn't like it when you're home late."

"Oh, well. I'm not going to flunk out of school just 'cause he doesn't like it. If you stay here, everything will be fine. Just don't sass or get too friendly so he coaxes something out of you."

Ashley nodded and Jack walked away. She sat on the bench Henry had made and watched Ronny and Katie. She was disgusted with them. She thought of how easy it would be to kill them. She could throw a rock at their heads and it'd be over. *I wonder if I'd get in trouble if I said they just died? That wouldn't be my fault.* But Ashley wasn't brave enough to find out.

Ashley rubbed her mittens together, but it didn't do much to warm her fingers. Her boots were poor protection against the icy snow, and her flimsy cloak was practically useless. During the coldest weeks, Mr. Berk built a pen inside the barn for Ronny and Katie. He wouldn't let them stay inside as long as the sun was shining, though. They could get sick.

Ashley was good at entertaining herself. She knew all about cloud formations, the wind in the trees, and the squirrel that lived nearby. She even knew how to tell which way the wind was coming from, and whether or not it would storm that day. Boredom was something Ashley didn't even consider anymore. It was no use being bored. It only made the hours pass slower.

At ten o'clock, Mrs. Berk banged on a pan on the porch. Ashley secured the chicken coop and went to the house.

She swept all the snow off the porch and did the dishes. She hauled two buckets of water from the creek, then went back to the chickens. She threw them some corn and watched them pick at it through the snow.

Ashley watched the chickens until sunset. Bonnie brought her supper and tried to convince her to come to the house, but Ashley wouldn't until Jack got home. Mr. Berk had brought a bottle home that night. She'd rather freeze.

Nighttime fell quickly on the countryside, and the lamps went out in the house. Ashley wasn't afraid of the dark anymore. She liked to look at the stars.

She went to the barn loft and stretched out in the straw. She lay with her head close to a hole in the side of the barn so she could watch Ronny and Katie. She put her hands behind her head and studied the stars through the dilapidated roof, covering her face with her scarf. She heard Ronny and Katie settling into their corner.

Something touched Ashley's shoulder. She sat upright and blinked her eyes open.

"It's me," Jack whispered. "You were asleep."

"How late is it?"

"It doesn't matter. Let's put the chickens away."

Jack climbed down from the loft and unlatched the gate to the chicken coop. He felt around the snow with his boot. When it hit something, he reached down and picked up both chickens. Katie squawked and complained, but Ronny lay still. Jack carried them into the barn and Ashley followed. When they got there, Jack lit a lamp. When he set Ronny down, her head flopped. He gasped.

"What's wrong?" Ashley asked, her heart pounding.

"I think she froze to death." Jack poked at Ronny but she didn't move. He slammed the cage door shut and kicked it. "Stupid chicken," he yelled. "What are we gonna do now?"

"Can we get another one?" Ashley could barely speak for the lump in her throat.

"No. Not without Pop knowing."

"I'll get in trouble, Jack."

"I know. Just go to bed. I'll figure this out."

Ashley walked out of the barn and shut the door. When she heard Jack's boots on the stairs several hours later, she didn't let him know she was awake. She didn't want to know if Ronny had died.

In the morning Mr. Berk found the dead chicken, and Katie was gone. Jack didn't try to defend Ashley and Mr. Berk didn't give her a chance to look for Katie. Ashley saw the woodshed before breakfast.

Mr. Berk forced Ashley to eat, telling her that she was ugly and skinny, and so she ate. But every bite made the lump in her throat grow bigger. Mr. Berk told her he would strap her every day until Katie was found. Tomorrow he was going to make her pay for Ronny. Today was the discipline for being irresponsible.

The next morning, Ashley tried to hide. He found her curled up in a ball under the bed, and didn't bother taking her to the woodshed. She had nightmares about the bedroom that night.

After breakfast, Ashley went searching for Katie. Getting dressed was painful, but she did it bravely, and Bonnie helped. The two girls searched for the hen all day while Henry dug a hole for Ronny and buried her.

Jack made Ashley come back to the house late that night. Katie had not turned up, and Ashley refused to go home until she found her. Only when Jack came to the forest and carried her screaming and kicking did she return. He told her that it would be better to see the belt than to freeze to death.

That night, Jack tried to defend Ashley, but his father threatened him, so he let him have his way with Ashley.

"Get up, Ashley," Bonnie demanded early the next morning. "Father's gone. We can search for Katie some more."

"I can't." Ashley winced, and her legs burned. "Please, Bonnie. Get more rags. I can't get up."

"You have to. Jack will have to belt you if you don't. None of us are going to school today. We're going to find Katie."

Jack appeared in the doorway. He pulled her out of bed and threw her dress at her. Henry went down the stairs to get a bucket of corn from the barn. Maybe Katie was hungry enough to come home.

As Ashley walked through the forest, the snow stung her legs. She tried to ignore it. Soon, her legs were numb.

"I'm going to strap you tonight if we don't find this hen," Jack told Ashley as they walked. She looked up at him. "I think Father will keep his hands off you if Mother tells him I really did strap you. He knew I was lying before."

Ashley imagined Jack's belt on her legs. "Just pretend, Jack."

"I can't. You have to cry."

"I will."

"No. You have to cry from pain. Mother will know. She won't lie to Pop. At least I won't leave scars, Ashley."

Ashley wondered how Jack knew that she had scars.

"Please don't." Ashley pulled her scarf up to her chin. She knew she couldn't fight against Jack's strength.

"What do you want me to do?" Jack's jaw clenched. "Listen to him beat you like a dog and wonder if you'll make it out alive? I have to take matters into my own hands. I would rather have you hate me than listen to him do that to you again."

"I don't want you to do it. Let Henry." Ashley knew she could convince Henry not to touch her.

"Henry's a baby. He won't get near you."

Ashley reverted to silence, but tears came to her eyes. For the rest of the day, she frantically searched for Katie, but there was no sign of her. Bonnie found a black feather in the snow, but no blood. Katie was probably still alive. The children walked for miles in every direction, and returned home in time to do chores before Mr. Berk came home.

Ashley sat in the barn loft and sobbed when she thought about Jack strapping her. Jack would probably cry as hard as she would. He would tremble, and his eyes would look at her in pity. He would make himself do it, though.

After chores, Bonnie and Henry went to the house, but Jack stayed in the barn with Ashley. He slowly climbed the loft ladder. He bit his lip as he neared Ashley. She was curled up in the corner; her shawl wrapped around her little body. She looked up at him with pleading eyes.

"Please, Jack."

His eyes filled with tears and he blinked them away. He sat next to Ashley and rested his forearms on his knees. "He'll be home soon."

Ashley trembled.

"We could get it over with now."

"I don't want to."

"You want him to do it?"

"He'll do it anyway."

"Not if I do."

Ashley squiggled away from him. "Please don't touch me."

"I won't hurt you as badly as he will. You know that. I'll just do what's necessary."

Ashley's stomach tightened. She didn't want to know if Jack was capable of hurting her.

Ashley saw his belt buckle in the lamplight. She couldn't imagine Jack using that on her. It was too painful of a thought. Better Mr. Berk. She already knew that he was capable of it.

"You'll get it when he gets home, then," Jack said. He clenched his fists. "If I stand in his way, it'll be worse. I'm just warning you. I gave you your options. It's your choice."

"Let him do it."

"I can't believe you're saying that."

"I want him to do it!" Ashley's voice was hoarse. "Leave me alone!"

Jack got up and walked away. Ashley sobbed until she couldn't breathe, then went to the house. Her exhausted body rested for less than an hour before Mr. Berk came home.

Ashley shrieked as Mr. Berk dragged her through the snow to the woodshed. She smelled the repugnant odor of the bottle on his breath. She shook violently, and her stomach was a painful knot.

Ashley screamed for Jack, but no one came.

She fought as hard as she could. She begged Mr. Berk. But nothing helped. When the woodshed door opened again, Ashley was choking on her sobs, but she wasn't fighting. Now she could go to bed.

The little girl felt utterly abandoned. Jack and Henry had gone to bed. Bonnie hadn't even rolled over when Mr. Berk yanked Ashley into the night. The nighttime air was silent and still, and nobody was around.

Little Ashley couldn't see the footprints that had been made over an hour earlier, and led to the back of the woodshed. She couldn't see the person who was crouched down, freezing in the nighttime chill, with his face buried in his hands and tears streaming down. Every time she had called his name, an arrow had drawn blood from Jack's heart. He had tried to be angry with her and blame her for not letting him do the job, but he ended up torn to pieces and openly bleeding with the sting of the wound. Desperation. Anger. Helplessness.

If Ashley ever fell silent in the woodshed, Jack would kill him.

TWO

The Upper Crust

Luke unlatched the iron gate and his feet tapped briskly on the brick path to the orphanage door. He forced himself not to look over his shoulder for fear of being reported as suspicious. But he was burning with curiosity as to whether anyone was watching him.

The air was crisp and cool, and the smell of wood smoke was thick. Luke's white uniform and the stethoscope that hung on his neck were meant as a disguise. He had not come to the Galesburg orphanage to doctor a sick child, even though he wished that were his mission. He had come to inquire of a little girl his wife had her heart set on adopting. A "penny parcel," as the Galesburg orphans were called.

Luke shook his head. *What am I doing?*

A young, dimple-chinned maid answered Luke's knock on the door, and she faltered when her eyes shot up to the face of the tall man. "May I help you?" she said in a squeaky voice.

"I'm here to see Mrs. Harms," Luke said as he removed his hat. He nervously entered and shut the door. "Is she still in her office?"

"She's preparing to retire for the night," said the maid.

"I'm here to see about an application that I made almost a month ago." Luke fingered his hat impatiently. "We were interested in a little girl from the orphanage, but we never received a reply."

Miss Elizabeth, a tall, dark-haired woman strode into the room, her shoes clacking loudly on the wood floor. "Mr. Tanner, it's a pleasure to see you," she said. "Hattie, I'll see to Mr. Tanner. Thank you."

The maid nodded and left.

"Have you come to see about your application?" Elizabeth asked.

"It's been almost a month." Luke noticed a hole in the rug just inside the door. The entrance of the orphanage was poorly lit, but he imagined spider webs in the corners, dust on the staircase, and dirty little children poking their heads out the bedroom doors.

"I apologize for the delay." Miss Elizabeth's eyes narrowed, demanding Luke's attention. Luke squinted back at her, his arms tensing.

Elizabeth shrugged. "Unfortunately, there have been many distractions. Mrs. Harms hasn't had a chance to consider your request. I'll be sure you receive a letter as soon as possible." She nodded toward the door.

"All right." Luke replaced his hat. "Good evening, Miss Elizabeth."

This is crazy, Luke thought as he boarded his carriage and clicked to the gelding. On the brief strip of brick on Main Street, the horse's trotting was loud—too loud. Galesburg was quiet and dark, and in the silence, Luke's thoughts screamed at him. *How did Grace get this idea into her head? And why did I make that stupid promise to her?*

He'd done it to console his wife after Emma died. But seven years had passed, and he figured Grace would forget. An upper crust adopting a penny parcel? *I might as well say goodbye to my reputation. I can't believe this is happening.*

Luke shook his head. In their early years together, he had agreed to be open to adopting children since he and Grace couldn't have their own. They had adopted two children from neighboring counties and Luke had been eager when his wife said that she wanted another one. But he had never expected to adopt a child from Galesburg, where parentless children were called "penny parcels" because people said they came for a penny a parcel. Orphans were highly scorned in Galesburg. With a penny for paperwork anyone could adopt one.

The "upper crusts," on the other hand, were the most refined and esteemed men in Galesburg's social classes. This assembly of approximately fifteen socially advanced men formed an elite circle that determined the health of Galesburg's economy as well as religious response and popular opinion. The upper crusts were opinionated, critical, and completely self-sufficient. Becoming an upper crust was a feat that few men had the stamina to tackle, and even fewer lived long enough to complete.

Dr. Luke Tanner was an upper crust.

In fact, Luke was deemed "the model upper crust"—the epitome of perfection in the social class, though only in his thirties. He had ruddy hair, blue eyes, and stately height that was almost unmatched in the social circle. He walked with confidence, talked with ease and poise, and held a spotless reputation in the town.

He had shown up in Galesburg with his young bride eight years previous. The first day he went job seeking, he had been hired at the Galesburg Institute of Medicine, and within a month had secured a large piece of property west of town. Luke hadn't had to try to fit into the upper crust. He was a natural. Decisive. Respectable. Christian. He followed the unspoken rules and responded to the secret pressures of other citizens like a pro. Luke never questioned the hidden codes or inserted his opinion on anything if it was contrary to popular view. Yes, he was the model upper crust.

Unfortunately, his wife was also barren, and there was a little girl in the Galesburg orphanage that she had her heart set on adopting.

"How did it go?" Grace asked the minute Luke arrived home and swung open the farmhouse door.

"Fine." He tossed his gloves on the table.

"What did Mrs. Harms say?"

"Elizabeth said we'll be receiving a letter as soon as possible."

"Excellent!"

Luke glanced at his young wife. Her eyes were glazed with blindness. They reminded him of her barren womb. "I think we're making a mistake, Grace."

"A mistake?" She gasped and dropped her knitting to her lap. "Why?"

He sank into the rocker. How could he explain it to her?

"You mean by trying to adopt again?" she asked.

"No. I mean by trying to adopt *her.*"

"Is there something wrong with her?"

"No." Luke banged his head against the back of the rocker. "Never mind. I'm sure it'll all turn out OK in the end."

"Just think, Luke. We'll be giving Wes a sister his own age." Grace's voice was gentle and quiet. "He's so excited."

"I know." Ten-year-old Wesley had been begging for a sibling close to his age ever since Luke could remember. Ashley was two years younger.

"We'll just have to see how it works out," Mr. Tanner said at length.

At least she would only cost him a penny.

Defend the poor and fatherless: do justice to the afflicted and needy.

—Psalm 82:3

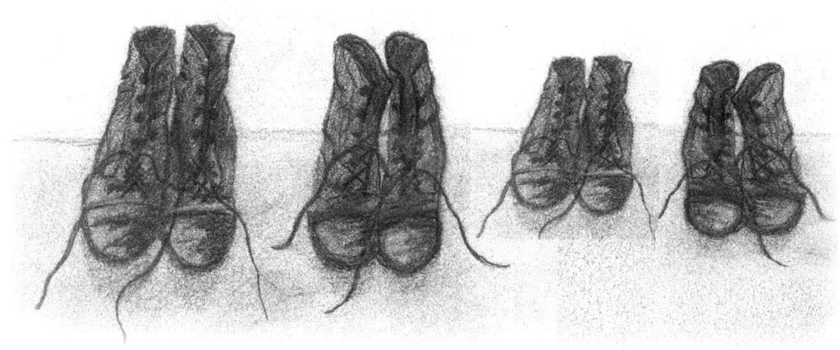

THREE

The Orphanage

Four iron headboards lined the wall of the girls' room, all slightly rusted, all covered with heavy quilts and stark white pillows. Four white nightgowns hung from hooks in the wall. Black shoes sat along the bottom of the rickety wardrobe, and although they had once been shiny, no amount of polishing could make them like new again.

Eight-year-old Ashley Kant had lived in this room as long as she could remember. There had once been a crib against the wall where she had slept most of her babyhood away. So little had changed since she had come to Galesburg Orphanage that not even the adults could remember the asylum being any other way. It was big, brick, and brutal, and every child who lived there had a history as bleak as the barren bedroom. Somehow, the thick walls weren't enough to protect against the cruelty of life.

Life.

For Ashley, life was a schoolroom every day except Sunday. It was an unhappy teacher, an old mistress, and a yard bordered by an iron fence. It was boys teasing her and no one standing in her defense; it was the constant worry that someone would come along and adopt her someday. It was the utter sense of loss that only her soul could understand. Life was four iron beds lined up against the wall, and four pair of scuffed shoes against the wardrobe.

Ashley sighed as she tidied the bedroom. This had been her only chore since she had returned to the orphanage. School took up the rest of her day.

"Ashley," a serious voice sounded, and the girl saw Miss Elizabeth standing in the doorway. "Play time is almost over; don't you want to join the other children?"

"No."

"Then you won't have any play time."

"I know."

The dark-haired lady stared. "Ashley, Mrs. Harms needs to see you in her office after school."

"Why?" The girl's braid whipped over her shoulder as she met Miss Elizabeth's cold, dark gaze.

"Run along to the schoolroom now; I'm going to ring the bell." Miss Elizabeth strode away and Ashley stacked the last shoe and left the bedroom.

"What are you up to, Ashley?" Miss Jolie asked, dusting a dresser in the hall.

"Just going to school."

"Why so gloomy?"

Ashley shrugged.

Miss Jolie glanced up. "Did you hear that the seamstress is coming on Monday?"

"Monday!" Ashley shrieked. "That's only two days away."

Jolie smiled. "Do you think she'll make you a dress?"

"Oh, I hope so. Won't she?"

Miss Jolie dropped her dusting cloth and tweaked Ashley's chin. "You'll smile when she comes?"

"Yes."

"Then I think she will. But you'd better run along to the classroom; here come the girls."

Ashley raced down the hall. The other three orphan girls followed, breathless and flushed from their afternoon run.

"I told you I'm faster than Nate," said eleven-year-old Melissa, dropping into the nearest desk.

"That's because Nate's only ten," said thirteen-year-old Gretchen.

Five-year-old KatieAnne settled into her desk across from Ashley. Her dark hair was braided in poky pigtails that barely brushed her petite shoulders. KatieAnne's big brown eyes looked at Ashley with concern. "Are you sick? You don't play anymore."

"Of course not," exclaimed Ashley. "Did you hear the seamstress is coming on Monday?"

Melissa bounced to her feet, banging the bucket of drinking water. "Oh, won't that be grand, Gretchen? I bet she'll make us all new dresses, and the boys will get shirts, and we'll be the smartest-looking children on the street come next month. I bet Ronny will even get a pair of trousers, since he put a hole in his today. Oh, Gretchen, do you suppose we'll get new pinafores? Mine is so dirty. I've needed one for *ever* so long, but Miss Elizabeth says we haven't the money. I will keep my things nice this time. I didn't care so much last time until I saw how quickly I wear things out and how terribly hard it is to mend. Do you like mending, Ashley?"

"No." Ashley had learned to relapse to silence when Melissa was excited.

"I won't get a dress," KatieAnne said.

Wisps of sandy hair fell over Melissa's rosy cheeks and clear blue eyes. "Why ever not, Kate? Well that's silly; of course you will. If we look bad enough, we may even get new shoes from the store in town. Have you ever had new shoes?"

"Stop!" Gretchen pounded her fist on her desk. "You sound like a baby, chattering on. You make a fool out of yourself."

Melissa's brow creased slightly, but she didn't respond.

"You will get a dress, Kate," said Gretchen. The thirteen-year-old nodded her dark head firmly, narrowing her green eyes. She put her hands on her hips the way she always did when she gave commands or promises. "Even if Miss Elizabeth tells you that you won't, you just have to ask Miss Jolie, and she'll get you one."

KatieAnne smiled a baby-teeth smile and Melissa sat down and began clicking her shoes together.

Ashley dropped her chin into her hands, staring at the blackboard. The sloping eaves above the teacher's desk had lately been decorated with white paper chains draped about the little corner. The small windows, which sat slightly off the floor, had been opened to let the spring breeze in.

"Here come the boys," Melissa said, and her shoes clicked with more vibrancy than before. The boys thundered into the schoolroom, laughing so loudly Ashley plugged her ears.

"Boys!" Melissa shouted as all seven of them rushed for the water dipper with a great shove that sent most to the floor. Water splashed on Melissa's feet. "Settle down. Ronny, stop it. Mark, get up."

Mark, who was at the bottom of the pile, looked up with a hearty chuckle. "Why don't you help me up instead of standing there like a dumb sheep?"

"Get up yourself," she retorted.

Mark reached for the dipper and slurped noisily. The other boys dropped their weight on his back and he let out a squeak of complaint before surrendering the dipper to Darien, the oldest, biggest boy.

Melissa brushed the drips from her stockings as the boys slowly rolled off the pile and splashed one another. When they returned to their desks, each sweating youngster tweaked and pulled at Melissa as they passed.

When Miss Elizabeth arrived a few moments later, she found her students sitting quietly in their desks, awaiting instruction. The schoolteacher eyed the students warily and sat behind her massive black-painted desk. Her crooked, pointy nose stuck out on her face as if it told her more about the children than her thin, dark eyes, and every hair on her head was drawn into a tight knot at the nape of her neck.

Ashley scooted against the wall and leaned on her elbow as she started her spelling lesson. She gazed out the window and then at Miss Elizabeth, who towered over the third graders at the blackboard with height that was unmatched inside the walls of the orphanage.

"Ashley," came a stern command, and she looked into the teacher's eye. "Do your lesson without daydreaming."

Ashley returned to her studying, although the sunshine that streaked through the window caught her attention more than once when Miss Elizabeth wasn't watching.

Melissa slumped at her place around the girls' table. "Miss Jolie says we might be able to play before bed."

"Before bed?" Gretchen said, situating her napkin on her lap. "'I don't believe it."

"We had to do extra school today, so she said she'd see if we can have an hour to play after supper."

"And what day is it?" Ronny's voice mocked from the table beside them.

Melissa glared at him. "It's Saturday," she said.

"We have to take baths and go to bed early on Saturdays, remember?"

"Miss Jolie still said that."

"Did you hear that a new girl is coming in tomorrow, and KatieAnne is leaving?" Gretchen nodded toward the littlest orphan, who ate in silence beside Miss Elizabeth at the grown-up table.

Ashley gasped. "Leaving where?"

"A new home, of course. A family came and wanted a girl her age, so they're going to take her for a while."

"Just a while?" asked Mark.

Gretchen nodded. "She's going for HOPES."

This last statement produced a general sigh from all ten of the orphans.

"Hanna went for HOPES," Melissa said.

"I hate HOPES," Mark said.

"How would you know?" asked Nate, laughing. "You've never been out of the orphanage for HOPES."

"But you have, and you hated it."

Nate nodded, and the countenances of the children fell. Mrs. Harms had founded the Helpful Orphans Provisional Education Society, a program meant to help families in temporary need with an extra hand, and let the orphans see what the world was like so they could capably step into it when they were old enough to take care of themselves.

Ashley knew all about HOPES. The Berks had taken her through HOPES. Poor KatieAnne.

Ashley swallowed hard and glanced at her plate. She dropped her fork.

"What's your problem?" Nate asked.

"I'm not hungry."

Ronny pounded the table with his fist. "Who could not be hungry?"

Miss Jolie passed by and Ashley caught her dress. "May I be excused?"

The woman nodded slowly. "I can't let you go outside, then."

"I know."

"Very well. Up to bed."

Ashley scooted her chair back and dropped her napkin onto her nearly full plate. She stepped out of the dining room and turned the corner to climb the wide stairs.

Ashley went up to the girls' bedroom and closed the door with a bang. She wandered down the row of beds and sat on the one with the white quilt.

"Poor KatieAnne."

Ashley unlaced her shoes and pulled her stockings off her feet. As she ran her hand down her leg, a lump stuck in her throat. After returning to the orphanage, Ashley had obeyed Jack. What went on in the woodshed was nobody's business, so she had not squeaked a clue to anyone. When Mrs. Harms asked her why Jack brought her back, she told her what Jack had instructed her to say: that the Berks didn't need her help anymore. It was true, Jack had said. The chickens were dead.

Ashley had been in terrible pain when she returned, but she dedicated her life to making sure no one found out. When the wounds healed, Ashley kept the scars hidden. She couldn't control the nightmares, but only Melissa knew of those. Gretchen always slept through them, and Melissa covered Ashley's mouth every time she screamed, so none of the maids knew. Melissa never asked questions, and Ashley was glad. Every orphan had a past, and Melissa seemed to know that some things were better left unsaid.

Ashley lay back on her bed and pulled the curtain closed, sealing out the striking hues of gold and purple that came from the sinking sun. She closed her eyes and sighed, placing her hand on her chest. She breathed in the stale smells of old wallpaper and sweaty sheets, and heard excited screams from the other orphans, who had just been released outdoors.

As sleep threatened to overcome her, Ashley forced her eyes open, afraid to surrender to sleep because of the nightmares.

"Poor KatieAnne," she whispered again, and she brushed away a tear.

I am desolate and afflicted.

—Psalm 25:16

FOUR

Mr. Bowtie and the Baby

Ashley closed the bedroom door and tiptoed down the stairs, hoping Miss Elizabeth would pass by. The woman barked one more command to Miss Hattie and climbed the stairs.

"Ashley, you didn't talk to Mrs. Harms last night," said Miss Elizabeth. Ashley tried to hurry past, but Miss Elizabeth grabbed her arm.

"I don't want any excuses." Her grasp tightened. "You also left the supper table eating hardly a bite, and you neglected your bath."

"Miss Jolie said—"

"You are to ask me, not Miss Jolie." Miss Elizabeth released Ashley's arm, and she rubbed it gently. "We leave for church in fifteen minutes. After that, you are to go directly to Mrs. Harms's office. Without breakfast."

Ashley tried to ignore her burning hunger.

"Now, go get your hair done."

As Ashley walked away, Gretchen and Melissa stepped out of the bedroom. They rushed down the stairs to catch up with her.

"Why did she talk to you?" Melissa whispered.

Ashley opened the door to Miss Hattie's room, trying to contain her tears. "Because I didn't eat supper, and I forgot to see Mrs. Harms."

Gretchen gasped. "You got Death Sentence?"

The orphans scorned meetings with Mrs. Harms so much they were called Death Sentence.

"I'm awfully sorry," said Melissa. She patted her friend's back.

Ashley felt the knot in her stomach tightening. Miss Elizabeth always made her pain worse.

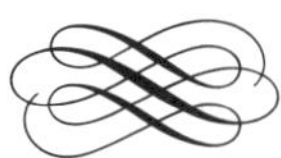

The children's clacking shoes disrupted the morning quiet of the little town. KatieAnne was first in line, and then there was a bashful seven-year-old newcomer. The boys brought up the rear, followed by Miss Elizabeth. Mrs. Harms led the procession, her kind face smiling with pride and her silver hair in tight curls, as was the Sunday fashion.

The walk to church was brisk and damp in the mid-April weather, and Ashley stomped her feet to keep them warm. It was nearly four blocks to the church from the orphanage. All of the children despised the walk more than any other activity in their week. Ashley didn't pay as much attention to the scorn on the townspeople's faces as Gretchen and Melissa did. She knew the old men frowned on her, and the children were told to "keep away," but she didn't know why. She didn't care. She was happier being left alone, even though the other orphans seemed to be attracted to the idea of belonging in Galesburg. Gretchen and Melissa always whispered to each other as they walked, and Melissa once told Ashley that they never actually said anything; they just did it so the Galesburg people would think they didn't care a bit about their dirty looks.

When the orphan party finally reached the church, Ashley was delighted to see Miss Jolie go in just before them. Sunday was Miss Jolie's only day off, but she still sat with the orphans in church, and she came to the orphanage in the morning to start the girls' day with a smile. The rest of the day was bereft of her sunshine.

Miss Jolie held the door open for the children and said a motherly "Good morning, children" as they quietly entered the little white church. Several of the boys nodded as they passed by, but with Miss Elizabeth herding from the rear with a scorning frown, the orphans didn't dare break the rules by returning her greeting.

"Might I sit by you, dear?" whispered Miss Jolie as she scooted down the bench and settled beside Ashley.

"Good morning!" a male voice boomed before Ashley had the chance to reply. The minister held up his hands in greeting. "It's good to see you this bright April morning. Let's stand and sing 'Amazing Grace' together."

As the congregation began the restful song, Ashley fumbled through the words while staring at the minister with rapturous concentration. He had always baffled Ashley. Every Sunday, the stout, elderly man came to church dressed in black trousers, a stiff white shirt and collar, a black coat, shiny black shoes, and a freakish bow tie. A strange chain hung from his pocket watch, and a gaudy ring adorned his pinky. He spoke with an unusually gruff voice and faltered about so horribly during his sermons that he threatened to topple over the bouquets of flowers that had been set about to liven the stark, white walls.

Every Sunday since Ashley could remember, a group of men had stood outside the church door when the children began to walk home. Their only topic of discussion seemed to be the preacher. Ashley had once heard them say the preacher would have to find a new job, and she had often heard one man loudly proclaim that this Sunday would be Mr. Harris's last sermon. The older orphans had explained to Ashley that no one liked Mr. Bowtie, as the town called him, because of his bizarre tastes. But no matter how many weeks the subject was discussed, the same minister always took the pulpit on Sunday morning, and his "last sermon" was always followed by another.

"Please be seated," Mr. Bowtie said at the closing of the song.

The sermon began. Ashley was perplexed at how one man could talk for so long, and how he seemed to capture his audience. It looked as if most of the congregation actually enjoyed listening. His words hardly made sense to her, and the way he put them together, using "thees" and "thous" and "hithers" and "thithers" in large phrases, made it impossible for her to sit still through the entire service.

Ashley's mind wandered, and she sat silent and still while she examined the congregation, occasionally glancing at the pulpit and the ungainly old man.

A small family with two children caught her attention. They were seated across the aisle, nearly at the front, all of them listening intently to the minister. Even the boy who looked just slightly older than Ashley had his eyes fixed on the preacher. Ashley leaned forward to see the mother, who sat straight on the bench, holding a tiny baby. Then she looked behind her at Gretchen and Melissa, but they were whispering between each other and didn't see her. The girls always told Ashley about babies they had taken care of. Ashley had never seen one as small as they said babies came.

"Miss Jolie," Ashley whispered, tugging on the woman's sleeve.

Jolie lent her ear.

Ashley nodded toward the baby. "Do you think I could hold that baby after church?"

Jolie shook her head.

Ashley settled against the bench and felt a tug on her braid. She turned to see Ronny leaning forward in his seat.

"You want to hold that baby?" He motioned toward the woman and Ashley nodded. "That baby has a blind mama."

Ashley's eyes widened and she glanced forward again, staring at the family with new wonder. *Blind?* She'd never seen a blind person.

Full of curiosity, Ashley stared at the woman, hoping she would turn her head so she could see whether she really was blind. The boy, who sat next to the tall father, shifted his feet and brushed back his thick, blonde hair. Ashley shivered when she looked at the father, for he was big and strong. She watched to see if he would slap his son's hand or scold him for moving. But he didn't.

Miss Jolie touched Ashley's shoulder and nodded for her to sit still. She leaned back against the bench and hooked her feet together to keep them from moving.

Ashley heard clicking on the floor and glanced around to find the source of the noise. In front of her sat a girl with a fancy, pale green dress, and she clicked her white shoes together and banged them on the floor repetitiously. Ashley thought of Bonnie, and quickly pushed the memories aside. Bonnie never had shoes that were that pretty.

The sermon finally ended and the preacher retired to his position at the back of the church to shake hands. Ashley watched him from the back pew and noticed that every child touched his attractive bowtie when they passed. Ashley smiled when the bowtie began to slump and hang twisted on the preacher's collar.

Before Ashley had the chance to ask Miss Jolie to see the baby, she learned that the baby's family had already left.

The orphans were soon lined up outside the church door, ready to begin their trek to the edge of town. Breakfast wasn't served until after church on Sundays, and the children's stomachs growled and burned, causing their feet to tap hastily on the boardwalk.

Ashley watched the other church families start for home. Some boarded big, fancy carriages with two horses pulling them, and a driver sitting on top. Others had smaller carriages, and still others walked. The mothers were laughing, and the fathers carried their little girls on their shoulders or boosted them into the carriages and bundled them with lap blankets.

The orphans passed one particularly merry family, slowly strolling along the boardwalk. The parents talked in sweet voices, and the three boys poked and teased one another in a heartwarming way that made Ashley shiver. A general spirit of compassion and charity hung in the Sunday air, and for a moment, Ashley forgot she was an outcast.

Reality came in a sudden sweep when the rambunctious lads stared mercilessly at the row of marching orphans. Ashley's eyes followed the boys as they passed, but Gretchen tapped her shoulder and commanded that she look ahead. Ashley noticed that Gretchen and Melissa were marching with their backs unusually stiff and their mouths set in thin lines.

"I told you what I think," Ashley heard Gretchen say in a seething whisper.

"I don't care what you say; they can take away my pride just by their nasty looks," Melissa returned.

Gretchen's voice was hard. "All Galesburg children are spoiled. They can't make me ashamed just because they think they're better."

That family must not be truly happy, Ashley thought, squaring her shoulders like Gretchen and Melissa. *Anybody with a family can't be truly happy.*

Ashley looked straight ahead and pushed the memories away.

And it shall come to pass in the day that the Lord shall give thee rest from thy sorrow, and from thy fear.

—Isaiah 14:3

FIVE

A Baby Doll Family

Miss Elizabeth opened the door to the office and Ashley quickly stepped through it. She was careful not to sigh when the slam of the big door reminded her of the clanking of bars that she sometimes heard when she walked past the jail on Main Street.

Death Sentence, Ashley thought, wishing there were a better way to "develop character" than to sit through another one of Mrs. Harms's sermons.

"Hello, Ashley," the silvery-haired woman greeted from behind her massive desk. Tight curls bounced about her face. Ashley stared at her through the dark shadows that the lamp cast and thought that a cheerful greeting was a hypocritical way to welcome a child to Death Sentence.

"How are you today?" asked Mrs. Harms, moving a stack of papers and putting her bony hands on the desk.

"I'm fine." Ashley forced her voice to sound strong and confident.

"I've been needing to talk to you. Why don't you sit?"

Ashley sat in the hard-backed chair in front of Mrs. Harms's desk, and she heard her stomach growl.

"Since you've been back from HOPES, I haven't really been able to talk to you." Mrs. Harms pulled her wiry spectacles from her nose and set them on the desk. "The Berks enjoyed your stay, Ashley."

She looked down and her cheeks warmed.

"But Miss Elizabeth says you aren't doing very well in school. I know you didn't go to school when you were with the Berks, but you couldn't have forgotten your lessons. Ashley . . ." The little girl glanced up at her. "I need you to do well in school. Everyone has to try their hardest. Elizabeth has a difficult job getting you caught up from a whole year without school, and I need you to help her. Do you understand?"

"Yes, ma'am." Ashley listened absent-mindedly, for she was hardly able to distract herself from her hunger. She had been brought to the office to be scolded so many times that Mrs. Harms's words bounced off her mind like rain on a rooftop.

Mrs. Harms glanced at the clock on the wall. "It's breakfast time."

Ashley glanced at the floor. "I can't have breakfast."

"No breakfast? Ashley, you hardly ate any supper."

"Miss Elizabeth said that since I didn't come see you last night and I didn't finish my supper, I couldn't have any breakfast."

"After the walk to church?" Mrs. Harms shook her head. "Really, I think that's too much. Come have breakfast."

"But Miss Elizabeth . . ."

"I'll talk to Miss Elizabeth." Mrs. Harms stood and opened the door, motioning for Ashley to leave.

Ashley refused to say goodbye to KatieAnne when she left that afternoon. The other girls did, but when they begged Ashley to come along, she yelled at them and slammed the bedroom door. Ashley hated HOPES and every family who ever applied for HOPES, and she knew that if she had said goodbye to KatieAnne, she would have spilled all her secrets in warning.

When the girls returned from sending the youngest orphan with her new family, Gretchen, Melissa, Ashley, and the new girl, Della, sat in their room and pretended to be mothers. They held their babies (who were blankets wrapped tightly around large wooden blocks) and cared for them in the only ways they knew how. Ashley watched Gretchen to see how she held her baby, but even though Gretchen was thirteen years old, she was clumsy and inept.

"Melissa, have you ever taken care of a really, really little baby?" Ashley asked, patting her lumpy blanket.

"I once held one that could almost talk, but he wasn't very little." Melissa pretended to kiss her baby, and then wiped her lips on her dress.

Della watched the girls in silence, her eyes darting from one to the other.

"Well, I touched one that was just a few weeks old," said Gretchen, "and at the Sarters' house, there was a baby girl who was starting to crawl."

"How old are babies when they start to crawl?" Ashley asked.

Gretchen shrugged.

"How do they look when they're just a few weeks old? Do babies smile then?"

Gretchen laughed. "Of course not! All they do is sleep and eat then. You hardly even see their eyes open."

"Really?"

"Someday, I'll have a baby," Melissa remarked proudly. "A little girl with red hair."

"I don't like red hair," Gretchen said.

"Fine. Then maybe blonde, or brown would even work. Maybe she'll look like me, and I'll name her Lissa after me."

"Or Mel," Della piped up. All the girls looked at her.

"That's an ugly name," Gretchen said. She looked at the ceiling and then said with conviction, "I'll have more than one baby. I'll have six, like the Sarters. They had seven with me, but I wasn't really their child." Gretchen glanced away and patted her doll briskly, banging it against her shoulder until the blanket fell off to reveal the wooden block innards.

Melissa looked at Gretchen. "How come they sent you back?"

Gretchen shrugged. "They didn't need me anymore, I guess. Their baby was walking and talking when I left, and Paul, the oldest boy, didn't have a broken arm anymore. There was nothing else to do." Gretchen wrapped her blanket around the block again and set the reconstructed baby on the rug while she fumbled with a tea set made of acorns.

"I don't want a family when I grow up," Ashley announced.

Melissa's eyes grew wide. "What do you mean?"

"Families aren't really happy, like they look. I'll just stay here for the rest of my life and take care of the children, like Miss Jolie. Maybe I'll even have Mrs. Harms's job."

"I wouldn't want her job," Gretchen mumbled.

"Ashley, if you don't have a family, then . . . then you'll never have a baby," Melissa exclaimed. "That's just awful!"

"Not really." Ashley noticed that Della's eyes were glued on her. "Maybe sometime I'll *hold* a baby, but I don't want to be married, because fathers aren't happy."

"You wouldn't know," Gretchen said. "You've never had a father."

"I did so." Two blocks fell from Ashley's blanket onto her lap. "You know I did."

"Oh, fiddlesticks, Ashley. Mr. Berk wasn't a father. He doesn't even *like* children."

"Well, you've never had a father either," Melissa said.

Gretchen's eyes widened. "Don't you ever say that again, Melissa!" Tears filled her eyes. "I did too have a father."

"Yeah, but he died 'fore you were big enough to remember him."

Gretchen threw an acorn and shot to her feet. Wrath covered her face. "I remember him. You have no idea how much I remember him. You're cruel, Melissa. You're cruel, and I wish you'd leave!" Gretchen stomped her foot and threw herself onto her bed, bursting into tears.

Melissa briskly patted her baby and said with a shrug, "Well you don't have to cry about it, Gretchen. It's over, ya know."

"It's not over." Gretchen's jaw clenched as she seethed into the pillow.

"Don't fight," Della begged.

Melissa put down her baby and picked up the acorn Gretchen had thrown. "At least you remember someone who loved you, unlike most of us. You should be thankful instead of always being so grouchy. Come on, Della, let's go play with the boys."

With a clack of her shoes, Melissa threw the acorn on Gretchen's bed and left with Della behind.

"She's a jerk," Gretchen said.

"I did have a father," Ashley insisted.

Gretchen sniffed. "Then I hope you've already learned never to trust a man, no matter what he tells you. Fathers promise to take care of you, and they break their promises."

The morning light on the dining room floor made the hard wood glow. Ashley's black shoes echoed off the barren walls as she walked up to the doorway. Miss Jolie had drawn back the curtains to the tall windows and she was now on her hands and knees, scrubbing in the far corner.

Ashley watched her for several minutes. "It isn't that dirty, Miss Jolie."

Jolie glanced up, and her familiar chuckle made Ashley smile. "Yes, dear, but I might as well get every spot while I'm down here."

"When do we get breakfast?" Ashley asked. The clock on the wall had rung in the breakfast hour nearly fifteen minutes ago.

"The cook is behind this morning." Jolie dropped her rag into the bucket and sat back on her knees. "Mrs. Harms is helping make breakfast, and as soon as it's done, we'll call you. What have you been doing?"

Ashley shrugged. "Nothing. Gretchen and Melissa were fighting last night, so they're not talking to each other. Della doesn't really talk to anyone, and the boys are still cleaning their room, so there's nothing to do."

"Nothing at all?" Jolie's eyes twinkled in the sunlight, and her smile made Ashley's spirits brighten. "You only have a little more than two hours before the seamstress comes."

"She's coming today?" Ashley said in a gasping whisper. She felt excitement surge to her toes.

"I didn't expect you to forget." Miss Jolie clicked her tongue. "Why don't you find Della and play with her? She's new, and she could probably use a friend."

"I don't like her." Ashley leaned against the doorway.

Miss Jolie smiled. "That's not unusual. You never get along with new children until you decide that you can stand to play with them. You didn't like KatieAnne at first, either."

Ashley felt her cheeks sting. "Why didn't the people take Della? They could've left KatieAnne here."

Jolie's brush made a dry sound on the floor as she scrubbed. "Because Mrs. Harms doesn't allow new children to leave the orphanage for six months. KatieAnne has a good family, Ashley; I met them."

Ashley bit her cheek. Mrs. Harms had told her the Berks were a good family.

"At least make sure Della isn't sitting in a corner by herself somewhere, 'ey? Show her the library."

Ashley sighed and her shoulders slumped as she walked away.

Breakfast was served an hour late that morning, and by the time the children were called, Ashley was so exhausted from trying to entertain Della that she was in a sour mood.

"Do I get a new dress?" asked Della as she picked at her food.

"Everyone does," Gretchen said. "And stop eating like that, Della; it's getting on my nerves."

"I'm going to ask for my dress to be red," Ashley said.

"Red?" Melissa gasped. "If I were you, I'd keep mine blue."

Ashley looked down at her threadbare blue dress. “I hate this color.”

Gretchen chuckled. “I have to agree, your dress is really ugly. But not because of the color.”

“Blue is second best to yellow,” Melissa said.

“Then you can have my dress. Or Della can. I want a new red dress.”

“Have you ever had a new dress?” asked Melissa.

Ashley shook her head. “This one was already dirty when I got it.”

Gretchen sniffed. “I’ve only had one new one since I’ve lived in Galesburg. I’ve been here nine years, and I got my new dress a month after coming. We’ve gotten cast-offs ever since.”

“What are cast-offs?” asked Della, knitting her hands in her lap.

“Orphans are cast-offs,” Gretchen said. “It’s stuff people don’t want. We get cast-off clothes ’cause they’re so worn out that nobody else wants them.”

“But not anymore,” Melissa said with a hopeful glance at Gretchen. “This time Mrs. Harms is getting us new clothes ’cause someone donated the fabric. I figure I’ll have new dresses every year from now on ’cause I’m planning on getting adopted this year.”

Gretchen looked at Melissa, her eyes sharp. “You’re setting yourself up for trouble. Every person who says they’re getting adopted this year has at least five more to wait. I think God makes it like that to teach us a lesson. Now you’re going to be sixteen before anyone wants you, and by then you might as well live on your own ’cause you’ll be too old to be somebody’s child.”

Ashley saw the color drain from Melissa’s cheeks. The eleven-year-old swallowed and cleared her throat, then said to Della, “Gretchen always says the worst about everything, so you can’t ever believe her. You and I will both get adopted this year, ’ey?”

Ashley was beginning to feel uncomfortable when she heard her name spoken at the grown-ups table. She leaned back in her chair to listen.

"Ashley didn't bathe Saturday night," said Miss Elizabeth. "Should I have Rose heat some water for her this morning?"

Mrs. Harms nodded, and Ashley's heart sank.

"What time is the seamstress coming?" Mrs. Harms asked.

"Just before school. I'll have the boys see her first so they can begin classes on time. The girls can neglect reading to see her."

"Does everyone need dresses?"

"Hattie and Rose and the cook are in need."

Mrs. Harms's eyes widened. "All of them?"

Miss Elizabeth nodded. "I'm not sure about the girls. Gretchen has grown, but her dress is still in good enough condition to be worn. Maybe we could pass that one along. I don't think enough material was donated for all the girls."

Mrs. Harms cocked her head. "It would've been enough if Della hadn't come. We could pass Gretchen's dress to Della, but it'd be too big, wouldn't it?"

"Much too big."

"Melissa is Gretchen's size already." Mrs. Harms tapped her fingers on her water glass. "I suppose we could give it to Ashley. She has to get rid of that worn-out blue dress, but I guess she doesn't have to have a brand new one. She could get some use out of Gretchen's dress, couldn't she?"

"Gretchen's dress still has a year of wear in it," Miss Elizabeth said. "It might be a bit big for Ashley, but she could make do."

Ashley's chin sank to the back of her chair, and her eyes filled with tears.

Ronny interrupted her thoughts by tapping her drooped shoulder. "Hey, Ashley, did KatieAnne leave her schoolbooks when she went away?"

"I don't know."

"You know she had the second primer, don't you?"

Ashley shrugged. "What does that matter? So do I."

Gretchen laughed. "Your book is ripped up and stained. You should take KatieAnne's book and leave the old one for her when she gets back."

"Children," Miss Elizabeth's voice rang out, and the table fell silent. "The seamstress will be here soon. Boys, go to the library and I'll call you when she arrives. Girls, all of you stay here."

Chairs squeaked on the floor as the boys barreled out of the dining room. Miss Elizabeth turned to the girls. "Gretchen, Melissa, and Della will be getting dresses this time. While the seamstress is measuring them, Miss Rose will heat water for you to bathe, Ashley."

"What about a dress for me?" Ashley's throat tightened.

"You'll get Gretchen's dress as soon she has a new one."

Ashley glanced at the frock, which was an ugly brown color and hung with unflattering limpness on the girl's form. "But Miss Elizabeth, I . . ."

"Don't argue. Go to the kitchen and Miss Rose will get your bath. Gretchen, Melissa, and Della, go to the library and sit quietly. No walking around and absolutely no fighting with the boys."

The girls paused, staring at Ashley as a tear rolled down her cheek. Miss Elizabeth turned toward the library, but paused when the girls didn't follow her. "Girls!" she exclaimed. "Off you go. You're not to dawdle."

They stepped briskly out of the dining room, but Ashley stood frozen. She clenched her fist and felt herself tremble.

"Please, Miss Elizabeth," she mumbled, and received a cold stare when Elizabeth looked back at her. "Can't I have a new dress? I've been waiting all week."

Elizabeth's eyes widened. "If there's another word spoken about a dress, you won't get one next time, either. This orphanage only has enough material for the other three girls. Now, go to the kitchen."

"Can't I at least see her?"

Elizabeth threw her hands in the air. "Why? I'm sure she looks like every other seamstress."

Ashley's brow creased. It had never occurred to her that all seamstresses looked alike. "I'll just sit quietly while the other girls get measured. Please, Miss Elizabeth?"

"It would be ridiculous for you to miss school just to look at a seamstress. The other girls will tell you everything about her, I'm sure. Now, go, or I'll give you a real reason to cry."

Ashley turned away, hot tears streaking down her cheeks. She rushed through the swinging kitchen door just as Miss Tabitha, the volunteer gardener, came in from the other side. She crashed into Ashley with a pot of dirt and a shovel in her hands.

"Ashley!" Tabitha exclaimed as the pot fell to the floor. "Don't be in such a hurry. What a mess!"

Ashley rubbed her head, trying to hide her tears. Miss Tabitha scooped the dirt back into the pot. "Aren't you supposed to be seeing the seamstress?"

"I can't. Where's Miss Rose?"

"In the kitchen."

Ashley hurried away, brushing her cheeks until she was sure there were no streaks left.

"Well, what would you know—Sara Harms finally went through with hiring a seamstress," said Miss Ella, the cook, as Ashley entered the pale-green kitchen.

Miss Rose chuckled, shoving her hands into a basin of dishwater. "I didn't believe it would happen until this morning, when Sara still hadn't cancelled her. This is—what?—the fifth time she's hired a seamstress, but the first time she's actually let her come."

Miss Ella shook her head and laughed. "Elizabeth says Sara backs out because of finances, and continually chooses to give the children cast-offs. I say it's a shame for the children to have nothing."

"Who is the seamstress this time?" asked Rose.

Ella shrugged. "A woman named Grace, I heard. No one knows her last name, but Hattie mentioned that she's blind."

"A blind seamstress?" Miss Rose laughed in her loud, hearty way.

Ashley's eyes widened and she felt sick with jealousy that the other children were getting to see a blind person.

"Miss Rose," Ashley said, biting her lip, "Miss Elizabeth sent me in."

The plump woman turned to Ashley. "For your bath, 'ey?"

Ashley nodded.

"Very well; come along."

Miss Rose wiped her hands on her smudged apron and led Ashley to a small, cozy corridor off the back of the kitchen. There, she swung open a tall linen curtain to reveal the bathroom. The little apartment was furnished sparsely, consisting only of a sap-smelling potbelly stove, a little washstand, and a large iron kettle that the children knew as the bathtub.

As Miss Rose poured several pots of hot water into the tub, Ashley watched her carefully, thinking how frightening it would be to hang in that pot like a batch of syrup over a roaring flame. Ashley stared as the searing water melted into steam above the tub, and she breathed in the piney smell of crackling cedar and burning sap. Steam rested so heavily in the air that Ashley could feel the weight of it press in on her already aching shoulders, and she wished there were a window to let in a breeze.

Miss Rose cooled the bath with several buckets of cold water and set a bar of soap on the washstand. She turned to Ashley, brushed her hands on her damp apron, and nodded.

"There ya are," she said, planting her hands on her hips. "Hurry up, child, or you'll miss your lessons altogether."

Ashley had always disliked bathing. Since returning from her stay with the Berks, no one—not even Miss Jolie—had seen Ashley without her pantaloons on, for she refused to take them off to sleep or change, and barely tolerated bathing without them. It was impossible for Ashley to obey Miss Rose's command to "hurry it up," for she procrastinated every part of this activity so thoroughly that the hurried kitchen staff often scolded her, declaring that she was "an obstinate, fractious little creature."

Ashley soon settled in the warm tub and water seeped over her shoulders. She couldn't help but breathe a sigh of relief that Miss Rose had left her to bathe herself, for this new way of doing things had only been practiced since she returned from her stay with the Berks.

Ashley glanced at her legs and covered as many scars as she could with her hands. Her head pounded from the collision with the flowerpot, and her stomach churned and stung with emotion. She imagined the orphan boys being fitted for their clothes, and she could almost hear the happy chatter and see the line of orphans straining their ears to hear every word the seamstress said. Gretchen and Melissa would each remember a distinct part of the visitor's looks, and they would talk about her in bed that night, combining their memories to paint a permanent picture. The boys would tease the seamstress and see how she responded, and some of them would test her gentle side by reporting sob stories of their life as orphans. By the time the seamstress had finished her work that day, the orphanage would be buzzing with stories and excitement.

And Ashley was missing it all.

With a fresh burst of silent tears, Ashley seized the slippery soap and vigorously washed her thin form until she squeaked, and was scolded through the curtain for being so slow.

After Ashley's bath she was sent to the schoolroom, where the boys were already studying. Ashley stepped through the door and another wave of sadness overcame her when she saw that Gretchen and Melissa and Della weren't there.

"Where are the other girls?" Nate whispered when Ashley sat down.

She shrugged and dug for her spelling book. "I don't know."

"Weren't you with them?"

"No."

"I thought you all were getting dresses!"

Ashley's lip quivered. "I'm not."

Nate looked at his arithmetic book when Miss Elizabeth glanced up from her desk. Ashley opened her flimsy, brown-covered speller. When Miss Elizabeth looked down, Nate leaned forward again.

"All us boys get shirts, but only Ronny gets knickers, 'cause he ripped his." Nate's voice lowered. "I'm gonna rip a hole in my knickers this year, if I have to steal a knife from the kitchen to do it. Imagine another year in these pathetic clothes." He sat back in his desk and banged his pencil against his book. Miss Elizabeth glared at him and Ashley couldn't help but look up from her slate with a guilty stare.

"I'll have no more disruption," the teacher rebuked.

Out of the corner of her eye, Ashley saw Nate shake his head in disgust, and she wished she were brave enough to do the same.

Ashley opened her speller and wrote the words on her slate, sighing with boredom from their repetition. She saw a flash of green and looked out the window to see the seamstress walking away from the orphanage. A boy who looked a little older than Ashley accompanied her, and he carried a covered basket and his short, black hat. Ashley gasped aloud, then covered her mouth when she realized this was the woman and the boy she had seen in church with the tiny baby. The blind woman. Ashley welled with excitement and felt Miss Elizabeth's eyes upon her.

I wonder if she brought her baby, she thought. *I wonder what her baby's name is? I wonder . . .*

"Ashley," the teacher's voice interrupted, "you'll have to study through break if you don't apply yourself."

"I was just—"

"Do your spelling," Miss Elizabeth commanded.

"Ashley, the seamstress is blind!" Melissa shrieked, catching Ashley in the hall after school. "It was terribly strange to talk to her because she couldn't even see us." Melissa laughed. "One time, she was talking and Gretchen moved, but she kept talking just like she was there! It was so funny I almost laughed, and Gretchen just answered her and acted like she had been listening the entire time."

"That wasn't very nice," Ashley scolded, continuing down the hall.

"Oh, but you should've seen how funny it was! Can you imagine if you were blind? Wouldn't that be just awful?"

Ashley shrugged.

"She was mighty pretty," Melissa said. "She showed us the fanciest dress I've ever seen and said that she made it."

Disappointment rushed over Ashley again. "Is she going to make you a dress?"

"Of course. I wanted a yellow one, but the donated material is red with blue flowers. I told Grace I hate red, but she said that red usually looks good on sandy-haired people, and Miss Jolie told her that I have sandy hair." Melissa laughed and stopped short. "Where are you going?" she asked.

"Nowhere." Ashley's cheeks felt hot.

"Then why are you walking this way? It's free time. You can go outside with us."

"I don't want to."

Melissa's eyes lit up. "Well, I do! See you at supper." She trotted off.

Ashley continued down the hall and up the stairs. She closed the bedroom door and fell onto her bed. "Their dresses are going to be red. And Della is getting the dress I was going to have. I hate her! No one is ever fair to me!"

Ashley clenched her jaw until her temples stung. She closed her eyes and buried her face in her hands. She stuck her pillow over her head and held it there until the air was so hot that she couldn't breathe. The pillow dropped off the bed and Ashley glanced out the window. She felt the cool breeze that beckoned springtime to arrive and she stared at the airy clouds in the sky. Her trained eye saw pictures. There was a horse, a snake, and a skillet. Then she saw a man's face. Ashley turned away. No matter where she went, he was always watching her.

Why is thy spirit so sad?

—1 Kings 21:5

Decision & Dread

I don't know, Elizabeth," said Mrs. Harms. "Since the mother is the way she is, maybe we shouldn't allow it. I'm sure they'd be satisfied with someone a bit . . . easier."

Elizabeth shook her head. "Ashley's been here for eight years. We might as well give her a chance with a family. She's not doing well at the orphanage."

"But she was better before she went away." Mrs. Harms clacked the papers against her desk. The window behind her let in a breeze that tossed the lace curtains against the wall. "I'll think about it for a few days."

"I was hoping they could pick her up before next week."

"That soon?"

Elizabeth shrugged. "They applied a month ago."

Mrs. Harms's mouth gaped. "Why wasn't this request brought to my attention earlier?"

"You were dealing with the application for KatieAnne. The financial case that came last month was causing so much stress so I decided to wait. I dare say my decision was in your best interest?"

"No." Mrs. Harms's pulse quickened. "I'm in a bigger mess now. I've had no time to think this over and I have to make my decision.

It's an unusual request, asking for a specific child! I'm not sure this is the best thing for Ashley. She's so . . ."

"Outlandish," suggested Elizabeth.

"I suppose that's one way to explain her. Do you think she'll do well with a family?"

"It's hard to tell. But Ashley deserves a chance to be outside the orphanage again. She's never known anything other than an institution, except for her stay with the Berks."

Mrs. Harms's brow creased as she searched her memory. "She was a pleasant baby. Always smiling. She wasn't a miserable toddler, either. Was it Melissa or Ashley who went through the first primer in half a year?"

"Ashley," Elizabeth said in a low tone.

"But she's so odd now." Mrs. Harms tapped her desk. "Well, Elizabeth, I'd like to be left alone now. I have some paperwork to look at, and I need to think about the girl. We'll discuss this more at dinner."

Elizabeth nodded and bowed out.

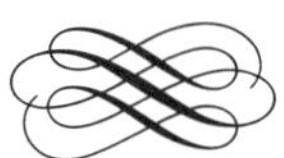

A week after the seamstress brought the new clothes, she was still the talk of the orphanage. Ashley heard a dozen stories about her hour-long visit to the asylum, for everyone had a different tale to tell, or at least their own twist to an old one. The boys talked of her gentle voice, the color of her dress, the motherly touch of her hands. Georgie, the youngest boy, admired the long measuring tape the seamstress used, and he repeatedly described the tickle it made when it touched his neck. Gretchen and Melissa told every detail of the woman's face, from her glassy eyes to her "distinguished" nose and rosy cheeks. They told Ashley that Grace was "the perfect mother; just like the ones you read about in fairy tales." It seemed to Ashley that this Grace was some sort of heroine to the entire human race—or at least the society of waifs.

"She doesn't do the measuring," Melissa said one Tuesday during recess. She sat on the porch steps and arranged her dress on the floor as if she were a princess in the company of suitors. "She can't read the tape."

Ashley pushed the swing. "Who does it, then?"

"Miss Jolie did the measuring on us girls, and Grace's son measured the boys. Mark said he could read a tape faster than anyone could write what he read."

Ronny trotted in from the yard and tapped Melissa with his foot as he bounded up the stairs. He sat next to Ashley, panting. "You're funny," he said, jerking the swing.

"Why?" Ashley asked.

"You never play. Don't your legs work?"

"My legs are fine. I just don't want to."

"You never want to. You're not normal."

Melissa narrowed her eyes at him. "Just 'cause you got tagged doesn't mean you should pick on someone else."

"I didn't get tagged." Ronny stuck out his tongue. "Besides, you know I'm right. Della's new here, and even she doesn't act like Ashley. Normal girls don't sit on swings all day long and walk around looking so gloomy that they could scare a fly away."

"I don't do that." Ashley's back stiffened.

Ronny laughed. "Now you're lying."

"Go away!" Ashley shrieked.

He smiled and rocked the swing. "I can stay if I like."

"I'll leave, then." Ashley stomped away, and as the orphanage door slammed behind her, she heard Mr. Berk's voice in her head telling her how stupid and strange she was.

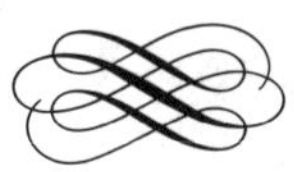

That afternoon, Sara Harms spent an intense hour considering sending Ashley with the Tanners. How could she deny their request, especially since they'd asked for her specifically? The family had waited a full month to bring Ashley home. It would be almost unbearable for them if she refused the application now. Still, she felt uneasy about sending Ashley away while the girl was failing in school, and always seemed sad and distant.

Mrs. Harms set her spectacles on the desk and stood from her high-backed chair. She looked out the window over the orphanage grounds. Her gaze settled on Miss Tabitha, who was working in one of her brilliant flower beds. Miss Ella came out the kitchen door and splashed a pail of dishwater onto a patch of poky lily buds, puffing so terribly that Sara wondered if the cook's health was fading.

Sighing heavily, she turned from the window and sat on her yellow fainting couch. She pressed her fingers against her temples and wondered how much longer she could endure the headaches. Twelve years of running an orphanage was finally catching up to her.

She pulled the chain that rang a bell in the kitchen.

"Yes, Mrs. Harms?" rang a cheery voice moments later.

Sara glanced up, surprised to see Miss Elizabeth standing in the doorway. "Aren't you teaching school?"

"The children are studying quietly, so I decided to lend Ella a hand since Rose is sick."

Sara nodded and moved behind her desk, folding her hands on it. "I've decided to send Ashley with the Tanners."

Elizabeth smiled.

"When are they coming into town?" asked Mrs. Harms.

"Thursday."

"The day after tomorrow?"

"It's probably better if Ashley doesn't have a lot of time to think about leaving. We can tell her after supper tonight and pack her things tomorrow." Elizabeth peered at Sara. "Are you all right, Mrs. Harms? You look ill."

"Quite all right," Mrs. Harms said spiritlessly. "We'll need to type copies of Ashley's papers. I'll pull a HOPES form for the Tanners to fill out when they come."

"Oh, this isn't for HOPES," said Elizabeth. "Mr. Tanner's letter stated that they don't plan to send Ashley back."

Mrs. Harms glanced up. "Aren't they from Galesburg?"

Elizabeth nodded. "They live just west of town."

"And they're adopting permanently? Are you sure?"

"Quite sure, Miss."

Sara shook her head. "Have they ever even met the girl?"

"It's doubtful."

"Very well. We'll see how long their resolution lasts. But it's not fair to expect them to sign the adoption form without trial, so we'll start with the temps form. Is Hattie available to type a copy of Ashley's papers?"

"I'll make sure she is."

"All right, then. See to it that Ashley is ready on Thursday morning."

"Yes, ma'am." Elizabeth started to leave, then turned and paused. "Why don't you lie down for a while? I can keep the children busy for another hour."

Mrs. Harms attempted a smile. "Thank you, but I'm all right. Just a little bout with a headache. It'll pass."

After supper that evening, Mrs. Harms escorted Ashley to her office and cheerfully told her about her upcoming adoption. But the little girl didn't respond to the news with cheer. Her face turned a ghostly pale color, and her eyes widened in disbelief.

"It's a good family, Ashley," Mrs. Harms assured her.

"I can't go." Ashley stared at the mistress and the brick-wall look on her face made Mrs. Harms falter in surprise.

"The decision is already made," Mrs. Harms said.

Ashley's eyes glistened with tears. "Please don't make me leave. I promise I'll do better in school. And I won't fight, not ever."

Mrs. Harms embraced Ashley's stiff body. "You'll be happy with the Tanners, just like you were with the Berks."

Ashley cringed.

"And I'm sure they'll bring you here to visit from time to time."

Ashley squeezed her dress in her fingers and rocked on her heels. "Please, Mrs. Harms. Don't make me go. I can't do it."

"No more arguing." Mrs. Harms sat at her desk. "Miss Elizabeth will help you pack."

With tears streaking down her cheeks, Ashley turned and raced down the hall. Mrs. Harms heard Jolie follow the girl upstairs and she stood and shut her office door.

"Why is Miss Elizabeth packing all your things?" Melissa asked as she entered the library after breakfast the next morning.

Ashley leaned against the armchair and didn't look up. "Because I'm leaving."

"Leaving?" Melissa shrieked, covering her mouth. "That's awful, Ashley! But you already went for HOPES. Do we all have to go twice now? Oh, goodness! Do you know the family? Are they from church? Will I ever see you again?" Melissa threw herself around Ashley's neck. "This is terrible. It's the worst news I've heard all day. I have to tell Gretchen. She's going to be so upset. When are you leaving?" Melissa stared at her, finally waiting for an answer.

"I'm leaving tomorrow."

Melissa's eyes widened. "Where to? I thought you were going to stay here forever."

Ashley's throat tightened. "I don't want to leave. But Mrs. Harms says I have to."

"Where are you going?"

"I don't know."

"Is it just for HOPES?"

"No." Ashley bit her lip. "It's not for HOPES."

Melissa fell into the overstuffed green chair. She glanced at Ashley and said in a breathless whisper, "Forever?"

Ashley felt as if her world were crashing down on her in one, harsh tumble. She sat on the ottoman and looked at her friend. "I don't know. What if I never come back? What if the Tanners are

. . ." The fear rising in her throat nearly strangled her. "What if they're mean?"

Melissa stared at Ashley, her eyes wide with panic. "Oh, Ashley, how horrible! Does anyone else know?"

"I don't think so."

"You should tell Gretchen and Della."

"I don't want to."

"Can I tell them?"

"It doesn't matter."

Mrs. Harms stepped into the library and her wrinkled brow was knit with concern. Her skirts brushed against the furniture in careless sweeps. "Melissa, you're supposed to be in school," she said as a book fell to the floor.

"It's break," Melissa said with a stubborn set of her shoulders.

Mrs. Harms grabbed Ashley's wrist and pulled her from the ottoman. "Come, Ashley."

"Where are we going?" Ashley's shoes shuffled on the floor as Mrs. Harms dragged her out of the room.

"Luke Tanner is here," she said.

Ashley's heart leapt. *Already?*

"He came earlier than we thought." Mrs. Harms stopped in front of the staircase. "Now, Ashley, you be a good girl and don't cry or fight when he takes you. Do you understand?"

"But I don't want to go," Ashley said, fighting tears.

"Hush. We already have your things in the carriage."

"Can't I say goodbye to everyone?"

"We don't have time."

Ashley pulled away. "But I have to!"

"Stop this nonsense."

As Mrs. Harms pulled her down the hall, Ashley tried to swallow the panic that threatened to choke her.

Entering the office, Ashley saw a tall, ruddy-haired man leaning against the wall by the office window, examining a stack of papers. He had broad shoulders and big hands. He wore a blue-checked shirt and black trousers. When he looked up, he tried to smile, but he looked just as afraid as Ashley felt.

"This is Ashley," Mrs. Harms stated, patting the girl's head in a surprisingly tender way.

"Hello, Ashley," said the man, folding the papers into his pocket. His tall frame sent a shudder through her whole body.

"I'm sorry we're not entirely prepared, Mr. Tanner," Mrs. Harms said. "We weren't expecting you until tomorrow."

"That's quite all right," the man said. He avoided Ashley's gaze.

Miss Elizabeth stepped into the room. "We've gathered Ashley's belongings. Everything's ready."

Mr. Tanner nodded at Elizabeth, then turned to Ashley. "Are you ready?"

Ashley looked at him and then she burst into tears. She turned her face into Mrs. Harms's dress and felt her cheeks turning hot.

Mr. Tanner knelt in front of her and he was still taller than she, even when stooped on one knee. "The people at home are mighty anxious to see you," he said, though his voice was tainted with displeasure.

Ashley was so overcome with fear that her knees trembled. She clutched the old mistress's dress as if her life depended on her hold.

"Elizabeth," Mrs. Harms said, "would you take Ashley out? I need to talk to Mr. Tanner for a moment." Mrs. Harms tore Ashley from her skirt with painful force. "Hush, now, Ashley. Go outside like a good girl."

Sara Harms turned to Mr. Tanner and nodded at the papers in his pocket. "The girl has never seen what's in those papers, so she knows nothing of her past. We choose not to tell the orphans how they got here until they're thirteen. Now that you're taking Ashley, it's your choice whether you'll read her the papers or tell her what they contain."

Mr. Tanner's brow creased.

"Ashley's last name is Kant, and it should remain thus, unless you formally adopt her."

"We're already planning on that."

Mrs. Harms nodded. "Then her name will change when the adoption papers are signed. To help her get settled, I'll be keeping the other children away from church for six weeks. It could cause problems for Ashley to see them right away. Hopefully, over time, she'll forget somewhat. I'll be stopping by in a couple of months to check on Ashley. In the meantime, I hope you'll stay in touch."

"We will. Thank you."

"Take good care of her."

"We will."

Luke sucked in his breath, put a penny on the desk, and stepped out the door.

Mr. Tanner glanced at his cheerless passenger and wished she would say something. Anything. Silence made him imagine rebellion, and he hoped he hadn't just adopted a rebel.

That morning, after Grace and Wes eagerly sent Luke off, it had taken him almost an hour to travel the four miles to Galesburg because he repeatedly stopped the carriage to wrestle against his thoughts. Was it still early enough to back out? He could tell Grace that God had told him Ashley wasn't the child for them. Couldn't that be true? God could speak through hesitance, couldn't He?

But Luke had made himself go. He groaned every time he remembered that he was accepting an orphan. True, he had done it twice before, but Wes and Cherish had come from different towns, and nobody really cared. Ashley was from Galesburg.

"How long have you lived at the orphanage?" Luke asked as the harness jingled on the horses' backs.

"Eight years." Ashley clutched the side of the seat, staying as far away from him as she could.

"And you're eight years old, 'ey?"

She nodded.

Luke clicked to the horses, and they quickened their pace with a lurch that would've sent Ashley to the floor had he not reached out and caught her.

"Careful, darlin'," he said, braving a smile.

Ashley settled herself on the seat with blushing cheeks.

When the silence became uncomfortable, Luke began whistling and Ashley sat perfectly still. He saw her battle tears and her knuckles turned white as she clung to the seat.

She'll warm up to me, Luke thought as he repeatedly glanced at her. *I'll just wait for tomorrow. She'll soon forget where she came from and be comfortable in our family.*

Luke looked at his passenger again and shook his head. He could hardly believe a child could make him feel so powerless.

If I speak of strength, lo, he is strong.

—Job 9:19

Larissa L. Hitch

SEVEN

"Forever?"

The monotonous sound of the horses trotting was disrupted long before Ashley set eyes on the house. She heard a boy's voice screaming and then a door slammed.

Mr. Tanner's mouth creased slightly. "I reckon Wes is mighty excited to see you."

Ashley loosened her grasp on the carriage seat. She couldn't feel her fingers.

Mr. Tanner turned up a long dirt lane toward a white farmhouse that was nestled in a grove of budding trees. Ashley squinted and saw a boy standing on the covered porch, wildly flailing his arms. She felt her body tense and she held her breath.

The door to the house opened and out stepped a dark-haired woman with a blanketed bundle in her arms. As the horse took her closer, Ashley slowly let out her breath.

"Mama's blind, so you be kind to her," Mr. Tanner said.

Ashley's eyes widened and she bit her lip. With a rush of surprise, she remembered seeing that boy at church, and the blind woman with the baby.

It's the seamstress! Ashley gasped, then held her breath again. *And that must be the boy who read the measuring tape.*

"Here she is," Luke said as he stopped the carriage at the tarred hitching post. He jumped from the wagon and went around front. "An' she looks just like you, Wes, my boy."

The lad's smile covered his entire face. He stood holding his mother's arm, his eyes as blue as his father's shirt.

"Welcome, Ashley," the mother said tenderly.

Ashley sat in the carriage, frozen to the seat. Mr. Tanner reached and swung her down. She let him set her on the ground before she realized what he was doing, then scurried from his reach.

Ashley stood at the bottom of the porch stairs, staring at the boy and the blind woman. What a nice story this would be to tell the orphans when she got back.

Mr. Tanner touched Ashley's arm and she shied away. "Come inside," he invited.

Ashley stepped onto the porch and found herself shoe-to-shoe with the grinning boy.

"Hi. I'm Wesley." The lad thrust his hand out to her. Ashley shook it. She glanced at Grace, the blind seamstress, and squinted at her hollow, glazed eyes.

Mr. Tanner opened the screen door and nodded toward the dimly lit foyer. "Come inside," he said with a weary glance at Ashley.

Wes led his mother toward the door. "Hey, Ashley," he said, excitement making his voice squeak, "have you ever been in a forest?"

A picture of Mr. Berk flashed across Ashley's mind and her cheeks stung.

Mr. Tanner chuckled. "Let her get settled before you take her anywhere."

The smell coming from the house was like Christmas Day at the orphanage, and Ashley's stomach churned. She pinched her dress in her fingers as she followed Wes into the house. When Mr. Tanner shut the door behind her, she was overwhelmed by vulnerability.

Ashley followed Wes into the sitting room, where a fire burned in the fireplace, and the tantalizing smells of sizzling sap and hot bread hovered in the air. The papered walls were decorated with shelves adorned with rag dolls, dried flowers, and two ancient-looking samplers.

"This is Cherish," Wes announced, taking the baby from his mother. "She looks nothing like you and me, huh, Ashley?" Wes showed her the baby. All Ashley saw was pink skin, brown hair, and brown eyes.

Mr. Tanner dropped his driving gloves onto the mantle and sat in a wooden rocker. He sighed heavily, and Ashley felt his eyes on her.

"You want to hold her?" Wes asked

Ashley nodded and Wes's eyes lit up. He held the baby toward her.

"Have you ever held a baby, Ashley?" Mr. Tanner asked.

Ashley shook her head, unable to find the tongue to speak.

"Then let her sit down first, Wes."

Wes cradled the baby in his elbow while he pulled a chair away from the wall.

"Be careful, Wes," Mrs. Tanner said in a kind voice like Miss Jolie's.

Baby Cherish melted into Ashley's arms. Ashley rubbed her fingers over the soft, pink blanket and found herself smiling. Cherish sleepily blinked her eyes open.

Wes dropped to his knees in front of her. "She's pretty cute, 'ey?"

Ashley nodded. She wanted to ask how old Cherish was, but her mouth wouldn't open to say the words.

Mrs. Tanner made her way to a tall rocker and sat down. Ashley was surprised at how capably the woman handled herself and how pleasantly she smiled, even though she couldn't see.

"She's tiny, isn't she?" Mrs. Tanner asked.

Ashley nodded.

"She nodded, Mom," Wes said. He leaned close to Ashley. "She can't see you nod," he whispered with a wink.

Ashley bit her lip in embarrassment.

"She isn't going to look like us when she grows up." Wes touched Cherish's fuzzy head. "She's going to look like Mom and Dad, I think."

Ashley thought how unlikely it was that dark-haired Cherish would someday have the ruddy hints of Mr. Tanner's thick hair.

Wes craned his neck to look at his father. "Ashley and me look like brother and sister, don't we, Dad?"

Mr. Tanner nodded, and Ashley's brow creased. *He's my brother?* Like Jack and Henry? Oh, well. Brothers weren't permanent.

"Dad, can I show Ashley around the farm?" asked Wes, jumping to his feet.

Mr. Tanner squinted. "Does Ashley want to go anywhere right now?"

Wes looked expectantly at Ashley. "We've got animals and everything."

When Ashley slowly nodded, Wes plopped the baby into his mother's arms and raced for the door.

"Stay close to the house," Grace said.

As Wes and Ashley strolled toward the barn, Ashley felt the spring wind nip at her legs. She looked at Wes's stiff, black knickers and glowed with excitement when she wondered if she would get a new dress now that she lived with the seamstress. Ashley wanted to ask Wes about his visit to the orphanage and how he had measured the orphan boys, but before she could mention it, Wes swung open the tall barn door and eagerly went inside.

Wes showed Ashley pigs and lambs and she was captivated. She stared for a long time at the colorful tom turkey roosting in the corner of the barn, and she giggled when he fanned his tail. But when Wes opened the chicken coop door, Ashley's heart sank.

"Why do you have chickens?" she squeaked.

"For eggs. We get a dozen every day. You wanna gather them now?"

"No." Ashley backed away. *Labor,* she thought. That's all she was good for. Watching chickens. So every family really was like the Berks.

Ashley retreated from the chicken house, and Wes shut the door behind them. "We have a cow too," he said, excitedly trailing her. "I didn't milk her this morning 'cause I was waiting for you. You wanna do it now?"

Ashley felt sick to her stomach, but she nodded. Soon she found herself in the stall, face-to-face with an enormous milk cow. She breathed in the thick smell of musty hay.

Wes filled a bucket with foaming, silky milk. The milking stool fell under the cow when he stood up. "You wanna taste it?"

"Sure." She tried to smile.

Wes fetched a glass from the window ledge, cleaned it out with his hand, and poured milk into it from the bucket. "Here."

Ashley put the glass to her lips and drank. "It tastes just like real milk," she said, laughing uneasily.

"That's because it is, silly. All milk comes from cows."

"Cows like him?"

"That's a girl. Boy cows don't have milk, same as boy sheep or boy horses. Only girls nurse their babies, so that's why they have milk."

Ashley stared at him. "It's for their babies?"

"Yeah." Wes tossed his blonde hair away from his face. "That's how they get fed."

Ashley took another drink of the sweet, warm milk and wiped her face on her sleeve. "Then why do you take the milk?"

The boy rested his thumbs in his belt loops. "The babies don't need it after a while. Same as Cherish won't need milk when she gets bigger."

"Where does she get milk?" Ashley asked.

"Most babies get it from their moms," Wes said.

"Moms have milk?" Ashley exclaimed.

"'Course! All girls have milk when they have babies."

"They do?" Ashley sputtered.

"Yup. Well, at least most of them. Not our mom, but that's 'cause she's blind."

"But where does it come from?"

Wes shrugged. "Hey, can I have some of that?"

Ashley gave him the glass and he drank the rest of the milk. Then he smacked his lips and smiled. "I guess it comes from God." He slapped the milk cup against his dusty trousers, scattering drops on the dirty window and the pile of straw beneath. Then he set the glass on the window ledge and strode toward the door. "Want to go to the forest now?" He opened the barn door and held it for her.

"No."

Wes cocked his head. "Why?"

"What's in there?"

"A surprise I made for you."

"What else?"

"Nothing." Wes sounded confused. "Trees. A creek. Bushes. What do you think?"

"I don't know."

"Well, do you wanna see?"

"I guess."

Ashley hesitantly followed him into the dark woods, staying close on his trail. She soon found herself surrounded by trees and brambly bushes. There wasn't a path, yet she felt strangely confident. The forest got darker and cooler the deeper into it they walked, but she didn't say a word. Ashley knew all about trees. At least today she didn't have to search every branch for Ronny or Katie.

"There it is," Wes announced when they arrived at a brush heap topped with fallen-in saplings, pine needles, and dabs of tar.

Ashley stared at the pile with a critical glare. "What is it?"

"The surprise. Can't you see it?"

She looked closer, but all she saw was tar.

"Ashley, haven't you ever seen a fort before? Look, here's the door." Wes knelt and stuck his head into a hidden opening at the base of the tall mound. She dropped to her knees and followed him.

Inside the camouflaged hut were two rooms with an opening adjoining them, and a ceiling high enough to sit up or even squat comfortably.

"Isn't it great?" Wes said, his face engulfed in a smile.

"How did you make it?"

"I cut down a couple of small trees, and I searched all over the forest for the right-size branches. This is the biggest one I've ever made. I put two rooms in it 'cause I thought maybe you might want to share it with me. This could be our special place and we'd never tell anybody else about it."

"Nobody?"

"Nobody."

Ashley clapped her hands together. "So it'd be like our own secret house."

Wes gazed at her with sparkling eyes. "Yeah. Just for you and me—and maybe Cherish when she grows up. What do you say?" He stuck out his hand, ready to strike a bargain.

"I like it," she agreed, shaking his warm hand tightly. She giggled and felt her cheeks blush.

Wes pulled out a watch from his trouser pocket. "Supper's at five thirty. We should be getting back."

"What's that?" Ashley pointed to the watch.

"It's a pocket watch. Dad gave it to me when I turned nine 'cause he said he wanted me to learn to be on time." Wes chuckled. "I used to come to meals late and sleep in when Dad was doing chores. Now I don't 'cause I got my own watch."

Wes crawled out the door and Ashley followed. The cold air sent a chill over her.

"How old are you, Wes?"

"I'm ten. My birthday is March eighteenth. When's yours?"

Ashley shrugged and looked away. "I don't know. Miss Elizabeth always tells me."

"Who's Miss Elizabeth?"

"The lady who takes care of us at the orphanage."

"You mean the lady who *used* to take care of you," Wes said with a confident nod. "You don't live there anymore."

"But I might again."

He flashed his eyes at her. "Why? Don't you like it here?"

"Yeah, I like it all right. But most of the orphans come back when they go to live with a family."

"Well, you aren't going back," Wes said.

As they made their way through the forest, Ashley's heart sank. So even if things became brutally horrible, Wes wouldn't be her rescuer. There was no Jack in this home.

Wes looked at her, his eyes searching hers. "You're my sister now, Ashley, and Dad and Mom are your parents. You get to stay here forever."

"Forever?"

"Well, why would you leave? We want you to be in our family, so there's no reason to go back to the orphanage. I mean, there's not even a dad there."

Ashley wondered why not having a dad was a bad thing.

The sun was beginning to make its way into the horizon by the time the children came out of the forest. Ashley glanced at the landscape and sighed. The white farmhouse with its blue shutters and trim stood out against the green hills with striking beauty. No shoes or toys were scattered about the yard, like at the orphanage, and the porch swing was so inviting Ashley could hardly resist sitting on it. This place was much nicer than the Berks'. *Probably rich people,* she thought. Melissa had told her that rich people made slaves out of children.

"Are you hungry?" Wesley asked as they reached the porch.

Ashley shrugged. She hadn't had a good appetite since she returned to the orphanage.

"Well, I am." Wes held the door open for her. "We can help Mom with supper, so it'll be ready faster. Dad's probably out doing chores already."

"Is that you, Wes?" Grace asked when the screen door slammed after the children.

"Me and Ashley," he replied cheerfully.

"I need you to help me with supper."

Wes led the way to the kitchen at the back of the house. "Ashley wants to help too . . . don't you?"

She shrugged.

"Maybe one of you could hold Cherish," Mrs. Tanner suggested. "She's been fussy and I can't hold her when I cook." The warm tone of her voice made Ashley's heart race.

"Do you wanna hold her, or do you want me to?" Wes asked.

Ashley shrugged again.

He smiled. "You should. But don't be afraid if she cries. That usually means she wants you to pat her or move her around. She'll smile if you make a funny face."

Wes took Cherish from the cradle and handed her to Ashley. She noticed how easily Cherish formed to the shape of the cradle she made with her arms.

"You can sit if you like," Grace said from where she worked at the kitchen counter. "But if you're very careful, I don't mind if you stand."

"Aw, she'll be careful," Wes piped up. "I think Cherish likes her, Mom."

Mrs. Tanner smiled. "I'm sure she does."

Ashley glanced at Cherish and thought about Gretchen and Melissa and Della, wondering if she would ever get to tell them about the tiny baby she got to hold. A smile spread across her face. Certainly none of the girls had ever held a baby this small.

"I was thinking about supper before you got here, Ashley," Wes chatted as he set the table. "Now I get to set four places instead of three. When Cherish grows up, it'll be five, and that's actually a lot, I think. Did you ever think you'd have three children, Mom?"

Ashley watched Mrs. Tanner as she moved gracefully about the kitchen. "I was hoping so."

"Do you think we'll ever have four?" asked Wes.

Mr. Tanner stepped into the kitchen and burst with laughter. "We haven't even had three children for a day and you're already wanting four." He rustled his son's hair. "You are something, Wesley, my boy."

"But do you think we will, Dad?"

"It depends on what God says," Grace said with a patient smile.

God, Ashley thought. Mrs. Berk talked about God a lot. He was that person everyone went to church for; the One who let some people be rich and some be poor. "Providence" is what Mrs. Berk called everything God did. It was Providence that had made Ashley such a perfect chicken-watcher.

Ashley glanced at Mr. Tanner. He was taller and stronger than any man she had ever known. She felt nervous in his company, and wished Wes would offer to go to bed early, like Bonnie often did.

I will have mercy upon her that had not obtained mercy.
—Hosea 2:23

EIGHT

A New House

Ashley peered out the window of her new bedroom, but all she could see was a glittered expanse of stars. She turned and fell on the bed, spreading her arms and swinging her feet over the side. Ashley had dreamed of having her own bedroom, but the closest she had ever come to having anything of her own was the little bed at the orphanage. She had learned to appreciate that after sleeping on a lumpy, creaky mattress with Bonnie.

Her new bed had a four-post oak frame and a rosy-pink quilt. She had her own chest of drawers that sat by the door, and a large wardrobe all to herself. Lacy curtains brushed the top of the desk under the window. A pretty pink-and-white rug covered most of the floor, and the lamp on the bedstead touched the room with cozy light.

Ashley ran her fingers over the smooth, cream-colored wall. She glanced at her dresser and noticed that the enormous mirror above it reflected a brush and a gold-speckled box. She jumped off the bed, clutched the box in her hands, and lifted out a pink baby-doll dress with miniature pearl buttons and a stiff, white collar. Ashley held the dress up to her shoulders and looked in the mirror.

"It won't fit me," she whispered, "but I'd like to keep it all the same." She stuffed it back into the box and dove into bed with a gleeful giggle.

Ashley gazed around the room. A wooden shelf on the far wall held a bouquet of dried flowers. A small wreath and sampler hung beside the window. Above her headboard was a large painting of a father in a rocking chair with a little girl on his lap. The girl was dressed in a fluffy silk frock, and the man was laughing.

Ashley felt her heart sink. She had once been that little girl, perched on Mr. Berk's lap, smiling just like that. He had told her stories and tickled her neck and called her sweet names. The man in that painting looked much happier and more handsome than Mr. Berk, but the very fact that he was a man made Ashley cringe.

She wiggled her bare toes under the cool sheets as grief rushed over her. She tried to tell herself that she was the luckiest orphan in Galesburg because she had her own bedroom, but she knew the truth. She was a slave again. Not to labor, not to chickens or boredom or chores, not even to Mr. Tanner. She was a slave to life. To fear. To injustice.

A slave to memory.

"Does the girl know how to talk?" Grace perched the baby on her hip as she opened the bed and then wearily sat on it.

"She told me how long she's been at the orphanage," Luke said, "but that's all I've heard out of her."

"How long has she been there?"

"All of her life."

"Do you know anything else about her?"

Luke brought the papers from his pocket and tossed them on the dresser. "Mrs. Harms gave me some papers. We'll look at them later."

"Wes seems to have taken a liking to her," Grace said.

Luke unbuttoned his sleeves. "Yeah, he took her to that secret spot of his in the forest."

"Jolie said she was the most adorable orphan in the place." Grace stood and placed Cherish in the cradle beside the bed.

Luke shrugged. "She's cute and she seems to have an agreeable personality." It was obvious that Ashley was detached from everything, but sometimes those kinds of children were best. The attached ones were often bullheaded.

"Well," she said as she slid under the covers, "we have three children now. God has done it for us again."

Luke lay down beside her and the quilt was heavy on his chest. Grace put her hand on his arm and kissed his cheek. He patted her and blew out the lantern and as he lay back against the headboard, his stomach flipped with sickening anxiousness.

When Ashley awoke the next morning, she sleepily opened her eyes and glanced out the window, which was letting in bright sunlight. She leaned over the bed, pushing the curtain back so she could see the outdoors. She gasped at a beautiful field dotted with pink and blue wildflowers, and a barn far off in the distance. Trees lined one side of the field, their budding leaves shaking in the breeze and glittering with sunlight.

Ashley's smile grew so big her cheeks ached. She reveled in the fresh feel of her new room, free from musty air and dust balls. A mockingbird sang a song from the sugar maple tree outside the window, and Ashley saw a baby squirrel run up the trunk, chattering to itself in a squeaky voice.

"Hey, Ashley!" Wes's voice called through the door.

She stood quickly and exchanged her nightdress for her shabby dress.

"Are you awake?"

"Yeah."

"Come on; you can help me with chores."

Ashley glanced at the mirror and cringed at her tangled hair. She took the brush and pushed her hair together at the back of her head, tying it with her piece of string. She put on her stockings and shoes and opened the door with a happy rush.

Wes stood on the other side, his trousers wet and his cheeks rosy. "Dad left for work, but he said I could see if you're awake so you can help me with the rest of my chores."

"What do we have to do?" Ashley followed Wes down the stairs.

"Milk the cow and feed the chickens. But we have to hurry, 'cause Mom's already making breakfast."

The sweet smell of bacon and brown sugar wandered up the stairs, and Ashley's stomach growled loudly.

Wes glanced at her and laughed. "Hungry?"

Ashley nodded, giggling.

The two children scurried to the barn. The spring air felt brisk, and Ashley wrapped her arms around her shoulders. She squinted against the bright glow of the rising sun. The comforting bellow of the milk cow echoed through the valley.

Wes smiled. "Maymie likes to be milked early so she can go out to pasture."

The horses stood grazing in the dew-covered meadow, and the brown-spotted cow stuck her head through the top door of her stall.

Wes began trotting when the cow kicked the stall door, and Ashley was hot on his heels. The stinging wind made her eyes water.

Inside the cozy barn, dust danced in the light that came through a window at the peak of the roof. Ashley remembered pretending with Gretchen and Melissa that the glittering dust was magic powder that could carry them out of the orphanage. Ashley had refused to play that game since she returned from her HOPES family.

Wes shut the top door of the cow stall. "Think you can milk Maymie while I feed the chickens?"

"Do you have to put the chickens outside?" Ashley asked.

"Naw. Not today."

Ashley turned toward the cow stall. "What if she kicks me?"

Wes smiled. "She won't."

Ashley nervously took the large pail from the wall. She stood on tiptoes and stared at quiet-eyed Maymie, thinking how frightening it would be to get squished by a belly-swaying cow. She fumbled with the latch on the gate, pretending she didn't know how to open it.

"This latch is really easy," said Wes, coming up behind her. "Just pull up and push to the left, and it comes right out." He opened the stall. "You don't have to lock it, 'cause she won't try to get out this way. She knows she can only get to the pasture the other way."

Ashley stepped into the stall. She took the stool from the corner and set it beside the cow. Maymie turned her head and Ashley jumped. "I won't hurt you," she promised as butterflies replaced the hunger in her stomach. "You can go with the horses as soon as I milk you, Maymie. Be a good girl now."

Ashley patted the warm belly and cautiously sat on the stool. The tin bucket banged against Maymie's leg and Ashley eyed her warily. When the hefty cow chewed her cud and heaved a sigh that sounded like a kitten purr, Ashley reached for her udder.

"Like this?" Ashley glanced over her shoulder and her eyes met the fond ones of her new brother.

"You got it."

Ashley squeezed the milk from Maymie's teats, and she laughed. "I'm doing it, Wes! And she doesn't even care!"

Wes laughed on his way to the chicken coop. Ashley heard the chickens squawking and scolding as he threw corn on the floor. She glanced behind her and saw Charlie, the white-and-gray rooster, push his way through the hens, scurrying after an ignorant bug. As she watched them fight, Ashley wished she could wring every one of their scrawny necks.

"Have you seen our filly, Ashley?" Wes hollered.

"No."

"Well, she's not really a filly anymore. She's gonna be two this May. Dad got her at the Hendersons' auction last fall. I think she's part draft."

Ashley didn't know who the Hendersons were, or what a draft was.

"Did you go to the Hendersons' auction?" Wes tossed the last of the corn crumbs on the hens' rosy backs.

"I don't think so."

"It was a really big one. A bank auction. Barry Lee Financial foreclosed on the whole farm. The Hendersons left before the auction 'cause Mrs. Henderson couldn't stand to see her things sold off. Dad says Mr. Henderson was always irresponsible, and he borrowed more than he was worth, so it was only right that Barry Lee Financial foreclosed. That's only the second foreclosure in Galesburg in ten years."

Ashley's cold fingers went up and down Maymie's teats. The foamy milk hit the sides of the tin pail.

"We have notes at Barry Lee Financial, too, but Dad says we'll never have foreclosure," Wes continued as he hung his feed bucket on a nail and absently kicked at the loose straw on the floor. "He's a doctor at the hospital—one of the head doctors, actually—so he won't lose his job unless the railroad stops bringing supplies and Galesburg becomes a ghost town."

Ashley's brow creased, wondering what a ghost town was.

"But that won't happen, either." Wes shrugged. "The railroad is really successful, and this town uses it a lot, so there'd be no reason for it to stop coming."

Ashley hummed in agreement.

"Larry Henderson used to be my best friend. We went to Galesburg Academy, and we were in the same grade. But then his dad started doing bad business, so Dad said I shouldn't play with Larry anymore. It was kind of a statement, Dad said. It wasn't Larry's fault that his dad wasn't being wise, but if I played with Larry like he was my best friend, people might think Dad and Mom supported Mr. Henderson."

Ashley pulled harder on the teats, wondering what it would feel like to lose your best friend because your dad wasn't wise.

"After the Hendersons moved, a new family bought their house, and the boy that lives there now is my best friend. His name's

Galen Hendricks, and he's exactly my age. Our birthdays are one day apart. He goes to Galesburg Academy too. We do everything together—all the church socials and the baseball games and the fair. He's gone right now, though; he had to go out west to visit his grandpa. He'll be gone for most of the summer, I guess. I've got a couple other good friends, too, but none as good as Galen. His dad's a lawyer, so Dad likes him well enough. Sometimes Mr. Hendricks has to represent one of the patients at the hospital when they think they haven't gotten the right kind of care. Mr. Hendricks doesn't really want to, but he's the only good lawyer in Galesburg, so he has to. He never wins the cases for the patients, though. It's kind of his sign of loyalty to the hospital."

"He doesn't even try?" Ashley said to the stomach of the cow.

Wes leaned on the stall door. "I suppose he does sometimes. But usually the patients are telling stories, 'cause Galesburg has the best hospital in Caledonia County."

"Don't the doctors ever make mistakes?"

Wesley shrugged. "I guess everyone does sometimes. But they're probably not big enough mistakes to need a lawyer. One time, Mr. Hendricks had to go all the way to district 'cause a patient wouldn't settle with the county court."

Ashley didn't understand all this business, and she was tired of discussing things that were meant for adults.

A short time later, Wes and Ashley entered the house with eggs in Ashley's dress and the pail of foam-covered milk in Wes's hand.

"Shut the door so the baby doesn't get cold," Mrs. Tanner called from the kitchen.

Wes closed the door, then swung the bucket of milk onto the counter. Grace put her arm around her son's shoulders and kissed his head. Ashley stared wide-eyed. She had never seen a mother kiss her child.

Then Ashley felt the motherly grasp around her own shoulders and a little kiss on her tangled mass of blonde hair. She stood frozen, not knowing how to react.

"I heard you're a good helper in the barn," said Grace.

Ashley merely nodded.

"What have we here? My goodness, Wesley, did you make Ashley carry the eggs in her skirt?"

"They didn't break," replied the boy.

Mrs. Tanner gathered the eggs, giggling and patting Ashley so that she couldn't help but like the woman.

Cherish started fussing soon after Grace had emptied Ashley's skirt. "Ashley, do you want to pick her up for me?" asked Grace. "She seems to get along with you, and I need Wesley's help."

Ashley approached the oak cradle, eager to see the baby again. "What's the matter, little one?" She lifted the infant into her arms and sat in the chair. Cherish squirmed and as Ashley sat silently admiring the rosy cheeks and long eyelashes, she wondered if squiggles and waves of chubby hands were how babies communicated.

Wes washed his hands in the basin and shivered when he splashed his face. After drying off with the towel, he took three china plates from the cupboard.

Wes sidled up next to the stove, which was laden with fancy breakfast treats. "Hey, Mom," he whispered, and Ashley strained her ears to hear. "Did you notice Cherish doesn't cry when Ashley holds her? And she's smiling."

Grace uncovered a pan of cinnamon rolls. "Ashley does a good job, doesn't she?"

"She must've held babies before, don't you think?"

"Probably. Now, hurry and set the table. The bacon's going to be cold if we don't eat soon."

Ashley glanced at Mrs. Tanner as the woman worked and she noticed how easily Grace handled herself. The blind woman knew where each cupboard knob was and where her pans hung on the wall. She knew how to manipulate the broken handle on the water pump, and she never forgot where she placed the gloves she wore to take things out of the oven. Even Grace's tidy hairstyle was a reflection of her capability.

I can't even do my hair, the little girl thought, blowing a loose strand from her face with the hint of a smile.

After breakfast, Wes and Ashley cleaned the kitchen while Grace dressed the baby. Wesley instructed his sister on how to wash dishes and which cupboards everything belonged in.

As soon as the dishes were done, Wes burst out the front door with a whoop. Ashley followed close behind. She noticed with a start that Wes had bare feet.

"You don't have shoes on!" Ashley shrieked, stopping on the porch.

"Of course not!" He turned back. "I never wear shoes in the spring. You should take yours off too."

"And go barefoot?" Ashley gasped. This transgression always resulted in Death Sentence at the orphanage.

Wes nodded toward her brown shoes with an air of disgust. "Who needs shoes when the weather's good? Even Mom doesn't wear shoes in the spring."

Suddenly Ashley's feet felt cramped. She plopped down on the porch and pulled off her shoes and stockings with a naughty smile that made Wes laugh.

With their shoes abandoned on the porch, the children strolled to the forest again, Wesley whistling a merry tune.

"Hey, Wes," Ashley said, shoving her hands into her shallow dress pockets, "how old is Cherish?"

The lad thrust his arm at a weed that was in the path. "About three months. She was born January twenty-sixth."

"What's today?"

"I think it's May fifth."

"How long have you lived here?" asked Ashley.

"Since I was six. Dad and Mom bought this place so we could be close to the grandparents and Mom's sisters."

"How many children are in your mom's family?"

Wes stopped abruptly and Ashley bumped into him. He turned and stared at her. "How come you call her my mom?"

"What do you mean?"

"She isn't just *my* mom, you know. She's your mom too."

"She is?"

"Yeah. And my dad's your dad. Don't you understand that?"

Shivers went down her back at the thought of Luke Tanner. Wes patted Ashley's shoulder. "If you don't call them Mom and Dad, people will think we're not really sister and brother."

As they continued through the trees, Ashley wondered if real moms and dads and brothers and sisters lasted forever, like Wes said. She knew that Jack and Henry and Bonnie had been brothers and sister since they were babies. Ashley squirmed when she thought about calling Mr. Tanner "Dad."

"Mom has three sisters, and Dad has one brother," Wes continued. "Dad's family lives a long way away, though, so we don't see them. Have you ever had grandparents?"

Ashley shrugged. "I don't know." She kicked a pebble out of her way. "How do you get grandparents?"

"Mom and Dad's parents are our granddads and grandmas. Orphans don't have grandparents, but now that you're not an orphan, you have two sets of grandparents."

"I have grandparents?" She gasped, and then added quickly, "I'm not an orphan?"

"Of course not! We adopted you. Orphans who go to live in families with moms and dads and brothers and sisters can't still be orphans, you know."

Ashley felt confused, but before she could ask any more questions, they arrived at the fort.

Wes crawled inside. "I think this side wall needs to be stronger." He pushed on the wall. "See how it bows?"

Ashley scooted in behind him. "What does *bow* mean?"

"It kind of leans, like it's going to fall over. Come on; let's fix it."

"How?" asked Ashley as they backed out of the fort.

"We have to find some really straight sticks. You go that way, and I'll go this way, and we'll meet back here as soon as we find a bunch of sticks."

Ashley brushed hair from her face. "What if I get lost?"

"In this little forest?" Wes laughed. "If you stay where you can always see the fort, you won't get lost. And if you do, just start walking and you'll make it home."

Ashley glanced at the fort, which still looked like a pile of brush to her, and she wondered if she could distinguish it from every other dilapidated mound under the tall pines.

"Be careful only to bring the really good, strong sticks, OK?"

Before she could argue, Wes trotted away, and she began stick-searching.

Wes and Ashley spent the entire morning mending their fort. Wes was only satisfied when the wall was so strong that both children could have run at it and not broken it down. Shortly after the two were finished, a bell began ringing in the distance.

Wes reached for his pocket watch. "It's only eleven-thirty. I wonder why Mom's ringing the bell?" He shrugged. "Come on, we have to go."

"Why?"

"When Mom rings the bell, that means she needs us."

Wes stuffed the watch back into his pocket and the two picked their way through the forest. Ashley tried not to squeak when her bare feet stepped on sticks and rocks.

Wes stopped short when he spotted a team of skinny black horses tied to the hitching post. "Somebody's here," he said, glancing at her excitedly. "I bet it's somebody to see you!"

"Me?" she exclaimed. "Why?"

"People want to meet you." He stared critically at the bony horses. "I bet it's Granddad and Grandma Jackson. Those horses are Arabians—probably the ones Granddad just got from the Jensons. They don't look too good. I hope they don't die on the way home."

Ashley stared at the horses, wondering if such skinny creatures really would collapse under harness.

By the time the children stepped onto the smooth, painted porch, Ashley's feet ached terribly. She scooped her shoes into her arms and clutched them tightly.

"Granddad and Grandma Jackson are Mom's parents," Wes said, peeking into the front window. "They really like children, so we won't get away now."

"What do you mean?"

"Just come see," he said, giggling.

Wes and Ashley stepped into the farmhouse, and Ashley peered into the sitting room. There she saw a white-haired man sitting with Cherish in his arms and talking to her in a lively, warm voice as if she could really understand him. He looked like the kind of man she'd heard about in the heartwarming stories Miss Elizabeth read in school. He had smile wrinkles around his eyes and mouth, a full white beard, twinkling green eyes, and a belly that reminded Ashley of Saint Nick. But what captivated her most was the man's cherry-red shirt. That was the very color she wanted for a dress.

"Hello, Nathan!" he exclaimed when the children stepped into the room.

Nathan? Ashley wondered. *Who's that?*

Wes beamed. "Hi, Granddad! I didn't know you were coming."

"Well, of course! We wouldn't miss out on a special day like this, the day our little girl finally comes home." Granddad glanced at Ashley with a kind smile that seemed to approve of every part of her, from the stringy blonde hair to the unsightly dress. "I'm guessing you're Ashley," he said, his voice dripping with pleasure.

Her eyes fell to the floor and she nodded.

"I'm Granddaddy Jackson."

The fire crackled in the fireplace.

"Is Grandma here?" Wes asked, tossing his jacket onto the hat tree.

"She's in the kitchen with your mother," Granddad said. "My goodness, you must be feeding your baby sister well, Nathan. She's twice as big as the last time I saw her."

"She's about three months old now." Wes bounced into the sofa. "She likes Ashley a lot."

"Does she?" Granddad winked at Ashley.

She turned away, but glanced back a second later to admire the shirt again.

A tall, silvery-haired woman came in from the kitchen, carrying two mugs. Her pretty face was identical to Grace Tanner's.

"There you are, Nathan," the woman greeted, offering a mug to Wes. "I brought some water for you and Ashley. Are you thirsty?"

"I am," Wes said, eagerly taking the drink.

"How about you?" Grandma looked at Ashley. She took the mug and sipped from it.

Grace came in behind Grandma. "Wes, did you introduce Ashley to your grandparents?" she asked.

Grandma smiled. "No, but we knew who she was. She's absolutely lovely."

"Ashley," said Mrs. Tanner, "this is Granddaddy and Grandma Jackson. They came to visit because you're here. Isn't that special?"

Ashley leaned against the wall with a rush of awkwardness. Her mind raced with the words *absolutely lovely.* If *lovely* meant what she thought it meant, it certainly didn't fit her—not when Granddad was sitting across the room in a cherry-red shirt, and she had an ugly brown dress.

"Granddad, did you give Ashley her gift?" Grandma asked.

Ashley's heart skipped a beat.

"I haven't had a chance to present it properly. Nathan, fetch that box by the door and give it to your new sister, 'ey?"

Wes eagerly went after the gift, which was wrapped with pretty pink paper and tied with a large white bow. When it was set in her arms, Ashley stared at it. She had never received a present this large and fancy in her entire life—not even for Christmas.

"It's not my birthday," Ashley told Wes with an embarrassed blush.

"It's not for your birthday." He laughed in delight.

"Then why?"

"Because we've been waiting a long time for you," Granddad said, "and we're very happy that you've finally come."

Ashley looked at him, puzzled.

Wes groaned and untied the gift's strings. When he began to rip the paper off, she pulled off the bow. When Wes lifted the lid off the box, Ashley saw a lacy white hat with a netted veil and pearls swirled on the brim. She shrieked. "It's a hat!"

Granddad gave a hearty laugh. "That's the latest fashion—the very best we could find in all of Galesburg. Now our little girl can walk the town in style."

Ashley set the hat on her head and giggled when she looked through the veil, which was scattered with sparkles.

"It looks beautiful," Wes said. "Mom, you should feel all the pearls and sparkles on it."

It's all my own, Ashley thought, moving across the room to sidle up to Grace.

"It's wonderful," Grace said when she felt the netting. "Say thank you to your grandma and granddaddy."

Ashley bit her lip.

"Ashley loves it, Grandma and Granddaddy," Grace said. "Don't you, Ashley?"

Ashley couldn't hide her grin.

"She'll have to wear it whenever we go to town," Wes said.

And every other day.

Grandma gave her a kind wink. Ashley noticed that her silver hair was braided in a crown on her head. She wondered if Grandma did her own hair, and she wished she could wear her hair like that.

"Are you expecting more company today, Gracie?" Grandma asked.

"Not today. Harriet Elton and Susie said they might stop by tomorrow."

"We'd better start cleaning then. Granddad has the baby, so if Wes and Ashley can run errands, we'll get a lot accomplished today."

"Once a week," Wes whispered to Ashley, "Grandma helps Mom cook and clean and sew. Last week they sewed and Miss Maggie cleaned, but Dad said he doesn't want Miss Maggie to come this week."

"Who's Miss Maggie?"

"The maid. She comes about once a month to do all the dusting and cleaning that Mom can't do very well."

Ashley fell silent when she noticed Granddad watching her.

"The kitchen needs cleaned the worst this week, Mum," Grace said with a shake of her head as the women started for the kitchen. "Wes said there are cobwebs in the corner."

"Maggie didn't get them last week?" Grandma asked.

"Or maybe they came since then."

The kitchen came alive with the sounds of sweeping, dusting, pumping water, and happy chatter. Ashley sat on a stool beside the couch, thinking what a difference this kitchen team was compared to the scolding, gossipy one at the orphanage. She smiled at the realization that plump Miss Rose wouldn't be giving her a bath the day after tomorrow.

Ashley watched Wes and Granddad talking. Granddad laughed more than he talked, and patted Cherish's bottom so often that Ashley felt pity for the baby, who was trying to fall asleep. Granddad spoke to Wes as if he were a grown man, asking Wes's opinions on how the syrup crop would be this year, and listening to Wes tell stories of his last day at school, his plans for the summer, and his new duties as the older brother of two little girls.

"How did your grades end up in school this year?" asked Granddad.

"I got second best out of thirteen in our class. Next year Ashley will be going to school with me, won't you, Ashley?"

She wished her brother wouldn't take notice of her.

"Have you had a tour of your new home, Ashley?" Granddad asked, winking at Wes.

"No." She tucked her chin into her shoulder.

Granddad's eyes bulged. "No? Well, what has your brother been up to?"

"I haven't had time," Wes said, his blue eyes sparkling. "I showed her the barn and the forest. She's seen some of the downstairs too. Is that all, Ashley?"

She nodded, not wanting to mention that she had peeked into Wes's blue-and-white-striped bedroom earlier that morning.

"So you haven't shown her the outhouse yet?" said Granddad.

Wes's face dropped, and he looked at Ashley with sudden surprise. Her cheeks blushed. "I found it."

Granddad laughed loudly. "I still say you should give her the tour, Nathan."

"Come on," Wes said. "I'll show you around."

Ashley got the grand tour of the Tanner home from the tip of the attic to the bottom of the cellar, in every wardrobe, out every window, and through every door. Wesley showed her the trinketry treasures that he kept in his room, and they admired the wallpaper in his mother's purple sewing room in the corner of the hall upstairs. Wes showed Ashley the little pink room adjacent to her own bedroom, which was called "the baby's room," though Cherish slept in her parents' bedroom.

The children searched the guest bedroom (the only bedroom on the main floor) to find a beautiful lace doily that Grandma Jackson had made. In the cellar they discovered a box of Mr. Tanner's medical books, and they got distracted trying to pronounce the names of diseases and fractures.

Then, with ceremonial gracefulness, Wes opened the door to the parlor and tiptoed in reverently.

The parlor was a pretty, bright room set just off the foyer at the front of the house. It was decorated so beautifully that Ashley was afraid to step onto the gorgeous flowered rug or bounce onto the green fainting couch like Wesley did. She merely stood in the doorway and admired the silvery white paper on the walls, the quiet painting above the fireplace, and the cozy-looking chairs and sofas surrounded by end tables holding bouquets of fresh wildflowers.

"Nice, isn't it?" asked Wes, watching her with a smile.

"We shouldn't be in there," Ashley said quietly. She stepped back from the doorway.

"Why not?" Wes bounded off the couch, glancing with alarm over his shoulder.

"'Cause you'll get it dirty," whispered Ashley as she backed farther into the foyer.

Wes's shoulders slumped. He stared at her and shook his head. "You act like it's dangerous. Mom doesn't mind if I show you; we're just not supposed to play in there. I help her clean it, and we have company in the parlor. She won't mind, Ashley, really."

Ashley stood silent for a moment. "Are you sure?"

"Of course. Now, come on—let's go see what Granddad's doing."

"Grace, are you planning on making Ashley a dress?" Grandma asked as she scrubbed a shelf in the pantry.

"Actually, I wasn't. Does she need one?"

"Yes. Hers is a plain brown, and it's too big at the sleeves. If you have time, it would make her look more kempt to have a calico dress."

Grace scrubbed a pot in the sink. "That's a good idea, but I'm very busy sewing for the society right now. They're helping the hospital expand, and they've asked me to make twenty shirts to use as uniforms. I guess Ashley's dress will have to wait. I've already committed to the society."

Grandma shook her head. "Really, Gracie, you should consider pulling out of the aid society. There are plenty of women who have more time to sew than you do. And you don't make a cent at it."

"But I want to do it, Mum. It's the only real sewing Luke will allow me to do. He doesn't want me to share in providing for the family."

"It really is his job," Grandma agreed.

"But I could help," Grace said in a frustrated tone. "I'm a trained seamstress. The only thing that holds me back is being a doctor's wife."

Grandma laughed. "I don't think that's something to complain about." She shook out her rag on the dusty pantry floor. "Don't worry about Ashley's dress. I'll help you with it whenever you're ready."

"Does she need anything else?" Grace thrust the squeaky pump handle up and down. "How are her shoes and her hair?"

"Her hair is just pulled back with a string. I don't suppose she knows how to braid. Someone at the orphanage probably did it for her."

"Is it pretty?" Grace brushed her hands on her apron.

"Very pretty. But it's thin and scraggly at the ends. If she'd let you to trim it, I think it would be prettier."

"Luke says it's light colored."

"She's a beautiful blonde. Gracie, she's the daughter you've been waiting for. Do you realize that Ashley was born the same year as Emma?"

"I know," Grace said in a quiet voice. She set a large pan upside down on a towel on the counter. "It would mean a lot to me if you would do her hair today. I'll do it after you get the first snarls out. I want Ashley to feel good about herself. Jolie said she hasn't had a lot of self-esteem. And no wonder. The poor child, living in the Galesburg orphanage her entire life. Mum, if it were in my power, I would do away with orphanages altogether and place all the children in happy families. But there are so many of them."

"You're changing the lives of three children, Gracie."

Grace stopped washing and turned toward her mother. "Do you think Ashley is happy?"

Grandma paused. "She's cheerful, but I can't tell if she's genuinely happy. Of course, I haven't known her even as long as you have."

Grace leaned against the counter. "I haven't even had the chance to hold her. I'm still waiting for an opportunity to sit with her and tell her stories, like Wes loved."

"It's only the second day." Grandma reached for the broom. "You'll have time. It's obvious that Ashley admires you."

"Does she?" Grace's cheeks blushed.

"Of course. She watches you whenever you come in the room."

Silence ruled the kitchen as Grace returned to her scrubbing and the broom whisked across the pantry floor. The teapot squealed and Grace took it off the burner.

"Do you know if Ashley has ever done cooking or cleaning?" asked Grandma.

"She did the dishes with Wes this morning and she seemed to do fine, but I don't know if she's done much on her own."

"She could be a great help to you eventually. You may even be able to replace Maggie if you train Ashley well enough. How old did you say she was?"

"Eight."

"That's old enough to sew even. I'm sure she could help you make a dress, or you could start her on a sampler."

"I'm not ready for that yet." Grace patted her hands on the edge of the basin and reached for the towel. "I want to build a comfortable relationship with her first."

"The child trained young is a child trained well."

"She'll be plenty young enough even if she's nine years old. I'll let that wait for now."

That evening, after the grandparents left and the house was clean, Wes and Ashley sat on the floor in the sitting room, playing a counting game and attending to Cherish when she fussed. Mrs. Tanner sat in her rocking chair, stitching the hem of a pillowcase and listening to the children play their game. She touched each stitch after she had taken it to make sure it was straight and strong.

Ashley stared at the sea of dominoes that made a winding, cutting pattern on the rug. "Now, where do I have to lay mine this time?"

"Do you have one with four dots, like this one?" asked Wes, showing her one of his.

Ashley plucked a domino out of her stack and laid it against the four-dotted one at the end of the dizzying maze.

The kitchen door opened and heavy shoes pounded on the floor.

"Hey, Dad!" Wes exclaimed when Luke Tanner's tall form stepped into the room.

"Hello, Son. How are you?"

"Good. We're playing a game. Wanna play?"

Luke shook his head. "I'll just watch this time." He touched his wife's shoulder and kissed her cheek. "Hello, Grace," he said softly.

"Granddad and Grandma Jackson came over today," Wes announced, resting his chin on his knee after he had found a place for another domino. "They got to meet Ashley, and they gave her a new hat."

"Is that right?" Luke groaned as he sat in his rocker, and Ashley wondered if the uneasy scowl on his face meant that he was in a sour mood.

"I showed Granddad the new buggy," Wes said.

"What'd he say about it?"

"He liked it."

Mr. Tanner lifted Cherish into his arms. Ashley stared at the dominoes stacked on the floor, trying to stop her heart from racing.

Wes turned his attention back to the game. "I can lay one here, and then I'll only have two dominoes left." He placed one piece on the rug and smiled. "Your turn."

Ashley reached for her top square and found that her hand was trembling.

"Did you get your chores done, Wes?" Mr. Tanner asked after kissing Cherish.

"I haven't gone out yet."

"Better do that 'fore supper is served; otherwise you'll be doin' it in the dark."

"Can we finish this game first?"

"How soon will it be over?"

"As soon as one of us runs out of dominoes. I think Ashley's going to win."

Mr. Tanner smiled, but Ashley thought his smile was fake. "She's catchin' on pretty well, 'ey?"

"Yup."

Ashley agreed to do chores with Wes that night, grateful to escape from Mr. Tanner's sight.

"Watch me milk," she begged the boy.

Wesley patiently watched her, chatting amiably, engulfing Ashley in a world where she could forget her fears.

"Do Granddad and Grandma live a long way away?" Ashley asked, leaning her head on the belly of the cow and keeping her eyes on the milk that slowly streamed into the bucket.

"About an hour's drive. They usually come to our house every week, and they go to the church in Galesburg on holidays."

"Why do they call you Nathan?"

Wes stuffed his hands into his pockets. "That's my middle name. Granddad's name is Nate. They call Cherish 'little Cherry' sometimes. Granddad calls Grandma 'Granny.'"

"Gretchen had a granny once," Ashley said. "But then she came back to the orphanage."

"Why do orphans leave and come back all the time?" Wes asked.

"That's just the way it happens. Nobody keeps orphans for a long time."

"Well, I think that's silly. Parents should keep kids forever." Wes's heavy sigh caused the cow to swing her head to look at him.

Ashley smiled. "Then there wouldn't be such a thing as orphans."

Wes gazed at her. "I guess you're right. Boy, you're smart."

I'm smart? Ashley blinked in surprise. She had never been called that before.

Edify one another, even as also ye do.
—1 Thessalonians 5:11

The Apothecary

Ashley awoke to the sound of rain gently falling on the roof. Her window let in a cold breeze that sent shivers down her spine. She wrapped the quilt around her shoulders and gazed out the window at the dark early-morning world.

Ashley sat up. She followed the streaks of moonlight to the picture at the head of her bed.

A father in a rocker with a girl, she thought with a nervous rush. She sank back into the quilts and tried to imagine why someone would paint such a scene.

When she heard rustling downstairs, Ashley quickly dressed and stepped into the hall. Wes's bedroom door was slightly open as she tiptoed by. The parents' bedroom was at the end of the hall, and Ashley didn't dare get close to it. Mr. Berk once strapped Henry when he sleepwalked into the parents' bedroom.

Creeping down the stairs, Ashley stayed close to the wall, hoping to see who was talking before she showed herself. She had hardly made it down five stairs when Grace called in a quiet, gentle voice, "Is that you, Wesley?"

Ashley crouched down on the step.

"I think it's Ashley," whispered Mr. Tanner.

"Ashley?" Grace's voice rang out.

Ashley slid down three more stairs and slowly poked her head around the corner. She saw Mr. and Mrs. Tanner sitting in their rockers with a fire blazing in the fireplace.

"Come sit on Mama's lap, baby," Grace invited.

She hesitated on the step. When Mr. Tanner gave her a friendly nod, she scooted onto Mrs. Tanner's lap. Ashley fidgeted with her nightdress and stiffly laid her head on the woman's shoulder. Grace rocked as the fire sent shadows dancing on the dark walls.

"Did you sleep well?" Grace asked.

Ashley nodded against Mrs. Tanner's chest, afraid to move or speak. The crackling fire drowned out the sound of the rain on the roof, and the little girl stared into it until her eyes blurred and she had to look away.

Mr. Tanner nodded at Ashley. "Have you lived anywhere besides the orphanage?"

Ashley shook her head. Her cheeks blushed, knowing she had just lied.

"I thought Mrs. Harms said you lived with another family at some point." Mr. Tanner shrugged. "Well, I guess we'll be the first ones who show you what a family is like."

The rhythmic movement of the rocker made Ashley's eyes heavy but she refused to let them shut.

"Is anyone coming to see Ashley today?" Mr. Tanner asked at length.

"Susie and the children will be here for dinner," Grace said.

"You'll have a houseful, then." Mr. Tanner crossed his knee and winked at Ashley. She glanced away at the cheerful gesture, her heart racing.

"I have to do some sewing before the day's over," Grace said. "Will you be able to come home early?"

Mr. Tanner sighed. "Not very. Zeke hired two new doctors, so I have to show them around. I'll likely be home just before supper." He shook his head. "I don't know where the hospital comes up with these city boys, but I often wonder if they come to Galesburg only to build their reputations, since Galesburg Medical Institute is reputed in all the colleges."

Ashley squirmed in Grace's arms as Mr. Tanner stood and started toward the stairs. "It's five thirty; time for Wes to do chores."

"What's going on at the apothecary?" Grace asked with presumptuous disgust.

"It's Friday, Gracie," he replied. "We meet a half hour earlier on Fridays, remember?"

"I feel bad for Wes," she said tenderly, "having to get up before dawn."

"He'll be fine." Mr. Tanner began climbing the stairs. "He's almost a man."

The apothecary on Fifth and Selly was a tiny, white-painted brick building that attracted Galesburg's high social circle for no apparent reason. It was the only store in Galesburg that didn't have a glass window front, and the rug outside the door gave the only indication that it was occupied. Inside, the walls were painted stark white from floor to ceiling and were lined with soaps, medicines, candles, salts, tonics, and herbs. It smelled of castor oil and lye soap in the afternoons, and cigar smoke and men's cologne every morning.

Mr. Dale Gildey, the store owner, was a passionate politician, and his morning visitors were limited to sophisticated white gentlemen no younger than twenty. Everyone else was too ignorant, colored, female, or low class to dare walk through the apothecary doors between seven and eight in the morning, even though the sign on the door read OPEN. Galesburg's higher class didn't have time to be interrupted by uneducated conversation, and every native knew that well.

When Luke arrived at the uninviting building on Friday morning, he was ten minutes early, as usual, but Judge Baker, banker Barry Lee, and an odd assortment of twenty-something-year-old practicing politicians were already there, all gathered around the trim, balding Mr. Gildey. A piece of paper hung next to the OPEN sign, with NO CHILDREN ALLOWED in thick, bold letters. This was Mr. Gildey's way of telling parents that he wouldn't pay for broken merchandise.

A gold-plated bell announced Luke's arrival. He brushed his feet on the brown rug and tried to push away the nervous knot that had formed in his stomach. He hadn't decided what he was going to say if one of the men asked about Ashley. He wanted to break the news to them slowly over a matter of weeks, so that by the time they realized that he had adopted from Galesburg, Ashley would be a part of his family enough that it wouldn't matter if she had once been a penny parcel.

"Good morning, gentlemen," Luke said as the door sucked shut behind him. "I have a surgery at eight o'clock, so there's no faking the timecard. Make the coffee strong, Dale; I'm going to have a long day."

"Not half as long as Freddy Hall here," Barry said, nodding toward a skinny youth. "He made the mistake of scheduling an appointment with Preacher Bowtie today." He winked. "Seems Freddy's been having some spiritual issues, and Bowtie says he's got the answers."

Judge Baker clicked his tongue. "I reckon you'd be better off waiting for your 'spiritual issues' to figure themselves out, rather than subject yourself to ol' Bowtie."

Freddy was hunched in a chair, staring at the floor with reddening cheeks.

Luke settled into one of Dale Gildey's squeaky leather recliners. "I don't know for myself, but I've heard rumor that Bowtie gets mighty intense in those counseling sessions of his. Good luck, Freddy. You'll have to give us your report on Monday."

The bell above the door rang again and a stream of men flooded the apothecary, hanging their stylish black hats on the three hat trees by the door. They swarmed the coffee and cigar table. As discussion rolled on, the white walls became saturated with smoke, and nearly every chair in the sitting room became occupied.

One of the men who arrived with the rush was Dan Sulka, a carpenter and father of four. Of all the men who came into the apothecary every weekday, Dan was easily voted the most peculiar. Nobody knew why he came, for he certainly didn't fit into this classy meeting. He didn't smoke the expensive cigars or even drink coffee, and his opinion usually contradicted everyone else's. He was a fairly tall man, with a clean face, dark, earnest eyes, and a voice that rang with honesty. Dan was just gentleman enough to be counted in the high class of Galesburg, so he was welcome at the apothecary, but he always made everyone nervous.

Mr. Gildey greeted all the newcomers . . . except Mr. Sulka.

"Morning, Dan," Luke said.

"Morning, Luke. How are things at home?"

Luke cringed. That was a question only Dan Sulka would ask. "Good. How about you? Are the children well?" His eyes wandered to the other men and he wondered if they were listening.

"Very good. If I remember right, you adopted a new little one this week."

Luke felt several sets of eyes turn toward him and his cheeks turned hot. "Sure did," he said without pause.

"A little girl this time, 'ey?" Dan asked, sitting in a wide chair that would have drowned a smaller man.

"Yeah."

"Healthy and happy?"

Luke shrugged. "Could use a little help with both, but that'll change with time. My wife sure is proud; I guess that's all that matters."

"I heard you got this one from Galesburg," Barry Lee said with a sniff.

Luke cocked his head. "I didn't realize you were keeping such close tabs on my life."

"Oh, don't worry, Tanner; I don't mind. If you have to get your children by adoption, you might as well keep your business local. Every placement gets us one step closer to closing that asylum."

"Actually," said Patrick Cummings, an outspoken Democrat who took pride in his Irish brogue, "adopting orphans doesn't help society at all. Children like that turn into adults who upset the balance of humanity. It's better that they live without parents, without being related to anyone, and live alone on the streets of New York when they're grown."

Luke bit his tongue. He wished he could punish Dan for bringing up the subject in the first place.

"You're a brave man, Tanner," Patrick added. "Foolish, but brave."

"Does this new little girl of yours behave?" asked Judge Baker with a raspy cough.

Luke saw the warning in the old man's eyes and decided not to answer. He wouldn't brag about Ashley until he was sure she would never cross him in public.

"More coffee! More coffee!" Barry Lee broke the silence, and the men thrust their cups in the air as if cheering on the awkward confrontation.

The bell rang as the door opened again. Lawyer Jonathan Hendricks entered alone, as he always did, just so everyone would acknowledge his arrival. Dressed in the most expensive suit to be found in Galesburg, with shiny black shoes and a brass-polished cane, Mr. Hendricks was a walking fashion statement. He took up most of the doorway.

His waxed mustache creased into a mocking smile when he laid eyes on the large gathering. "A delightful morning to you, gentlemen. The coffee is being called for already, Mr. Gildey?"

Luke blushed and hoped that no one would mention the reason for the call.

"It's the start of a good, political day," Mr. Gildey replied. "Lots of confrontation to keep the men sharp at work."

As Hendricks passed by Luke's chair he patted his shoulder in an older-man fashion. Luke didn't look up at him or greet him for fear of receiving another scowl like the one Judge Baker had given him.

The rumble of low voices began again.

"How's the wife?" Hendricks asked Barry Lee as he took the last available chair.

"Don't think I'll ever understand that woman," he said with a grunt. "Insists on making her own clothes, when we've enough surplus to buy three wardrobes full." Barry cocked his head. He always made sure everyone knew of his successful financial position. "She works for the aid society like it were a paying job, but never accepts a cent. Not only that, she made me hire a trophy shiner for this year's baseball trophy; says she doesn't have time to do it herself."

"Doesn't she work at the bank anymore?" asked Freddy.

"Not a lick, and I've had a terrible time finding a trustworthy replacement. Accountants these days all want more money, more time off, and more credit than they're worth. None of them will even shine my trophy."

"What kind of child did you find for your trophy-shiner then?" Patrick Cummings asked with a warning glance at Barry.

"It better not be a child," grumbled Mr. Hendricks. "Even though you design it, Barry, that trophy is public property, far as I'm concerned. And when the Class wins the ball game in June, it'd better never have been touched by a child."

"Don't worry." Barry Lee whistled through his teeth. "I hired a regular professional to shine it—Mr. John L. Mason himself."

"Is he from around here?" asked Freddy.

Barry Lee cocked his head and shifted in his seat. "Not at all. Comes from Bennington County. I searched long and hard before I came up with him. Yes sir, that trophy will be the prettiest one in the showcase. After all, it's a new decade. A winning game in the year 1910 deserves an especially fancy trophy."

"Haven't you even finished designing it yet?" asked Mr. Cummings, puffing on a cigar.

Barry tapped on the table. "I finalize the drawing today. It'll be here in plenty of time to sit in the bank's front window so the Class will have a motivation to get the victory."

"The Tariff Act was the most pathetic move Taft's made yet," a voice from the cigar table said loudly. Several of the men cocked their heads to listen as Judge Baker began his weekly scolding. "Completely cripples American progress."

"Some people are happy about it," Dr. Gere, a middle-aged man, replied. "It was good for the businessmen, and I dare say the bankers didn't protest."

"Not at all," said Barry Lee, turning in his seat to join the debate. "Baker, if you owned an industry that had to fight against cheap foreign goods, you'd be glad the tariffs were raised so there wasn't as much competition. The businessmen have to know their products are going to sell. And if we bankers didn't have successful businessmen investing in our establishments, we'd end up poor and homeless—not that I've ever been close to either."

Luke was about to insert his opinion when he glanced across the room and saw that Dan Sulka was watching him. He quickly looked away and sealed his lips in silence. He resolved to keep quiet as long as Dan was in the room to avoid the possibility of the conversation turning back to Ashley.

Luke shook his head at himself. He thought about Ashley and wondered what was so special about her that Grace couldn't have chosen a child from an orphanage outside of Galesburg.

Judge Baker grumbled at Barry Lee. "Businessmen and bankers shouldn't be our concern. We should be concentrating on the Midwest—the land of promise that will see our country to honest gain. Farmers were hit square in the gut by the Payne-Aldrich Tariff Act! I've heard of three already who've gone under because they can't afford to buy imported goods."

"They went under because of a raised tariff?" Dr. Gere asked skeptically.

Judge Baker snorted. "Well, I suppose there could have been other small contributing factors."

"Even if three went under solely because of the Tariff Act," Dr. Gere argued, "that's three out of how many?"

"There are thousands still in operation," Patrick put in. "And some who've actually benefited from the Act."

"Not farmers." Jonathan Hendricks tapped the floor with his cane. "The only people benefiting from that Act are the Standpatters."

"I guess I can't exactly agree with the Act," Mr. Gildey said as he set out a new pot of coffee. "Especially since Taft promised lower tariffs during his campaign. But it doesn't sit right with me, knowing that industries are losing money because of foreign competition."

Judge Baker gulped down his cold coffee and went for more. "Taft has broken every promise he made during the campaign. He's not a man of his word. I'm ashamed of Roosevelt for voting for him."

"I reckon between Taft and that Democrat Bryan, anyone would choose Taft," Dan Sulka said.

Patrick Cummings blew out a puff of smoke. "Roosevelt said, 'There could not be found in the whole country a man so well fitted to be president.' But Taft isn't half the man some of our senators are."

"And not a quarter of ol' Roosevelt," Freddy said.

"A quarter?" Judge Baker choked on his coffee. "For shame! Saying Taft is anywhere near a quarter of Teddy Roosevelt. Willie Taft doesn't have a hair on his head that compares in quality to Theodore Roosevelt."

Dr. Gere returned from the coffee table and mumbled to Luke, "In Baker's eyes, no one will ever compare to Teddy—not even George Washington himself."

"I hope Taft's life is stolen clean out of him before his term is over," Judge Baker said. "The way I see it, James Sherman could take over and repair some of the damage."

Mr. Gildey firmly shook his head. "Schoolcraft Sherman is just a vice. That's all he's good for."

"He's a good vice, though," Barry Lee commented.

The clock on the wall chimed quarter till eight, as if to announce the start of round two. When it finished, Jonathan Hendricks leaned back in his chair and asked, "So, Dr. Gere, what is your opinion on the builders who were recently hired for the construction of the new sheriff's station?"

"They're qualified," Gere said calmly.

"And expensive," Dan Sulka added. "The new station isn't going to be big enough to hire a crew like Valley. The plans have some lavish extras, but nothing a regular carpenter couldn't tackle. The city is paying far more than that building is worth."

Mr. Cummings cocked his head. "I'd say you're a bit biased, having had your bid denied, Mr. Sulka." Several of the men snickered quietly. "I think Valley Construction is sufficiently qualified. If we hired lower-class workers, it would slow construction time and heighten the chances for mistakes that will cost more in the long run."

"There's a price to pay for community safety." Barry Lee smiled broadly. He had already secured a contract for the note on the extravagant sheriff's station and jail.

Mr. Sulka sniffed, but said nothing.

"Socioeconomically disadvantaged citizens must be securely kept," Freddy added.

"Not that we've ever had a breakout," Mr. Gildey pointed out.

"Even the worry of a breakout isn't worth the risk," Judge Baker said. "I hesitate to sentence lawbreakers to jail anymore, out of anxiety over the possibility they'll escape." Several of the men looked at Judge Baker with wide eyes. "Not that something like that would ever distort my sense of justice. Of course duty prevails over personal concern for safety."

The men nodded.

"Speaking of safety," Dr. Gere announced abruptly, "I have a baby to see into the world." He retired his coffee cup to the cigar table, nodding at Luke. "And I believe you are to be in surgery in a few minutes."

Dr. Tanner surrendered his cup after one last swig. "Good morning, gentlemen. I hope you all have a fine day."

"Give our best regards to your penny parcel," Patrick Cummings said with a little laugh.

Barry Lee scooted to the edge of his seat and said firmly, "And remember that an upper crust keeps society as his main focus, whether or not his wife is barren."

Luke reached for the door handle and his cheeks turned hot with shame as he left.

Even so ye also outwardly appear righteous unto men, but within ye are full of hypocrisy and iniquity.

—Matthew 23:28

TEN

Gray Skies

Ashley sat on the wood floor of Grace's sewing room and snipped threads from the white gowns that her new mother had sewn. She wore her new hat to give the impression of a professional seamstress, and occasionally sang a little tune to herself:

> If you can't sing at all,
> a whistle will have to do;
> If you don't know how to whistle,
> you'll have to hum this tune.
> Doo-dee-doo, doo-dee-doo.
> If you don't know how to whistle,
> you'll have to hum this tune.

The window on the north side of the sewing room was slightly open, and the smell of rain made Ashley want to cuddle under a blanket and fall asleep. Cherish slept in her cradle near the window, snuggled under a heavy quilt, occasionally smiling in her dreams.

Grace sewed in silence. She had asked Ashley several questions about herself, but the girl couldn't answer most of them because she knew very little about herself. What she did know of her past, Ashley was unwilling to admit to. She didn't know her last name or the day she was born or why she had been brought to the orphanage. All she told Grace was that she had lived at the orphanage for eight years, and that Miss Elizabeth said she was in the second grade.

Wes came in from chores with his blonde hair dripping. His boots banged on the stairs as he climbed them, and when he approached the sewing room, he left a trail of footprints. "Mom, can we go to the forest now?"

"Isn't it still raining?" asked Grace.

He shrugged. "Well, yeah."

"I don't suppose that's very wise, then."

"But it's only sprinkling. Please, Mom?"

"Your dad said he saw lightning earlier. Did you?"

Wes sank into a chair and sighed. "Yeah."

"Then you know you can't go into the forest, Son. Why don't you get that book you were reading earlier?"

"I don't want to read a silly old book. When's Aunt Susie coming?"

"I don't know."

"Is she bringing Kenny?"

The sewing machine purred. "I think so."

"I wish Galen were here."

"Is he still gone?"

"Yeah; he won't be back for the whole summer."

Ashley looked at her brother with wide, curious eyes. She had never seen Wesley discontent.

Grace pumped the pedal up and down. "At least you have Ashley to be your friend. You'd be very bored if she weren't here."

The boy stared blankly. "Yeah, but she's helping you."

"Did you make your bed today, Wesley?"

"No." Wes slumped further.

"Then do that and try to find some way to entertain yourself inside," Grace said tenderly. "You could read to me later, or maybe we'll make cookies when I finish this shirt."

Wes kicked off his boots and shuffled to his bedroom.

Ashley stared out the sheer white curtains, smiling when she saw puddles in the driveway. She loved rain, and wondered what it would be like to jump in a puddle after the sun came out. Rainbows often glided on the tops of the puddles, and Ashley wanted to know if they would disappear if she stepped on one.

"Is the baby sleeping, Ashley?" Grace asked.

"Yes."

The machine stopped and Grace straightened the fabric she was piecing into a hospital uniform. "Then why don't you leave that gown and go get a brush? As soon as I'm done with this sleeve, I'll do your hair really prettily. Does that sound good?"

"No." Ashley wasn't convinced that Mrs. Tanner knew how to braid, especially since she couldn't see to do it.

Grace looked surprised. "It's not nice to tell Mama no, darlin'. Please do as you're told."

Ashley set down the scissors and meandered to her bedroom, gently removing her special hat and then pulling the string that held her hair at the back of her neck. She moved as slowly as possible, hoping the woman would forget by the time she returned to the sewing room.

But Grace didn't forget. When Ashley came back in, her mother's sewing project had been put away and the machine was covered. Mrs. Tanner sat in a chair by the window, her face illumined by the outdoor light.

The moment Ashley put one toe in the sewing room, Grace asked, "Are you ready, darlin'?"

Ashley answered with a meek, "Yes." She handed Grace the brush and plopped down on the floor. When her mother touched her hair, she shivered and giggled.

"My, your hair is long," Mrs. Tanner said as she ran her fingers across the thin ends. "Has it ever been cut?"

"No."

"Would you like it cut?"

"No."

"Who did your hair at the orphanage?" Grace asked.

"Miss Hattie."

"Did she make one or two braids?"

Ashley smiled. "Could you do it in a crown?"

Grace chuckled. "I'm afraid you'll have to ask Grandma for a crown."

"Then just one braid."

Wes came banging down the hall and slipped on the slick floorboards in the sewing room. He caught himself against the doorframe. "Aunt Susie's here!" he yelled.

Cherish's eyes popped open and she stirred.

"Don't be so loud, Wesley," Grace said, quickly pleating Ashley's hair. "Go greet them. I'll be down when I'm finished."

Wes ran out the door and Grace laughed. "He's such a silly boy."

Ashley had often been called silly, but she had never heard the word used as a compliment, or said in love or adoration. She smiled to herself as Grace began braiding, thinking that *silly* sounded like a wonderful word when Mama said it.

Mrs. Tanner tied a pale pink ribbon at the bottom of Ashley's braid and lifted Cherish into her arms. She carried the baby downstairs, with Ashley following.

Ashley heard excited voices on the front porch. She took Cherish from her mother's arms so she would have something to look at when everyone started asking her questions.

I should have put my hat back on. She could have hidden her face under the brim.

Ashley stood on tiptoe to look into the mirror that hung on the foyer wall. To her surprise, the braid looked neat and tidy, every hair in place.

As she dropped down to her flat feet, Wes stepped in, accompanied by two boys about his size.

"This is Ashley," Wesley said to the boys, pride sparkling in his blue eyes. "She's my new sister. Ashley, this is Kenny and Len. They're our cousins."

"Hi," Ashley said in a shy voice. Kenny was dark and brawny, and Len was skinny with sandy hair. She stared between the cousins, thinking how much they looked like Jack and Henry.

Wes turned to the boys. "You want to go to my room for a while?"

"Sure," Kenny replied.

"You wanna come?" Wes asked Ashley.

She shook her head, blushing in spite of her efforts to look composed.

After the boys took off, Grace came into the house, a dark-haired, slender woman beside her. She looked almost identical to Mrs. Tanner, and the baby she held in her arms looked just like Cherish.

"Ashley?" Grace called as she closed the door.

"Yes?" came a small, timid reply.

"Darlin', this is Aunt Susie and her daughter, Mary. They came to meet you."

Ashley leaned against the wall, wondering why these people would make a visit just to meet her. In all her eight years, Ashley had not received as much attention as she had in the past two days.

"Hello, Ashley," Aunt Susie said with an approving nod. "It's nice to meet you. We've been waiting a long time for you to come."

Baby Mary squiggled in her mother's arms and pushed to get down, but Aunt Susie held her and whispered in her ear. Ashley watched Susie's gentle pats on her baby's back, and her brow creased. After two days of scrutinizing her own new mother, Ashley had come to the conclusion that Mrs. Tanner was an exception to the female race, or perhaps the epitome of human beings altogether, for her gentle style was unlike any other person Ashley had ever known. But now she wasn't so sure, for Aunt Susie appeared to be equally as kind.

"Ashley, be polite," said Grace, interrupting the girl's thoughts. Silence fell, as if the women were waiting for something. Ashley stared at Susie, wondering how to "be polite."

"At least say hello," Grace urged.

"Hello," Ashley replied, then let her gaze fall to the floor.

"My, my, you're handy with that baby," Aunt Susie said in a slightly hoarse voice. "She must like you. I'll bet Ashley's a great help, isn't she, Gracie?"

Mrs. Tanner stepped into the sitting room. "Yes, she is. Ashley and Wes help me with Cherish all the time. Would you like a seat, Susie?"

Aunt Susie sat in Mr. Tanner's rocker and situated her baby on her lap, smoothing her little pink dress. Ashley sat on the floor beside the fire and put Cherish on her shoulder, patting her when she wiggled. She stared at baby Mary and questions danced in her brain.

If she can walk, Gretchen and Melissa will want to know how old she is. They'd often speculated about how old babies were when they began to walk. *I wonder if she sleeps all the time? She probably can't talk yet. I wonder how old babies are when they talk?*

Aunt Susie smiled at Ashley. "Would you like to hold Mary?"

A big smile spread across her face.

"If you'll let me hold your sister, I'll let you hold Mary. How's that?"

My sister? Ashley thought. "Oh. Sure."

Aunt Susie set Mary on the floor and the baby stood beside the rocker, clutching her mother's dress. Her tiny white shoes tottered shakily, then balanced out as Aunt Susie stepped away and took Cherish. She sat on the floor close to Ashley.

Much to Ashley's surprise, Mary toddled to her mother with a wide smile on her face and her arms waving in the air.

"Can you sit with Ashley, baby?" Susie said. "Just sit right here on your cousin's lap."

Mary eyed Ashley, then smiled and sat with a bounce.

Ashley touched her soft, chubby hand. "How old is she?"

"Thirteen months. She's just learning to walk, so she's a bit shaky. Do you like your cousin, Mary Rose?"

Ashley wondered why Aunt Susie called her daughter by two names.

"I think she does," Aunt Susie said.

Ashley touched the lacy back of Mary's bonnet, admiring the softness of the fabric.

"Have you heard from Ruthie lately?" Aunt Susie asked.

"Not since she came back at Christmas," Grace answered.

Susie kissed Cherish's forehead. "She wrote me in January, but I haven't replied yet."

The stairs pounded as Wes barreled down them, with his cousins tagging along, and approached his mother. "Can we go outside now?" he said excitedly.

Grace touched his arm. "Did it stop raining?"

Wes glanced out the window. "It's sprinkling."

Grace patted his arm. "Stay in the barn or one of the buildings as much as you can, then."

"Can we go to the forest?"

"You have to come in immediately if there's any thunder or lightning."

"Yes, ma'am." Wes started for the door.

"Wes," Grace called, "maybe you should invite Ashley to go along."

Wes turned around. "Do you want to come?"

She shook her head.

"All right. If you change your mind, we'll be in the forest." Wes approached his little sister and whispered in her ear, "Don't worry; I'll keep them away from our fort."

Ashley smiled, and as the boys raced outdoors, she rubbed her cheek against Mary's soft hair, whispering to herself, "He's gonna keep our secret." She was brimming with delight.

Much to Ashley's dismay, Luke returned from work shortly after Susie and her family left. He found his children in the barn, doing chores, and Grace in the kitchen. He went to the sitting room and sat in his chair, sighing heavily.

"Are you home, Luke?" Grace called.

"Yup."

She came into the room, her hands dripping with water. "Come talk to me while the children are outside. Supper's almost ready."

Luke got up with a groan and followed her to the kitchen. Grace immersed her hands in the basin of dishwater, saying lowly, "Ashley was so difficult today."

He leaned against the counter and crossed his arms. "Oh? How?"

"Susie and the children came over and Ashley didn't even greet them. I had to remind her over and over to be polite, but she never did it on her own. It was exhausting."

Luke clenched his jaw. He had been thinking about that morning's apothecary meeting all day, and he was severely disappointed that he ever allowed Ashley into his life. "I'll talk to her tomorrow."

Grace's hands were still. She turned her head toward him. "I don't expect you to do anything about it."

"I was already planning on talking to Ashley about a couple other things. I'll mention what you said."

"What other things do you need to say to her?" Grace's tone was worried.

"What does it matter? I have a right to speak to my daughter."

"I just think she's more sensitive than Wes was. You had a talk with him when we first got him, but I don't know if giving Ashley a whole bunch of rules right away will work for her."

"I guess I'm capable of figuring that out."

"I'm not trying to insult you, Luke."

He sniffed. "I've already been insulted about Ashley today. I don't need anyone else telling me how to raise her."

"How were you insulted?" Her voice became gentle.

Luke shifted his feet. He thought about the look Judge Baker gave while asking if Ashley would behave, and it made him bristle. And Patrick Cummings—everyone knew that he was an opinionated man, but what he said about penny parcels had struck Luke. He hadn't thought the upper crusts' disapproval would haunt him like it had that day.

"The men at the apothecary have their opinions. It can be hard to take," he said.

"They're against us adopting Ashley?"

"Yes, Grace." Hadn't she figured that out by now?

Grace's cheeks turned red. "That's pathetic. The upper crusts have no right to give their opinions on what we should and shouldn't do."

"Yes, well, maybe that's what you believe."

"You think it's their right?"

"I think it's the way things are, whether or not it's their right. Being socially advanced is a privilege."

"And that's what you are? Socially advanced?"

"Yes."

"Are you going to let them dictate what we do?" Her voice was rising.

Luke clenched his jaw. "Well, I guess if I were planning on doing that, we never would've adopted Ashley. I just think she needs some direction. She has to know what I expect from her."

Luke imagined taking Ashley into the public and cringed. She was definitely not trustworthy enough to be introduced to anyone in the upper crust.

"What do you expect?" Grace asked quietly.

"I expect her to behave."

"I see. What exactly did the men say to you?"

"People don't have to say a lot in order to communicate."

"Well, they can take their communication and shove it down the throats of people who care. But it won't affect us."

Luke stood up and went to the sitting room. There he picked up the latest issue of the *Caledonia Record* and sat reading until Wes and Ashley came in.

Luke was quiet during supper, even though Wes excitedly told stories of the day spent with his cousins. Mr. Tanner was watching Ashley. The more the girl cowered at the end of the table next to her mother, the more irritated he became. Yes, a talk with Ashley was definitely necessary. How she responded to it would be her choice, but he decided that the end result would be spotless behavior. It had to be. There were people watching.

My grace is sufficient for thee: for My strength is made perfect in weakness.

—2 Corinthians 12:9

ELEVEN

The Reputation

Ashley opened the door of her large wardrobe and stared at the long, empty rack. "Even Cherish has more clothes than I do," she whispered.

She turned and gazed into the mirror. She pushed aside a few loose hairs that had fallen from her braid and scrubbed jelly off her face with her hand. Then she remembered that she had one item to hang in her wardrobe. She picked up her nightdress from the floor, placed it on a hanger, and hung it up. "There. Now my wardrobe isn't empty." She stared at the threadbare gown for a long while.

Ashley shut the tall, heavy door and sank into the hard-backed chair by her desk. She started opening the drawers, but every one was empty. When she pulled open the top drawer, she gasped at the sight of a few sheets of paper and an inkwell and feather. "My very own paper! I should write something."

Ashley thought for a long while about what she could write on the three sheets of paper. At length, she took up the feather and dipped it in the ink. She scribbled her name several times, wondering at how plain and short it was.

Someday, somebody will call me 'Miss Ashley.' Or maybe I'll get two names, like Baby Mary Rose.

Ashley put her writing things away and opened her bedroom door. She heard Grace working in the kitchen downstairs, and Wes was talking to Cherish in the sitting room. Ashley wandered into Wes's bedroom, which was right next to hers, and stared at the blue curtains and the dark oak furniture. Wes had a four-post bed like hers, and his bookshelf was filled. His wardrobe was slightly open and Ashley saw that it was almost completely full.

When she saw the white quilt that covered Wesley's bed, Ashley remembered her white quilt at the orphanage. She closed the bedroom door to seal out a rush of loneliness.

Ashley wandered down to the kitchen. Cherish's diapers soaked in the sink and the smell of lye soap permeated the air.

"Who's here?" Grace called when Ashley's feet tapped on the floor.

"Ashley," she said bashfully.

"What have you been doing, my dear?"

"Nothing."

"Would you like to help Mama for a while? I could use your help planting some pots outside."

"Pots of what?"

"Flower seeds."

"More flowers?" Ashley's fingernails were still dirty from planting three new roses, six flower pots, and a full bed of pansies and forget-me-nots the day before.

Grace laughed, her pretty smile shining with passion. "Why don't you fill a little pitcher of water from the pump and then come to the porch and we'll work together?"

"All right." Ashley took the pitcher and skipped outside to the well pump. She pulled the heavy handle up and then let it sink back down as cool water came rushing out.

When Ashley returned to the porch, she found Grace standing there, holding a seed packet and two pots nearly filled with dirt. Wes was sitting on a wicker chair beside his mother, Cherish squirming in his arms.

"Hey, Ashley," Wes called. "You wanna take Cherish and I'll help Mom?"

Ashley shrugged. "Sure, I guess. Is she crying a lot?"

"She's just a little bit fussy. But you can probably handle her since she likes you so much." Wes's eyes sparkled with a hint of flattery, and he stood to give his sister the chair.

"You have to take her back if she starts crying," Ashley said as she sat down.

While Grace and Wes planted the pots, Ashley wrapped Cherish's blanket tightly around her tiny form and held her close, delighting in the feel of her soft skin and fine hair. She stared at Cherish's long eyelashes and hands that were creased with dimples on every knuckle. Cherish began to quiet in Ashley's arms and her eyes fell closed.

"How come babies sleep so much?" Ashley asked.

Grace giggled. "They need a lot of rest when they're tiny."

"Will Cherish always sleep that much?"

"Oh, heavens, no; only for a few months longer. Then she'll start moving around and she won't want to sleep much."

Wes clapped his dirt-covered hands together. "When's Dad gonna be home?"

"Just before supper."

Wes pulled his watch from his pocket and pushed open its cover, blowing the dirt from its face. "It's already two thirty, so I guess that isn't very long."

"Why do you want him to come home?" Ashley asked.

He looked at her with a confused countenance. "I like it when he's here. Don't you?"

Not wanting Mrs. Tanner to hear her answer, she merely shook her head. Her new brother met the gesture with wide eyes.

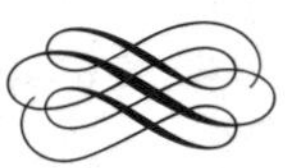

While Grace made supper that evening, and Wes began his chores, Ashley held Cherish on the sofa in the sitting room. Shortly after Luke got home, he came into the sitting room and took a seat in the rocker across from Ashley. She didn't look up at him.

"Ashley, I need to talk to you," Luke's voice boomed. He tried to sound as stern as possible so she wouldn't dare to cross him.

She kept her eyes on the baby.

"Look at me."

Ashley slowly looked up. She poked at Cherish to try to make her cry so she would have to comfort her.

"I want to go over a few rules of our house, and tell you what I expect from you, as my new daughter," Luke said. The word *daughter* rang through his ears with unpleasant familiarity. "We all have to work together to make a happy home and family."

She looked away. A happy family. That was impossible.

Luke began to list his expectations, and his words bounced off her mind. She heard something about doing chores . . . sewing . . . watching Cherish . . . sweeping the kitchen . . . getting along with Wes . . . then her head popped up. Chickens. He said she was responsible for the chickens.

Ashley searched Luke's face as he continued listing her duties, and she forced herself not to cry. He began telling her that if she didn't do things properly, he would discipline her. She didn't ask what that meant. She already knew.

"Are you listening to me, Ashley?" Mr. Tanner prodded.

She didn't answer.

"I'm serious about you doing things well. Wesley is very obedient, and you have to be like him. It's important to keep your priorities straight." He could see that he wasn't penetrating the brick wall in front of her face. "I don't want to discipline you, but I will if it's necessary."

Of course he would. And it would be necessary someday. Someday when she lost one of the chickens.

Ashley's eyes filled with tears when she thought about the scars she had not being her last ones.

"Do you remember what you're expected to do?" Luke asked, his voice full of displeasure.

"Watch chickens," she blurted.

She felt his eyes burn into her.

Snapping out of her reverie, she tried to blink away the tears.

"Mom will tell you what you're to do, and if you don't do it nicely, I'll hear about it when I get home," Luke said slowly.

She sat frozen.

"Ashley, respond to me when I'm talking to you."

"I know."

"You know what?"

"I know what I have to do." She swallowed a lump in her throat.

"Good." Luke stood up and hesitantly turned away. When he looked back at Ashley, she was rubbing Cherish's blanket on her cheeks.

He shook his head and went outside, thoroughly aggravated.

The next morning, when Wes went to do his chores, he found Ashley already in the chicken coop. She was standing in the doorway counting the mob of birds that loudly scolded her.

"What're you doing?" he asked as he came up behind her.

She startled and then grumbled, "I was counting, but you messed me up."

"Why are you counting?"

Ashley's eyes darted back and forth as she began again. "To see how many there are."

"Why does it matter?"

Ashley looked at him. "'Cause I don't want to lose one."

"Oh." He watched her count for a few moments, then slung his thumbs in his pockets. "There's about thirty."

"Thirty?" Ashley's braid whipped over her shoulder and she looked at him in panic. "Why so many? I'll never be able to watch them all."

Wes's eyebrow went up. "Why would you have to watch them?"

"So I don't lose one." Ashley sank down against the wall, right in the middle of the chicken manure. She rested her chin in her hands and shook her head.

"I usually count about once a week," Wes said. "It's not that hard if you count as they're going out the door."

Ashley's back stiffened. "Going out where?"

"I let them in the yard sometimes in the summer. They eat the bugs that ruin Mom's gardens."

"You let them out?"

"Sure. Why not?"

"Don't you lose any?" Ashley's eyes squinted.

Wes shrugged. "Haven't yet."

"What would happen if you did?"

He twisted his thumbs in his suspenders. "I don't know. We'd probably get a new one."

"Wouldn't your dad be angry?"

"Maybe, but not for long." Wes looked at the corn bin just outside the chicken coop door. "Are you done feeding them?"

"No."

"Well, I'm going to milk, so after you're done, you can help me clean Maymie's stall. All right?"

She nodded.

After Wes left, Ashley stared at the brood of chickens for a long while. When she noticed Charlie pecking at the hen's backs, she remembered Ronny. What a worthless bird, always fighting and teasing and making holes in the fence. And always making Katie follow her. If Charlie ever got out, he would probably take all twenty-nine hens with him.

Ashley stepped outside the coop and stuck her hand into the corn bin. Wes had taught her to give the chickens three scoops a day. She scattered one scoop on the floor and the chickens scrambled after it. She filled the scoop a second time, then paused. What would happen if she only gave the chickens two scoops? Maybe they would all die, and when Mr. Tanner asked her what happened, she could honestly report that she had fed them every day. It might be a slow death, but at least it would happen before winter.

Ashley filled the second scoop and threw it in front of a timid white hen. Then she tossed the scoop back into the bin and snapped the lid. Stupid birds deserved to starve.

For the next week, Ashley kept her distance from Luke Tanner. She retreated deep into her brick castle and barred the door like a prison. He seemed to understand what she was doing, but he didn't bother her as long as she obeyed. It was easier to make her behave when she trembled in his presence, anyway.

As she grew more distant from Mr. Tanner, Ashley fell in love with Wes and Grace. She and Wes did chores together every morning, and Ashley learned to delight in the smell of the barn, the feel of Maymie's stomach, and the sound of milk squirting into the tin pail.

Wes introduced her to the filly, whom Ashley named Kate, after her best friend. He spent two days explaining horse breeds to her, until he finally convinced her that Kate did indeed have draft blood.

Ashley loved sitting with her mother when she sewed in the afternoons, watching the belt spin on the wheel as Mrs. Tanner pumped the pedal. While Cherish was hummed to sleep by the whirr of the machine, Grace chatted and praised Ashley for every good quality she could think of. Ashley came to enjoy her mother's company so much that she never missed a sewing session. She gladly helped by trimming all the scraggly threads that were left on the white gowns and shirts her mother was preparing to deliver to the hospital.

Ashley often thought about the orphanage, and whenever her mind wandered that far back, it took her even further. She wondered about Jack and Henry and Bonnie. She didn't know where they lived now, but she felt sure it was probably too far to walk to visit. Of course, she would never mention anything to the Tanners about her past, not if her life depended on it.

The nightmares grew more intense after Luke's talk with Ashley. She tried to avoid them by thinking of happy things as she fell asleep, but nothing helped. She awoke in a cold sweat at least twice a week. Lately, she didn't just see Mr. Berk's cruel face, she also heard Jack's voice, though she could never make out what he said.

So far, Ashley had been able to keep herself from screaming, so the Tanners never knew she struggled with terrifying dreams. That was the way it should be. What went on in the woodshed was nobody's business.

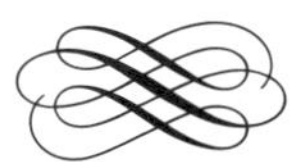

Luke sat in his rocker and scanned the paper, listening to the dry sound of Wes's knife as it scraped the bark off a stick. He read the front page article and his eyes fell to the name of the reporter who had written it. Luke sighed. It was an upper crust.

He turned the page to read the police reports and his eyes fell to a report about the status of the local church. It was written by an upper crust, as was every other article on the page.

Luke dropped the paper onto his lap. He studied Ashley, who had her hands clenched in her lap on the couch. She hadn't been off the Tanner property since arriving almost two weeks ago, but tomorrow was Sunday, and Luke knew he had to take his family to church. He had avoided it last week and Patrick Cummings questioned him about it on Monday morning.

"What do you say we go to church tomorrow?" Luke said abruptly.

Wes stopped carving and looked up. "I forgot tomorrow's Sunday."

Grace snuggled Cherish into her lap and rocked back and forth in her rocker. "Of course we should go. It'd be nice to get out of the house."

"Then everyone will have to be ready by seven o'clock in the morning. Do you think we can handle that?" Luke eyed Ashley warily. She was always still in her bedroom when he went to work in the morning. Dragging her out of bed in time for church might cause an issue.

"We can do it, Dad," Wes promised. "Ashley and me will get ready real fast."

"That means there'll be baths tonight," Grace said, and Ashley squirmed.

Luke glanced at the clock. "We'd better start right away. It's already almost eight."

"Would you fetch the water, then, and I'll get the tub?"

Mr. Tanner stood from his rocking chair. "Wes, come help me."

Grace gave Cherish to Ashley and the fuzzy bundle melted in Ashley's arms as she followed her mother into the kitchen.

"Can't we just take sponge baths and wash our hair in the sink, like we did last time?" Ashley asked, her voice squeaking.

"I only allow that on really cold nights," said Grace. "It's high time you had a regular bath, Ashley. I don't think you've been in the tub since you came to live with us."

"Where will we take baths?"

"We'll hang a curtain in the kitchen. You'll be first, since you're the youngest."

Ashley swallowed hard. "What about Cherish?"

"After your bath, you can help me wash her. Would you like that?"

Grace went into the dark pantry, where she retrieved the big tub from its hook and set it on the kitchen floor with an echoing thump.

"Why can't Wes go before me?" Ashley asked.

Mrs. Tanner uncovered a wiry towel stand. "Don't you like baths, honey?"

"No."

Grace dug out a massive pot and set it on the warm stove. The oven door creaked open and she took out the bread that was rising there. Within minutes, Grace had a fire roaring in the stove.

Ashley sat on her mother's tall stool and glared at Cherish, who smiled back. She wished she were old enough to make her own decisions about bathing.

"We'll make your bath a quick one." Grace donned her apron. "Then you can go to bed and get your rest for church."

Luke and Wes returned with four buckets of water, which they poured into the pot on the stove. Grace covered the burners with cast-iron kettles and one tiny pan. The men fetched bucket after bucket until every vessel was filled. Wes cleaned out the tub with a cloth and Grace fetched the soap and towels from the linen chest while Mr. Tanner hung a long, dark curtain over the door. Ashley felt sleepy from the steamy heat of the water on the stove.

"Ashley, run upstairs and get your nightdress," Grace directed. "The water is almost ready."

Mr. Tanner reached for Cherish. "Here, I'll put the baby in her cradle." He took the infant and left the room.

"I don't want to take a bath," Ashley whined when she returned with her nightdress.

Grace wiped her hands on her apron. "You have to be fresh for church tomorrow."

"I'm fresh already. Please don't make me take a bath."

"Nonsense. Now, take down your hair and I'll brush it for you."

Ashley slowly tugged the ribbon from the bottom of her braid and loosened her golden hair. Her stomach churned as she examined the thin curtain that covered the doorway. It would be very easy for Mr. Tanner or Wes to peek in on her.

Grace brushed Ashley's hair and then left her to undress herself while she went to feed Cherish. Ashley unbuttoned her dress and stared at the tub, which was nearly full of warm water. She had never taken a bath in such a small tub. The one at the orphanage was big enough to fit all the girls.

She glanced to make sure the curtain was pinned securely, then stepped into the water, letting it rush over her until it was all the way up to her chin. She took the soap from the tray beside the bathtub and it slipped out of her hands into the water. Ashley grabbed at it, but it slid through her fingers and sank to the bottom by her toes. Embarrassed at her awkwardness, she grabbed the soap, fumbling a dozen times until she was ready to cry with frustration.

"Are you ready to do your hair?" Grace asked, stepping through the curtain. The soap slipped from Ashley's hands again, and her eyes welled with tears.

"I can't do it," Ashley said.

Grace knelt beside the tub and touched Ashley's arm. "What's wrong, darlin'?"

"The soap keeps slipping out of my hands."

"Can I help you?"

Ashley stared at the woman, whose blind eyes seemed to stare right back at her. She was thankful Mrs. Tanner couldn't see her naked body.

"I can't catch the soap," Ashley said, plunging her hands into the water in another attempt. "It's too slippery."

Grace laughed. "Try again. Once you have it, I'll do the rest."

Ashley looked at her mother and couldn't help but smile.

Nearly twenty minutes later, Ashley was in her nightdress with her hair combed through by a gentle hand, and her body so clean she squeaked. Grace brought Cherish in for her turn, and Ashley smiled at the sight of the sleepy baby.

"Does she like baths?" Ashley asked.

"She doesn't like to get her ears wet or have her hair washed, but I think she likes the warm water."

Ashley stared at the deep tub. "Won't she drown?"

Grace chuckled and unbuttoned Cherish's long gown. "No, darlin'. I'll be holding her up."

"What do you want me to do?"

"I need you to hand me the soap and help me wash her with the cloth."

Grace soon had Cherish undressed, and the baby fussed in the cold air. Grace carefully lowered her into the water and the child's eyes grew bright. She kicked and squiggled in her mother's arms.

"Can you hand me the soap now?" Grace asked.

"Why does she kick all the time?" Ashley asked as she handed her mother the soap.

"Kicking makes her feel good 'cause she doesn't know how to walk yet."

"Mom?" Wesley's voice rang through the curtain, making Ashley jump.

"What do you need, Wes?"

"Mr. Sulka is here."

"Why?"

"I don't know. Dad's talking to him on the porch, but he said to come tell you. He brought his baby. He probably came to meet Ashley."

Grace cocked her head. "Ashley isn't dressed."

Ashley glanced at her nightdress and felt her cheeks blush.

"Can't she get dressed?"

Grace sighed. "We'll be right there. Let him in; he doesn't need to stay outside."

After Wes left the curtain, Grace said mercifully, "Can you put your dress back on, Ashley?"

Ashley had cold feet and eagerly went for her stockings. "Who's Mr. Sulka?" she asked.

"He goes to our church. He lives about five miles from here, with his wife and children. Where's a towel?"

"Right here." Ashley tossed a towel onto Mrs. Tanner's shoulder. "How come he came to visit so late?"

"I don't know. Let's get dressed and we'll find out, 'ey?"

Ashley helped her mother dress Cherish in a fresh gown. Then Grace buttoned Ashley's dress and brought her hair out of it. Ashley pulled her wet hair over her shoulder because it stung like ice on her back.

When Grace and Ashley arrived at the sitting room, the front door let in a gust of cold air as Luke, Wes, and Mr. Sulka stepped inside. Mr. Sulka was carrying a little girl who bashfully ducked into his shoulder.

"Grace, I apologize for the late hour," the man said. "I was on my way home and I wanted to meet your new little girl. Laura is out for the evening, so I thought this would be a good time since she's not waiting for me at home."

Grace smiled and strands of dark hair fell over her face. "Well, we're very pleased to have you. Come and sit. I was just giving the girls baths, so the baby is a bit fussy right now."

Mr. Sulka laughed a deep, warm laugh and patted the toddler. "Laura left the baby with me tonight, and I've had quite a time keeping her warm. The wind picked up on the way to town and hasn't quieted yet."

Luke took a seat in his rocker and Mr. Sulka sat on the sofa.

"Is this your youngest?" Luke asked.

"Yes." Dan Sulka's cheeks were rosy with pride. "This is Elaine. She's almost two now."

Almost two, almost two, Ashley chanted to herself, wishing she could retreat upstairs for a slip of paper to write down those words so she wouldn't forget them. *I don't think Gretchen and Melissa have ever seen a baby that's almost two. I wonder if she's older than Mary?*

Wes sank into the overstuffed chair and Ashley leaned against Grace's rocker.

"I'm guessing this is your new little girl," Dan said, nodding at Ashley.

Mr. Tanner gave a smiling nod, and when Ashley looked up at him, her heart dropped to her toes. She had never seen so much warning in his eyes, and her whole body surged with panic. That was exactly the way Mr. Berk had looked at her the night she talked to the prying lady.

"Are you going to church in the morning?" Mr. Tanner asked Dan.

"Yeah, we'll be there. A couple of the younger children are sick, so I think my oldest daughter will stay home with them. I didn't see you there last Sunday. Are you going tomorrow?"

The gentleness in Mr. Sulka's eyes calmed Ashley's racing heart. She wondered why Mr. Tanner's face was so much harder and his body so stiff and tense.

"We're planning on it," Luke said.

Dan's chuckle rolled off the walls. "That Mr. Harris sure has been preaching up a storm. He's been hitting Galesburg with heart-to-hearts. Can't go to church and remain passive anymore. Some of the folks say he's trying to start a revival in Caledonia County. I wouldn't be surprised. That preacher has enough fire to see the whole state to revival."

"I just wish he'd keep to his notes and not stumble over the words," Luke replied with a smirk. "I don't think Mr. Bowtie polished his speaking skills very well in whatever seminary he went to. Then again, I heard old Bowtie lived real rustic in those years—didn't even have a well to draw water from. For all I know he could've been living in a monastery, wearing those long black robes and saying prayers all day."

"I don't believe Mr. Harris went to a monastery," Dan said with a cock of his head. "If so, he'd be an ordained priest, and I doubt he's that."

"I doubt he's ordained as a minister, even." Luke shook his head. "Not with his speaking skills. Reminds me of Moses—except our preacher didn't ask God to help him get over his impediment."

Grace laughed. "Mr. Harris doesn't exactly have an impediment, Luke."

"Well," Dan said slowly, "if he keeps preaching like he has been lately, not a soul in Galesburg will care about stuttering or wandering from notes. The fire of God will make up for all of Mr. Harris's deficiencies."

Ashley saw Mr. Tanner's jaw clench.

"Did you hear we have new neighbors to the east?" Dan asked as Elaine crawled off his lap and waddled to the fireplace.

"Yeah," Mr. Tanner said. "I saw their house going up. It looks like a right fine place; I'm guessing the folks don't lack in finances."

Dan smiled. "That's Barry Lee's new place."

"They sold their mansion on the south side of town?" asked Mr. Tanner. "I wonder why Barry didn't mention it to me."

Dan held out his hand so Elaine wouldn't get too close to the fire. "I heard one of the doctors bought his old place—was it Gere or Keller?"

"Probably Keller," Luke said with a nod. "The bird brain. He's hardly so much as toured the hospital and already he's counting on a job that will pay the note on that mansion. Well, I guess three foreclosures in ten years isn't a terrible blow to Galesburg. It does raise doubts for the out-of-towners who read the paper, though. We don't need the start of a bad reputation in this town."

"That's impossible." Dan shook his head. "I reckon most of this town would lie down right on the railroad tracks before they'd let Galesburg get a bad name."

"Did you hear the new sheriff's station is finally going up?" Luke asked.

Dan nodded. "Next spring. Sheriff Bilt has a committee figuring out how to raise funds. You know my opinion on that. Even if my bid hadn't been rejected, I would oppose spending so much money on a building that isn't even necessary right now."

"Barry Lee already secured the note," Luke said. "Why is Bilt raising funds?"

"He wants to invest in one of those Tin Lizzys. He's been wanting one of them things since he first heard about them two years ago. Says a horse can't outrun 'em and a bullet'll stop halfway through."

"They are nice." Mr. Tanner smiled. "I've seen the inside of one. They've got seats softer than any carriage. I could send Wesley to town with one of those and never have to worry about a rider-less horse returning. They're more dependable than mules, I've heard, and twice as stubborn."

"And not worth the expense of maintenance," Dan said. "People in the big cities are constantly trying to figure out how the things run. Unless you're Henry Ford himself, you don't have a chance."

Dan pulled Elaine onto his lap and kissed her dimpled cheek.

Luke looked at Ashley, who had been leaning against her mother's legs, practically falling asleep during the men's discussion.

He thought about what a good first impression it would make if Dan saw him cuddle Ashley on his lap. He called her name in a low voice.

"Do you want to sit on my lap?" he asked.

Ashley's heart began to pound, and her cheeks grew hot. She shook her head and kept her eyes on the floor.

"Go ahead," Grace encouraged. "You'll be more comfortable there."

Mr. Tanner stood and gently took her into his arms. She pushed against his arms.

"Hey, now," he coaxed, "what's wrong?"

"I didn't say anything," Ashley whispered in a hoarse voice. "I won't say anything. Just let me go."

He settled into his chair with her on his lap. "You can sit with Daddy for a while."

Ashley squirmed under the weight of his hand, but he held her tightly in place.

"Sit still now, and let us talk."

Luke turned back to his guest, hoping he could distract Dan enough that he wouldn't see how Ashley struggled against him. "Did I tell you about Hendricks's latest case?" he asked deliberately.

Ashley felt his deep voice rumble through his chest. She could hardly breathe.

Dan shook his head.

Ashley tried to squiggle under Luke's arms but he put his hand on her leg.

"A young couple lost their son as he was being born, and they're blaming it on Dr. Gere," Mr. Tanner said. "They say Doc didn't take the proper procedures. The baby came fast and early, and they say he was too casual about it. Truth is, the baby was no more than thirty weeks developed. Gere didn't want to tell the little mama that she'd been carrying a dead baby for two weeks, so he just pronounced him dead at birth. He obviously didn't expect a lawsuit."

"What was the parents' name?" Dan asked, his voice full of compassion.

“Valentine. James, I believe. They live on Maple, just west of the barbershop.”

Ashley’s body began surging with terror. Her only goal was to escape Mr. Tanner’s grasp, no matter what it took to break his strength. A full-force shove against his arms ended the men’s conversation and sent her into a fit of tears.

“Let me go!” she screamed, tearing at Luke’s arms with her fingernails. She kicked and struggled and her scratching stung Luke’s arms so forcefully, his grip finally loosened. He caught her just before she tumbled to the floor.

“You’re going to sit with your daddy,” he commanded, bringing her back onto his lap. His fingers left white marks on her arms. Luke saw that Dan was watching, and he knew that he was going to fight this battle until he won. He had to, lest the rumors fly.

Tears ran down Ashley’s cheeks. The strength she felt in Mr. Tanner’s arms was getting stronger. He was closing in on her, just like Mr. Berk used to do. As soon as the company left, she would be seeing the woodshed for sure.

“No more fighting,” Luke hissed into Ashley’s ear. She fought harder. “Ashley, stop or you’re going to regret it.”

“I won’t be bad,” Ashley begged. “I just want to sit with Mama. Please? Please let me go!”

“No.”

Dan murmured something into Elaine’s ear, then stood, swinging her into his arms. When his eyes met Ashley’s, she saw mercy in them. She began to sob.

“Guess I’ll be going,” Dan said.

Luke stood with Ashley and furiously realized that Dan was going to leave without seeing him conquer. Ashley’s feet barely brushed the floor as he pulled her across the sitting room. He swung her onto the third stair so she looked straight into his face. His brows pinched together. “You’ve made me very angry,” he said roughly. “Go to bed.”

Ashley fled up the stairs and Luke slammed the door after her.

It was only because of Grace's pleading that Luke left Ashley alone after Dan left.

Ashley lay in her bedroom and wept, waiting for Mr. Tanner to burst through her door with his belt in hand. She didn't even undress, but lay in the darkness, listening to him hollering downstairs. He sounded angry enough to kill a horse.

When his voice quieted somewhat, she could hear Grace talking in calm, gentle tones. Ashley wanted to run to her arms for protection, but she knew if she entered Mr. Tanner's presence, she would be sealing her own sentence.

Ashley glared at the picture above her bed. The father in that rocking chair was nothing like the man who was exploding with anger downstairs. Standing on her thin pillow, she lifted the large frame off the wall and laid it facedown in her wardrobe, slamming the door.

Ashley lay on her bed and thought about the painting for a long time. She imagined Melissa or KatieAnne sitting in the lap of the loving man in the rocker. Maybe Elaine would fit. Or Cherish. Or even baby Mary Rose.

A thought crept into Ashley's mind. Maybe she could be that little girl. Maybe she could have cheeks that weren't pale, and a smile that was content on a man's lap. Maybe she could talk to him like that little girl was. Maybe she could even giggle and show a dimple like the girl in the picture.

Mr. Tanner's voice grew louder downstairs, and Ashley shook her head. No matter how hard she wished for her imagination to take her there, she decided that she would never be that little girl.

All the ways of a man are clean in his own eyes.
—Proverbs 16:2

TWELVE

Crossfire

Luke stopped the horse at the church hitching post and jumped down. He helped Grace to the boardwalk and then reached for Ashley's hand. She pulled it away and shied into her mother's dress.

"Ashley, stay close to Daddy on the street," Grace said.

"But I want to stay here, by you."

Luke looked away in disgust. He should've strapped her last night. Maybe she would have a little respect for him.

Grace patted Ashley's back but said firmly, "I'm holding Cherish right now, honey. Walk with Daddy."

Luke reached for her hand again, and Ashley just looked at him. He waited, and as she slowly let go of her mother's skirt, Luke's stomach twisted painfully. What would the upper crusts think of Ashley's distance?

"Ashley," he said, engulfing her little hand in his big one, "let me lead you so you'll be safe."

Ashley hid behind her white hat. *Safe* was not a word she related to any adult member of the masculine race.

Luke hooked arms with Grace on the other side and started down the boardwalk. Ashley glanced at Wes, who gave her an encouraging nod. As they walked, she stared at the ground and her legs trembled, but she didn't fight. She was too scared to fight again.

The church was crowded, and Luke kept hold of Ashley's hand once they were in the building. He led his family to one of the front benches and sat quietly. He sensed the glances of the men, making him feel like a little boy, suffering under the scrutiny of his father. So much for coming to Galesburg to find freedom.

Ashley sat between Wes and Grace so Mr. Tanner couldn't scold her should he see her fidget.

"Dad said you went to this church when you lived at the orphanage," Wes whispered to her before the service began. "But I never saw you here."

Ashley's throat felt dry. "I saw you."

"You did? When?"

"A few weeks ago. You were sitting with your dad and mom."

Wes's eyes narrowed. "You mean *our* dad and mom."

Luke called the children's names, and Ashley's throat tightened. "Quiet now," he said, in a kinder tone than Ashley had expected.

Wes leaned back on the bench and stared straight ahead. Ashley wondered at his willingness to obey.

The little door at the back of the sanctuary clicked open, and the congregation became silent. Mr. Bowtie glided out, accompanied by a young, homely minister carrying a Bible. Mr. Bowtie took his place at the pulpit and cleared his throat. "Good morning! I'm glad to see so many folks out on a beautiful Sunday morning. I'll be joining you in the pews this morning to listen to a message given by my new friend, Minister Joseph J. Plain."

Ashley thought that "Plain" was an awkwardly appropriate name.

"I met Mr. Plain on a visit to Virginia last year, and invited him to speak from our pulpit if he ever came this way. He recently graduated from seminary and is traveling while waiting to be assigned to a congregation. I was surprised to see him this week, but nonetheless, delighted." Mr. Bowtie stepped back from the pulpit and swept his hand toward Mr. Plain as if introducing the star of a Broadway production.

Joseph Plain smiled a large, bug-eyed smile. The second he set his Bible on the pulpit, his voice boomed. "On behalf of Galesburg and Mr. Harris, welcome to all of you. Let's stand and sing 'Sweet Hour of Prayer.'"

The piano rang clearly, and voices filled the little white building. Mr. Plain sang in a loud, well-trained tenor voice. Ashley noticed that the three old women in the bench behind her forced their vibrato-drenched voices louder and louder, but Mr. Plain couldn't be matched.

When the last note was sung, Mr. Plain looked over the congregation with a satisfied nod. "Isn't it wonderful to have a 'sweet hour of prayer,' as the author of the hymn calls it?"

"I don't think anyone ever prays for an hour straight," Wes whispered to his sister.

She had her head cranked over her shoulder and her eyes were wildly searching the congregation.

"What are you doing?" Wes murmured.

"They're not here." Ashley shook her head.

"Who are you looking for?"

"My friends from the orphanage."

He shrugged. "They're probably busy today."

"No." Ashley turned toward the front and her eyes were wide with concern. "Mrs. Harms never misses church."

Mr. Plain opened his Bible and began his sermon. He seemed eager to share his message, which was titled "A Christian of Good Repute." All eyes gazed upon the scrawny youth as he spoke.

"Well, do you love God, or don't you?" Mr. Plain shrieked and his voice cracked. "And are you serious about keeping a good reputation, or aren't you?" He puffed for breath, clacking his notes on the pulpit.

Mr. Tanner shifted his feet and crossed his arms.

The minister glanced over the congregation, the wrinkles on his forehead making a deep furrow. "Jesus' commission to His people was to 'go and preach the gospel,' but it's completely impossible to be heard unless we have established our reputation in our community. Unsaved souls won't listen to a man who doesn't have his children in order, because they know that his method won't work. They won't pay attention to someone who lets his wife run his household. Am I making sense?" He didn't wait for an answer. "It's absolutely essential that Christian men keep their reputation spotless so they can be heard when it's time to preach the gospel." Mr. Plain blushed. "And besides that, the rewards of a good reputation are well worth the effort."

Ashley sat perfectly still but her eyes still searched for the orphans. She saw a flicker of yellow and settled on Mr. Bowtie, who was sitting in the front row. His bright bowtie was crooked on his neck and he was squirming in his seat.

"Being spoken of in social circles as a conqueror of the more difficult things in life will bring pride to a man's heart," Mr. Plain was saying. "Men, you won't regret the energy you put into building your reputation."

Ashley heard someone cough on the other side of the building.

"Reputation starts in the home." Mr. Plain left the pulpit to stroll the stage. His shiny shoes clicked on the floor, and he folded his pale hands behind his back. "Make sure your wife understands the biblical concept of submission, as well as the proper way to train your children. You're the head of the house, and your entire family is a reflection of your methods. Thus, your family becomes your reputation."

Mr. Tanner glanced at his wife with a subtle air of authority.

"After your wife is in order, or at least understands *how* to be in order, examine your children. Whether you have one child or fifteen, they should all respect you when you set the rules, listen when you speak, and fear you when they have provoked your anger. Children must understand that their father is to be revered and obeyed. When the family has company, the children are to be seen and not heard. If your children don't respect you, they must be disciplined—biblically, of course, but thoroughly. There's no reason for disorder in any Christian home, and excuses won't count on Judgment Day."

Just then, Cherish began to cry. Grace put the baby to her shoulder, patting her back and rocking gently. But her efforts were to no avail.

Mr. Tanner offered to take the baby out.

"I need to feed her," Grace whispered.

"Do you want help?"

"No; I'll be fine."

"Where's she going?" Ashley whispered to Wes as Mrs. Tanner slunk up the aisle.

"Probably to the carriage house."

Ashley debated whether she should follow her mother. Sharing a bench with Luke Tanner was terrifying enough, but being in the same room with Mr. Plain added a new, uncomfortable twist.

Ashley leaned against Wes. "Can I go find your mom?"

"*Your* Mom? No. Dad will get mad."

Mr. Tanner glared at his whispering children, his face filled with scorn.

"Children," he hissed, and they shot their eyes to him. "Absolutely no more."

When Ashley turned away and fell silent, Luke looked back at the preacher and straightened his shoulders. If the upper crusts were watching his pew, they couldn't deny that he had Ashley under control.

"So, what do you think of the young preacher?" Luke asked a group of black-suited businessmen assembled in a corner of the churchyard. He was trying to keep the conversation from turning to Ashley.

"He's miserable," grumbled Lyle Elton, a middle-aged man and new father.

Luke rolled his eyes and several of the upper crusts smirked with him. Lyle was certainly not an upper crust, but he was just bold enough to join their after-church discussions and insert his opinion.

Lyle continued. "Mr. Harris made a grave mistake when he invited that young man to the pulpit. Plain is fresh out of college. He needs a taste of the real world before he goes preaching about things like reputation. Of course that's what we should've expected him to preach on—that's all any college graduate cares about these days. But that sermon was certainly not for Galesburg. I think Joseph Plain completely broke the cycle of Thomas Harris's revival."

"What revival? I don't know that there's anything to be revived," Judge Baker said.

"I agree," Mr. Hendricks said. "Our town has always been a generally Christian place. In fact, our church attendance exceeds most, according to Mr. Cummings."

"Quite true," Patrick Cummings agreed. "I've attended many churches that don't have half as many members as Galesburg."

"I'm glad Plain preached on reputation," Luke said. Many of the men hummed in agreement, and Luke was glad to have their approval. He glanced at Dan Sulka, who stood with his arms crossed, not offering his opinion on either side.

Lyle shrugged. "I think reputation is overrated in Galesburg. How many times do you think reputation is mentioned in the Bible compared to pride? If Mr. Plain would've preached on humility, he would've made the difference he aimed to make when he wrote that sermon."

"You don't strive for a good reputation?" Luke asked quickly. He was unwilling to accept the guilt he had just managed to shed during the sermon.

Mr. Sulka shifted his weight and Luke saw it out of the corner of his eye. It made him uncomfortable to have Dan in the circle. That man could look through ten layers of clothing and see a man's soul.

Lyle smiled and slapped Luke on the back with an oblivious chuckle. "You and I both know the balance of a good reputation," he said, and Luke didn't know whether to feel convicted or complimented. "I believe reputation is a result of godliness in the home. My children will never be forced to perform so everyone can think highly of me. I don't agree with Mr. Plain's method. It's just as important to have a good reputation with your family as it is with the outside world. As long as there aren't problems in the home, and children aren't pushed away to keep friends thinking highly, that's the right kind of reputation."

Luke couldn't agree. He excused himself and gathered his family into the carriage. As he drove away, he saw Dan Sulka talking to Barry Lee on the boardwalk. Luke shook his head. It would only be a matter of time before Dan reported the story of Ashley's rebellion the previous night.

Luke forced himself not to look at Ashley in the back seat. Small and scared as she was, that girl held the power to ruin him.

When the family arrived at their farmhouse after church, Grace was just as stirred about the sermon as Luke was, and it happened that the couple had contradicting views. Luke had finally decided to take young Mr. Plain's advice to make reputation his priority, instead of agreeing with Lyle Elton. He had contradicted the upper crusts enough lately, and was unwilling to wage war with them by accepting Mr. Elton's point of view.

Instead, he waged war in his own soul.

Grace put Cherish to sleep and then tackled her knitting. The sermon that morning had made her cringe. In a town that was less socially demanding than Galesburg, Joseph Plain's message might have stirred hearts and brought about revival. But Grace knew her husband would use the sermon as a defense of his actions.

"I thought the message was exactly what our family needed to hear, didn't you, doll?" Luke asked, joining Grace in the sitting room. She could almost taste the sugar in his words.

"It settled a lot of questions for me," her husband said as he settled into his chair.

"Questions that now have the wrong answers," Grace muttered. She worked her fingers through her knitting. "Mr. Plain just brought trouble by preaching about reputation to a town where status is already valued more highly than family and friendships. What he said doesn't excuse you, or somehow justify you."

"I disagree," said Luke. "Your reputation reveals who you are to the unsaved world. If my children don't obey me, I'm setting a bad example for non-Christians."

"Not in the case of Ashley. And not in the presence of friends who are saved and know perfectly well that Ashley is a new child and that perhaps she has some . . . problems." Grace lowered her voice, not wanting Ashley to hear. "Luke, think about it," she whispered. "Last night was your first chance to reach out to Ashley, but because Dan was here, you pushed her away. Which is more precious to you: your friends and your reputation, or your new daughter, who's watching to see if you're trustworthy?"

Luke said with almost bitter revenge, "'Excuses won't count on Judgment Day.'"

"It's pathetic that he said that," Grace returned with a detestable shiver. "What I'm saying has nothing to do with excuses. It's the plain truth because Ashley has come to us differently than most children come to their parents."

"In any case, I think reputation, friends, and Ashley can all mix."

"Not if you're going to put her below the first two."

"She's not below, but she must come to understand how important my reputation is, not only to me, but to our whole family. You wouldn't want all of Galesburg judging us for not having our children in order, would you?"

Grace spoke through clenched teeth. "I would rather all of Galesburg wonder about us than for Ashley see you the way you were last night."

Luke felt anger rise in his chest. "I did nothing to harm that girl."

"Nothing to harm her!" She dropped her knitting into her lap. "It doesn't take physical pain to harm a child. Don't you think she heard you screaming in the kitchen? You threatened to belt her or take her back to the orphanage. How do you think that made her feel? Performance is what you want. Not a relationship. Ashley must perform in front of company or she'll be beaten or rejected."

"I only asked for obedience."

"Without compassion or mercy. You don't even try to understand her. Maybe she's afraid of you."

"She has no reason to fear me."

"You don't know what her life's been like. She's been an orphan for eight years! You have no idea what kind of trauma she's been through. You're expecting her to act like Wesley when she hasn't even had a chance to heal."

"Heal from what?" He panged with guilt but he shoved it away.

"I have no idea. But I believe she needs to rest for a season."

"And ruin my reputation while she's at it?"

"Or transform it. Maybe turn your reputation into something genuine. Take away the hypocrisy of it."

"I am not a hypocrite." Luke's voice seethed with anger. "Don't tack sins like that on my head."

Grace let the silence rest. She'd said enough.

Luke clicked his tongue. "I'm not lowering my standards. That girl can conform or see my wrath. It makes no difference to me. I'm the head of this house, and she must be in order."

Grace stood and walked away. She had fought this battle with Luke for too many years. Ashley might be caught in the crossfire, but God was going to have to rescue her. Grace had done all she could.

I will love them freely.

—Hosea 14:4

Larissa L. Hitch

THIRTEEN

Discipline & Disaster

Ashley brushed biscuit crumbs from her dress and stretched out her legs on the floor of the fort. "Have you ever eaten in here before?" she asked Wes.

The boy wiped the milk from his mouth. "Nope."

"I think we should do it every day, don't you?"

Wes shrugged. "If Mom will let us. I don't think she will, though."

"Why not?"

"'Cause she likes us to be in the house with her. That way we can help her if she needs something."

Ashley leaned back on her hands. "Wes, when did your mom get blind?"

Wes squinted at her. "Why do you call her *my* mom? Don't you want to be part of our family? She's your mom, too."

Ashley ignored him. "But when did she get blind?"

"After she married Dad. She was pregnant, and she got really sick. Her eyes went blind and the baby died."

Ashley gasped. "Why did the baby die?"

"I don't know. I guess it was just too little."

"You were born after that, right?"

Wes looked at Ashley with a puzzled expression. "No. Dad and Mom didn't get me till I was six."

"What? But I thought . . ."

"I was adopted too. Didn't you know that?"

"No. I thought they were your real parents."

"They are. Just like they're your real parents, even though you didn't know them until you were eight."

Ashley stared at Wes in astonishment. "So you were an orphan?"

Wes nodded. "Yup. I was really bad too. I used to hit people when I got mad, and I'd yell and run away. I hid from Mom 'cause I knew she couldn't see me. I even told Dad I hated him once. Finally he told me I had to stop acting like that. The next time I did something bad, he strapped me."

Ashley felt the breath go right out of her. "He strapped you?" she squeaked.

"Yeah." Wes's cheeks reddened. "Once, I stole something from a store, and Dad made me take it back and then I had to work to pay for it. The work was so hard that I never stole again, and I never will, either. It makes you feel bad inside, you know?"

Ashley didn't understand why stealing would make a person feel bad inside.

"I've changed a lot since I came here." Wes's eyes brightened. "I used to be really sad, but Dad and Mom showed me how to be happy."

"But Cherish is their real baby, right?"

"No." He looked at her with a puzzled stare. "She was adopted too. Dad and Mom had to go to a place that's almost two days from here to get her. I stayed with Granddad and Grandma Jackson while they were gone. When they brought Cherish home, she was so tiny she hardly opened her eyes for a whole day."

"So your mom doesn't have any children of her own?" Ashley asked.

"Dad and Mom can't have any babies. That's why they adopt. Mom said someday we might get a new kid from an orphanage about ten miles from here. I hope we get one a little bit older than

Cherish so we could have one between you two girls. Wouldn't that be fun to have three brothers and sisters?"

"I don't know." She remembered Jack and Henry and Bonnie. Mr. Berk told her that they were her siblings. "There were lots of children at the orphanage, and we were kind of like brothers and sisters. But the boys were mean."

Wes sifted a handful of dirt, creating a miniature dust storm in the fort. "I don't really remember the other children at the orphanage I lived at. There were a lot of us, so I didn't know most of them. There was one boy who was five, like me, and we were best buddies until I left. Did you ever have a friend like that?"

"Not really." Bonnie had been her friend when Mr. Berk was mad at Ashley, but she wasn't very friendly otherwise. Ashley's throat felt pasty from the dust. "KatieAnne was my friend most of the time. But she left."

"You know Mr. Sulka, the man who was here the other night?"

Ashley nodded.

"His dad died when he was eleven, so he and his brothers and sisters all had to go live at other people's houses. I think that'd be worse than being an orphan, don't you?"

"Why?"

"'Cause you'd already know what it's like to have a family."

Ashley leaned against the fort wall and clicked her shoes together. "I don't know what I think." It would be better to never have lived in a family. "Do you remember going to the orphanage I lived at?"

"Yeah. But I only went there once, to measure the orphans so Mom could make clothes for them. We thought we'd get to see you, but you were in school."

"I hate school," she grumbled.

"Why? You're good at it, aren't you?"

"No." Ashley felt herself blush.

Wes stared at her. "But aren't you in the second grade?"

"Yeah."

"Well, then, you're good at it." He nodded. "Anyone who's in second grade when they're only eight years old has to be good at school."

Ashley thought of the countless hours she had sat on a hard desk, laboring over catechisms, figures, sentence structures, and spelling words. She would be happy to leave those days behind forever.

Ashley glanced at the roof of the fort, and bright sunlight revealed every hole and flaw.

Wes glanced at his pocket watch. "It's one thirty," he said with a sigh. "Mom said we had to be back by one o'clock."

"Is one thirty later than one o'clock?" Ashley asked.

"Yeah."

"Shouldn't we get heading back, then?"

Wes laughed. "Mom's blind. Unless she listens to the clock, she doesn't know what time it is. She doesn't usually listen to the clock, either. She only cares what time it is when she has to make supper."

Ashley poked at the ceiling, wondering if she should suggest patching it.

"Dad was talking about taking some time off work next week," Wes said, and Ashley stiffened. "He tried to get off last week, but his boss said he couldn't."

A lump stuck in Ashley's throat. "Why would he want to take time off?"

"To be with us, of course."

"Oh." Ashley's heart sank.

Wes searched her face. "Aren't you happy about that?"

"No."

"Why not?"

"I'm just not." A memory streaked across her brain. Three beatings in a row. If Mr. Tanner came home, he would probably require perfect behavior every day. That would mean lots of pain.

Wes stared at her with a crooked brow. "You're strange, Ashley."

Bonnie had told her she was stupid. At least strange was better than stupid. Being stupid was dangerous.

Wes stood and snapped the lid shut on the tin lunch box. "C'mon. We should be going inside now."

The children were just stepping out of the forest when they heard Mr. Tanner yelling Wesley's name from the porch. "We're coming, Dad!" He nervously glanced at his pocket watch. "I guess Dad got off work early. We'd better hurry." Wes quickened his step.

Ashley's heart beat intensely in her chest as she trotted behind Wes. As he ran toward the house, she ducked into the barn and opened the chicken coop door. All twenty-nine hens and one rooster were there. She counted them three times. If Mr. Tanner told her she was lying, she would show him the number Wes had carved into the chicken coop wall. There was proof that they started out with thirty.

When Ashley came out of the barn, she saw Wes stepping up to the porch. "Yeah, Dad?" he said, panting.

Mr. Tanner stood in the front doorway, his tall frame casting a mammoth shadow on the much smaller form of his son.

"Son, Mom told you to be back at the house at one o'clock, didn't she?"

Wes's gaze dropped to the wooden floor.

"Wes, what time is it now?"

Wes reached into his pocket and brought out his watch. He clicked it open and squinted. "Quarter till two," he mumbled.

Ashley ducked behind the house, trembling.

"Where's Ashley?" Luke asked.

Wes glanced over his shoulder. "I don't know. She was following me."

"Ashley!" Mr. Tanner called.

She cringed. His deep voice reminded her of Mr. Berk just before he exploded in violent anger.

"I can go find her," Wes offered.

"Go on then."

As soon as Wes stepped off the porch, he spotted his sister standing close to the side of the house, trying to disappear into a shadow. "What are you doing, Ashley?" he asked with a perplexed stare.

"Nothing."

"Dad wants you."

Ashley swallowed hard, trying to shake away the cold feeling that gripped every inch of her body. She stepped onto the porch and stared at Mr. Tanner, wishing she had enough strength to flee, but thinking she would probably faint if she tried.

"There you are," Mr. Tanner said, his voice sounding more grieved than angry. "Go inside, Ashley. Mom needs you."

As Ashley darted away, Wes looked up into his father's stern face.

"Why didn't you come in at one o'clock?" he asked.

Wes bit his lip. "I guess time got away from us."

"Didn't you check your watch?"

Wes rubbed his fingers together. "I looked once, but I didn't think it was very late."

Luke stroked his chin. "What time was it when you looked?"

"I don't know." Wes's shiny watch mocked him from his pocket. "Probably one thirty."

"Probably?" Luke's eyes narrowed. "Since you knew you were already late, why didn't you come in at one thirty?"

Wes bit his cheek. "I figured Mom wouldn't know what time it was since she can't read a clock."

"So you were planning on lying to her?"

"I wasn't gonna lie." Wes felt a wave of guilt, and his palms started sweating.

"And you didn't think anyone would find out if you were late?"

"I didn't know you were coming home early."

Luke cocked his leg and his expression was confused. "Wes, I thought we already had this deception thing taken care of. You know you can't take advantage of your mom's blindness and get away with it. That's no way to treat her."

Wes glanced at his father. "I'm sorry."

Luke slowly nodded. "Son, that's what you said the last time you deceived her, and I let it go at that. Sorry isn't enough if you're not going to change, and we've been working on this issue for long enough for you to have changed."

"Dad, it's not really that big of a deal if we were late," Wes said bravely. "Mom didn't need us for anything anyway."

"That's not an excuse to disobey. Was Ashley involved in this?"

"No."

Luke stood in silence for a moment, and Wes tried to swallow the lump in his throat.

"I can't let you go with an apology this time," his father said. "I wish you would just obey so we wouldn't have to go through this." Luke nodded toward the door. "Upstairs with you."

Wes lingered for a moment, his mind racing with a dozen arguments and twice that many excuses. He quickly decided that arguing wasn't worth the risk since he couldn't even convince himself of his innocence. He opened the door and went straight to his room.

"Where's Wes going?" Ashley asked from her stool in the kitchen when she saw him dart up the stairs.

"I'm sure Daddy's going to take care of him, darlin'," Grace replied.

Mr. Tanner stepped into the kitchen, his mouth a thin line. "How are you today, Ashley?" he asked in a strangely cheerful voice.

She stared at him.

He stepped up to the counter beside his wife and spoke in low tones. "He knew he was late but he didn't think anyone would find out."

Grace pounded the bread dough on the counter. "Are you going to deal with it, then?"

"Yeah." He sighed heavily. "Grace, keep Ashley down here, would you?" he whispered.

"Of course. Is Cherish still sleeping?"

"Yeah."

He strode away, and Ashley sat still and silent on her stool. She heard Mr. Tanner climb the stairs and then the bedroom door shut.

Ashley fooled with a loose string on her dress. She forced herself to believe that Mr. Tanner was just talking to Wes and not belting him.

"What's made you so quiet, my girl?" Grace asked at length.

"Mama, when is he going back to work?"

"Daddy? He just got home. It's the weekend, so he won't go back until Monday."

"Monday? But what about Saturday?"

Grace chuckled. "Darlin', you know Daddy gets Saturdays and Sundays off. Now, why would you want him to leave?"

Ashley broke the loose string from her dress. "Why is Wes upstairs?"

Grace placed her bread dough in a pan. "Wes was disobedient, Ashley."

"So why is he upstairs?"

Grace set her teapot on the burner and said in an emotionless voice, "Daddy has to strap him."

"Strap him!" Ashley shrieked. "You can't let him get strapped!" She bounded off her stool and fled to the sitting room. "*Tell him to stop!*"

Grace hurried to catch her and stumbled over a chair.

"You can't let him get strapped!" Ashley screamed from across the sitting room, where she was headed toward the steps. "Mama, you can't let him! How could you? You have to go! Tell him to stop! Mama, tell him to stop!"

"Ashley, stop right now," Grace commanded.

Ashley froze in her tracks just as she was reaching for the upstairs door. Fear gripped her when she contemplated rescuing Wes. What good would that do? Then they would both have new scars.

Ashley retreated to her mother and fell in her arms. "You can't let him." She yanked on Grace's dress. "Mama, please. Go up there. Tell him to stop. You can't let him strap Wes."

Grace sat down in the rocker and pulled the little girl onto her lap. Ashley trembled from the sobs that escaped from her throat, accompanied by a flood of tears.

Faces streaked across Ashley's mind, and everything danced in her head: the degrading remarks, the scolding, the yelling, the fighting, and finally the pain of the belt. It was a cycle. And she was caught in it again.

"When children are naughty," Grace said in a tender voice, "the Bible says that parents must use the rod to make them good again."

"What's the rod?" Ashley shivered with dread.

"It's what Daddy uses to discipline. Darlin', Wes knows he was wrong, and that Daddy has to use the rod in order to obey God."

"No." Ashley stiffened. "You don't understand. Mama, how could you? Why do you let him do that?"

"Why are you crying, Ashley?" Grace asked earnestly. "Tell Mama what's wrong."

"I don't want Wes to get strapped." Ashley's sobs increased with every breath. Panic seized her, and she tore at Grace's arms. "Mama, you can't let him! Let me go! I have to help him!"

"Ashley, stop," Grace said, half begging. "Listen to me; I want to talk to you."

Ashley was too hysterically involved to listen. She heard footsteps on the stairs, and the door creaked open. When she laid eyes on Luke Tanner, Ashley fought so desperately that Grace finally lost her grasp.

Mr. Tanner caught Ashley as she fell to the floor, his strong hands gripping her shoulders. "What's wrong?" he asked with astonishment.

Ashley winced, and her legs trembled so badly she could hardly hold herself up.

"She's afraid," Grace said, sounding ready to cry. "She didn't want you to strap Wes."

Mr. Tanner's eyes searched Ashley's face. A sob escaped from her throat and she stood perfectly still, cowering.

"What are you afraid of, Ashley?" he asked in a voice that reflected concern for the first time.

Ashley stared at his belt, unable to breathe between her sobs.

"You don't need to be afraid. Wes is fine."

Just like Jack was fine. Just like she was fine. Mr. Berk always told Mrs. Berk that the children were fine.

"Please let me go," Ashley squeaked. "I'll be good. I'm sorry. I didn't hurt Mama. I'm sorry."

Luke knelt before her. "Tell me what you're afraid of," he prodded. He tried to see some glimpse of answer in her eyes, but they were dark and hidden. Full of secrets.

"Just don't." She closed her eyes and involuntarily imagined the strength of Mr. Tanner's enormous hands. He must be even crueler than Mr. Berk.

"Wesley!" Mr. Tanner yelled, making Ashley jump.

She heard the bedroom door open.

"Yes, sir?" Wes's voice echoed down the staircase.

"Come here, would you, son?"

The feet stomped down the stairs and Wes showed his face in the sitting room. Mr. Tanner nodded for him to draw near, which he did, staring at his sister with curious eyes.

"Yeah, Dad?" Wes asked softly. Ashley saw tear stains on his cheeks. She had never seen her brother so quiet. He must still be in pain.

"Ashley's upset," Mr. Tanner said tenderly. "I need you to tell her that you're OK."

As Ashley looked at Wes, all she could think about was Jack. Jack always smiled like that to cover up the pain. He always told his father he was fine. But Ashley knew Jack was dead inside. He lied because if he told the truth, he'd be as much of a baby as Henry. He said "yes, sir," because if he didn't, he'd get strapped again. It was all a game, and Ashley felt sickened that Wes knew how to play it too.

"I'm fine, Ashley," Wes said. "Why are you crying?"

A crushing weight came over her when she saw the brass buckle on Mr. Tanner's belt. "I want to go back," she squeaked. "Please take me back."

Mr. Tanner sat on the floor and brought Ashley into his lap. She didn't fight because she knew he would use that belt on her if she did. She sat on his lap just like she had sat on Mr. Berk's lap. She could laugh and pretend that he loved her. She could respond to tenderness. But it was all a game. She wasn't stupid.

"I don't want you to cry anymore, Ashley," Mr. Tanner said in a soft, soothing voice.

Or I'll strap you, Ashley thought.

"I want Mrs. Harms," Ashley whimpered.

Mr. Tanner patted her arm. "When you're a good little girl, and you learn not to be afraid of Daddy anymore, then we'll go see Mrs. Harms. She doesn't want you to be afraid, so you must show her that you're not."

Ashley suddenly understood. Mr. Tanner was afraid she was going to tell Mrs. Harms what he had done, just like when Mr. Berk belted Jack because he thought Ashley had talked to that nosy lady. Mr. Tanner thought he had to teach her not to talk. Well, she already knew. What went on in the woodshed—or the bedroom—was nobody's business.

"I won't tell," Ashley blurted. "I'll be good. You can trust me—honest. It's nobody's business."

Silence covered the room like a dark cloud. Mr. Tanner wrapped his arms around Ashley and tried to penetrate beyond her skin. But he wasn't touching her. His hands were around her skinny body, but she was completely detached. She had no life in her body; no life in her spirit. It was all gone. She was a walking skeleton.

"What do you mean, Ashley?" Wes broke the silence. His eyes were glued on her. "What do you mean you won't tell?"

"It's nobody business." Ashley's eyes flashed. "I know. Tell him, Wes. I know."

"Tell who?"

"Mr. Tanner." She squiggled, but he held her back. "I promise!" Ashley burst. Her heart beat faster when she realized that he wouldn't let her escape.

"You're not making any sense." Luke shook his head. "Stop saying that. I don't know what you're talking about."

"Please don't strap me."

"I'm not going to."

Ashley swallowed hard. She didn't believe him.

"I'm just holding you. See? Ashley, look at my hands." Luke opened his palms in front of her. "I don't have my strap. I'm not going to hurt you. I'm just holding you."

Ashley felt the belt against her back and knew he was lying. He did have his strap. He could unbuckle it at any time.

"Please don't hold me anymore," Ashley begged, pushing against him. "I'll do whatever you want. I'll do any chores you say." *Performance.* If she were good enough, he would leave that belt around his waist.

"I'm glad you're going to be good. That makes me happy. But right now, I just want you to relax and stop fighting me."

"Can't I go?"

"No. Just let me hold you." Luke rubbed her arm. "Stop trembling, Ashley. It's all right. Don't fight anymore."

Ashley grit her teeth and closed her eyes. She forced herself to relax, even though she could still feel his belt buckle on her back. She tried to push away thoughts of Mr. Berk and Jack and Henry and Bonnie. She couldn't look at Grace for fear of crying. Ashley had hoped that Mrs. Berk was the only woman alive who would let her husband strap her children. It was no consolation that Grace didn't fight for Wes.

Several minutes passed, and Luke began a casual conversation with his wife. Wes sat on the sofa, looking at Ashley like she was the most baffling creature he had ever known.

At length, Luke loosened his grasp slightly. Ashley breathed deeply, still laboring through intense fear.

"You can go now," Luke said.

She timidly moved away from him and went upstairs. She locked her bedroom door and fell onto the bed as the crushing weight of betrayal and lies and fear threatened to choke her before she had a chance to cry all the tears.

For I am poor and needy, and my heart is wounded within me.
—Psalm 109:22

FOURTEEN

Six Sundays Spent

A letter from Aunt Ruth arrived on Monday morning, and Wes was so excited he practically burst by the time he finished reading it to Ashley.

"Do you know what this means?" he cried out. "In only six days, five of our cousins are coming. For a whole week!"

"Stop jumping around, Wesley," Grace said. "You're going to wake up Cherish."

"Do you know how much fun this is going to be?" he said, grabbing Ashley's shoulders. "A whole week with Norm and Gerald! And there's two girls in the family, Krissa and Deborah. They're just about your age, so you'll have friends too."

"Wes," Grace said, "settle down. I just got Cherish to sleep."

When her brother collapsed into dreamy silence in a chair, Ashley asked, "Why do the boys have to come? How old are they?"

"Fourteen and ten," Grace answered.

Ashley's heart sank. Jack and Henry were around those ages.

Grace felt around the table for the letter and Ashley handed it to her. "Why wouldn't you want the boys to come? They're Wes's friends."

"I just don't want to meet them."

Grace stood and brushed her hands on her apron. "You'll have fun; I promise. Wesley, I need you to run to the Hendrickses' and tell Maggie I need her to come tomorrow morning. If possible, she should plan on being here every day next week. It's time for a real house cleaning."

Wes bounded out of his chair. "You want to come, Ashley?"

"If she goes, she has to wear shoes and be polite and friendly," Grace said.

"Where are we going?" Ashley asked as her brother tugged her out of the room.

"To the Hendrickses' house across the road. Miss Maggie is cleaning there today, so we have to give her Mom's message. Where's your hat?"

"In my room."

Before Ashley could pull her shoes on, Wes ran up the stairs and came back down with the white hat. He set it on Ashley's head and nodded in satisfaction, then hollered goodbye to their mother. As Ashley was being pulled out the door, she heard Cherish cry and her mother call, "Wesley, I wish you wouldn't yell."

Ashley squinted against the bright sun as she and Wes started up the lane toward the road. Her hat sat cockeyed on her head when she pulled it down to shield her eyes. The breeze was chilly, even though it was the second week in June, and Ashley wrapped her arms around herself.

"Aunt Ruth is Mom's oldest sister," Wes explained as they neared the road. "She and Uncle Mark live four hours from here, so they usually don't come except for holidays. I wonder if they're coming to meet you?"

Ashley looked at her brother and her brows creased.

He shrugged. "They came when Mom and Dad adopted me, so maybe that's why they're coming this time."

She shook her head. "I don't think so."

"Well, you've been here for almost six weeks. If they didn't come till Christmas, like they normally do, you would've already lived with us for over six months by the time they met you. I bet that's why they're making a special trip. You'll really like them."

"I don't like company."

Wes ran his hand along the weeds in the ditch as a large carriage passed by and sent up a cloud of dust. Ashley felt the dust stick to her cheeks. "And I hate it when people are rude. They should slow down so there's not so much dust."

"That was Mr. Barry Lee," Wes said, "so I'm sure he didn't mean to be rude. He likes Dad, so he's always nice to us."

The children climbed the hill up to the road and Wes held Ashley back while he looked for traffic. A young boy whizzed across their path on a bicycle. As soon as he passed, Wes grabbed his sister's hand and ran across the road.

Ashley stared at a meadow on the other side of the road. "I thought you said the Hendrickses live just across the road."

"They do—and a little to the west. See that blue house over there?" Wes pointed to a building a quarter of a mile away.

Ashley thought it looked like a long way to walk just to fetch a maid.

"That's where Miss Maggie lives. The Hendrickses live over the hill a little bit farther."

"How far?"

"About half a mile from here. It won't seem so bad once we can see the house."

"Can't we just wait at her house till she gets home?" Ashley asked.

"She gets mad if we bother her after working hours."

"Why does she get mad?"

"I don't know." Wes giggled. "She yelled at me once."

The children walked on in silence. Ashley wondered what Miss Maggie would look like. She painted a picture in her mind—it was a memory, really. She pictured a tall, thin woman with a crooked, pointy nose, thin, dark eyes, and every hair on her head pulled into a tight knot at the nape of her neck. This woman could inflict pain just by the look in her eyes—pain that would leave permanent wounds on the spirits of innocent children.

"Is Miss Maggie married?" Ashley asked.

He shrugged. "I don't know. Do you think there are any tadpoles left in our creek?"

"I don't know." Ashley disliked tadpoles. "Why are some people always unhappy, Wes?"

"Probably because they didn't have good parents, or maybe because they don't know about God. Will you help me make fishing poles tomorrow?"

"I don't know how. Does Miss Maggie really yell?"

Wes shrugged. "She probably won't yell at us. We should make a fort for Norm and Gerald to play in next week."

Ashley's eyes shot to her brother. "A fort? But you promised you wouldn't show anybody our fort."

"I'm not. I said we should make another one."

"Oh. Well, I don't think we'll have time."

"Why not? If Miss Maggie cleans the house, we won't have to do our chores every day. We'll have plenty of time to build a fort."

"Maybe you will, but I won't. I have to take care of the baby, you know." Ashley set her shoulders with an air of importance. "I also have to help Mama sew, and Grandma will be coming tomorrow, so I have to cook."

They crested a large hill and Ashley saw the Hendrickses' bright yellow house.

"You can build your own fort."

"I can't make a big enough one without you." Wes looked utterly disappointed. "Don't you think you can fit it into your schedule somehow?"

Ashley bit her lip as if mentally examining a hectic calendar. At length, she answered, "I suppose I can get up early and get my chores done, and then we can work on the fort in the afternoons."

Wesley's eyes sparkled. "Thanks, Ashley."

Upon arriving at the Hendricks residence, Wesley led his sister to the back door and loudly knocked.

"Is Miss Maggie here?" Wes asked when a plump woman answered the door.

"She's cleaning right now." Mrs. Hendricks looked at Ashley over the top of the white hat. Ashley saw her frown. "And Galen is still working with his granddad."

"Mom sent me with a message for Miss Maggie."

Mrs. Hendricks managed a smile and opened the screen door. "Come in, then. Wipe your feet on the rug. I'll get Maggie for you. Get a drink if you like."

The Hendrickses' grand house was lavishly furnished and decorated, and every inch of it was spotless. The kitchen had three ceramic sinks, a polished wood floor, cupboards with painted china handles, an oversized gas stove with a tin-top cupboard, and a walk-in pantry the size of Ashley's bedroom. A china cabinet, which took up one entire wall, was filled with so many exotic treasures Ashley couldn't count them all.

Glass and porcelain vases sat on the oak counters, each one filled with a different kind of flower—brilliant pink roses, plum blossoms, iris, forget-me-nots, and Queen Anne's lace. Ashley's nose tickled from the mingled scent.

A freckle-faced young woman with a red braid entered the kitchen. "Has your mother taken sick?" she asked harshly.

"No," Wes replied. "She just wants you to come clean our house tomorrow."

Ashley stared at the maid and tried to undo her mental picture of Miss Maggie.

"We're having company next Monday," Wes continued, "so Mom said you'll probably have to come every day this week."

"Every day?" Miss Maggie smirked. Ashley thought that such a sneering grin did not belong to a freckle-faced young woman.

Wes shrugged. "I guess she wants to do spring cleaning or something."

"Spring cleaning the week of June the sixth? Wesley, I guess the season for spring cleaning is already over."

"I don't know what she wants, then." Wes didn't flinch at Maggie's argument, although Ashley wanted to disappear under the thick, floral rug. "Can you come? Mom wants you in the morning."

"Very well." Miss Maggie pushed a pair of thin spectacles farther up on her nose and looked at the clock that hung on the wall. "I'll be there at nine o'clock. Tell your mother I can work for her until Thursday, but I'm completely occupied on Friday. Whatever we get done in that time will have to be enough."

"Thanks, Miss Maggie." Wes smiled, then led his sister out the door.

"She's cross," Ashley said once they were out of earshot of the Hendricks mansion.

"I don't think she had a good dad," Wes mused.

Ashley wondered what that had to do with anything.

"One time she said something about not liking her father, so I think he must've made her unhappy for life." Wes stuck his hands in his pockets. "She doesn't really mean to be rude, though. Dad told me to treat her like I'm her boss."

"Why would you be her boss?"

"We pay her. That means she has to please us."

Ashley slumped her shoulders and dropped her head. "You can tell her what to do, but I won't."

"You have to."

"She's too cross. I don't even want to talk to her."

"Ashley, you can't always be intimidated by people. Miss Maggie won't hurt you."

"She acts like she will."

Wes put his arm around his sister's shoulders. "But she won't. And that's all that matters."

The end of the week came quickly, and with it, the last preparations for hosting Aunt Ruthie's family. Miss Maggie did a thorough job of cleaning the Tanner home. Ashley thought it was too clean to be comfortable, for she couldn't walk on the kitchen floor without being asked if her shoes were dirty.

Sunday morning began as a bright, happy day. When the Tanner family came into town at quarter till eight, they found the streets of Galesburg unusually crowded. Wes had told Ashley that this was the week of the big baseball game.

Every year in June, the Galesburg Class went up against their most valiant challenger, the Harrison Boys. Everyone in Galesburg called this game "the championship," even though it wasn't a final game in the real world of baseball. The trophy that Barry Lee awarded wasn't an official cup, but it had the reputation of being more handsome than any trophy either team would receive in the official championship.

Monday's baseball game would be full of intense competition. Many of Galesburg's businesses would close for the day, and the town square would be so crowded during the trophy-awarding ceremony that Sheriff Bilt's whole company would be on duty. The big game began on Monday morning, and if the Class won, Galesburg would be swarming with guests for a full week of wild celebration. Already the streets were packed with baseball fans who eagerly awaited the big day.

"Do you suppose there'll be room in the church for everyone?" Grace asked her husband as the horse pranced through the noisy streets.

He shrugged. "The men might have to stand."

"I'll stand with you, Dad," Wes offered.

"We'll see if you need to, son." Mr. Tanner stopped in front of the tavern alongside an empty hitching post. "Hold your mother's hand, Wesley. Ashley, keep my hand so you don't get lost." Luke jumped from the wagon and took Cherish from Grace's arms. When he reached for Ashley's hand, she shied into the corner of the carriage.

"Come on," he said with a smile. "You'll get lost in such a big crowd if you don't have my hand. Now, obey Daddy."

Ashley reluctantly let him take her hand, though she gripped her mother's skirt as they walked.

Luke saw many of the upper crusts entering the church ahead of him and he squeezed Ashley's hand tighter. The weakness he had seen in Ashley recently should've made him confident of his ability to force her to behave in public, but it made him feel crippled, instead. If she threw a fit like the one she had thrown when Wes got strapped, he had no idea how he would restrain her.

In the sunny chapel that morning, visitors had already taken the Tanners' normal pew. Luke saw Lawyer Hendricks, Barry Lee, and Judge Baker settled in the wooden pews, so he quickly took a seat on the far side of the church, where Ashley remembered sitting with the orphans. This pew was one of the last empty ones, and while Wes hesitated, wondering if his father would suggest standing, Luke sat next to his wife with an air of significance.

Ashley looked all over the congregation, but the orphans weren't there.

The deafening congregation became suddenly silent when Mr. Bowtie stepped onto the stage. Just then, Ashley heard the door at the back of the church open and close. She glanced over her shoulder and stifled a gasp as she watched Mrs. Harms walk in with the orphans. The old woman's eyes searched for an open pew, but they were all full.

Just when Mrs. Harms started lining the children against the back wall, a visiting family stood in the pew ahead of the Tanners, and the father offered their pew to Mrs. Harms.

Wesley's cheeks turned red when he saw two little girls follow their daddy out of the pew. "I should have offered my seat," he whispered to Ashley.

But Ashley wasn't paying attention to him. She was too busy searching the orphan group for familiar faces.

As they filed into the empty bench, Ashley saw many changes. Gretchen was taller, Melissa and Della had ribbons in their hair, and Ronny had new shoes. Georgie, the smallest of the boys, was wearing a bandage around his hand and a patch on his dark head.

Ashley stared at the group until they were all squished into the row in front of her. Gretchen and Melissa turned their heads and gazed back, examining Ashley's new family critically. Wes nodded at them.

"The orphans are sitting in front of us," Luke whispered to his wife.

"Does Ashley see them?" Grace asked.

"Yes."

Mr. Bowtie assigned a hymn, and the sound of turning pages and people standing filled the room.

Mr. Tanner looked at the words in the hymnal as the congregation sang. "All to Jesus I surrender; all to Him I freely give . . ."

"I hope we don't have a problem with this." He glanced across the aisle at Doctor Gere, who was dressed in a stuffy gray suit, with his dark hair parted down the middle, his deep voice ringing out as if he really meant what he sang.

Mr. Tanner's hands clutched the hymnal.

"I surrender all, I surrender all, all to Thee, my blessed Savior, I surrender all . . ."

"She's not singing, Dad," Wes said.

"Just let her be." Luke was just glad that Ashley hadn't yet created a mortifying scene. He glanced at the back of the church and saw that the door was still open. Good. If she started acting up, he could escape with her quickly.

"Make me, Savior, wholly Thine; let me feel the Holy Spirit, truly know that Thou art mine. I surrender all, I surrender all, all to Thee, my blessed Savior, I surrender all."

The organ's last note faded away and the congregation took their seats. Luke took Cherish from his wife so he could busy his tense hands. He dared not look at Ashley for fear of being noticed.

When Mr. Harris began his sermon, Grace leaned forward on the bench. "Ashley," she whispered, "come sit by Daddy and Mama today."

"Why?"

"I just want you to."

Ashley scooted toward her mother, but when Grace made room between herself and her husband, she hesitated.

"Why do I have to sit there?" Ashley stared at the big man.

"Please don't complain."

Ashley eyed Mr. Tanner, and he glanced at her with a mingled look of pleading and warning. She sat as close as she could to her mother and stared straight ahead.

As the passionate Mr. Bowtie presented his message, Ashley heard whispering from the orphans' bench. She sat very quietly in order to listen in on her friends' conversation.

"Is that Ashley's new family?" Melissa asked Gretchen.

Gretchen shrugged. "I guess so."

"She's still wearing that ugly brown dress. And her hair is done the same way it was at the orphanage, except she has a new bow."

"I bet they're too poor to get her anything else." Gretchen snickered.

"Except a hat."

Ashley couldn't tell if Melissa's tone indicated envy or disgust.

"She looks ridiculous with that hat sitting all cockeyed."

"Did you see their baby?" Gretchen asked Melissa.

"Ashley's never held a baby in her life. The lady probably doesn't let her touch her."

Mrs. Harms tapped Melissa's shoulder and the girls fell silent.

For six weeks Ashley had looked forward to seeing her friends at church. Now she was sitting right behind them, yet she felt as if she were in a completely different world. She was tense and anxious during the sermon, and she never took her eyes off of the orphans.

Luke watched Ashley carefully and his cheeks burned with embarrassment. He glanced over his shoulder several times to see if the upper crusts noticed her detached behavior. He tried to listen to Mr. Bowtie's sermon but he heard nothing but the voices that danced in his head. They whispered failure and shame.

Luke set his jaw and pushed away the panic that was rising in his chest. Ashley was going to have to change quickly. Before she ruined him.

Ashley stood by her mother's side, searching the diminishing church crowd for Wes. She sighted him in a group of boys at the back of the church.

Ashley approached her brother and eagerly pulled on his sleeve, boldly interrupting the story he had been telling his friends. "Wes, I need you."

"Why?"

"I want to talk to Gretchen and Melissa. Come on; we have to hurry."

Wes let Ashley lead him outside the church to where her friends were lining up for the march home. Mrs. Harms was saying her usual encouraging words to Mr. Bowtie.

Ashley ran up to her friends. The orderly line dissolved into a shambles when the children saw her approaching. They gathered in a lopsided half circle, staring at her.

Ashley tumbled into the circle and stood there for several seconds, trying to catch her breath.

"Hi, Ashley," Gretchen greeted her.

Ashley smiled. "Did you see the baby I was sitting by?"

Melissa nodded. "Yeah."

"That's my sister. Isn't she cute?"

Melissa shrugged. "I didn't really look at her."

"Is that big, tall guy your dad?" Ronny asked with wide eyes.

Ashley shrugged. "Kind of."

"Kind of?" Wes blurted. She glanced at him and saw that his eyes were wildly searching hers.

Melissa pushed closer. "Do you have a real mom too?"

"Of course," Ashley replied. "Hey, do you think you could come over to my house sometime? It's just a little ways from here."

"Can we, Mrs. Harms?" Melissa asked.

Ashley turned around and saw Mrs. Harms approaching. "Hello, Ashley," she said with an air of disappointment.

"Hi, Mrs. Harms."

"Ashley wants to know if we can go play at her house," Melissa said.

"We'll have to discuss it," she said coldly. "But it won't be soon." She glanced at Ashley. "Besides, your parents would have to invite the girls, not you."

"Oh, I don't think Mama would mind; do you, Wes?"

He shrugged. "We'll have to ask Dad."

Just then, Mr. Tanner approached. "Mrs. Harms," he said, removing his hat.

"Hello, Mr. Tanner." The old woman nodded at Ashley. "I suppose you were looking for your children?"

"Yes, I was."

Ashley glanced at Mr. Tanner and his face was smeared with displeasure.

"Well, we'd better get going," Mrs. Harms said. "The cook doesn't like to hold breakfast. Back into line, children."

A wave of loneliness and fear rushed over Ashley. She reached for Melissa's sleeve.

"Maybe we'll see you next Sunday," Gretchen said, pulling Melissa away.

"I don't want you to go!" Ashley followed the marching line, but Mr. Tanner took her arm to hold her back.

"Ashley, they have to go home." His voice was calm, but his eyes darted around the church crowd swarming the boardwalk. He saw faces from the apothecary.

"No," Ashley whimpered, backing away from him.

Luke tried to catch her arm, but she yanked it away. Ashley remembered Wesley's strapping and darted toward the orphans. He pulled her back and buried her in his arms, covering her mouth as she screamed.

Mr. Tanner pushed through the crowd and ducked behind the church. Ashley kicked and fought against him until he pinched her leg. Then she fell silent.

Luke set Ashley on the ground and held her shoulders tightly in his hands. Her face was streaked with tears.

"Stop it," he commanded, shaking her shoulders. "I'll strap you right here and now if you make another squeak."

Ashley sucked in her breath and tried to bring her hand up to wipe her cheeks but he grabbed it and held it at her side.

"You're going to be punished when we get home," Luke said through clenched teeth. He tried to control the anger that made him want to get it over with right there. At least if he did that, the upper crusts would know he had done his job well. But what would she do if he started strapping her? She could multiply his problems.

"I want to go back," she squeaked, glancing into his face before her eyes dropped to the ground. She felt the strength in his hands and her knees became weak. She wanted to crumble on the ground but knew that he would yank her back up.

"You can't. You don't belong there anymore." His eyes shot fire at her. "If you make one more sound, you'll get it even worse when we get home."

She tried to wriggle out of his grasp.

"Stop it." Mr. Tanner squeezed her and she winced. "Don't fight me. Ashley, I swear, you're going to regret anything you attempt."

The submitted slump in her shoulders didn't comfort him.

"You're going to stay by me and not say a single word unless I tell you to. You're not going to go with Mom or Wes, and if you so much as ask to go with the orphans, you'll be right back behind this church and I'll strap you right here. Do you understand?"

Ashley breathed heavily. A whimper came from her throat and she pinched her mouth together to avoid making another sound.

Mr. Tanner stared at her and his jaw was clenched together. "Answer me," he demanded.

Ashley was afraid to speak so she nodded her head.

His hands clenched her arms harder. "Answer me properly."

She sucked in her breath and said in a tiny voice, "What do you want me to say?" A tear fell down her cheek.

"Yes, sir."

"Yes, sir," she repeated.

Luke stood and her hand disappeared into his grip. He told her to dry her tears and then took her out from behind the church.

Ashley was trembling so badly she could hardly walk, and his grip pinched her knuckles. But she sealed her lips and refused tears.

Ashley saw Wes as she walked sheepishly beside Mr. Tanner, and his compassionate glance made her want to sob. When she laid eyes on her mother, she wanted to run. But she behaved.

Mr. Tanner approached a group of men and began talking with them. In their presence, Ashley played the part of the perfect little girl. She trusted her daddy. She loved her daddy. He was always kind, always considerate, and he always tried to understand her. She obeyed out of love, not fear of force. She was a happy little girl in a happy little family, and all was well.

Ashley's stomach felt sick from the charade, but she performed.

Luke was determined to strap the girl. No matter how much Grace begged him or Ashley sobbed, he was going to do it. She had to learn her boundaries and the consequences of bad behavior. If he avoided it any longer, she would learn to play him, and it was a downhill slide from there.

All the way home, Ashley's hands trembled. Every turn of the carriage wheel twisted the dagger in her stomach, and every word Wes said to her made the situation worse. He whisperingly tried to comfort Ashley in the backseat but it only made her more nervous.

"Don't worry, Ashley," Wes said. "You don't need to shake like that. Dad's not going to kill you."

She didn't dare say anything, although she wanted to argue.

"Just 'cause you did something wrong doesn't mean he doesn't love you," Wes continued. "What are you worried about?"

Ashley looked at him and he tried to read her eyes.

"So what if he straps you?"

Tears filled the blue pearls.

"It's not that bad. It'll be over in just a couple minutes."

That's what Bonnie used to say.

"You can say you're sorry and accept your discipline, and that'll be the end of it. Just relax." Wes sat back and put his hand over hers. "You can talk about it when we get home."

But Ashley didn't say a word when they got home. Grace and Ashley went inside while Luke and Wes went to the barn to see to the horse. Ashley darted to her bedroom and climbed into the wardrobe, wishing she could change colors like a lizard.

While Luke hung the harness, he fought a vivid internal battle between Ashley and his Galesburg friends, and it made him angrier by the second. He had received many cold stares and a few scolding words from his apothecary friends after the incident with Ashley, and the more he thought of it, the more livid he became.

How dare she ruin my reputation? She should be thankful to me for saving her from orphanage life. She deserves to be strapped. She'll see my wrath and never dare to cross me again. Good. If anyone at the apothecary asks me about this morning's events, I'll tell them about the thorough punishment I gave her. She'll shape up quickly. She's utterly . . .

Luke stopped. The harness jingled in his hand. What was she? Disobedient? Prideful? Rebellious? Selfish? *Embarrassing.* That's what she was. Luke shook his head. How was he going to explain that to an eight-year-old?

Luke hung the harness and tapped the dirt off his boots. A knot formed in his stomach.

I'm still going to do it.

Don't, Luke.

She deserves it.

She's not ready. Love her.

Love comes through discipline. "He who spareth his rod hateth his son."

Mercy rejoices against judgment.

Luke shrugged his shoulders to rid himself of the weight. He walked out of the barn and headed toward the house but then veered off to the forest. He tried to make himself go back. He tried to talk himself into it. But the voice of truth haunted him, forcing him to leave Ashley alone.

Luke never spoke about the event at church that day, or ever after.

For he shall have judgment without mercy, that hath shewed no mercy; and mercy rejoiceth against judgment.

—James 2:13

Larissa J. Hitch

FIFTEEN

Ruth's Family

When are they coming?" Ashley asked her brother.

Wes shielded his eyes from the sun as he watched the road. "They were supposed to be here by now."

Ashley stepped up higher on the splintery rail fence. "What are their names again?"

"The mother is Ruth and the children are Norman, Gerald, Krissa, Deborah, and Neal."

"And how old are they?" Ashley flipped her braid over her shoulder and squinted her eyes in the intense sunlight.

"Norman is about fourteen, and Gerald is my age, ten. Krissa is eight, Deborah is six, and Neal is just a baby. The last time I saw him, he was about Cherish's age."

Ashley couldn't help but notice the excitement in her brother's voice. She had butterflies in her stomach at the thought of meeting new people. *At least there isn't a man,* she thought.

Wes stepped down from the fence. "Let's go inside."

"What for?"

"It's hot out here. Maybe we could look for them from the parlor or your bedroom."

"I don't want to go in." Mr. Tanner was in there, and she still hadn't received the strapping he'd promised her yesterday. She intended to keep out of his presence as much as possible. "Let's go to the barn or the fort."

"But then we won't know when they get here!" Wes exclaimed. "I'm going inside. You can come if you like." Wes began walking away. "Are you coming?"

Ashley sighed and climbed off the fence. "Yeah, I guess."

As the children walked across the meadow and over the hill toward the farmhouse, Wes brushed his hand atop the wildflowers and occasionally plucked one off the stem.

"You know, my name didn't used to be Wesley," he said, shredding a blue flower and throwing the petals in the air.

Ashley cocked her head. "What was it?"

"When I was born, my mom didn't name me, so the people at the orphanage named me Edsery Janeson."

Ashley's eyes grew wide. "Edsery? That's a name?"

"Yeah." Wes laughed. "The orphanage named the children alphabetically. The first boy there was Art, then there was Barry, then Clarkson, Donny, and I was Edsery."

"How many boys were in the orphanage?"

"A lot."

"Did they ever run out of letters?"

"No. Some of the boys already had names when they came."

Ashley plucked a daisy. "So, did your dad name you Wesley?"

He rolled his eyes. "Why do you still call him my dad?"

"What does it matter?" She stiffened.

"You still have a problem with him, don't you? Is that why you didn't eat supper last night?"

"I fell asleep in my room." Her neck still ached from spending the night in the wardrobe.

Wes cocked his head. "He came home late, you know. He spent a long time walking in the forest 'cause he was so mad at you. You should've apologized before you went to bed."

Ashley stiffened. "For what?"

"For embarrassing him."

Ashley looked at the ground.

The children fell silent for several steps, then Wes said, "You still can apologize."

Her head shot up. "No."

"Why not?"

"I don't want to. Maybe he doesn't even remember. Don't remind him, Wes. Promise you won't."

Wes's hair danced on his head as he shook it. "You're prideful, Ashley. You're not even humble enough to apologize."

"Just promise me you won't remind him, no matter what."

"Fine. But if I were you, I'd want to get strapped."

"Why?"

"To take the guilt away."

Wes and Ashley ducked under the fence and started toward the house. Ashley thought about humility and decided it wasn't worth intense pain. She would rather be prideful and live with guilt, whatever that was.

When the children stepped into the kitchen, they found the parents talking while Grace prepared supper. Ashley followed Wes into the room only because she knew that Mr. Tanner would notice if she ran off.

"Why isn't Aunt Ruthie here yet?" Wes asked. "I thought they were coming after lunch."

"It's only two o'clock," Mr. Tanner said.

"Well, that's after lunch."

Grace giggled. "'After lunch' could mean anytime before supper, and supper won't be for several hours."

Ashley shifted her eyes to the floor when Mr. Tanner glanced at her. She felt his tall frame towering over her. The disgusted look in his eyes made her squirm.

"Have you heard the scores on the game, Dad?" Wes asked as he climbed onto his mother's stool.

His father leaned against the cupboard. "Haven't gotten a report yet. But the Class will win; they have the past three years."

"I heard the Harrison Boys are extra hard to beat this year," said Wes with a smile. "Kenny thinks Harrison will take home

Mr. Barry Lee's trophy. He's going to the game, so he promised to tell me all about it."

"I would've taken you if we weren't having company. But I'm sure we'll hear about it. The game will be the talk of the month in Galesburg."

Wes nodded. "There sure are lots of people in town."

Luke crossed his arms and tried not to let Ashley's distance bother him. He blushed with embarrassment that he had been too cowardly to strap her last night. He still had no idea what had stopped him.

"They've come from as far away as Essex County, from what I hear," Luke said uneasily. "Some live almost to the Canadian border. Can you believe they'd drive that far for a baseball game?"

"I heard most of them take the train," Grace said.

"I guess that's good for the economy," Wes decided with a mature shrug. "The city council probably knew that a good attraction would boost train ticket sales. It really was smart to start a team here."

Mr. Tanner beamed at his son.

"Have you seen the trophy?" the boy asked. "Uncle Paul took Kenny and Len to see it, and they said it's the biggest and perttiest one yet." Wes whistled through his teeth. "It's gold, and there's never a speck of dust on the whole thing 'cause some guy shines it every day."

"Mr. John L. Mason," Mr. Tanner said.

"I bet Mr. Barry Lee would be really disappointed if the Class lost," Wes said.

"That would be a shame."

"If the Class wins, do you think I could go to the college and see the showcase with that big ol' trophy in it?"

"We'll see if we can get you in. That showcase sure is something to see. All the locals have their horse racing cups displayed, and every blue ribbon won at the fair. It takes up a whole wall."

"The college must have a full-time employee just to dust," Grace said with a grin.

Wes giggled. "Do you have any ribbons or trophies in there, Dad?"

"Should, but I don't."

"What should you have one for?"

Luke shrugged and glanced at Ashley again. "I suppose if a medal were given for every miracle we doctors perform at the hospital, there'd need to be an entire building to hold them all. Ribbons for hogs and pies are given out more freely than medals for saving lives. I reckon I could make a considerable contribution to that showcase if there were such things as awards for doctoring."

"There should be." Wes sighed. "If I ever get on the city council, that'll be the first thing I change in Galesburg." He paused. "Can girls be on the council?"

"Heavens, no," Grace said. The pump handle squeaked when she thrust it up and down.

"That's too bad." Wes gave his sister an apologetic shrug. "Well, Ashley could tell me how to vote. That'd be the same as her being on the council."

"I hope by the time you make it to the council," Grace said, "Ashley will be supporting a kind Christian husband."

Ashley thought it highly unlikely that she would ever support any kind of husband.

"Maybe her husband will be on the council with me," said Wes with a faraway look in his eyes. "That'd be grand to have two of your sons influencing Galesburg, 'ey, Dad?"

"Grand," he echoed, his brow creased.

"Cherish's husband could be on the council too . . . 'cept he probably wouldn't serve the same term as me."

"The council doesn't serve terms," Mr. Tanner said. "Everyone on the city council is tenured, which means their position is permanent. They can't be voted off or replaced unless they resign or retire."

Wes whistled. "That's a bigger job than I thought." He shrugged. "I suppose I might as well be prepared to serve for life, then."

Grace banged a head of lettuce on the counter and plucked out its core. "I suppose you won't run for council at all if it's not God's will?"

Wes crinkled his nose. "I hope I can tell God's will."

Just as Grace opened her mouth, no doubt to lecture about the enormous importance of God's will, Wes shrieked a girlish announcement that the company had arrived.

Emptying Aunt Ruth's wagon was a long, tedious chore, and the cousins weren't introduced until afterward. Wes and Ashley were engulfed in a parade of luggage-carriers who went back and forth from wagon to bedrooms at least a dozen times.

"Can we go now?" Wes asked as he dropped the final bag on the sitting room floor. Two boys stood beside him and Ashley watched them like hawks. They looked almost exactly like Jack and Henry.

"Go where?" asked Grace.

"I was going to take Norm and Gerald to the forest. You can ring the bell when supper's ready."

"Fine, but you need to invite the girls to come along."

"I don't want to go," said Krissa, a tall, skinny girl of eight.

"Me neither," echoed pretty-eyed Deborah.

When Wes invited Ashley along, she sat on the hearth and shook her head.

After the boys left, Ashley examined her girl cousins. Krissa and Deborah sat on the rug in front of the window, staring back at her with curious dark eyes.

Mr. and Mrs. Tanner sat in their rockers and Aunt Ruth stood, holding baby Neal.

"The girls have been talking about you all day, Ashley," Ruth said with a pleasant smile. "They didn't think they'd get a girl cousin who was their age, so they're very excited that you're part of the family now. Isn't that right, girls?"

Deborah nodded slightly, but Krissa gave her mother a critical glare.

"Maybe you girls want to go find something to do," Ruth suggested. "I'm sure Ashley has plenty of toys. You could have a tea party or play dolls."

"I don't have a tea set," Ashley said.

Grace smiled. "You have plenty of other toys. Why don't you take the girls upstairs and see what you can find?"

Ashley's back stiffened. "I don't want to."

Mr. Tanner glared at her and her mouth snapped shut. "Go," he said, and Ashley was on her feet and up the stairs before her cousins were off the floor.

"This is my room," Ashley said as she flung open her tall, wooden door. Krissa poked her head in while Deborah finished climbing the stairs.

"We've slept in your room before," Deborah said. "Before you came."

Ashley gave the girls a sassy lift of her shoulders. "Well, it wasn't my room then, but it is now, so you won't sleep in here."

"Mama said we could!" Krissa exclaimed.

"You can sleep in the spare bedroom. Unless you want to sleep on the floor." Ashley had meant the comment to discourage her cousins, but Deborah's eyes lit up. The girls agreed that they would be happy to sleep on the floor if they could only spend the night with their new cousin.

Ashley closed her bedroom door and took the girls outside, hoping to bore them with some uncreative chore so they would leave her alone.

"Do you like Uncle Luke and Aunt Gracie?" Krissa asked as the girls walked along the pasture fence.

"Mama's nice," said Ashley. She carried a rope in her hand and scanned the pasture for the horses.

Krissa looked at her. "Uncle Luke is my papa's favorite brother-in-law."

"I don't like him much."

"Why not?" Deborah asked, slipping her hand into Ashley's palm.

"I just don't." Ashley shrugged Deborah away. "I guess the horses are at the creek. Wes and I will have to get them in before dark."

"Can we go with you?" asked Krissa.

Ashley scowled. "No."

"Why not?"

"'Cause that's Wes's and my chore. You can feed the chickens."

"Can I?" Deborah pleaded.

Krissa pouted. "I wish I could get the horses. Do you ride them back to the barn?"

Ashley shook her head. "I tried once, but it's easy to fall off without a saddle."

"Could we saddle the horses sometime?"

"No."

Krissa's shoulders slumped. "Why not?"

"We have to have Mr. Tanner to do that." Ashley nodded matter-of-factly.

Krissa's eyes lit up. "You call him Mr. Tanner?"

Ashley's cheeks burned, and she swung the rope in circles until it made a noise that was distracting enough to surprise the girls.

"Can you do tricks with that?" Krissa asked.

"Wes can. He's teaching me."

Deborah sighed. "I'm tired of walking. Don't you have anything fun to do here?"

"Don't whine, Dee," Krissa warned. "Ashley's our hostess."

Wondering what a hostess was, Ashley's brow creased. She wished she didn't have to entertain the girls.

"We should've stayed at the house and played tea party," Deborah said, yanking on her dress when it got stuck on a twig.

"I don't like tea," Ashley said.

Krissa looked astonished. "You don't like tea?"

"Nope."

"All ladies like tea."

Ashley shrugged. "Well, I don't. Hey, look. There's a deer rub on that tree."

"What's a deer rub?" Deborah asked.

"It's where a buck rubbed his antlers as a marking. Wes and I hunt deer."

Deborah stared at her. "You hunt deer?"

"Yup." Ashley licked her lips and smiled.

"Do you shoot them?"

Ashley kept swinging the rope. "I don't, but other people do."

"Papa does," Krissa said. "But we ladies don't eat them."

Ashley looked at Krissa. "Being a lady must be boring."

The girls fell silent for several moments. Finally, for lack of a better pastime, Ashley took her cousins to the barn.

Krissa told Ashley that she knew Maymie when she was just a calf, but Ashley refused to believe her. What a silly idea that a calf could grow up to be a cow like Maymie. When Deborah begged to see the chickens, Ashley opened the coop door and made the girls go inside if they wanted to see. Then she climbed in with them and shut the door tightly for fear of Charlie escaping.

"How many do you have?" asked Deborah as she stared at the sea of feathers.

"Thirty." Ashley eagerly searched for any sign of starvation, but the chickens looked healthy. She had cut down their feed to one and a half scoops, and they still thrived.

"Do you get lots of eggs?"

"We used to get more."

"Then what happened?" Deborah looked up at Ashley with innocent eyes.

Ashley shrugged. Then her eyes widened. Mama had been complaining lately about the hens laying poorly. Maybe that was the first sign of starvation. "I think they're getting old."

Krissa laughed. "These chickens were chicks last year. They're not old, Ashley."

"Well, I don't know, then. Maybe they're dying." *Lord willing.*

"That's awful." Deborah looked at the hens. "You should give them medicine."

"They're fine." Ashley stepped out and her cousins followed. She led them into the forest on a search for their brothers. Krissa and Deborah followed Ashley nervously, for it was getting dark, and the farther they went through the trees, the thinner and colder the air became.

"Maybe we should turn around," Krissa suggested as she plucked out the third sticker vine from her shoe.

"Why?" asked Ashley, maneuvering masterfully through the brush and trees.

"It's getting awful cold. Makes me feel like we're under water, like we'll suffocate 'cause the air is so light."

"How do you think the animals live?" asked Ashley.

"I don't know, but I'm not an animal, and I can't live in here, not even for ten minutes longer."

Just as Krissa said this, the girls happened upon the trio of boy cousins. They were sitting on a grassy area, catching tadpoles in the murky water of the creek, their pant legs rolled up to their knees and their shoes in a heap on the bank.

"What're you girls doing?" Wes asked.

"Trying to find you," Krissa said. "We walked forever and almost got lost."

"We did not," Ashley snapped.

Wes glanced at his sister and laughed. "What'd you do to your hair?"

Ashley blew a strand of blonde from her face and all three girls sank to the ground. "I was trying to push through a thicket and my hair got caught in the brambles," she said.

Gerald suddenly slapped the water. "No luck again. They're too fast for me, Wes."

Norm hunched over, intently watching a swarm of tadpoles swim around his feet. "Too fast? They'll float right in front of you if you'll just stand still."

"I am standing still. They don't like me."

Krissa giggled and fell back on the grass. "That's 'cause you smell like Papa's cologne. I told you not to put it on this morning."

"It's not 'cause of Papa's cologne," Gerald retorted. "It's 'cause I ain't fast enough. We should've brought nets, Wes."

"We don't have any good ones. All of ours have holes in them."

"We should fix 'em, then. I'm not gonna have any bait to fish with if I don't catch something soon."

"You can have some of mine." Wes nodded toward the metal bucket on the far bank. "Are you girls coming fishing with us?"

"I'm not," Krissa said firmly.

"I am," Ashley said.

Krissa made an ugly face and stuck out her tongue. "You like catching those stinky fish and cutting off their heads and ripping their guts out?"

"The boys cut off the heads," Ashley said. "We can just catch them. Wes will bait your hook, so you don't even have to poke the tadpoles."

"We're going tomorrow morning," Wes said. "If you girls are coming, we'll have to make more poles."

Krissa sat up on her elbows. "I guess I'll go if Ashley does. I'd rather play tea, though. That's more ladylike."

"We'll never have enough tadpoles if we have to bring all the girls," Gerald complained, rubbing his eyes. "Maybe we should use worms."

Wes shook his head. "Naw. We'd have to dig 'em up, and that takes forever."

"Not any longer than catching tadpoles." Gerald sighed. "Dee, you know how to do this; help me."

Deborah scooted back on the bank. "It's too cold to get wet."

"Cold? It must be a hundred degrees out here. Isn't that right, Wes?"

"Maybe not quite that hot." Wes slapped the water and brought up a tadpole.

"C'mon, Dee," Gerald pleaded. "I bet Ashley helps Wes."

"Catch tadpoles?" Ashley shrieked. "I don't like touching slimy things."

"They're not slimy," Gerald argued. "They're not any worse than a lump of butter, and I bet you press butter all the time."

"Yeah, but butter doesn't move."

"And you don't have to get wet to press butter," said Deborah.

"And butter doesn't stink," Krissa complained.

"And it doesn't have a head." Ashley giggled.

"Or a tail," said Krissa.

"And it can't bite," Deborah added.

"Tadpoles don't bite," said Gerald with drooping shoulders.

Deborah looked at him shyly. "They could . . . if they were hungry enough."

The children laughed, and Norman splashed the girls with a handful of water. They squealed and fell back onto the grass.

For the rest of the afternoon, Norm and Wes walked up and down the creek catching a full bucket of tadpoles while discussing the baseball game that was happening in town. Gerald tried to keep up with them, but eventually retreated to a dirty spot under a fir tree and unsuccessfully dug for worms.

Ashley and her girl cousins lay on their backs on the sunny side of the bank and discussed the vitally important subject of whether or not one could be a real lady and not like tea.

Even a child is known by his doings.
—Proverbs 20:11

SIXTEEN

OPEN

I've never asked for help before," Grace said as she poked her needle through a button and felt to be sure it matched the rest. "It seems so strange."

"I'm sure many women of the town would be happy to share with you," said Ruth.

"But they all have families and responsibilities of their own."

Ruth clasped her hands together in her lap. "Grace, you're a new mother, and you already have three children. If those kids had been born to you, all the women would have blessed you then. I think it'd be right to give them the opportunity now."

"I don't know . . ."

"You won't have to do a thing; I'll arrange the details. You'll only have to show up at the folks' house on Friday afternoon. I'm sure Jolie and Susie would help, and Dod and Mum also. Maybe I can find someone who has a dress to give Ashley. Just think of the things people have in their wardrobes! I know several mothers in Galesburg who would love to see their girls' clothing being put to good use again."

Grace tried to swallow the lump in her throat. "You don't understand Galesburg's women. I'm afraid all you're going to find is a hodgepodge of harsh words."

"Nonsense." Ruth giggled. "If the society is as high as you've told me, everyone will respond out of sheer politeness."

Grace cringed. "Inviting people to attend a shower for Ashley is one thing, but to ask them to bring gifts? It's a daring request."

"I'm a daring sort of person," Ruth said with a careless shrug. "Gracie, think about it. How many girls does Galesburg Academy have enrolled in the third grade?"

"I have no idea."

"Probably at least ten, judging from the size of the school. Certainly those little girls have closets full of things they don't need. I'll say that the shower is for an orphan, and they'll give for charity."

Grace's needle stopped half-way through the fabric. "No, Ruthie. Please don't mention the orphan part. We don't need that kind of charity. Luke makes enough money for me to buy fabric for a dress; I just haven't had time yet."

Fiery-eyed Ruth sat back in her chair. "Grace Katherine," she said with an impatient groan, "you can't expect God to bless you if you refuse to be blessed."

The thread twanged as Grace tightened it on another button. "I'm not talking about refusing to accept God's blessings. I'm talking about asking the wrong people. You wouldn't ask unbelievers to support the church; they wouldn't have the heart. And I can't expect Galesburg to give to Ashley because they don't appreciate orphans."

Ruth threw her hands in the air. "Then we'll give them a new appreciation! Good lands, Gracie, this town has been distorted long enough." She stood up. "Can I borrow a horse and carriage tomorrow morning?"

Grace followed the sound of her sister's voice. "Why?"

"I need to go to town. You can come or stay; it makes no difference to me. I'll be glad to change this town if no one else is willing."

Grace heard her husband's big boots bang on the floor in the foyer. "It's not that no one is willing," she muttered under her breath. "It's that they don't want to be changed."

The apothecary was especially lively on Tuesday morning, and the conversation was devoted to the previous day's baseball game. When Luke entered the little store at quarter after seven, he was surprised to find all the men already gathered, hollering and laughing as they recalled the "fantastic" way Galesburg took the trophy that year.

"It was perfectly splendid; a game that Galesburg will be proud of forever," Barry Lee said.

"I reckon that game was the best I've seen since '72," agreed Lawyer Hendricks. "Not a thing to be ashamed of this year."

"Except Jackson hitting two fouls in a row," Mr. Cummings added. "That Kenneth Jackson needs to find himself a different team."

As Luke hung up his hat he wondered why Lawyer Hendricks hadn't loitered in his buggy until all the other men had arrived so he could make his habitual grand appearance.

"Tanner!" Judge Baker called when Luke went to the table to fill his coffee mug. "What are you doing here? I thought you were taking a week off work."

"I came for my morning coffee." Luke motioned toward the casual clothes he was wearing. "Besides, I had to hear the report on the game."

"Surely you heard that Galesburg took the trophy," Freddy said. "The runners told us everyone in the city had been told."

"You better have heard," hollered Sheriff Bilt, a stocky, blonde-headed gentleman with a handlebar mustache and palms as big as Freddy's head. "I hired every one of those runners and paid 'em well."

"I heard from 'em," Luke said, taking a seat in a squeaky leather chair. "They came to our place about suppertime last night and told us the score."

"It was an impressive game," Barry Lee said. "Too bad you missed it. There won't be another game like that for a century."

Luke seemed to remember Barry saying the same thing last year.

"That pitcher, Bucky Forbes, was a star of stars," Barry continued. "I reckon he has every one of those world-class players already beat. I tell you, there's not another team like Galesburg in the entire nation. I'm surprised the big boys haven't found that out yet. They could make thousands of dollars if they'd take Galesburg to the big league. It's just a matter of gettin' discovered. And as soon as that happens, we'll be on the front page of every newspaper in the country."

"The Galesburg papers are already sold out," reported one of Freddy's chums.

Dr. Gere sucked on his cigar. "Everyone wants a memory of the day we whooped the Harrison Boys," he said with an arrogant nod. "Yes, sir, those Harrison Boys didn't stand a chance. This game will be talked about for an entire year."

Jonathan Hendricks tapped his cane on the floor. "Mr. Gere, I believe this game will be talked about for an entire ten years—maybe twenty, depending on how long some of us last."

"That trophy made everyone gasp," Barry Lee said. "I'm sure it was the finest Galesburg has ever seen."

"It sure was," Judge Baker said from a dark corner by the cigar table. "Mr. Mason shined it so you could spot it a hundred yards away on a dark night."

"It wasn't big enough," Patrick Cummings said with his eyes narrowed. "When you said the trophy was the best ever, I was expecting more gold, and at least three times the size. For goodness sake, Barry, you've never made a trophy that was bigger than the showcase; how do you expect it to attract attention over all those others?"

"It has to fit in the case," Mr. Gildey said. He opened a new box of cigars and tossed them to the men's raised hands.

"Nonsense." Patrick caught a cigar and plucked a match out of Dr. Gere's shirt pocket. Smoke rose from the cigar as he sucked it deeply. "That trophy would get twice as much attention if you made it so big that we'd have to make a new case to sit in the corner, all by itself. That's the kind of trophy Galesburg deserved this year."

Several of the men hummed in agreement.

"A trophy any bigger would've cost me as much as the new sheriff's station," Barry Lee defended. "I would've had to sell my entire establishment just to pay for it. This year's cup is as big and gold Galesburg can afford."

Patrick stared back at him. "Or as big and gold as *you* can afford."

Barry's dark, wrinkled eyes stared back at Patrick's gray, flashy ones, and for a second, Luke wondered if there would be an outbreak. The other men sat on the edge of their seats, and Mr. Gildey froze with the cigar box in hand.

Barry tugged on his black coat. "I beg your pardon, Mr. Cummings," he said smoothly, "but I consider my annual contribution to the city of Galesburg via my extraordinary trophy to be worth more than any other citizen contributes in any form, at any time, with all views taken into account."

"I beg *your* pardon, sir," Patrick returned sharply, "but I beg to differ. And I think you would agree with me, had not your gray head grown so very large when you inherited your wealth from a dishonest father."

Barry Lee's face turned red enough to explode.

Judge Baker raised his cup and yelled for more coffee, and the room erupted with laughter.

Mr. Gildey went for the pot. As he began filling cups, the bell above the door rang. "It isn't eight o'clock yet," he mumbled. "Why do customers visit before eight o'clock? Every soul in Galesburg knows my policy!"

"Maybe you shouldn't flip your OPEN sign," Dr. Gere suggested with a chuckle.

Gildey shook his head. "If I didn't officially open till eight, I'd only have my door unlocked for nine hours, and that Podunk drug store across town is open for nine and a half hours every weekday. I have to have that OPEN sign up for ten hours a day, or my business will plummet."

"Morning, gentlemen," a female voice called.

Luke's eyes bulged when he saw Ruth walk around the shelves. Before he had a chance to shrink into his chair, she said, "Morning, Luke. Grace told me you'd be here this morning, so I decided to stop here first. I need a few supplies from whoever runs this establishment." Her eyes searched the faces of the men.

"What do ya need at this hour of the morning?" Mr. Gildey groaned. "Good lands, woman, it's not even eight o'clock."

Ruth's face dropped. "The sign on the door said OPEN."

The old man set down his coffeepot and tied his apron strings. "What're you after?"

"Lye and peppermint."

Mr. Gildey went behind the counter and fetched the items. Handing them to Ruth, he announced the total without ringing it up.

When she held her items in a small, brown paper bag, Ruth glanced at Luke. "Will you be home for breakfast?"

"Don't know," Luke said, clenching his jaw.

"I'm sure Grace would appreciate it. Morning, gentlemen." With a smiling nod at the crowd, Ruth bowed out.

When the bell rang after her, the apothecary fell silent and the men turned to Luke. Their gazes tore into his pride.

"You know her?" Patrick Cummings asked.

"She's my sister-in-law," Luke said. "She doesn't live in Galesburg, so she has no idea that customers aren't welcome early."

Mr. Hendricks sat forward in his chair and said with a shake of his head, "You know, Tanner, I can't quite figure out what's going on with you. Are you trying to back out on us? First it was your penny parcel, and now it's this."

"Ruth honestly didn't know." Luke braced himself for a humiliating scolding.

"But none of the rest of us have our in-laws coming here," Judge Baker echoed.

Mr. Hendricks' glare cut to Luke's heart. "Does society not matter to you anymore? Are you giving up on that?"

"No. It was a mistake. I had no idea she was coming here."

Mr. Cummings smirked. "And you had no idea your penny parcel would show up on your doorstep, either."

Luke grit his teeth.

Mr. Hendricks sat back in his chair and all of the men had their eyes glued on Luke. "I just don't know," he said, sniffing. "I think you've forgotten your calling in Galesburg."

Luke turned his eyes away as the anger mounted in his chest.

"Good lands, Grace!" Luke yelled. "Why couldn't you have kept her at home for one more hour? One hour—couldn't you have asked her to wash the dishes or scrub the floor to keep her distracted for just one hour?"

"I had no idea Ruth was going to the apothecary straight off. I assumed she'd post her notice or buy groceries first," Grace said.

Luke sniffed. "You should have made sure."

"How? Ask her entire schedule and every stop she was going to make? Or explain to her the pathetic way Mr. Gildey technically opens at seven o'clock, but is deliberately rude to anyone who comes in before eight?"

"You could have at least mentioned it to her." Luke dropped his hat on the kitchen counter and leaned against it.

"I think that's an absolutely pitiful request," said Grace.

"It would have saved me a lot of embarrassment."

"I think that's pitiful too." Grace rinsed a large kettle and set it on the counter with a careless bang. "Those men act like children, having their 'private' meetings in the apothecary, as if they ever do anything other than gossip."

"We don't gossip," Luke snapped.

"Then why on earth wouldn't Mr. Gildey want customers?"

"Because it's an annoying interruption. Besides, it's his store, and he should be able to operate it any way he likes."

Grace shook her head. "That's a silly excuse, and the only reason you agree with it is because it was your sister-in-law who unintentionally shamed you."

Luke's jaw flinched. "Dale Gildey has the right to flip his OPEN sign any time he wants. And as the man of this house, I have the right to ask my wife to keep her sister at home until that OPEN sign means what it says. That's the end of it!"

Luke began to walk away, but Grace stopped him. "I can't believe you can get so angry over a two-minute interruption into your social circle. Can't you see how useless those meetings are?"

"Useless?" he shouted. "The men I socialize with are the very roots of Galesburg—the thread that holds this town together. Not only are they honorable businessmen, they're the ones who are seeing Galesburg to progress into the twentieth century. These men are going to be the pillars of our children's views and beliefs, the ones we can count on for wisdom, as a town and as a family."

"What kind of wisdom?" Grace challenged. "Godly wisdom or worldly wisdom?"

Luke's cheeks stung with guilt. "There's no use talking to you about this."

He stomped out of the kitchen, trying to act stern but weeping inside. What did it matter that Ruth came early? Why did Dale Gildey turn that OPEN sign, anyway? Luke was in a trap. A prison. He had been here all his life; he was born into it. Reputation and approval were the only things that mattered. *Performance.* He had to prove himself worthy because without works, he was nothing. His life was conformed to fit into everyone else's expectations, and the key that locked his prison bars was passed from hand to hand in a vicious, winding circle.

It was all a big game, and Luke Tanner was a star player.

There is none righteous, no, not one.

—Romans 3:10

SEVENTEEN

The Trophy

Grace Tanner lay in bed with Cherish cuddled in her arms. A warm breeze flowed in from the open window, and little Cherish's curls were wet with sweat as she slept. Grace heard her husband breathing shallowly beside her, stirring often.

She wished she could see her husband's form that night—just to look on his dark hair again, and understand the messages in his eyes; perhaps she could see a light into his soul. Maybe, if she could see pain or worry there, she could dismiss the feeling that her husband had become a very prideful man. Perhaps she would know how to minister to him—to make him see the truth that she knew was written in every chapter of the Bible. If nothing else, maybe she could once again feel completely thrilled to be touched by him, and all the pride and ignorance and theology wouldn't matter. Maybe if she could see him, she could repair the wounds to her heart and understand why he had given them.

"This isn't working." His deep voice shattered the darkness, and Grace's heart leapt. Luke turned over to face his wife. "Ashley is pulling us apart."

It's not Ashley, Grace thought.

"Are you awake, hon?" he asked.

"Yes."

"Tell me what I should do."

A lump stuck in Grace's throat. She wanted to convince her husband that his pride was what was dividing them, but she knew he wouldn't understand, and she wasn't prepared to be rejected again.

"I don't know."

Luke touched her hand but she didn't respond. "This is my week off work, and I thought I could make some changes at home. But I'm up against a brick wall." *A castle. With the doors barred like a prison.* "Ashley isn't responding to me. Do you know she runs the moment I step foot into any room?"

"I know."

"I haven't even been able to smile at her, much less impact her the way I planned this week." Luke supposed neglecting to strap Ashley had been his biggest mistake. "Things aren't working between you and me either. We've come too far to grow apart now."

Silence overtook the bedroom. Grace felt her husband's fingers dance on her hand.

"Talk to me, Gracie; please?" he said.

"I don't know what to say." Her stomach turned with a sickening flip.

"You're not helping me much."

"I don't know how."

"Tell me what to do!"

Grace closed her eyes, wishing she could open them to perfect sight. But when her glassy eyes looked again, all she saw was perfect darkness.

"You won't like my solution, and I don't know how to find a common ground," she said timidly.

"We never argued before Ashley came."

"Luke, if I could make myself agree with what you believe, I would do it just for the sake of peace."

"But you can't, 'ey?" he whispered.

"I think you're too hard on Ashley and too concerned about your image to reach her selflessly."

Luke pulled his hand away from his wife's arm.

"I don't think you've subjected all your beliefs to the Bible, and I have a hard time going against God's Word," she continued.

He snorted with disgust. "God's Word says that if your heart doesn't condemn you, you're not condemned. I'm just not feeling condemnation like you want me to." *Or at least not admitting to it.*

Grace sighed. "I don't want you to be condemned; I want you to be convicted."

Luke rolled over and said with an unsatisfied groan, "Let's not talk about it anymore. I'm tired of arguing."

Grace slid her hand across the sheets and reached for his. "I still love you," she said in a painful whisper.

He gripped her hand, but said nothing. Even with her hand held tightly in his, Luke felt like everything was slipping through his fingers.

Luke Tanner watched as his son pranced back and forth, his eyes shining with excitement. It was Wednesday, June 15, 1910, and the postgame festivities were still progressing in the town of Galesburg. The remarkable trophy had been set in the glass case at the college the evening before. While those who had attended the game wasted themselves in reckless celebration, a small crowd lined up outside the college door to see the trophy. These were the few souls who hadn't attended the game or the ceremony afterward, and at nine o'clock that Wednesday morning, Luke, Wes and the cousins were numbered in the impatient crowd.

"I bet they have a lock on the showcase door," Gerald whispered to Wes.

Norm stood on tiptoe to see over the top of a short man's shoulder. "I can see it."

"You can?" burst Wes, and he and Gerald tried to poke their heads over the crowd.

"Boys, don't push," Aunt Ruth said from behind them. "We'll get our turn, and it'll be worth the wait."

Deborah stood beside her mother and bit her fingernails as her eyes wildly searched the crowd. Baby Neal tugged on her braid from Ruth's arms, and Deborah shrieked and pulled it from his hand.

Luke stood behind his sister-in-law and dug in his trouser pocket for his money clip. He pulled a dollar from the shiny clip and held it in his hand. A fee for seeing the trophy was only applied the week of the game, when the city officials knew they could raise a hefty sum.

"You could've taken Wes next week," Ruth said to her brother-in-law. "Then you wouldn't have to pay."

Luke shrugged. "Your boys might as well see it too. It'll only be a dollar for all of us."

The crowd took a step forward, and Wes and his cousins were on the heels of the little man in front of them. Krissa and Deborah followed more shyly.

"Did Grace get to see the showcase before her sickness?" Ruth asked.

"She did, several years ago. 'Course, that was before the big trophies. Five years ago the Class got medals, and they weren't very impressive."

"Someday Ashley will appreciate the showcase, but she's probably too young yet," suggested Ruth.

Luke knew that lack of interest in the showcase was not what had kept Ashley at home with Grace that day. When the little girl was invited, she gladly accepted until she heard that her mother would be staying home with the baby. Then she threw a tearful tantrum until Luke let her stay. Before he relented, though, he made it clear that he wasn't happy.

"Dad," Wes said, "how much do you think the trophy cost Mr. Lee?"

"I have no idea, Son."

"Do you think it cost a hundred dollars?"

Luke's eyes grew wide. "That's a lot of money."

"I bet it could've cost that much. I heard it's pure gold."

"It's not quite pure. It's gold plated, which isn't the same."

Wes turned to his cousins. "It had to have cost a hundred dollars," he decided. Norm and Gerald danced with anticipation. "If it's the best trophy yet, Barry Lee had to have spent at least that much on it. Especially since it's pure gold."

"Gold-plated, Wes," Luke echoed.

Wes smiled. "Well, that's almost the same, anyway."

The line inched forward and a stringy-haired, gangly young man stood in the doorway to collect fees. The boys smiled at him, but he stared back with a threatening glare.

Luke smirked as he put the dollar bill in the man's hand. "Lighten up, Freddy. They won't squeak by as long as you're standing there looking so mean."

"Mr. Tanner." Freddy's cheeks blushed. "I didn't expect to see you here. All the other cary men were at the ceremony."

"The what kind of men?" Luke looked at him critically.

"The cary men. You know; the apothecary group? I was sure and certain you'd see the ceremony for yourself. Guess you didn't, 'ey?"

"I couldn't make it."

Freddy looked at Luke as if he were a soldier fallen from rank. He stepped to the side of the doorway. "Come see her, then. She's a beauty. 'Course, she was a lot prettier Monday night, with the lights shining on her and the whole baseball team waiting to receive her. Oh, well. I guess the showcase is second best."

With a hypocritical smile, Freddy stuffed the dollar into his overflowing money bag.

Entering the doorway of the college added a whole new dimension of excitement for the children. Impatience surged even more intensely than before. The children couldn't see that the showcase was halfway down the hall, and there were at least fifty people ahead of them. From his position towering over most of the heads, Luke could barely see the beginning of the glass case. He didn't have the heart to tell the children that they would be standing in line for a good half hour longer, so he let them whisper and giggle and count the minutes on Wesley's pocket watch.

While Ruth entertained Neal by pointing out the paintings and photographs that lined the hall walls, Luke searched the crowd for any of the "cary" men, hoping to reclaim his pride after spiteful Freddy had dashed it. But he was very disappointed to find that he was the only reputable citizen in the crowd. He scolded himself for not being aware of the importance of attending the award ceremony.

"Who actually makes the trophy, Dad?" Wes asked, interrupting Luke's thoughts.

"I don't know, son. After Barry Lee designs it, he sends the plans to a company."

"Do they mail it when it's done?"

"I suppose so."

Wes whistled through his teeth. "It must cost a lot to ship it. Maybe somebody delivers it on the train."

"I doubt it."

"But I don't think a mail carrier could handle it, since it's so big."

Luke patted his son's shoulder. "Let's wait to see the trophy and then we can guess, 'ey?"

Wes beamed and turned forward again, chatting with his cousins about the exceptionally qualified escort who must have been hired to transport Galesburg's trophy.

By the time the Tanner group reached the showcase, the children were complaining of hunger, and Ruth had surrendered Neal to Luke's arms because the toddler was wrinkling her dress with his squiggles.

When the trophy came into view, the children fell silent.

"That's it?" Wes asked, staring at a two-foot-tall silver block topped by a gold-plated baseball. All of the cousins' faces dropped, and Wes looked up at his father.

"Pretty, isn't it?" asked Luke dryly. He stared at the sickly excuse for a decade-deserving trophy and tried to smile. "See the baseball? It's as shiny as you can get. Pretty impressive, 'ey?"

"Yeah," Norm said without conviction.

"I thought the whole trophy was gold," Gerald remarked.

"Are you sure that's this year's trophy?" Wes asked.

Luke nodded. "Compare it to the rest of them, Wes. It's the best in the showcase."

Wes glanced at the glass case's collection. He couldn't argue that the 1910 trophy was the most impressive. All the others were copper or silver, and not one was more than eighteen inches tall. "I guess Barry Lee did mail it. A trophy like that could fit in my book bag."

"I think it's pretty," Deborah said. "I wish I had a trophy like that."

"I don't," Krissa argued. "You can't even read the engraving on it. I like my spelling bee awards better than that silly thing."

Wes backed away from the case. "I guess if the Class is happy, that's all that matters. Some trophy! Barry Lee must not be as rich as I thought."

Lo, this is the man that made not God his strength; but trusted in the abundance of his riches.

—Psalm 52:7

EIGHTEEN

A Visit from Mrs. Harms

Krissa and Deborah sat on a little bench underneath an enormous, knotty hackberry tree and looked into the distance. Six-year-old Deborah swung her feet and Krissa squinted her eyes in an attempt to read lips.

"They're not obvious enough," Krissa said with a sigh. She sat back and shook her head. "I can't understand a single word Ashley's saying, and that old woman keeps repeating herself."

"What does she say?" asked Deborah, chewing on a piece of wheat gum.

"Something about Ashley being naughty."

Deborah looked at her older sister. "Well, she is naughty, you know. Papa would call us *rebellus* if we acted like her."

"It's rebellious, not *rebellus*," Krissa corrected. "And anyway, what does it matter? We're not orphans."

Deborah cocked her head. "Is it all right if orphans are rebellus?"

"No. Only sometimes. Why do you keep saying rebellus?"

"That's how Granddaddy says it."

"Granddaddy is wrong."

"Granddaddy is never wrong." Deborah set her shoulders confidently. "And neither is Papa. So I think Ashley is rebellus, 'cause that's what Papa would say. And I don't think it's 'cause she's an orphan, either."

Krissa leaned forward and tried to make out the words, but gave up when Mrs. Harms turned her back and her mouth was out of view.

"They've been talking for a long time," Deborah said.

"Of course they have. Ashley hasn't seen her real granny in nine years."

"That's her real granny?" Deborah gasped. "And she hasn't seen her in nine whole years? Ashley must really miss her."

Krissa nodded. "Well, I think that's her granny, anyway. It has to be. Why else would she come to talk to Ashley?"

Deborah pulled on her fingers as she counted out eight of them. Her little brow creased. "But you said Ashley is only this many." Then she held up one more finger. "Nine is this many. That's more than Ashley."

Krissa giggled. "You don't know how to subtract, Dee. If you did, it would make sense."

"Oh."

Deborah folded her hands in her lap and continued to swing her feet. A warm breeze blew on the girls' cheeks, and the hackberry leaves rustling in the top of the tree sounded like a song.

"Where did the boys go?" Deborah asked.

Krissa plucked a velvety-red hollyhock from a tall stem beside the bench. She turned it upside down and chose a slightly larger one to make a hollyhock doll. "They went to see the horses after Wes got sent to his room."

"Why did Uncle Luke send Wes to his room? Was he naughty?"

"Terribly naughty."

Deborah's brow rose in curiosity, but Krissa continued to make her doll without offering any more information. When little Dee begged her sister to tell, Krissa whispered, "When Mrs. Harms showed up this morning, she talked to Uncle Luke and Aunt Grace in the parlor, and Wes sat on the porch trying to hear what she had to say. When the old lady asked to talk to Ashley privately,

Wes said he wanted to talk to Ashley first. Uncle Luke wouldn't let him, but Wes was terribly determined, so Uncle Luke forced him to go to his room. Wes was piping angry! I bet Uncle Luke will thrash him."

"Do you think so?" wide-eyed Deborah asked.

"Our papa would, and Uncle Luke is a lot like Papa."

"Do you think Uncle Luke will thrash Ashley too?"

"What for?" Krissa glanced from her hollyhock doll to her sister.

"For being naughty, like that old woman says she is."

"I don't know. Probably not, 'cause she's an orphan."

"Orphans don't have to get thrashed?" Deborah said with surprise.

"Not Ashley, at least. I heard Aunt Grace tell Mama that Uncle Luke has never so much as touched Ashley. She'll probably never get thrashed."

"Are orphans real people?"

"Yeah. Well, kind of." A petal dropped off the hollyhock doll's dress, and Krissa threw the whole doll behind her and picked another flower to make a better one. "I mean, they're people, but they're kind of a different race. Not normal, like us."

"Oh." Deborah paused. "Is that why Ashley doesn't like tea?"

Krissa shoved a hollyhock upside down over the other one and smiled. "I guess that could be part of it."

Ashley climbed the stairs on tiptoe, trying not to make them squeak. The hallway was dark because the gray sky hid the sun outside. She turned the silver door handle of Wesley's bedroom and opened the door. The room was dimly lit with the glow of a candle, and shadows danced on the wall and floor. Ashley shivered with gloomy fear as Wes looked at her from where he was lying on the bed, his face smashed against his pillow.

"Did she leave?" he asked, his voice muffled.

Ashley stepped in and shut the door. "Yeah."

"Good."

"Why are you up here? Why aren't you playing with the boys?"

"Dad sent me up here."

Ashley's heart pounded. "Is he coming up?"

"Probably."

"I'm gonna go find the girls."

Wes shifted his eyes to his sister. When she reached for the door handle, he said seriously, "What did Mrs. Harms want to talk to you about?"

Ashley turned back and shrugged. "She wanted to know if I like it here."

"What did you say?"

"I said I like you." The siblings met eyes, and Wes's brow creased.

"Did she ask if you want to go back to the orphanage?"

Ashley looked at the floor. "Yeah."

"What did you say?"

"Nothing."

Wesley's head popped up. "Why didn't you tell her that you want to stay here? Ashley, she's going to take you away if you don't tell her you like it here! You really don't get it, do you? You really don't understand."

The door handle twisted and the door opened. Ashley stiffened when she saw Luke Tanner enter. The light from the candle seemed to drown in the shadow of the big man.

"What's going on in here?" Mr. Tanner asked quietly.

"We were talking," Wes answered.

Ashley stepped away from the tall man and couldn't force herself to look at his face. She kept her eyes on the door and when Mr. Tanner shut it, her mouth went dry.

"Mind if I join you?" he asked. Without waiting for permission, he sat at Wesley's feet on the bed. "What were you talking about?"

Wes bit his cheek. "Mrs. Harms."

"I see." Luke glanced at Ashley, and she felt his gaze cut into her very spirit. "Ashley, come sit with us."

Alarm surged through her. It took all the courage she had to sit beside Wes.

"What did you think of Mrs. Harms's visit?" Luke asked.

"It was fine," she said in a tiny voice.

"What did she say?"

"Nothing."

"She didn't say anything?" Luke chuckled. "Did she ask about me?"

Ashley looked into Mr. Tanner's face. The quiet light of dusk cast dark shadows on his eyes and she shivered. Mr. Berk had always come home in the evening, when nighttime was creeping up on the countryside. Almost every time Ashley had been strapped, it had been when darkness had made her vulnerable to Mr. Berk's power.

Ashley's eyes shifted to Wes, who laid on the bed resting, even though Mr. Tanner was so near. She remembered the picture above her bed and took a deep breath, resolving to do her part in becoming the girl in that picture. Somehow, she would believe Wes's faith in Mr. Tanner and try to trust him.

"Ashley," Mr. Tanner's voice boomed, "I need to talk to Wesley for a minute."

She jumped off the bed and dashed out of the room. "He's not the daddy in the picture," Ashley muttered to herself as she retreated down the stairs. "He's too angry and sharp to be a daddy like that."

"One more month," Ashley remembered Mrs. Harms saying to her. *"Stay here for one more month, and when I come back, if you still want to come with me, you can return to the orphanage."*

Ashley promised herself that she would be perfectly good for the next month. She could avoid Mr. Tanner that much longer and then she could go home.

For all that is in the world . . . the pride of life, is not of the Father, but is of the world.

—1 John 2:16

NINETEEN

The Pitiful Party

Friday morning dawned bright and beautiful at the Tanner house and Ruth pranced about in preparation for Ashley's party. Luke had consented to her idea of a baby shower on the condition that it wasn't called charity, and that no upper crusts were invited. He hoped he wouldn't come to regret his decision.

That afternoon, while the children were resting, Luke hitched up the carriage for Ruth and Grace.

"We'll only be gone a few hours," Grace said as he placed an empty basket on her lap. "If Ashley wakes up, tell her I'll be back soon, and that she should play with the boys."

He nodded. "She'll be fine."

"And Luke," she whispered, "please don't be hard on her."

"Don't worry."

Grace sat back. "All right. Go ahead, Ruthie."

Ruth clicked to the horse and they trotted away.

Luke strode back to the house with confidence in his step. When he opened the front door he heard crying from upstairs. He bounded up the stairs and followed the noise into Ashley's room. The moment he entered, she became hysterical. Luke tried to soothe her, but when Ashley wouldn't let him touch her, he called for Wesley.

"What's the matter with her?" Wes asked when he came up the stairs.

Luke's jaw clenched. "I don't know."

The boy's eyes were searching. "You can't help her?"

"Just go, Wes." Luke nodded toward the bedroom. "Don't ask questions. Just calm her down."

Wes entered the bedroom and approached his sister's bed. She had her knees tucked into her chest and the quilt was swaddled around her feet.

"Why are you crying, Ashley?" Wes asked gently. He sat down on the bed next to her.

Ashley stared at the closed bedroom door and wondered if Mr. Tanner were listening from the other side. She heard his boots go down the stairs. "I don't want him to be here," she whispered to her brother. "Tell him to go away."

Wes cocked his head. "Dad? Why? He wasn't trying to hurt you. He heard you crying, so he came to help."

Ashley hid her face in the pillow. "He's gonna get me in trouble. Don't let him hurt me."

Wes touched her hand. "Ashley, why do you always think Dad's gonna hurt you? He never has, has he?"

Her head shot up. "I don't like him."

"But why?"

"Every time he comes into your room, he hurts you."

Just like Mr. Berk. He never entered the girls' bedroom without his belt in his hand.

Wes's mouth dropped open. "Why do you think that?" he asked. "Have you ever seen him hurt me?"

"I know he does, 'cause Mama said so."

"What did she say?" Wes demanded.

"I know he strapped you."

"He strapped me once since you've been here." Wes shook his head. "And I deserved it."

Deserved it, Ashley thought. Jack said she deserved to be strapped after he had given her fair warning.

Wes looked at her with utter confusion. "You obviously don't know Dad. You don't give him a chance."

"I don't want him to ever come in my room."

"I wish you understood. I wish you would talk to him just once. You would change your mind about him."

"I don't want to."

Silence took over for a long moment.

"When are we going back to church?" Ashley asked.

"This Sunday, I suppose. Why?"

"I wanna see everyone from the orphanage. I wanna go back."

"You don't want to stay here?"

"No."

"Don't you like it here?" Wes's eyes filled with tears.

"I just wanna go back. When's Mama coming home?"

"I don't know."

"Will you stay with me till she comes?"

"Up here?"

Ashley nodded.

Confused and fighting tears, Wes merely glanced at his sister and tried to understand the burning grief he saw behind her eyes.

Ruth scurried around her parents' house, eagerly arranging the main living area for the party. Grandma helped Ruth set up a table for the gifts. They frosted the cake, which was large enough to feed fifty guests, put a white tablecloth on the table, and made lemon pudding to go with the dozens of strips of maple taffy. They draped stringers of brightly colored paper from the cupboards and ceilings, and hung a little sign from the front door that read, "Welcome, Ashley" in bold letters. Sunlight streamed in the windows, and a pleasant breeze swept through the house, spreading the tantalizing smell of cake, taffy, and pudding into every room.

When the house had been pronounced ready, Ruth sighed in satisfaction and leaned against the counter. "This is going to be a fun day for Ashley."

Granddad chuckled from the adjoining parlor. "You're a brave woman to take on such a task in Galesburg."

"Dod, is it really as bad as Grace said?" asked Ruth.

Granddad settled back on the fluffy sofa and folded his hands on his belly. "She probably didn't tell you the worst. Frankly, I'm surprised Luke adopted Ashley. He's considered one of those upper crusts, and they are all very much against the 'penny parcels,' as they call them."

Ruth rolled her eyes. "What a heartless label to put on orphans."

"No one seems to support those unfortunate children."

Ruth gazed out the window. "We'll see. Maybe the families of Galesburg just haven't had an opportunity to reach out to the orphans. They may prove us all wrong after today."

The first guests to arrive at the cheery Jackson household were Mr. and Mrs. Sulka. Ruth was elated when Granddad frantically told her that Dan Sulka was an upper crust, and that it was a miracle that he had come. Grandma and Ruth ushered the family into the parlor, where Granddad went about his duty to entertain them by striking up a conversation about syrup crops, weather, and children.

Minutes later, the door swung open again and Aunt Susie's family entered with Miss Jolie.

Susie and Jolie pranced about the house, exclaiming over the bright decorations and the bouquets of flowers. Baby Mary raided the toy chest, and the boys found their way to the parlor.

Ruth disappeared to her place in the foyer and paced between the door and the windows, waiting for the next guests to arrive.

But no one else came.

At ten o'clock, the Tanner family arrived with Ruth's children. A very small party of excited family and friends greeted them.

Ashley was so surprised by the decorations, desserts and presents that she could do nothing but hide behind her mother's skirt with a bashful but large smile, and watch the other children exclaim over it all. Deborah and Neal trampled baby Mary on their violent shove for the toy chest while Ruth's boys tore apart the stringers in their brave attempts to touch them. For a few minutes, the house was filled with loud excitement, and Ashley watched it all with a blank stare.

When Ashley spotted Miss Jolie, she stood frozen, staring. Jolie turned her face toward Ashley and Ashley shrieked and rushed into the woman's arms.

"Ashley!" Jolie exclaimed, scooping her into her arms.

"Where's everyone else?" Ashley squealed. "Did you bring Gretchen and Melissa? And where are the boys?"

"They're all in school today." Jolie kissed her forehead. "But I get to be here with you for your party! Did you see the cake that Grandma and Aunt Ruthie made for you? It's so exciting that everyone is doing this for you. How have you been? And how are Wes and Cherish?"

"They're fine." Ashley pinched Jolie's dress in her fingers. "Are you coming to my house? Will you bring Gretchen and Melissa?"

Jolie's eyes softened. "Someday I might bring the girls to see you. You look so beautiful today. Does your mama do your hair?"

Ashley nodded and Jolie patted her braid. "Well, now, let me say hello to your mama, 'ey?"

Ashley slid out of Jolie's arms. "You know her?"

Jolie laughed. "We're sisters, darlin'. Didn't Wes tell you? Granddad and Grandma Jackson are my parents, too."

Ashley glanced at Wes and his face was covered with a smile.

"It was a surprise," Wes said. "She's our aunt, just like Aunt Ruthie and Aunt Susie. Are you happy?"

Ashley watched Miss Jolie as she hugged Grace. Her heart pounded in her chest.

Wes bumped his sister's shoulder. "I thought you'd like to have an extra-special surprise. I knew you liked Jolie best of everyone at the orphanage, so I wanted to wait until you saw her before I told you that she's our aunt. I thought you'd like that."

Ashley glanced at her brother and found herself smiling. "I like it," she mumbled.

While the greetings were being said, the treats put out on the table and the children quieted, Ruth again took up her pacing between the door and windows in the foyer. She repeatedly peered out the curtains.

"Ruthie," said Granddad, approaching, "maybe we should get the children some cake."

Ruth glanced out the window again. "I suppose. Just to keep them busy until everyone else comes." She turned her back to the door. "Children, gather in the kitchen and get your cake. Mum, go ahead with the taffy too. Oh, and Gerald, get some for Neal."

Luke neared his sister-in-law. "Do you really think more people are going to come?"

She stared at him. "Luke, I invited more than forty people. I'm sure they're just running late. Let me hold Cherish so you can manage the boys." Ruth scooped the baby into her arms, sending Luke away with a decided nod that was obviously meant to silence him.

Ten thirty came without the door being opened again, and soon the chiming clock brought in the eleven o'clock hour. Ruth stayed at her post, but the door never opened again. By eleven o'clock, the children were growing impatient. Three gifts sat at the long table, and the little ones kept asking why Ashley had to wait to open them.

Finally, begged by a thousand tugs on her skirt, Ruth mustered a smile and said pleasantly, "Shall we open the gifts now?"

"That's a wonderful idea," Grandma agreed. "Bring them over here, Nathan. Ashley, they're all for you, so you get to open them."

The children gathered around Ashley, and the babies poked their fingers at the brown wrapping paper on the gifts. Ashley didn't open the presents fast enough to satisfy the children, so she was cheered on by quick commands to "hurry up." Before the eight-year-old had hardly had time to admire the crinkly paper, she found it shredded on the floor and her gifts set on the table.

After looking at the pair of soft pink mittens, two red hair bows, and an adorable cloth doll with black-button eyes and a crooked thread smile, the boys quickly abandoned the scene. Ashley stared at her presents with the rapture of a child who had only received ugly dresses, itchy stockings and tight, black boots as gifts. She scooped the ribbons and doll into her arms and tucked the mittens into her mother's pocket, giggling with wild excitement.

"It was a total failure!" Ruth erupted in the kitchen that night. "Never in my life have I come up against such a selfish, narrow-minded, altogether heartless society! It's dreadfully pathetic! Grace, if I were you, I'd move out of Galesburg and leave these people to suffer in their own carelessness. They've no heart, and I dare say they never will."

Grace calmly patted her sister. "Ruthie, it's not all that bad. Ashley was thrilled with everything today. Truly, you made a lasting memory."

"She didn't even get a new dress! No stockings, no shoes, no petticoats or playthings." Ruth burst into tears.

"Let's just sleep on it," Grace said tenderly. "It'll all seem better in the morning."

"Fiddlesticks." Ruth sniffed. "Galesburg will never be better, and I'll detest it for the rest of my days." She opened the spare bedroom door and slammed it after her.

Grace made her way into the sitting room with a helpless sigh. She sat in her rocker and brushed the loose strands of hair from her face, trying not to succumb to the defeat of rejection.

"Luke, are you in here?" Grace asked quietly.

He heard her call from the upstairs hall and started down the steps. "I'm coming."

"What are you doing up there?" Grace asked when he stepped down the last stair and joined her in the sitting room.

"Putting the children to bed."

"Ashley let you put her to bed?" Grace said with surprise.

"Not exactly." He had tried to instruct Ashley to lay in bed with her cousins but all he had gotten was a terrified look. When he went into her bedroom to tuck her in, Ashley shrieked for Wes and started crying.

Luke sighed deeply, trying to rid himself of annoyance. "Why is Ruthie upset?" he asked.

"She says the party was a total failure and that it proves what a heartless society Galesburg is."

Luke sniffed. "That's an unfair conclusion. I'm sure people were just too busy to come."

"All forty of them?"

"Grace, it's the week after the baseball game."

The stairs squeaked and Luke looked toward them. Ashley poked her head around the corner and Luke said quickly, "Ashley, why are you out of bed?" He felt like yelling at her for the embarrassment she continued to heap on him.

She darted up the stairs.

"Don't run away," he said loudly. "Come back."

"She probably just wanted to say good night," Grace said in a whisper.

"Not after she's been put to bed." Not if she couldn't say it to him when he was trying to tuck her in.

Ashley bravely came back to the bottom stair and the pleading in her eyes took Luke by surprise.

"You're not to get out of bed once you've been sent there," he said gruffly.

"Did you need something?" Grace asked.

"No," Ashley squeaked.

"Luke, can she sit on my lap for a little while?"

Ashley turned and started up the steps. "I gotta go to bed."

"Come back, Ashley," Luke called again.

Ashley came back down the stairs, and this time she looked petrified.

"Mom wants to hold you." The power in Luke's voice drowned out the crackling of the fire in the hearth. "Come sit with her."

Ashley started to argue but when Luke nodded toward Grace's rocker, she made a dash for her mother's lap. Luke watched her as she tucked her feet under her nightdress and lay her head back on Grace's chest and he was disgusted. She had done the same things to Jolie all day at the party, and she wouldn't so much as let him set foot in her bedroom.

She's controlling, Luke thought. *She wants to see how long she can make me do what she wants.*

"Did you have a nice time at the party?" Grace asked, stroking Ashley's arm.

Ashley nodded.

"The people were so nice to bring you gifts. God always provides for us, doesn't He?"

Ashley bit her cheek and saw a picture of God in her mind. God was a man. A big one, obviously, since He could be everywhere at one time. A mean one, because Bonnie said that God made Mr. Berk the way he was. If He were a man, God was very strong, and He had big hands and a voice that was angry and gruff. He was tall, like Luke Tanner, and fat and cruel like someone else she knew. He exploded at the least likely times, and He hurt people who got too near to Him. God was a man. It was very unfortunate that He was in charge of the world.

"Do you know much about God?" Grace asked.

She nodded again.

Mrs. Harms talked to God, and Miss Elizabeth taught Ashley about Him. He was that high and mighty Person you couldn't talk to unless you closed your eyes and folded your hands and sat perfectly still. Unless you had practiced your prayers every night, it was a dangerous thing to pray to God. He wouldn't answer your prayers if you stuttered through them. It was a sign of disrespect. And if you disrespected God, His angels would stop watching out for you, and that's when you were in danger of getting hurt or dying, and having to stand before the Judgment Seat to receive a real Death Sentence—the kind that would last forever. And that kind of Death Sentence was even worse than talking to Mrs. Harms.

Grace rocked back and forth and the soothing movement made Ashley relax.

"Did you read out of the Bible much at the orphanage?" Grace continued.

Ashley shrugged.

"Should we have Daddy read us a Bible story?"

Ashley looked at Luke and quickly shook her head.

He set his jaw and reached for the Bible from the mantle. He was glad for a chance to give Ashley another opportunity to obey.

"I think that's a good idea," Luke said as he began turning the pages.

"I don't wanna hear one," Ashley whispered to her mother.

"Why not? Don't you like stories?"

Ashley squiggled when Luke turned his attention back to her.

"Let's read one tomorrow, Luke," Grace said in a quiet voice. "Ashley doesn't really feel like listening to a story tonight."

Luke set the Bible open on his lap. "Reading from the Bible is good for us, Ashley," he said without looking up. "I think you can sit for a while and listen. Let's read about baby Moses."

"Luke, really, let's do it tomorrow," Grace pleaded.

This time, Luke looked at Ashley and she slunk back at the rebuke she saw in his eyes.

"Ashley, you've had a day of everyone spoiling you and now you're being selfish," he said. "Stop complaining to Mom and listen to me. I'm going to read a story and if you keep fighting about it, I'll strap you and then read the story. It's your choice."

Ashley scooted further into her mother's lap and made herself stay put. She wanted to flee up the stairs to the shelter of Wes's room.

"Are you going to sit quietly and listen?" Luke prodded.

"I . . ." She squiggled and felt the tears coming in her chest. "I'm really tired," she said to her mother.

"OK, then we're going to take care of this before we read," Luke said calmly. He set the Bible on the floor beside his chair and stood up.

Something in his spirit suddenly halted.

Luke, don't do it.

He pushed away the prodding inside. *I listened to You last time and was a cowardly fool.*

Son, please don't let your emotions get in the way. Look at her. Listen to her.

And skip the strapping, huh? I've had enough of this behavior!

Luke, look at her.

Luke saw Ashley gripping her mother's dress in her hand. Her knuckles were white and the color was drained from her cheeks.

He set his jaw and held out his hand toward her. *I'm not going to back out of this one.* "Come with me, Ashley."

He waited and then took a step toward her.

"Don't, Mr. Tanner," Ashley said desperately. Her voice was trembling.

Hearing her call him by that name made him more annoyed.

"I've given you plenty of chances to obey tonight. You're not listening, so I'm going to strap you, and then we'll come back here and see if you can listen better."

Son, don't.

"I think Ashley will listen better now," Grace spoke up.

Ashley's palms began to sweat as she clung to her mother's dress.

"Can't you, Ashley?"

She tried to swallow but the lump in her throat was too big.

Luke looked at Grace and shook his head. "Grace, she's not even responding to you. This is total disrespect."

Grace touched Ashley's hair and was surprised to find that the girl was broken out in a cold sweat.

"Ashley, tell Daddy you'll be quiet and obey," Grace said in a half-begging whisper.

"I will," she squeaked, and a tear fell onto her dress.

Luke stared at her for a long moment and felt the power go out of his hands. Here he was, finally brave enough to do what needed to be done, and his wife was standing up for Ashley.

"Go to bed, then," he commanded.

Ashley shot her eyes toward him and he looked away from the hollowness he saw.

"I'll come up and tuck you in in just a minute," Grace soothed. She moved Ashley off her lap but only when Mr. Tanner had sat back in his chair did Ashley dash up the stairs.

"Don't ever do that to me again, Gracie!" Luke exploded when he heard Ashley's bedroom door slam.

"She's not ready for you to strap her, can't you see that?"

He raked his fingers through his hair. "Yeah, well I'm not ready for her to treat me like I mean nothing and have absolutely no authority. That's a pathetic way for a girl to treat her father!"

"I'm going to go tuck her in." Grace stood and started toward the stairs. "She won't be ready to experience your discipline until she's experienced your love, Luke."

"She has experienced my love," Luke muttered under his breath as she walked away.

It was the last day Aunt Ruth and her children were to spend with the Tanners. Granddad and Grandma had come over to help prepare a feast for the farewell party, and they had done it well. As the nighttime hours crept upon the little, white farmhouse, everyone gathered in the sitting room to spend the last night together, being stuffed full of every sort of fancy treat the womenfolk could create.

While the adults talked about crops, children, and the economy, the boys played marbles by the fireplace. Ashley and her girl cousins stared at each other quietly for a long time. Then Ashley got some paper from her desk and went to the dining room. Krissa followed her and sat across the table as Ashley began to draw.

"I'm sorry, Ashley," Krissa said after an awkward pause.

Ashley looked up at her. "For what?"

"'Cause you're an orphan. That must be awful hard."

"Naw." Ashley looked back at her paper.

Krissa crinkled her brow. "It's not awfully hard?"

Ashley shrugged. "Not really." Being in a family was awfully hard.

"I'm sorry you never met your grandma before."

Ashley looked at Krissa with a scrutinizing stare. "What do you mean?"

Krissa leaned forward. "Your grandma. The one who came here the other day. I'm sorry it was the first time you got to meet her."

"I don't have a grandma who came here the other day." Ashley shook her head. "What are you talking about?"

"You know." Krissa looked confused. "The old lady with gray, curly hair."

"Mrs. Harms?"

"Yeah."

Ashley giggled. "That's not my grandma. That's the lady who took care of me at the orphanage."

Krissa looked astonished. "Really?"

A wave of loneliness swept over Ashley. She looked back at her paper. "I never had a grandma 'cause I never had parents. That's why I was an orphan."

"Oh. So why'd that old lady come here?"

"She was checking on me. I'm only staying with the Tanners for a little while longer. Mrs. Harms said I could go back in July."

"To the orphanage?"

Ashley began drawing again.

"You want to go back?"

"Yeah. I guess you don't really know what it's like being an orphan. I like the orphanage."

"So you're leaving the family?" Krissa stared at her. "Is this the last time I'll see you?"

"Yup." Ashley poked dots of ink on her paper. She tried not to seem disturbed, but inside, she felt tortured. Ever since her talk with Mrs. Harms, she had tried to kill the chickens quickly. She only had a month left to do it. The least she could do was get rid of the chickens before Wes had to be in charge of them alone again.

"That's sad," Krissa said.

Ashley looked at her. "What's sad?"

"You. I don't want you to leave."

Ashley was surprised to see tears in the girl's eyes. She shrugged. "I won't be very far away. You can visit me. And write to me."

"Can you come back here for Christmas?"

"Probably not."

Krissa watched Ashley draw, then asked, "What are you drawing?"

"I'll show you in a minute." Ashley continued to stroke the paper. After a long relapse, she held up the picture toward her cousin.

"What is it?"

"The reason."

Krissa looked at her. "The reason for what?"

"The reason I have to leave."

Ashley handed her cousin the paper. She watched as Krissa looked at the drawing of a tattered old house and a big kettle in the front yard. In the distance was a barn with a wire fence sticking out from it, and sloppy trees surrounded everything.

Krissa looked up and Ashley saw the confusion in her eyes. Ashley's mind raced with fear and dread and panic. She waited for Krissa to understand, but she just shook her head. She didn't even notice the woodshed in the background of the picture.

Why is my pain perpetual, and my wound incurable, which refuseth to be healed?

—Jeremiah 15:18

TWENTY

Chickens

When the first chicken died, nobody suspected anything but natural causes. It was a large, red hen that Ashley had been victimizing, and when she found the bird stiff in the coop one morning, she could barely keep herself from hollering in celebration. She picked up the hen and carried it to Wes, and the boy cried when he saw it. That was his favorite hen. The one who looked exactly like Ronny.

When the second and third chickens died the following week, Grace wondered out loud whether there was a disease running through the flock. But Mr. Tanner assured her that there were no signs of disease. It was true that the egg supply had ceased over the summer, but all signs pointed toward healthy birds. He figured the last batch of corn must've been rotten because all the hens looked skinny.

By the time eleven chickens had been buried, Mr. Tanner and Grace began to ask friends and relatives about chicken health. None of the doctors knew anything about chickens. Mr. Barry Lee suggested buying an entirely new flock or getting rid of them altogether and simply buying eggs. Not even Granddad could figure out why the chickens were dying. Ashley listened to their musings, surprisingly composed.

At last, one hot, early July day, the last hen was found crumpled in a ball in a corner of the coop, leaning against Charlie, the rooster, who had breathed his last. Wesley broke down. Seeing Charlie's poky-feather head dropped in death was more than he could take, and before Ashley had the chance to offer him the shovel, Wes ran inside, shedding tears.

"It's all right, Wes," Ashley said as the boy slumped on the couch in the sitting room.

"No, it's not." He glared at her. "All the chickens are gone, and we didn't even have a chance to figure out what was wrong. That was Charlie, Ashley. Dad gave him to me for my birthday two years ago. That was my rooster, and he's the only one on earth who looks like that."

Ashley bit her lip. "Maybe you could get a puppy." Bonnie said dogs were terribly protective of children.

"I don't want a puppy."

Ashley sat on the fainting couch. Everything in her urged her to confess. But she didn't. She couldn't. Wes wouldn't understand. Ashley was saving him a lot of heartache and wounds; he was just too ignorant to see it yet.

"What's the matter?" Grace asked as she came in from the kitchen.

"Charlie died." Wes didn't look at her.

"Charlie? Wesley, that rooster was the healthiest bird in the country last month. What on earth happened?"

"I don't know. Ashley found him dead this morning, along with our last hen. They're all gone, Mom; every single one of them."

"That's horrible. We'll have to get an entirely new flock."

"No." Ashley flashed her eyes toward her mother and felt her face sting. "Mama, don't get a new flock. They're too . . . expensive."

"Nonsense." Grace's brow furrowed. "Don't you want me to have more chickens, Ashley?"

"No. Please don't get any."

Grace set her hand on the back of the sofa. "Why not?"

"Just don't!"

"I want them for eggs and meat. Don't argue, Ashley."

Ashley got up and darted up the stairs at that. Her mind was racing. She had done her duty in killing the chickens. Now it was time for her to go.

In her dreams that night, Ashley saw Jack and Henry and Bonnie. Bonnie was crying and Jack was warning her not to say anything about the woodshed. When Ashley awoke in a cold sweat and tears, she saw faces in the shadow on the wall. She tried to keep herself from crying out but fear climbed up her backbone and she screamed into the night.

When Luke went to work the next morning, he had an excruciating headache and a mood that would make any sick patient even sicker. He snapped at every nurse under his order until they refused to make themselves available. All morning he grumbled about how miserable it was to be awakened by a shrieking child in the night.

Luke walked up to a small cot where a little boy lay in a leg cast. "How's that leg doing?" he asked.

"It hurts," the boy said through clenched teeth.

Luke slowly closed his eyes. Just his luck. A complainer.

"Have you been taking the pain medication?"

"It doesn't help much."

He tapped on the clipboard in his hand. "Is your mama here?"

"She's in the waiting room."

"The cast looks good. You'll be up and walking pretty soon." He turned toward the hall. "Jessica!"

A skinny, dark-haired nurse appeared in the doorway.

"Up his medication and tell his mama how to give it to him. Do I have any other patients?"

"The next room over," she said. "A boy with a broken wrist."

Luke started out the door and she caught his sleeve. "There's something suspicious about that one, Doctor. Be careful."

Luke shrugged her hand off his shoulder. He threw his chart on a nearby desk and pushed through the door to the next room. He hated it when women told him what to do.

When Luke stepped into the room, it was as if a rock hit him square in the chest. He stopped in his tracks. The room was dimly lit, and on the bed sat a teenage boy holding a crooked wrist in his hand. The boy's father, a grisly, chubby man, sat in a hard-backed chair. Both of them looked at Luke as if they were ready to slit his throat.

Luke touched the door handle, wishing he could escape. Then he tugged on his long white coat and said, "I'm Dr. Tanner." He thrust his hand toward the father and the man shook it. He looked strangely familiar.

"Broken wrist, 'ey?" asked the doctor.

The boy nodded.

As Luke neared the bed, every hair on his body prickled. When he touched the broken wrist the boy didn't pull away. "When'd you break it, son?"

"Last night." The boy's voice was deep and confident.

Luke looked at him with surprise. "And you didn't come in until this morning?"

"No, sir." His eyes looked straight ahead. They were solid and cold.

Luke let out his breath slowly, trying to sort out the messages his body gave him. There was something overwhelmingly dark about these men. Luke's mind was a jumble. Maybe it was because he had been disrupted by Ashley last night.

"Have you ever had a broken bone before?" he asked.

"I don't know."

"You don't know?" Luke's brows lifted.

"He hasn't," said the father. "Jack's been perfectly healthy all his life."

Luke nodded slowly. "Well, this bone is out of place and has to be moved back. In order to do that, I have to set it, and that's pretty painful. I'd like to give you some pain killer and come back in half an hour."

"I can handle it," the boy said.

Luke looked at him and squinted. "I would really rather you be on pain killer."

Jack sat up straight and said with a shake of his head, "I can handle it, Dr. Tanner, but thank you."

Silence hovered over the room for a moment. Luke acted like he was studying a chart on the wall, but from the corner of his eye, he looked at the grisly man, trying to place his face. He had seen him somewhere before. Somewhere not so good, Luke thought.

At length, Luke rolled up his sleeves and turned back to the boy on the table. "What's your full name, son?"

"Jackson Berk," the father said.

Jack's jaw clenched.

Luke turned to the man. "And you, sir?"

"Most people call me Berk."

"Mr. Berk, would you mind taking a seat in the waiting room while I set this wrist?"

"Stay, Pop," Jack commanded.

Luke looked at him with a baffled stare. "I beg your pardon?"

"I want Pop to stay."

Pop. That was what Luke had called his father. Dad was much too personal.

"If you want proper treatment, you're going to have to do what I ask," Luke said. He wanted that man to leave so he could talk to Jack. "An extra person in this room makes it too crowded to work. Is there a specific reason he has to stay?"

Jack looked at Luke with eyes as hollow as a cave. No sparkle or life or joy. Luke had only seen eyes like that in one other person. Ashley. The emptiness in her eyes made him want to throw up.

"I'll go, Jack," Mr. Berk said. "I don't like to see you in pain, anyway."

Mr. Berk went out and shut the door behind him. Luke took a tray from the counter and organized his tools on it. Just when he took a breath to question Jack, the boy interrupted.

"You won't get anything out of me, mister."

Luke looked at him. "What do you mean?"

"I don't answer questions unless they're directly related to my injury. Save your breath."

"Fine." Luke nodded. "How'd you receive your injury, Jackson Berk?"

"Call me that again and I'll wring your neck."

"You will, 'ey?" Luke tried to hide a smirk. "What would you like me to call you?"

"My name's Jack."

"OK, Jack, how'd you break your wrist?"

The boy looked off into a corner of the room. "I fell off a horse."

"No, you didn't."

Fiery eyes shot back at Luke. "You're calling me a liar?"

"Your eyes tell all the secrets."

Luke saw Jack's jaw clenching as his thumb vigorously rubbed his limp wrist. "I'm not going to betray your secret," he said.

"What are you talking about? You don't know anything."

Luke wondered why he felt so comfortable in spite of the hatred he saw in those eyes. Six months ago, that stare would've made him retreat, but he was strangely capable of pushing closer. Why did Jack remind him of Ashley?

"Does your father physically abuse you?" the doctor asked.

Jack shot him a glance that was meant to silence.

"Did he break your wrist?" he continued.

"No. I already told you that. Just fix it. I didn't come in here to be asked a thousand questions."

Luke took Jack's wrist in his hand and probed the injury. But no matter how hard he pushed on the broken bone, Jack didn't cry out.

"This is going to hurt," Luke said. Maybe Jack would talk after the pain had aroused his emotions.

Jack looked into the doctor's eyes and Luke's heart throbbed. It was as if pain were something the boy never lived without.

"Do you understand?" Luke persisted. "It'd be better for you if you'd let me give you—"

"Stop talking and just do it. Of all things, I hate a man who talks."

"Because his words hurt more than his hands do."

Jack sat utterly still. His eyes darted back and forth, searching Luke's face. "What are you talking about?" His voice was thick with anger. "Get it done! Just fix the wrist and shut up; you make me sick."

Luke put both hands on Jack's arm, and with a hard jolt, the bone cracked.

"Idiot!" Jack screamed, pulling away. "You didn't even give me a chance to get ready for it! Leave me alone! I'll fix it myself." Jack jumped off the bed and pushed past Luke. Luke grabbed his injured arm and pulled him back. If Jack hadn't already been in severe pain, he would've fought back. But he stood still, holding his wrist and groaning.

"Sit down. I'm going to finish."

Jack seethed as he dropped into a chair. "You don't help much, mister. All you are is a man, just like the rest of them. You're a cruel, nasty old man."

"So he does hurt you?"

"What are you talking about?"

Luke took a roll of cloth bandage out of a drawer and pulled a chair in front of Jack. The boy rocked in pain as he held his wrist. "He's cruel and nasty, which means he hurts you."

Jack looked up at him. "You couldn't begin to understand," he said in an excruciatingly painful whisper.

Luke's mind raced with images of Ashley. "How long has he been hurting you?"

"You still think you're going to pull something out of me, don't you? Well, I'll tell you what: all you do is injure me worse by trying. You want to see me back in here with my other wrist broken tomorrow? Keep talking. You'll kill me."

Luke began wrapping Jack's wrist. His voice was cool. "So he did break your wrist?"

Jack stiffened. "I don't have to answer that."

"Fine. Don't. Your eyes already have."

"You read a lot into eyes, don't you?" Jack sucked in his breath when the bandage put pressure on his bone.

"I'm a pro."

"How's that?"

"I've had three months of practice with a little girl who hates the whole world."

"And you think I hate the whole world?"

"No." Luke stared at him. "But you hate every man for walking the face of it."

"You have no clue."

"I do if you're anything like Ashley."

"Ashley?" Jack gasped.

"My daughter."

"Where'd you get her?"

Luke stopped wrapping. "What kind of question is that? She was a penny parcel."

"An orphan."

Luke nodded.

"You call her a penny parcel? How dare you say she's your daughter? You paid a penny for her; that's all."

"That's all it cost for the paperwork."

"And all you were willing to give."

Luke's cheeks stung. "I think you're speaking out of turn for a child."

"A real father would give his life for his daughter."

"I have given my life for her."

"I see." Jack gave him a sarcastic glare.

Luke began wrapping again and felt somewhat satisfied when he saw Jack wince.

"You don't deserve her."

"Ashley?" Luke's hands froze. "Do you know her?"

Jack looked away. "What does it matter? A man like you doesn't deserve anyone. That little girl needs more than your penny."

"You have no idea what you're talking about. That little girl has put me through more misery these past three months than I've lived through since I came to Galesburg. She's tried to ruin me a dozen times over."

Jack smiled. "And you're still alive? Surprise, surprise. You can endure more than you thought you could, can't you?"

Luke's eyes narrowed. "I think you're mocking me."

"Give her back, Dr. Tanner. Put her back in the orphanage. She deserves a kind life."

"You know her, don't you?"

Jack was silent.

"How do you know her?"

"I met her once. Hurry up and finish; I got work to do at home."

Luke stopped. "Tell me how you know her."

"I said I met her once. The orphanage is a safe place for her. I'm telling you, you need to take her back."

"I won't let her go back there," Luke said firmly.

"Why not? Because you're too selfish?"

"Because she's mine. That little girl will never leave my house."

"You live on Ninth Street, don't you?" Jack's eyes smiled. "In that big blue-and-white house with the bay filly in the pasture."

Luke didn't answer. His hands began to sweat. "Why do you care?" he said.

Jack cocked his head. "Just wondering."

Luke looked at the boy and fought panic. The way Jack sat, now with confident stiffness, made Luke's thoughts race. He wondered if Wes and Ashley were playing in the pasture like they often did in the morning. Ashley would be easy prey.

"I'll have the nurse get you some pain medication," Luke said when the wrist was stiffly wrapped.

"I don't need any medication." Jack stood.

"I want you back in here in three weeks."

Jack sniffed. "Not likely."

"Why not?"

The boy reached for the door. "I'm surprised you haven't figured that out by now, Dr. Tanner. Good luck with your penny parcel."

Before Luke could stop him, Jack slammed the door.

Be sure your sin will find you out.
—Numbers 32:23

TWENTY ONE

Escape

Ashley tried unsuccessfully to fall asleep. Mr. Tanner had come home terribly angry that evening, and all she could think of was his belt. She had gone to bed early, like Bonnie had taught her to do, and now she lay wide awake, staring at the dusky sky. She had locked her bedroom door but made sure the lock on her window wasn't rusted over so she could escape if she heard him coming.

Seeing something out the corner of her eye, she sat up and looked out the window. A lantern flickered near the porch. Ashley stood and approached the window, staring hard at the light. It was too dark to see who held the lantern.

The light neared the tree outside her window and swung back and forth as it went up the trunk on someone's arm. Ashley's heart raced and she smashed herself against the wall, but she couldn't get her eyes to leave the light. It stopped swinging and sat perfectly still on a branch in the tree.

Ashley heard an owl hoot. The sound was persistent—much more persistent than she had ever heard an owl. She gasped when she recognized Jack and Henry's secret birdcall.

When she squeaked her window open, the owl stopped. She knelt in front of the glass and the lantern went out.

"Henry?" she whispered. "Jack?"

The owl started again.

"I hear you! It's me . . . Ashley."

Ashley heard a match strike and the lantern blazed again.

"Ashley Kant?" Henry's voice called.

"Yeah."

"Pack your bags and come outside. Jack's going to take you back to the orphanage."

Ashley stood for a moment in dumbfounded silence. Then she carefully shut the window, threw open her closet, pulled out a bag, and shoved her dress and hat into it. She slipped on her shoes without stockings and tiptoed out of her room. Wesley's lamp was out in his bedroom, and the parents' room was dark. The only light in the house came from the smoldering fire in the sitting room.

Ashley crept down the stairs. Her heart chilled when she heard a door open upstairs. She held her breath and froze. She could hear her heart pound in her chest. The door squeaked closed and the house went quiet again.

She stood for a long moment, staring around the dark staircase. Then she continued down. When she reached the bottom, she rushed out the front door and ran toward the glow of the lantern, which was now on the ground where the yard met the forest. She looked up at the tall form there and stepped back.

"It's me . . . Henry," a deep voice said gently. He knelt in front of her and Ashley examined his face. Henry looked very much like Jack now. "Jack found out where you lived and we came to get you and take you back to the orphanage," he said in a thick whisper. "You wanna go, 'ey?"

"Yeah." Ashley sidled close to him as he moved toward the dark tree line.

"Jack," Henry called, "it's safe. Ashley's here. Come on!"

Ashley watched as a figure emerged from behind a tree. She saw a white bandage on Jack's arm. "What happened to you?"

"I got hurt."

Ashley knew how without him saying.

Jack looked down at Ashley from a frame that had grown at least six inches. "I met Dr. Tanner this morning when I went to the hospital to get my wrist fixed. I figured out where you lived and came for you. Are you all right?"

"Yeah." Ashley moved closer to him and felt engulfed in safety. Henry stood behind her and Jack in front of her, and her body relaxed.

"Where's Bonnie?" she asked.

"Back at home with Ma. Pop's in the tavern, so Henry and I snuck away. We're going home tomorrow." Jack knelt in front of Ashley, his eyes gentle. "We'll take you back to the orphanage. You're sure you're OK?"

"Yeah." Ashley looked over her shoulder. "Let's hurry."

Jack took Ashley's hand and they disappeared into the forest. Henry turned down the lantern until it was barely a spark in the thickness of the night. As they ran, Ashley felt the fear of the past three months shedding like layers of clothing.

By the time dawn had awakened the sleepy town of Galesburg, everyone in the city knew that Ashley was missing. The panic the Tanner family experienced when they found her bed empty was more heart chilling than anything Luke, Grace, or Wesley had ever experienced. In less than an hour, the police squad and dozens of relatives and friends were searching every inch of the countryside.

While the church bell rang in the lunch hour, Grace was vomiting because she was so nervous. Grandma Jackson took care of Cherish, and Granddad and Wes walked every step of the forest while Aunt Susie sat with Grace and tried to comfort her. Luke had declared a town emergency, and every business and home was emptied into the streets. Still, no one found a trace of Ashley.

"I don't know what else can be done," Sheriff Bilt told Luke around one o'clock.

"Keep looking." Luke's forehead was pearled in sweat, and his clothes were disheveled.

"I have every officer in the city on watch. We've searched a thirty-mile radius. No kidnapper could've made it that far during the night."

Luke looked at the sheriff desperately. "Has every building and home been searched?"

Bilt nodded. "Every house in Galesburg has been investigated. I don't know what to tell you."

"You're not sure the exact hour she went missing?" asked Judge Baker.

"How could I tell? We were all asleep. Some crook—" Luke swallowed hard and tried to speak clearly. "How in the world could they make it into the house?"

"Maybe she ran away," suggested Freddy.

"Impossible," Luke snapped. "She was perfectly happy. Bilt, you have to keep looking. I can't go back to my wife without knowing where that little girl is."

Sheriff Bilt shook his head. "We're doing everything we can."

A sickening knot twisted Luke's stomach with horrible, nauseating pain. He tried to remember the last thing he had said to Ashley, but all he remembered was coming home from work angry and demanding that the children do their chores. Ashley had gone to bed early without saying good night. Certainly she wasn't upset enough to run away.

The orphanage, Luke thought with a sudden rush. If she did leave on her own, that was the only place she would go.

"Has anyone checked the orphanage?" Luke asked.

The faces in the crowd stared at him in disgust.

"Maybe somebody took her back there after they found out she was a penny parcel." *A penny parcel.* The words slapped him in the face and left a blushing sting.

A group of apothecary men walked with Luke to the orphanage. They approached the gate suspiciously, hesitantly.

The knot in Luke's stomach grew bigger until he had to force himself to breathe. Surely Ashley wasn't here. But if she were, at least she was safe. He could bring her home to his wife.

Luke knocked on the orphanage door. The men behind him looked over their shoulders and fidgeted on the grass as if overwhelmed by disgrace.

Miss Hattie answered the door. Luke shoved past her into the foyer.

"What do you want?" the girl demanded, leaving the door open.

"Is Ashley here?"

"Go away, Mr. Tanner, or I'll have to call the authorities."

Luke smirked, sweeping his hand toward the open door. "The authorities are standing on your doorstep, ready to arrest you if you don't let me search every inch of this building for my daughter."

Mrs. Harms scurried in from her office. "What's going on in here?" she demanded.

"Ashley was stolen out of her bedroom last night," Luke said. "Do you have any idea where she is?"

"Stolen?" Mrs. Harms took off her spectacles and looked at Luke sternly. "Mr. Tanner, Ashley was not stolen. She ran away from you."

Luke's mouth fell open. Shame surged through every inch of his body. "Where is she?"

"I must ask you to leave this property at once," Mrs. Harms ordered.

Luke darted up the stairs. Mrs. Harms screamed. In an instant, he heard several men banging up the staircase after him.

Sheriff Bilt grabbed his arm.

"Let go of me!"

"Come on, Tanner."

"I'm not leaving until my daughter is back in my care."

Sheriff Bilt's strong hands gripped tighter. "Stop it, or I'm going to cuff you and throw you behind bars."

Luke took a step backward. "She doesn't belong here. I demand that she's given back to me immediately!"

"Just cool your temper so we can discuss this calmly."

Luke tried to shrug the sheriff off, but the brawny man held his arms in a vise grip.

When Mrs. Harms joined them on the steps, Sheriff Bilt asked coolly, "What is the problem, Mrs. Harms?"

The woman swept her hands over her dilapidated hairdo. "Ashley arrived at my doorstep at ten o'clock last night in her nightdress and begged me to take her back," she said. "She ran away from Mr. Tanner's home because she could no longer handle his abusive temper."

"Abusive!" Luke exploded. "You're a liar!"

"Ask her yourself!" Mrs. Harms said. "And get this man off my property before he sends that girl into terrified madness. She's fearful enough as it is."

"Ashley has been adopted by the Tanners, Mrs. Harms," the sheriff said. "You have no right to keep her, even if she came back to you. She'll have to deal with her problems."

Mrs. Harms shook her head. "She was never permanently adopted by the Tanners. They took her on a temporary home placement. They have no rights over her."

"She's lying," Luke said, struggling to get free. "That little girl is my daughter, and no law has the right to take her away. I haven't set a hand on her once since she entered my home. This is absurd!"

"You're doing yourself no good by getting so angry," the sheriff said, tightening his hold on Luke's arm. "Control yourself, Tanner."

"Let me talk to her," Luke demanded. "Let Ashley make the decision."

Sheriff Bilt looked at Mrs. Harms. "I'd like to have a meeting with the girl. Do you have a room we can use?"

"She'll be terrified if she sets eyes on him," the old lady said, her eyes bulging.

"I'll keep him restrained."

Mrs. Harms nodded toward the library. "You may go in there. But she's still asleep."

"Wake her up," the sheriff ordered.

With an exasperated sigh, she climbed the stairs.

"You have to settle down, Tanner," Sheriff Bilt said as he escorted Luke to the library. The apothecary men followed, and Luke blushed with shame.

"Everything she'll tell you will be a lie," Luke said. "You can't believe a word she says. She's always hated me."

Bilt's brows rose. "A little girl doesn't hate for no reason."

Luke sat down on a spring-poked couch and tried to catch his breath. Sheriff Bilt sat down nearby.

"Is Baker around?" the sheriff called.

"I'm out here!" a voice responded from the foyer.

The sheriff looked out the library door. "Get in here, Baker. I want you to write all this down."

Judge Baker entered the room and Luke's cheeks turned hot.

In a few minutes, Mrs. Harms came down the stairs with Ashley at her side. The little girl was pale and her hair was unbraided. She wore her brown dress but no shoes or socks, and her eyes were swelled from crying. When Ashley laid eyes on Luke, she gripped Mrs. Harms's dress.

The old woman sat on the couch opposite Luke. Ashley sat very close beside her.

"Hello, Ashley," Sheriff Bilt greeted. She didn't move a muscle. "Your family has been looking for you all day. Did you run away last night?"

Ashley nodded slowly.

"Why?"

"I wanted to come here."

"Why?" Luke demanded. "You were perfectly happy at home. You're going to break Wesley's heart. That was very bad of you to leave."

Judge Baker put up his hand. "Enough, Tanner. Let Bilt talk."

"Were you afraid of something at home?" the sheriff asked.

Ashley's face was turning ghostly pale. She looked as if she were forcing herself to breathe.

"I didn't want to. I'm sorry, Mr. Tanner. But I . . . I want to be here now. Please go away. I don't want to go back." Ashley turned her head into the couch, her hands shaking.

"Why do you want to live here?" Bilt prodded.

"It's nice here. I don't want to get strapped."

Luke sniffed. "That's crazy." His eyes darted to the doorway, where the apothecary men were crowded. "I've never strapped her in my life," he yelled. "Ashley, you're lying!"

Luke exploded like a time bomb. Before he knew it, he was being dragged through the streets with his hands cuffed behind his back.

Can thine heart endure, or can thine hands be strong, in the days that I shall deal with thee?

—Ezekiel 22:14

TWENTY TWO

The Tanners

Wesley settled back in the back carriage seat, sitting straight and tall like a man. Granddad drove and Grace sat silently beside him. Wes tried to ignore the awful feeling in his stomach.

"I'll wait outside," Granddad said when he pulled in front of the sheriff's station and helped Grace down. Wes took his mother's hand and led her toward the door.

"Don't say anything unless you're given permission," Grace directed.

When Wesley entered the jailhouse, he wondered how things had gone so wrong in just one day. Yesterday, his dad was talking about a drunk who had been released from this very jail and who "dishonored the town by being such a reprobate." Now, Wesley was walking through the doors to see his own father.

Sheriff Bilt opened the door to the cells and Wes thought he saw a smile on the brawny man's face. The boy led his mother to the last stall against the wall and there he saw his dad lying on a skinny cot with his shoulder pressed against the cement wall.

"What are you doing here?" Luke demanded the moment he set eyes on the pair. "Wesley, this is no place for you."

"I brought Mom."

"Grace, why'd you bring him in here?"

"He was helping me walk, Luke."

Wes looked at his father with tears clouding his eyes. The displeasure he saw in his dad's face made him turn away and leave.

"I can't believe you let him come in here," Luke said to his wife when they were alone.

"Just because you're embarrassed doesn't mean you have to hurt him. He has every right to be wherever you are."

"Not here—not in jail."

Grace wanted to scold but bit her tongue. She touched the bars and he stood and went to her. "Come home." Her voice was shaky. "I need you right now, Luke. I can't do this alone."

"I'll be home tonight."

Grace half smiled. "I doubt that. The sheriff isn't going to let you go so easily."

"He has no charge against me." Luke touched her hand. "I'm going to get Ashley back, Gracie."

Tears came to her eyes. "How? By breaking into the orphanage and kidnapping her? We've lost her, Luke. She's an orphan again."

A penny parcel, he thought. That phrase was beginning to haunt him.

"No, she's not. She's still our little girl. If I have to hire an army, I'm going to get her to tell the truth about our home. I won't let her go so easily."

"Why?" Grace squeezed his hand, her voice firm. "Because it's going to hurt your reputation, or because you love her so much?"

"She put me in this jail, Gracie."

Grace backed away, shaking her head. "You did that to yourself. Your anger got the better of you and landed you behind bars. This has nothing to do with Ashley."

Luke's jaw clenched. "She had no right to run away and make up a pathetic story to justify herself. She's a liar."

"I don't want to talk about this. I'm going home." Grace turned away.

"Don't leave me." Luke grabbed her wrist.

"Dod's waiting outside."

"Gracie, don't cut out on me."

She turned back to him. "I'll wait for you at home."

"I can't do this alone." He pulled her closer. "I need you."

"I won't leave you."

"Promise me."

"I already did." She touched her wedding band to the palm of his hand.

"I'm sorry." Luke's voice cracked. "I didn't mean to take it this far."

"Just come home and we'll do this together."

Reluctantly, he let her go.

That week was the worst Wesley had endured in his entire life. Being separated from Ashley was a heart-wrenching trial that haunted the boy day and night, and settled a burden on his shoulders that made him physically slouch. Going into Ashley's bedroom invited intense pain, and visiting the forest or washing dishes alone was as close to the lake of fire as the boy had ever been. Listening to his mother cry at night and watching the response of the town as they shunned the Tanner family was almost too bitter a strike for him to bear.

On top of all this, Wesley had become the man of the house. His father had expected to leave the jail quickly, but the sheriff kept him for a full three days and made him solemnly swear never to set foot on the orphanage property. Doing so would be punishable by thirty days in jail.

Wes eagerly waited for his father to come home so he could shed the responsibilities of housekeeping and comforting his mother. But even after his dad came home, he was worthless. He went to work as early as possible, came home late in the evening, and retreated to the barn every night.

Wes was forced to be the man of the house again.

Luke quietly stepped out of bed. He took his robe from the chest at the footboard and tossed it over his shoulders. Then he crept out of the bedroom and closed the door.

He made his way down the stairs and lit a lamp in the kitchen. Then he set the coffeepot on top of the stove and stirred the coals, adding a handful of firewood through the squeaky door at the bottom. He ran his fingers through his thick, ruddy hair.

Luke leaned against the counter and sighed. He turned the lamp down until it glowed as softly as the moonlight that came in through the window.

"Luke?" a gentle voice called out, and he looked up to see his wife coming into the kitchen.

"I'm here, Gracie," he said.

"What are you doing?"

"Putting the coffee on."

Grace stepped toward his voice, and Luke wrapped his arms around her. "Are you all right?" he asked, remembering the torrent of tears the night before, and hoping he wouldn't be forced to endure another outburst.

"I'll survive."

Luke squeezed her. "Gracie, I have to go to work today. I can't leave you here if all you're going to do is survive."

"I can't accept this yet." Grace gripped his shirt and the tears began down her cheeks again.

A pang went to Luke's heart. "I know how hard this is for you," he whispered. "And I'm sorry."

"It all happened so quickly. I just don't understand."

Luke couldn't handle any more tears. He was angry enough, and every tear Grace shed made him angrier. He pushed away from her. "I'm going to start chores. Send Wes out when he gets up, 'ey?"

"Isn't it too early?"

Luke glanced at the clock and through the dim light, he read the hands: five o'clock. It was an hour earlier than he usually started chores.

"Not this morning," he answered, and he retreated upstairs for his clothes.

The barn was still in darkness, but warm with the smell of feed and sawdust. The horses perked up from their stalls when they saw their master step through the door, and the cow swished her tail in welcome.

"All right, God," Luke burst out, throwing his hands in the air. "You have the power to control this situation, but apparently You're not choosing to. You know everything that's gone on in this house, so You're my witness."

The memories of his numerous mistakes pierced his mind and put him to shame. "Why are You asking me to give up everything I've earned?" He gazed at the tall, dusty ceiling and his stomach tightened.

"This isn't fair! I won't have my reputation ruined by her! Why are You doing this to us? Don't You understand what's happening? Haven't we been through enough? Did You just have to add this too?"

Silence greeted his questions.

"I can't believe You would let this happen. Do You realize what's going to happen now? The police squad searched every single house in Galesburg so every soul knows that Ashley was missing. The papers are going to be chock-full of this pathetic mess, and I'm going to be ruined. So much for a loving God! Forget what I've been trying to do for the past three months. Forget that good-for-nothing penny parcel. Forget the whole idea of following after God! You can't possibly expect a human to chase after You when You don't give a second glance at pain."

Luke kicked his workbench, making the animals bang in their stalls. He sank down against the barn wall and rubbed his face. "I already gave up my dream of having my own children. I willingly accepted the shame that I knew would come to my name when I adopted orphans, but I did what You told me to do." He paused. "So why did You have to give me a child like that?"

Wesley stepped into the house and the screen door banged after him. He trudged into the kitchen and dropped onto his mother's stool. "I can't do it, Mom."

"Can't do what?" She paused with knife in hand as potato chunks dropped off the counter.

"I can't do anything without Ashley. I even forgot how to latch the gate without her holding the rope, so the horses got out."

"Did you get them back in?"

"Dad did. But now he's mad. Before Ashley came, I could do everything by myself, but I can't anymore, and I don't even want to. It's stupid that she had to leave. Now Dad's going to be mad at me because he has to fix the gate before he goes to work so he'll probably be late. Everything's messed up."

Grace brushed her hands on her apron, oblivious to the shower of potatoes that had hit the floor until she stepped on a chunk.

"Wesley," she said, "God obviously has a different plan for Ashley."

"Then I don't think He knows what He's doing."

"Of course He does." Grace gave a weak smile.

"Then He's not very good at making it easy."

Luke came through the door and stopped when he saw Wes slumping on the stool and Grace standing silently at the counter. "Did I interrupt something?"

Grace sighed. "Not at all. We could use you in here."

Luke dropped his leather gloves onto the counter, examining the potato-adorned floor with a baffled stare. Then he plunged his hands into the cold water in the basin. "What's up?"

Wes slumped further on his stool. "Nothin'."

As Luke dried his hands on the towel, Grace scooped potatoes off the counter and dropped them into a pot of boiling water. Luke glanced between his wife and his son. "Guess we don't need to talk, then?"

Wes shrugged. "Nothin' to talk about."

Luke draped the towel over the washstand. "Well, then I'll go check on Cherish." He fled up the stairs.

"You can't run away from your son like that," Grace scolded as she entered the bedroom shortly after her husband fell onto the bed with a heavy sigh.

"Like what?" he replied, resting his hands under his head. "He said there was nothing to talk about."

"Fiddlesticks. You know as well as I do that he wants someone to talk to."

"Then go talk to him. You're better at explaining, anyway."

Cherish fussed from her cradle. Grace lifted the rosy-cheeked baby into her arms. "Please go talk to him."

"What am I supposed to say?"

"Just answer his questions."

Luke stared at Grace critically. "And what's he going to ask? 'Why did Ashley leave?' What am I supposed to say to that? 'Cause she hates me?' And then he'll ask, 'Can't we get her back?' And I'll say, 'Nope. Ashley's done for.' It's ridiculous to expect me to explain this situation to a ten-year-old."

"You have to do something; you're his father."

"And you're his mother."

Silence crept over the bedroom as Grace took a seat in the rocker.

"I have to go to work," Luke said, standing and kissing his wife and daughter.

Grace grabbed her husband's shirtsleeve. "Just tell him it'll be OK," she whispered.

Luke squeezed her hand. "Gracie, I've never lied to my son."

As he left, Grace burst into tears.

I will weep bitterly.

—Isaiah 22:4

THE REPORTER

Waif Doctor's Temper Slowly Recovers

TWENTY THREE

Of Social Situations

Luke didn't know how much longer he could endure the weekdays. It had been more than two months, and he was still watched like a hawk from dawn until dusk, and almost all of the upper crusts had stopped talking to him. The day after Luke's explosion with Ashley, the newspaper headlines turned to "The Penny Parcel" and "The Waif Doctor," and every day since, there had been a write-up about one side of the story. Most everything was against Luke, but the reporters took advantage of the opportunity to wipe out Mrs. Harms and the orphanage while they had a story to tell.

Even though Ashley hadn't accused Luke of physically abusing her, the public assumed that her retreat back to the orphanage was provoked by abuse. Mrs. Harms passionately confirmed this belief any time anyone asked her about the incident.

For the first two weeks following Ashley's return to the orphanage, Luke tried to defend himself against the accusations the public threw at him. He met with reporters and passionately declared his innocence, and he pursued many of the upper crusts and tried to get them to listen to his claim. But the more he defended himself, the more gossipy the newspaper articles became and the more critical the upper crusts' comments grew. He eventually gave up.

Sheriff Bilt became a regular figure in Luke Tanner's life, and by no means was his company pleasant. Every morning when Luke rode to work, the sheriff stood on the porch of the jailhouse and watched him with warning in his eyes. Luke cringed every time he got close to the building.

Worse than that, the sheriff visited Luke's home once a week and regularly questioned Mrs. Harms as to whether Luke had recently visited. Bilt's weekly reports were printed in the crime section of *The Reporter.*

"As if I were a criminal," Luke muttered to himself one day as he entered the hospital. He tried not to look at the newspaper stand, but couldn't keep his eyes turned away. "Waif Doctor's Temper Slowly Recovers," the headline read.

My temper—fiddlesticks. That little girl ruined my life with lies.

"You planning on having a good day, Tanner?" Sheriff Bilt asked as he was going out the hospital door while Luke was coming in.

Luke glared at him. "I think you enjoy belittling me."

"Belittling is against my job description. I'm just maintaining peace for all citizens. And I'd enjoy a quiet day, if you please."

Luke almost spit on Bilt's shoe as he left.

"I didn't see you at the apothecary this morning, Tanner," Dr. Gere said when Luke grabbed a coffee-stained chart from Jessica's desk.

Luke casually read the paper. "Don't reckon that place does me much good."

"We had a real interesting discussion on politics. You know how Baker gets—so sure about his view of Taft and Roosevelt. I haven't had such a quality discussion in several years. You working a full day today?"

"Might as well."

"I hear a circuit preacher is coming to town tonight—thought I'd go see him. You know, confession might do you some good." Dr. Gere slapped Luke on the shoulder.

Jessica, the nurse, came in and sat at her desk, and Luke turned to her to avoid strangling Doctor Gere.

"Did that boy with the broken wrist ever come back in?" he asked her.

"Haven't seen him. What a sad situation." She shot Luke a glance that put him in the same category as Mr. Berk.

"I can't imagine hurting a child of any age," Luke said, doing his best to remain calm. "But what do we know about the situation? Children lie and make their parents seem to be things they're not. Especially children like Jackson Berk. I could spot rebellion in him from a hundred yards away."

"It is a shame, Dr. Tanner. But younger children have a harder time lying than children Jack's age, I think."

I'm living in a nightmare.

"Is Gere taking this patient?" Luke asked, looking back at the chart in his hand.

"Is that the one for the baby?"

"Yeah."

"I told him to take it. Here. You can take this one." She handed him another chart. "He's been waiting for over an hour."

Luke dropped the chart to his side without reading it. "Lines are that long?"

"Yeah."

Luke sighed and made his way through the dizzying hospital halls until he entered a tiny room. There, he set eyes on Dan Sulka sitting on a stool in the corner. He paused and looked at the chart Jessica had given him. He scolded himself under his breath for not reading the name on the chart before he agreed to see the patient.

"You sick, or are you paying to sit in an examining room for an hour so you can poke fun at me?" Luke asked as he closed the door.

Dan's eyebrows rose. "I didn't think you'd be back to work yet. I figured you were taking some time off."

Luke dropped the chart onto the counter and stared at Dan. "You aren't the first patient who's used the excuse of aches and pains to antagonize my personal life."

Dan shifted on the stool, and Luke could see pain behind his eyes. "Actually, I was just thinking how inconvenient it would be if you came to look at me. I was hoping for Gere or Keller."

Luke smirked. "What's the problem?"

Dan touched his right leg. "I bummed up my knee about a week ago. I thought I'd get over it, but I've tried everything, and it seems like it hurts more every day. I was hoping someone here could make a difference."

"Have you tried Dale Gildey's salve?" Luke asked.

"I tried the cheap stuff. I didn't figure there was much difference between that and the expensive stuff he has."

Luke pushed up Dan's pant leg and saw that his knee was swollen. "What'd you do to it?"

"Twisted it, I think." Dan squinted when Luke touched it. "It happened real fast, so I'm not sure. My wife tried messing with it, but nothing's helped."

"Get some of Dale's expensive salve." Luke dropped the pant leg and stepped back. "Try that for a week, and if it doesn't work, we'll have to think of something else. Can I help you with anything more?"

"No." Dan winced when he stood. "Thanks for the advice." He looked at Luke. "Is there anything I can do for you? I guess your situation isn't so favorable lately."

"Down right pathetic," Luke said. He turned to the counter. "Everywhere I go I'm treated like a worthless sinner. It slaps me in the face every morning and goes to bed with me at night. People are ruthless."

"That they are."

"Have you read the newspapers?" Luke asked with disgust.

"Just what I can see when I walk by. I'm not real interested in your business. I will tell you one thing, though: The apothecary circle is not an example of Christ."

"Christ?" Luke sniffed. "I half expect Him to show up in a bolt of lightning and strike me dead one of these days."

"I guess you'll be waiting for a long time for that to happen."

"I might as well be in jail—at least people would leave me alone."

"You know how to get there," Dan said coldly. "You could try it and see if iron bars will keep you from God."

Luke's eyes flashed.

"Well, I guess I'll be going." Dan started for the door, but as he reached for the handle, he stopped and turned back. "Luke, I have no idea what went on at your house, and I'm not going to try to figure it out. You're probably telling the truth about everything you've said. But the road to freedom isn't easy. And defending yourself is only going to make the situation worse."

"So I should admit to crimes I never committed?" Luke blurted out.

"No." Dan's gaze was steady. "You should admit to the ones you have committed. You should admit to the motivations of your heart—whatever they are."

"You don't know what you're talking about."

Dan turned toward the door. "Sin is a part of the fallen human race. But shame is not one of God's tools. He's not trying to ruin you like everyone else is."

Luke's brow creased. "I'm not sure I believe you."

"God doesn't accept you on the basis of performance. You can't fall from God's approval and get Him to write up one of those nasty articles about everything you've done wrong. He doesn't base His love on what you've done. That's a pagan lie."

"Lots of things are pagan lies," Luke retorted.

Dan nodded. "And we believe many of them."

Luke looked at his chart and wished he had written something on it that needed to be corrected. He imagined God writing an article about him on that paper, and he wondered what it would say.

"I have to go." Mr. Sulka stuck out his hand to Luke and he shook it. "Stop by sometime if you're ever out our way."

When Dan shut the door behind him, Luke sank onto the bed. *A pagan lie*. Even if that's what it was, he still believed it.

School days for Wesley were almost as miserable as lonely days at home. The children of the opinionated Galesburg upper crusts were well on their way to becoming as heartless as their parents, and Wes took the brunt of most of their criticism. Galen returned to Galesburg and Wes was elated to have his best friend back in town exactly when he needed someone to stick by his side. Unfortunately, the lad had greatly changed over the summer, and his father's opinion of Luke Tanner ruined the friendship between the boys.

At lunch break a skinny redheaded boy sat beside Wes. The slump in his shoulders matched Wes's. "I guess you don't have much luck."

Wes turned away. "I don't believe in luck."

"I guess I don't either. It's too bad about your sister, though."

Wes held back tears.

"I'm Jimmy Sulka. My dad told me what happened to your dad and your sister."

"I guess people like to gossip."

Jimmy's brow creased. "He wasn't gossiping. He just figured we were in the same class and wondered how you were doing. I'm in fourth grade, too."

"I know. You sit in the back row, next to the door."

"I have two sisters who are in second grade."

Just like Ashley, Wes thought. "How'd they both get in the same grade?"

"They're twins."

"Oh. Figures."

Silence hovered over the boys, and Wes nibbled on his lunch, wishing Jimmy would leave him alone.

"I'm going to move," Wes said abruptly.

Jimmy leaned forward on his knees. "Oh yeah? Where to?"

"I don't know. As soon as I'm old enough to leave the house, I'm going to get out of Galesburg. Leave Ashley behind."

"You don't think you'll ever get her back, 'ey?"

"Are you kidding?" Wes glared at Jimmy. "If my dad so much as sets foot on the orphanage property, he goes to jail for a whole month."

"Have you seen Ashley since she ran away?"

Wes stared at his half-eaten cookie. "I pass by the orphanage once in a while." *Every day.* "But I haven't seen her." Not even through a window or playing outside.

"What do you think will happen to her?"

"They'll probably ship her west on the orphan train."

"Mrs. Harms doesn't really like the orphan train," Jimmy said.

"How would you know?" Wes snapped.

"My little sister told me."

Wes's brow creased. "And how would she know?"

"She used to be an orphan."

Wesley's mouth dropped open. "Your parents adopted a penny parcel?"

"My dad hates it when people call them that," Jimmy said. "We got her from Galesburg right before you got Ashley."

"What's her name?" Wes asked.

"KatieAnne. We mostly just call her Kate."

Ashley's best friend. "Ashley talked about KatieAnne."

"Kate talks about her sometimes too."

Wesley looked away to disguise his tears. "Look, I don't really want to talk about it. I have to forget about her, and you're not helping much."

The compassion Wes saw in the boy's eyes made him uncomfortable.

"I think it's all right if you're upset," Jimmy said. "You don't have to pretend it's easy."

"I'm not."

"You do when you're around Galen."

"That's 'cause Galen's my best friend."

"I reckon you can be yourself with your best friend."

"Why are you doing this?" Wes blurted. "I don't need your help."

Jimmy stared back at him. "I'm not trying to push anything on you."

"You're a liar," Wes mumbled.

"I just want to be your friend if you need one. I think it stinks what the other kids do to you, but it'd be a whole lot easier to like you if you weren't mad at anyone who tries to be your friend."

"Ashley was my friend." He couldn't hide the tears now. "She was a better friend than Galen or anyone else. And I don't much feel like making any new friends. So just leave me alone."

When Jimmy left, Wes swiped away the tears.

To him that is afflicted pity should be shewed from his friend.
—Job 6:14

TWENTY FOUR

Consequences

The apothecary meeting on Thursday, September 15, was especially lively, and filled with the rich dirt of gossip.

"I never thought this town would have to hire a night guard," said Judge Baker, clicking his tongue. "Can you believe what that man has come to?"

"It ain't pretty," agreed Patrick Cummings. "I don't reckon Bilt's gotten wind of it yet, else he'd already be at the hospital."

"He's watching Luke ride into town first," said Freddy with a sickly laugh.

"Do you suppose he'll make Tanner serve the full sentence?" asked Barry Lee.

"He'd better, or I'll put Bilt on trial," said Judge Baker. "Luke Tanner deserves a whole lot more than he'll get."

"It's too bad he can't get on top of things," said Jonathan Hendricks, tapping his cane on the floor. "I finally convinced Galen to stop hanging around with Tanner's boy, but I had to spill the whole story. Wesley Tanner will be a lawbreaking penny parcel himself in ten years."

"That's right," Patrick said. "But you know, I warned Tanner about adopting orphans the first week he brought that little girl home. Can't say it isn't his own fault."

"At least some of it," added Dr. Gere. "That Ashley came to him with a whole Lizzy of baggage. It's too bad he didn't see it right at first."

Barry Lee shook his head and sighed. "I still can't believe he made it worse with abuse, though. I never would've guessed that from Luke Tanner."

"Here comes Bilt," Freddy announced, and the apothecary fell silent. Mr. Gildey passed around a box of cigars, and as the sheriff walked through the door, the rumor quickly unfolded.

As Luke was coming out of surgery his head ached. He went to the washroom, threw off his coat, and put his stethoscope on the washstand, then plunged his hands into the cool water. The pain in his head pounded in his ears, and he wished he could go home.

Luke dried his hands and returned to Jessica's desk. She was sorting a stack of papers on the far wall, her back to him. Babies cried from rooms down the hall, and Luke could hear Dr. Gere's deep voice in a nearby room.

"What's next, Jessica?" Luke asked.

She flipped around and handed him a chart. "Burns from a stove fire. He's in a lot of pain."

"Just my luck."

Jessica smiled. "You're cranky today."

Luke tossed his head at her. "Thanks."

"Tanner," a familiar voice called down the hall, and Luke turned to see Sheriff Bilt approaching.

Luke sighed and leaned against the counter, folding his arms. "What do you want?" He stirred uncomfortably when he saw handcuffs in the sheriff's hand.

"You're in direct violation of our agreement." Bilt grabbed Luke's hand, and before the doctor could fight back, the chart crashed to the floor and the first cuff was locked.

“What are you doing?” Luke yanked his free hand away.

“You’re done for a month.”

“You have no right to do this. Get that cuff off of me!”

Bilt grabbed Luke’s arm and twisted it behind his back. Luke gritted his teeth and squelched a cry, swinging at Bilt. He felt the sheriff’s big hand on the back of his head and he stuck out his chest to protect his face from the wall. Bilt threw his shoulder into Luke’s back and pinned him, pressing his cheek against the brick. Luke’s vision blurred and his headache intensified. He felt the sheriff’s puffing breath near his face.

“Continue to fight me and get sixty days, Tanner.” The other cuff snapped tightly. “You don’t think the people of this town saw you snooping around the orphanage last night?”

“You can’t do this, Bilt.” Luke pulled his hand away and the cuff rolled on his wrist bone. “You can’t do this! Get these cuffs off of me!”

“Those cuffs are going to stay on until you’re under control.” Bilt’s shoulder jabbed into Luke’s back. “It’s your choice, Tanner. You either walk to the station like a civilized person, or I’ll drag you there and the whole story will be in the paper tomorrow.”

“Bilt,” Luke said with seething anger and mounting pain, “if you don’t get these cuffs off me, I’ll wipe your name out faster than a landslide.”

“So that’s the way it’s gonna be?” The sheriff grabbed Luke’s arm and yanked him toward the door.

“Don’t you dare take me out there like this,” Luke screamed, lunging toward Jessica’s desk. “You have no right to do this! You’re breaking every law in the book!”

By the time the sheriff and Luke had walked three blocks to the jailhouse, every soul in Galesburg knew that Luke Tanner had been arrested that day.

"Take these cuffs off of me," Luke demanded when the sheriff shoved him into a cell and slammed the door.

"Do yourself a favor and shut up," Bilt shouted as he walked away.

Luke kicked the bars. "You can't do this to me! I demand a trial!"

"Demand away!" The cell hall door slammed. "You're a fool, Luke Tanner! A doggone fool!"

Luke banged the handcuffs against the wall. His wrists were beginning to swell and his fingers tingled. He stood for a long moment in the middle of the cell and then fell onto the cot. Pain shot up his arms when he lay on them, so he sat up and pushed himself against the cool cement, muttering under his breath.

Luke tried to soothe the pain in his wrists by taking turns rubbing them. He slammed the handcuffs against the wall and cussed at them. His arm ached from being wrenched behind his back, and throbbing pain in his face made him wonder if he'd have a black eye.

"Stupid penny parcel," Luke said under his breath. "I wasted a good penny to buy a jail sentence."

An hour later Sheriff Bilt came back with the key to the handcuffs. He quietly opened the cell door and stepped through, leaving the door ajar. "Make a jump for it and you'll regret you ever lived."

Luke glared at him. "You're worthless."

Bilt pulled Luke to his feet and stuck the key in the handcuffs. "At least I haven't landed behind bars for sixty days."

"You can't leave me here for sixty days." Luke clenched his jaw. "My sentence was thirty."

"Until you fought. I warned you that it'd be sixty days if you fought. Don't argue with me, Tanner. You're just digging a bigger hole." The sheriff pulled off the handcuffs and turned toward the door. "Be good, Luke." He pushed the bars open. "Accept your sentence and shut up about everything. You'll be doing yourself a favor."

"When do I get a trial?" Luke demanded.

The bars slammed shut. "Whenever Judge Baker finds the time. Visiting hours are anytime except bedtime and lunch."

"I don't want any visitors."

"That's not your choice. If they come, they have a right to see you. Food comes from the hotel three times a day."

As Sheriff Bilt walked back to his office and silence took over the jailhouse, Luke felt the crushing weight of reality settle on his cramped cell.

Grace came to see Luke the moment she heard the news, but he sent her away. He promised he would be out of jail by the end of the week—just as soon as he had his trial and could prove his innocence.

For the rest of that first day, Luke lay on the cot and stared out the window. He yelled at Sheriff Bilt when he brought meals, and warned him not to let another visitor in. The sheriff answered Luke's threats by jingling the handcuffs in his belt and telling Luke that a gag was his next restraint. Luke continued to throw insults.

After one night in jail, Luke became incredibly bored, and at the first hint of sunlight he demanded a trial. The sheriff told him he would have to wait. Luke wanted to wring his neck.

Saturday passed, and Luke was left alone on Sunday. His meals were served in silence by a skinny officer Luke had never met. He hadn't realized how much he'd miss Sheriff Bilt's company. At least the sheriff talked to him.

Luke awoke on Monday morning to the sound of a key turning. He looked up and saw Sheriff Bilt walk into the cell hall. He was followed by a tall, clean-faced man.

Luke let out a groan that came from his very soul.

"You have a visitor," Sheriff Bilt said. Luke nodded at Mr. Sulka, acting perfectly composed. If this man were going to play a rescuing game with him, he would play along.

"Morning, Luke," Mr. Sulka said.

Luke faked a welcoming smile.

"Breakfast is in an hour, Tanner," the sheriff said. "I'm going to the apothecary. Behave yourself."

Luke glared at the sheriff.

For a moment there was silence in the jailhouse. Dan stood outside the bars and leaned against the wall, his arms folded. At last, breaking an awkward silence, he said, "I'm sorry about your situation, Luke."

Luke smiled at him. "This place isn't that bad. At least I don't have to work."

The bones in Dan's jaw clenched. "I checked on your wife and children this morning. Grace's parents are staying at your place, so it looks like things are OK."

Luke stiffened. "I don't want you going to my house."

"I don't mean any harm. Wesley's carrying an awful heavy load right now. I thought I could help him with the upkeep of the place."

"I'll take care of my own place." Luke shook his head. "I can catch up on it next week."

"When you get out, 'ey?"

Luke wondered if he were mocking him. "When I get out is nobody's business."

"I see."

Luke turned away and tried to suppress his burning anger.

"Accepting help isn't a crime, you know," Dan said.

Luke's eyes shot toward him. "I've never committed a crime in my life."

Dan eyed him coolly. "So, is there anything I can do for you?"

Luke leaned his head against the cold cement wall. "Be in court to defend me when the judge hears my case."

Dan shifted his big feet. "I couldn't do that. I have no idea what the charges are or what your defense is."

"You don't read the paper?"

"I make a habit of staying away from headlines."

Luke glanced at Mr. Sulka. "I don't know what kind of religious duty you're trying to fulfill, but I don't want visitors."

Dan's mouth barely creased into a smile. "Then I guess you and I are on the same page. I don't want to visit you either."

Luke felt a surprising pang of rejection. "Then go away."

"Can't." Dan's gaze was steady. "I'm in charge of jail ministry in this town."

"Jail ministry?" Luke blurted out. "You mean to come in here and minister to a man who's a Christian as if I were a drunk or criminal?" He shot up off his cot and turned his back to Dan. "I don't need your charity."

Dan rested his forearms on the bars. "I usually minister to thieves, drunks, and reckless teenagers," he said in a voice that rang off the cement walls. "I'm going to have to change my way of doing things for you."

Luke glared over his shoulder. "I told you to go away."

Dan didn't flinch. "I'm not here to minister to you, Luke."

He whirled around. "Then what do you want?"

"I want you to stop being a hypocrite."

Luke pounded his fist against the wall and every nerve in his body urged him to lunge at Dan Sulka.

"Well, then, let's get on with it." He turned to Dan with a mocking glare. "How about you tell me every way I've been a hypocrite, and I'll repent and beg forgiveness at your feet?"

Dan stared at him with a steady gaze. "What do you want, Luke? How do you want me to respond to you when you act like that?"

"I want you to leave me alone."

"So you can rot away in an empty jail, 'ey? So you can spend the next fifty-some days of your life without saying a word to anyone but Bilt? So you can worry over your family and hate Ashley and come out of here ready to murder anyone who goes against you?" Dan paused. "Luke, the only reason I came here is because I believe that God hasn't abandoned you, and He wants you to know that He's still committed to you. If you think you've got that message already grounded in your heart, I'll be glad to leave you alone for the rest of your life."

Luke turned toward the window with a heaving sigh. "I never laid a hand on that girl. Everything she's said about me abusing her is a lie. She's a deceitful little girl who deserves a good beating to teach her her place. She's manipulative and selfish and downright wicked. If I would've known I'd end up in jail as a reward for being kind to her, I would've beat every rebellious bone out of her body before it came to this. Ashley needs good, hard discipline to get her into shape."

Dan cocked his head. "I reckon she's just as confused about the whole situation as you are."

Luke sniffed. "She knows exactly what she did."

"I think she's going to come around to you."

"Come around?" Luke gave an angry laugh. "She's never coming back."

"So you've given up on her?"

Luke sensed the depth of that question and wasn't sure he could answer it. "No. If she came back, I would take her again."

"For the sake of reputation, or because you want to have another chance to love her?"

"Love her? I've already given every last drop of love I had to offer. She doesn't speak that language. She needs discipline, and if she ever came back to my home, I would be kind enough to give her what she needs."

Dan rubbed his thumbs together. "I think she's scared of you, Luke."

"She has nothing to be afraid of."

Dan laughed. "I'm not a little girl, but if I were, I reckon the anger I just saw would send me running for shelter."

Luke sat on the cot and shook his head. "I was never angry with her." Pictures danced in his mind of exploding anger he had shown because of Ashley, and they proved him a liar. "Ashley knew I loved her. But she needs boundaries set and respect established. She needs to know the price I've paid for her."

"A penny," Dan said, and it struck Luke like a blow to the face.

"I paid a penny because that was the cost of the paperwork." Luke's cheeks burned. "That doesn't mean that's all I would ever give for Ashley."

"She's going to cost you everything you hold dear."

"She won't take it away from me."

"Not unless you give it."

"It's wrong for a child to suck the very life out of her father." Luke's voice rose.

"She's not sucking the life out of you; you're willingly giving it for her," Dan said calmly.

"Ashley has robbed me of a reputation, a comfortable lifestyle, and every ounce of my freedom. I haven't willingly given those things for her."

"I don't know what to tell you, then." Dan shrugged. "I can't force you to give up your life to follow God's call."

"I'm not sure I'm willing to take God's call on my life if it includes Ashley."

Dan looked surprised. "Then I reckon that's the first thing you have to reconcile with."

Luke looked up at him with confusion. "God's call?"

"Yeah. I reckon you won't ever be happy if you're not giving yourself up for a higher purpose. God has incredible things in store for you, Luke."

"Yeah." Luke sniffed. "A jail cell. That's a bright future."

"I guess you can do what you want with it."

"What's that supposed to mean?" Luke glared at him.

"You can be angry at this situation for as long as you want, but you're only killing yourself."

"Thanks for the help, Dan." Luke turned away. "You can leave now because you're not doing me any good."

Dan paused at the bars for a moment and then walked away.

A wise man is strong: yea, a man of knowledge increaseth strength.

—Proverbs 24:5

TWENTY FIVE

Pain

Luke's trial date came more than a week after he had been put in jail. He had no warning of its arrival; he was simply taken from behind bars one morning and escorted to the courthouse, where Judge Baker was waiting for him, along with what seemed like the whole town.

Luke barely made it up the steps without hurling. The stress of the moment and the overwhelming shame and embarrassment were almost too much to handle. If he had known it would be like this, he would've skipped the trial. Sixty days in jail was better than one hour of public mortification.

The judge first heard the sheriff's testimony, and Bilt released all the pent-up anger he had been harboring against Luke. The more the sheriff condemned Luke, the further he sank into his wooden seat.

Judge Baker called five witnesses to the stand next. By the time they had finished telling the courtroom that they had seen Luke walking around the orphanage after dark the evening before he was arrested, Luke had all but given up in defending himself.

Luke's argument left him as soon as he was called to the stand. He had rehearsed a series of lies that would excuse him from the charge against him, but he couldn't say them. He knew he was guilty.

Surrounded by the condemning sighs and looks of the audience, jury, sheriff, and judge, Luke received the maximum sentence. Sixty days in jail.

Somehow he made it back to the jail without hurting someone. He felt so angry he could've killed anyone who crossed his path, but he was too embarrassed to act like he cared.

Behind bars again, with the word *guilty* running through his brain over and over, Luke lay on his cot in surrender. For the first time in his life, he felt completely condemned, completely alone, and completely exposed.

Grace sat at the table with her mother and forcefully dug at the meat of a cantaloupe. The house was quiet except for the crackling of a fire and Cherish's soft breathing as she slept. Grace had already shed plenty of tears. All she could do now was take her anger out on the melon.

"Granddad and I will stay until he's out," said Grandma Jackson. "We'll take care of the children whenever you want to visit him."

"I don't want to visit him there, Mother."

"He needs you."

"He needs to be alone so he can realize what he's done to himself and his family."

Marjorie was silent as she slid her knife through the peel of an apple. "I bet he'll get out in less than sixty days."

Grace sniffed. "I hope he doesn't. I want him to stay there for every second of his sentence. Maybe I'll take the children and move in with you."

"Don't do that, Grace. What if Ashley needs you?"

"Ashley?" Grace set her knife on the table with a bang. Cantaloupe seeds splattered against the wall. "Ashley's gone, Mum.

We have to give her up. Some other sweet mother who has been fortunate enough to marry a well-mannered, self-controlled, compassionate husband will adopt Ashley and my little girl will be raised by a stranger."

She swallowed a sob. "When Luke gets out of that jail, he'll be angrier than ever. He'll make Wesley into a bitter little boy who hates Ashley because she 'ruined our name.' I'll get even more sorrow and heartache than I have now."

Grandma reached for Grace's hand. "You're more important to Luke than anyone else in the world. You have to love him and accept him. He's a fallen soldier and everyone is trying to kill him while he's down. Don't you give up on him too."

Grace bravely wiped her tears away. "Dod can go talk to him and tell him we're all fine—at least financially. But I have to leave Luke alone or I'll ruin what I already have."

"Grace . . ."

"At least for a little while. He has to do this by himself."

Grace left the table with a firm set of her jaw and a heart that bled from the sting of her wounds.

Ashley tried to prevent more tears so her face could stop stinging. She curled up in a tight ball and pressed herself against the cool wall, her head pounding. The light from a tiny candle on the dresser flickered against the curtain and Ashley watched it, squinting her eyes in the heavy darkness. She reached out and touched the cold windowpane, and thought about the night she had seen a lantern in the tree and heard Henry's voice calling through her window. Now, when she looked out the glass, all she saw was an iron fence and a brick window frame. Where was the softness and security that was supposed to be found inside these walls?

Ashley heard the door click open and she buried her face in the pillow and tucked her hands into her chest. She imagined Miss

Elizabeth pulling her out of bed and forcing her into the schoolroom again, but the bedroom was quiet. Ashley almost looked up, but then she heard Miss Jolie's tender voice.

"What are you doing, sitting here in the dark?" she asked in a whisper.

Ashley heard footsteps near her bed, and the mattress jolted when Jolie sat on it. She felt shivers when Miss Jolie touched her back. She moved away and swaddled herself in the sheet.

"Ashley, there's no use crying anymore." Jolie's voice sounded like Grace Tanner's. "It won't do any good, darlin'."

Ashley held her breath to keep the tears away.

"You have to be a brave girl. Now, tell me why you're hiding in your bedroom in the dark? Why don't you play with the doll you got when you were at the Tanners? Gretchen gave you her old top; can't you entertain yourself with that?"

Ashley touched her fingers to the cold wall again. The coolness made the fire disappear from her face. "I don't want to."

"Ashley, sulking isn't going to make anything better."

"I don't care."

Jolie patted her shoulder. "Would you care if sulking made your mother unhappy?"

Ashley felt a sting. She glanced at Miss Jolie in the low candlelight. "No," she said, and turned away again.

"Now, Ashley," Jolie scolded, brushing the child's hair from her tearstained cheeks. "You know that's not the truth. If your mother told you not to sulk, you wouldn't sulk."

"But she didn't tell me," Ashley said to the pillow.

"I did." Jolie turned Ashley's chin toward her, and her cold hand felt like ice on Ashley's cheeks. "I'm your real auntie, and I think you should obey me as if I were your mother."

"I won't." Ashley pushed her away.

Jolie stood and lit the lamp with the candle flame. She set the lamp on the dresser and lifted Ashley into her arms. Then she sat on the bed, leaning against the headboard.

Ashley tried to push away from Jolie's touch, but her stiffness only provoked Jolie to hold her tighter. By the time Ashley relaxed in the tender arms, she was ready to cry another flood. She couldn't understand the vulnerability she felt when Jolie comforted her, but it made her feel like running away. *If only Jack would rescue me from here too.*

"I think I know something that you're afraid to tell the girls," said Miss Jolie as the lamplight scattered freakish shadows across the bed. "I think you want to go home."

Ashley wondered if that's what she wanted. Home? Where was that? Ever since she could remember, home had been inside the walls of the orphanage, sleeping in this room, against this window, on this very bed. Home had been the dirty library downstairs, the big dining hall, and the kitchen that was always bustling with gossiping old ladies. At some point in her life, Ashley had learned that this wasn't supposed to be home, and she had begun to dream about a home somewhere else, "with a good family," like the orphans told her. The Berks' house was supposed to be home after that. Perhaps it had been for a few days, but unless "home" was supposed to be a place filled with cruelty and hate and pain, the Berks' certainly wasn't it.

The Tanners. That was home, wasn't it? But how could it be, as long as Luke Tanner was there?

What about all the tender stories Melissa told Ashley about daddies who sat around the fire at night, reading to their children? What about Gretchen's memories of going to church and falling asleep in a strong set of arms, and waking up snuggled in bed on Sunday afternoon? Where was the nurturing environment—that warm, cozy place where fear never crept in and pain was healed? That was supposed to be home. But there was no place on earth like that.

"I don't want to go there," Ashley blurted, brushing her hand against her damp face.

"Your mama and daddy want you back very badly."

"I don't want a daddy," she said.

Jolie looked at Ashley with baffled eyes. "Why? Your daddy loves you."

Ashley stared at the lamp. If Daddy loved her, she must not know what love is.

Jolie turned Ashley around to face her. “Ashley, everyone thinks your daddy hurt you. You need to tell them that’s not true.”

Ashley wondered if Mr. Tanner had ever really hurt her. Not to any serious physical degree, but she felt wounded on the inside. She carried hurts that she couldn’t explain—ones that had made her run that night out of fear and neglect. Not all of them were Mr. Tanner’s doing, but certainly he held a great portion of responsibility.

“Your daddy didn’t hurt you, Ashley,” Jolie said firmly. “I know him.”

“He was angry.”

“But he didn’t hurt you, did he?”

“No. I mean—” Ashley covered her face and shook her head. “Stop, Miss Jolie! Please don’t ask me any more questions.”

“If you want to go home, you have to tell Mrs. Harms the truth. You have to tell her that your daddy never hurt you. You have to tell her that you’ve never had a bruise and that he never hit you or strapped you or pinched you or anything else.” Jolie was passionate. “Do you hear me? You have to tell her the truth.”

“I can’t.” Ashley winced.

“Why?”

She didn’t understand why. But saying that Luke Tanner never hurt her was a lie.

Jolie gripped Ashley’s shoulders and her eyes searched her face. “Did he ever hurt you?” she asked quietly.

“Yes.”

“When?”

“He pinched me. And he strapped Wes. Wes even said so, and so did Mama. He hurt him terribly.”

“He strapped Wes because he was naughty, right?”

“Yes.”

“But he never strapped you.”

Ashley’s eyes filled with tears. She wanted to scream from the captivity in her soul that kept her from explaining what she understood inside. “He told me he was going to. And he would have, but Mama stopped him. That hurts, Miss Jolie. It hurts! Listen to me!" She crumbled onto the woman's chest.

Jolie leaned against the headboard with a bang. She wrapped her arms around Ashley and rocked her. "What are you going to tell Mrs. Harms?"

"Nothing," Ashley said to Jolie's chest.

"You have to stick up for your daddy."

"I can't help him."

"Do me a favor. Tell Mrs. Harms that your daddy never hit you or caused you pain. Can you just tell her that one thing?"

"I don't want to talk to her anymore." Ashley sobbed. "I can't. Don't ask me. I can't tell her that."

"Why not?"

Ashley wanted to lift up her dress and show Miss Jolie her scars and tell her about every bruise and strike and blow Mr. Berk ever gave her. She wanted to tell her about chicken watching, sleeping in the cold, and searching for days on end for the chickens lost in the dense forest. She wanted to talk about Jack and Henry and Bonnie and how Mrs. Berk hummed off-key all day long. And then about the woodshed—the devastating pain of the woodshed and the belt, and the sound of Mr. Berk's words as he cut into her very soul.

Ashley wanted to tell someone about the day Jack had told her that she would die if she took one more beating. He had dropped her off at the doorstep of the orphanage that day, with specific instructions never to say a word about anything in her past. Never to show her scars or bruises, no matter who begged or bribed or threatened to kill her if she didn't confess. She was to be a good girl and leave it all in the past, where it belonged.

"I can't," Ashley whimpered.

Everything had to stay locked in the castle of her heart, where the pain was brutal enough to rob the life right out of her.

Thou art the helper of the fatherless.

—Psalm 10:14

TWENTY SIX

Being Free

Nothing lived in the jail. There was not even a lousy bug. No fly or spider or ant or flea. Nothing. No pictures hung on any wall, no design adorned the broken stool in the corner, and there was not a speck of color in the sheet or bedspread. No rug covered the monotonous gray of the floor; there was no change in shade from the metal cot to the cement wall. There wasn't even any dirt in the corner outside the cell, and every ray of sunlight was hidden behind the building next door by three o'clock. There was not even any sound. The place was perfectly silent and maddeningly still.

Luke lay on his cot and tried to imagine home—the fire in the hearth, Grace singing in the kitchen, Wesley laughing as he read a book. He remembered Cherish fussing in her cradle, covered in a pink blanket and sucking her thumb. Even Ashley fit into the picture, playing dominoes on the floor or blending into her mother's shadow in the dining room. He remembered a thousand colors and the smells of bread and flowers and soap. The feel and taste and smell of the barn haunted him like a long-lost dream that he had willingly let go of. And what for?

Luke squeezed his pillow to his chest. "God, what am I doing here?"

He waited for a reply, but there was only silence. It seemed to engulf him like a blizzard, freezing what warmth was left inside.

Luke banged his fist on the wall. "Why is this happening to me?" He pushed himself upright and the cot squeaked. "I'm losing everything—it's all slipping through my fingers like water. I'm losing it, God."

The sound of a key in the door made Luke groan.

"You've got a visitor," Sheriff Bilt's voice rang down the hall. Luke tipped his head into the corner when the sheriff appeared in front of his cell.

"Tell them to go away."

Dan Sulka walked in behind the sheriff.

"Go away, Dan," Luke said, raking his hand through his hair.

Bilt sniffed. "The top of the morning to you too. He has a right to stay."

"I don't need a preacher," Luke said.

Mr. Sulka raised his brow. "I reckon I'm no good at preaching."

Luke felt the man's eyes burning right through him, and it made him squirm. "I don't want to talk."

Dan stepped away, but Sheriff Bilt shook his head. "Stay, Sulka. He's gonna go insane if he's by himself much longer."

Luke heard the keys jingle as the sheriff walked off, and for a long moment, silence took over. Luke felt like a little boy awaiting one of his father's verbal and physical beatings. Dan Sulka—the honest, gentle-eyed giant—was staring at him from outside the cell. It was enough to make him go wild with desperation.

"So you're here for your jail ministry again," Luke said at length. He almost wished the big man were here to give him a beating. He would rather be bloody and bruised than staring into those eyes.

Dan nodded slowly. "I reckon. You picked a mighty fine time to get locked up, Luke. There hasn't been a single arrest 'sides you, so I've got no one to see but you."

"Just my luck. Well, if you're looking for a good, evangelistic day to list in your deeds of goodness, you might as well leave, 'cause this won't be it. Come back when I'm feeling happier."

"I don't suppose that'll be any time soon," Dan said.

"Not likely." It had only been four days since the trial; he had forty-eight more to go. The minutes passed like hours and the hours like weeks. "I've never been more miserable in my life."

"At least you recognize that."

Luke glared at him. "Are you mocking me?"

Dan held his hands up. "Not at all. I could be sitting right beside you."

"What's that supposed to mean?"

"I'm no less a sinner than you."

Luke's chest felt tight. "That's easy for you to say. You're on the other side, free as Dale Gildey's cigars. Nobody deserves to live through this."

"Least of all you?"

Luke's eyes narrowed. "I didn't say that."

"I thought that's what you were implying."

"I don't know why you're here. All you do is argue with me. I have enough time to argue with myself."

Dan shook his head. "Unfortunately, I can't leave until Bilt gets back. He locked me in here."

Luke smiled bitterly. "I'm a two-year-old, constrained by gates and keys and bars. I'm locked in a desolate building while the man with the key is having a grand ol' time at the apothecary across town." Luke pushed his hand through his hair. "This is insanity! While Ashley sits in her comfortable orphanage with maids at her service, I'm sitting on a puny cot behind bars. Aren't the righteous supposed to get rewarded?"

Luke's words bounced off the bare walls and haunted him.

"Judge Baker wouldn't have sentenced me if he would've believed the truth."

"What is the truth?"

"He shut me up in here for snooping around the orphanage, a direct violation of the agreement between me and the sheriff. But that's a flat-out lie."

Dan's eyes narrowed in disbelief.

Luke turned away. "Don't believe me if you don't want to."

"What were you doing at the orphanage, then?"

"Nothing. Walking."

"But you were there."

"I have a right to be near the orphanage," Luke said, setting his jaw.

"Didn't Bilt tell you to stay away?"

"He told me not to set a toe on their property. So I didn't."

"You didn't?"

"I didn't cross the fence."

Dan set his hand on the bars. "I thought you went around back."

Luke's cheeks flushed. "And I thought you didn't read the paper."

"Word gets out." Dan shrugged. "Luke, have you ever considered listening to what God has to say?"

Luke started to give a sarcastic answer but stopped. He squinted out the window at the fuzzy clouds. "I don't know what God thinks of me," he said with a pang of vulnerability. "But I reckon it's not good."

"You really think that?" asked Dan.

Luke glanced at him and then looked away.

"I reckon you'd do yourself a favor to find out the truth on that subject. Unless you come to grips with the fact that you've been justly sentenced, you're going to be bitter the rest of your life."

Justly sentenced. He knew it was the truth. What had he been doing in the back of the orphanage, anyway? He had been trying to get a glimpse of Ashley so he could force her to deny that he had ever laid a hand on her.

"I don't know how you expect me to come out of this a better person," Luke said.

"It's humanly impossible. Dependence on God is the only way."

"I wish it were that easy." A mattress spring poked Luke's leg. "You have no idea what it's like to be incarcerated. I have patients at the hospital who need to see me. My wife and children need me at home. For goodness sake, Dan, my wife is blind. I change the baby and buy groceries. How's she supposed to manage? There has to be a better way for the law to handle things."

"I guess jail was meant to be confining."

Luke clenched his jaw. "What are you trying to get at?"

"I'm just saying it the way it is. No sugarcoating. You're here for forty-eight more days; you might as well deal with it now."

Luke sniffed. "You want me to behave."

"No. But as long as you're concentrated on being in jail, you're going to miss what God wants to do for you. I want to see you as a free man."

Luke smiled and lay back on the cot. "Bring out the key."

Dan chuckled, his deep voice ringing off the cold walls. "I'm talking about spiritual freedom, Luke."

He waved his hand toward the bars. "Spiritual freedom in a tiny, confined cell like this?"

Dan shrugged. "I guess you have to choose whether or not these bars will keep you from being free."

Is My hand shortened at all, that it cannot redeem? or have I no power to deliver?

—Isaiah 50:2

HOLY
BIBLE

TWENTY SEVEN

Truth

The last days of September passed, and October was half over before Luke allowed Grace or Wesley to visit him. Winter made its way to Galesburg, and with it came a dreary rest. News about the Tanner crime still trickled into the paper occasionally, but life had moved on. The apothecary circle continued to thrive on political debates and gossip, but Luke was rarely the subject of conversation. It seemed everyone had forgotten about him.

One Tuesday afternoon, October 25, Luke was stretched out on his cot with his hands under his head. It was a cold day and the sky was a bitter gray. Luke wondered how much snow was on the ground.

Luke resisted the temptation to become restless. He had experienced enough restless days to count for a lifetime and couldn't afford another one. Restlessness made him anxious and angry.

Life at the jail had not gotten easier; it had only become more miserable, lonelier, quieter. His spirit was starving, fed by nothing but guilty silence.

Luke remembered Dan Sulka's words during his last visit: "Find truth, Luke. Whatever you have to do, find it."

Truth, Luke thought, shaking his head. *The truth is that I'm locked in a jail for another eighteen days, and when I get out, I'll have nothing. I might as well stay here—at least I don't have to deal with the ridicule of the town. When I leave this behind, my life is going to be even more miserable. I have nothing left for my name.*

Luke's cheeks burned with shame. He remembered Dan telling him that shame wasn't a part of God's gospel.

I don't know how to get rid of shame, he thought.

Shame was as much a part of Luke Tanner as the blood that ran through his veins. He had been born with it. It was impossible to get rid of. And truth? That was as foreign as freedom. The only truths he knew were that you had to earn everything in life, even if it killed you in the process; that men were brutal; and that everything had a price.

Just like the penny parcel.

Luke shook his head. *She's not even worth a penny.* She was a problem child. A little girl who didn't know how to behave and was a constant embarrassment. She had permanently ruined his good name.

That was the truth. He was worth nothing, just like his father used to say.

Memories of his childhood in Missouri made Luke squirm. He thought about his father, a powerful man who used his strength to hurt his son in every way possible. Luke had never been able to measure up to old Mr. Tanner's demands, so he had spent his entire life trying to prove that he wasn't who his father told him he was. He fled to Galesburg in search of refuge, but all he found was pressure to perform. For eight years he had been trying to prove to Galesburg that he was worthy, and now he was back at the beginning: a complete failure.

The weight of defeat made Luke's shoulders slump.

"I'm a bad Christian, aren't I, God?" he said with a mocking sniff. "Well, there's one more strike for me. So what if I were a good Christian? What if I did everything right and always made the right choices?" He cocked his head and a wave of loneliness made him shiver. "Good Christians do everything they're supposed to do, and they still end up just like me."

Dying on the inside.

A knot stuck in his throat. "What's this life about anyway? It's all just a jumble of confusion and pain and lies. And everyone ends up in the same place in the end. I might as well give up, because I'll be searching for a lifetime and still end up incarcerated."

In prison. Behind bars. A captive. In much more than a physical way.

He had to admit that Dan Sulka was right: These jail bars were only a physical reminder of the real prison.

"I don't have the keys, God," Luke said, his hands open.

Find truth. Luke remembered the words again.

"How?" he asked the empty air. "There's no one here to help me search."

He glanced at the Bible Mr. Sulka had slid under the bars the day before. He hadn't picked it up, but had been tempted to kick it into the hall several times that morning. Its very presence haunted him.

"I've already read Your Book," he said, turning his eyes away from it. Luke remembered his father forcing him to memorize a chapter in John when he was a schoolboy, and his childhood preacher had drilled him until he could dramatize dozens of Old Testament stories. He was prepared to take any man's challenge in a theological debate. But that black book lying on the floor made him uneasy. Dan Sulka talked about the Bible like a familiar friend, but to Luke it just meant law enforcement.

Dan had told Luke something about a pagan lie. What was it? Something about performance or acceptance or approval—yes, approval. God's approval was not based on what you've done.

"Then how do you get God's approval?" Luke said aloud. In his memory, his father's voice demanded that he try harder.

Luke slumped against the wall. *I can't try harder. I've tried for eight years in Galesburg and it's only landed me in this cell.*

"I have to stop." He closed his eyes and felt panic spreading over his body. "God, I can't think about Pop. Help me keep his memory dead. I killed it, and I don't ever want it back!"

Luke rose to his feet and kicked the stool in the corner, sending it into the wall with a loud crash. He laid his head on the cool brick and felt his heart pulse in his neck. His hands were fisted as if grasping to stifle something that was trying to take control of him.

He heard voices in his head, the ones that had taunted him for years—the ones he had worked so hard to ignore. His body tensed, and he fought to deafen his ears to the words, but they came over him full force.

Luke, you're worthless.

You'll never be what God intended you to be.

You can't do it.

You've failed; therefore, you're a failure.

God's waiting for you to mess up.

Everyone at the apothecary sees how unworthy you are.

Everyone else is capable of being a good Christian.

God wants you only for a servant.

Jesus died on the cross to make you behave.

God loves you because you're doing everything you can for Him.

God accepts you because you perform well.

You can—and will—fall from God's approval.

You're everything your father ever said you were.

God's disappointed in you, just like everyone else is.

Good works are what will get you forgiveness.

Your wife isn't going to stick this out with you.

God will approve of dying for you if you become a light to the world and bring people to Him.

God will forgive you if you repent and never return to your sin.

You are incapable.

If you don't get your act together fast enough, God will forget about you.

God is exactly like your father. He wants to hurt you.

You'll always be an illegitimate child.

No matter how hard you try, there will always be someone who can do it better than you.

Honesty with yourself is too dangerous to consider.

No one else has problems like you.

You're an ugly person.

You have to pretend that you're different than you are so people will respect you.

If you're not careful, the upper crusts are going to find out where you came from.

People give you compliments because they feel sorry for you.

Wesley will soon find out who you really are.

It was stupid for you to try to reach Ashley. She hates you because of who you are.

It's embarrassing to need God's grace.

God isn't interested in talking with you until you've cleaned up your walk.

You always make bad choices.

Your father hates you because you're a worthless person.

Everyone will run from you if you let them see who you really are.

You should be ashamed.

Your only hope is to move or die before people understand you.

Your marriage is sure to fail.

God made your wife barren because He knew you wouldn't be a good father.

You're a disgrace.

It's only a matter of time before you're ruined forever.

On and on and on the comments danced in Luke's brain, plaguing him and bringing back memories from the earliest days of his childhood. He heard his father's voice saying many of them, but others were said in the voices of his college professors, the apothecary circle, and the looks and deeds of hundreds of others.

Luke finally forced his mind to be silent. He stood perfectly still and the silence screamed. The voice of deception whispered one final time:

If you become the best person you can be and bear the name Christian with reverence and perseverance . . . if you do God's work humbly and try your hardest to stay true to the straight and narrow . . . then, and only then, will God fully love you.

Luke seethed. "If I can do nothing that will ever be good enough for You—if You put conditions on my life that I can never meet—why'd You bother to create me?"

He buried his face in his hands and sank down in the corner of his cell. For a long moment, the only sound was his own heavy breathing. He sat perfectly still and silent, concentrating only on pushing the voices out of his brain.

His eyes fell on the Bible near the bars.

"I won't read it, God," Luke said. "You wrote that book for people who are capable of making You happy. It'll do me no good. I have nothing to offer You."

How about your weakness?

No. Luke flinched. Letting God see his weakness was as dangerous as aiming a loaded gun at himself. *I can't give You my weakness. It's ugly.*

Give Me your ugliness, then.

Why would You want that? You're the epitome of goodness. I have nothing good enough to give You.

I don't want goodness; I want you.

Luke felt the breath go out of him. *God, let me die rather than pursue me. I'll always disappoint You.*

Luke felt tears swelling in his eyes and fear gripped him. *I can't cry,* he thought, swallowing the heaviness in his chest. He couldn't bear to cry, not when he was so alone.

Luke felt himself spiraling out of control, and fear made him rise to his feet and approach the cell bars. He peered down the hall but saw no sign of life. *If I were to die in here, no one would even know until it was too late.*

The thought of crying was as intimidating as death. He couldn't let himself get that far out of control for fear that he would never be able to pull out of it. He felt years of emotion attack him in rushes and he knew that if he let it affect him, there would be no end to the tears.

"What do I do?" Luke whispered as he broke into a cold sweat. He fell on the cot, and the mattress springs poked him. His hands trembled, just the way he'd often seen Ashley's do.

I have to be stronger than her, Luke told himself.

What if you're weak?

Then I die. He clenched his fists.

No. Then I'll be your strength.

You can't. I can't let You see inside me, God.

Why not? What will I do?

Hurt me.

I'll hurt you?

Luke's ears rang in the silence. *Yes.*

How?

Just like every other man on the face of the earth. If You know my weakness, You'll know how You can hurt me most. God, don't ask me to give You anything but the very best of my—

The abrupt halt in Luke's spirit made him gasp.

Performance, he heard as quietly as a whisper.

Luke stiffened. "Yes, my performance," he said aloud. "Ask me for something I know how to give!"

Luke laid his head on his pillow, breathing hard, his hands still trembling.

"Ask me for performance," the words danced in his head.

"*Truth,*" he heard Dan Sulka saying.

What about truth? Luke thought.

I want truth.

But You are truth.

I want truth from you. I hate performance.

The truth about me is revolting.

All I want is truth, no matter what it is.

"Truth, huh?" Luke sat up and threw his hands in the air. "Fine, I'll give You truth! The truth is that I am nothing. I have nothing. I've ruined my life trying to be somebody people would respect. And now I'm a prisoner, serving sixty days because I was justly sentenced for my own stupidity!" His voice trailed off to a whisper. "The truth is that I wanted Ashley to rise to my expectations and she couldn't. I wounded her, and that's why she ran away."

Luke ground his teeth and tears threatened again.

"The truth is that I can't measure up to Your expectations, God."

My expectations are for truth, Luke. You measure up.

A tear fell down Luke's cheek.

My gift is salvation to those who can't save themselves.

Stillness settled over Luke's spirit. His hands stopped trembling and the knot in his throat melted away.

"What's my purpose then, God?" he asked quietly.

To know Me.

Luke saw the Bible again and this time he picked it up. The sun sent a soft, orange glow on the cell as he thumbed through the pages. He was overwhelmed with exposure.

Luke heard Sheriff Bilt return to the jail. The office door slammed, then silence fell.

"It's too cold to be October," the sheriff muttered under his breath as he sat in a chair and propped his feet on his desk. He threw his hat into the corner and settled his big shoulders into the wooden chair. He folded his hands in his lap and closed his eyes, reveling in the silence.

Silence.

Bilt's eyes popped open. He cocked his head, wondering why Luke hadn't hollered some kind of demand or scolding like he always did when the sheriff returned to the jail.

A lyrical sound suddenly rang off the jail walls. Bilt's feet dropped off his desk. He opened the office door and stuck his head into the foyer. Quietly and deeply he heard Luke sing, "Just as I am without one plea but that Thy blood was shed for me . . ."

For by grace are ye saved through faith: and that not of yourselves: it is the gift of God: not of works.

—Ephesians 2:8–9

TWENTY EIGHT

Visitors

Wesley strolled home from school as slowly as possible on Friday, October 28. He kicked at pebbles and stones and swung his lunch pail at every spider web that clung to the weeds in the ditch. He shoved his hands into his warm trouser pockets, humming a sad tune to himself.

Several horses and buggies passed him by, but he paid no attention to the busy traffic until he heard the slow creaking of cart wheels behind him. Turning, he gasped when a fat donkey stopped short and Mr. Bowtie smiled from a squatty cart seat. Wes hardly recognized him without his Sunday bowtie.

"What's a schoolboy doing out on a cold day like this?" asked the preacher.

"Walking home, sir," Wes said, stepping out of the donkey's path.

"You're Luke Tanner's boy, ain't ya?"

Wes nodded and the preacher tossed his head toward the seat beside him. "Want a ride home?"

Wes started to refuse, but he could think of no good reason to decline such a kind offer on a dreary, windy day. He stuttered excuses for a moment before Thomas Harris jumped from his cart with a laugh and tossed the boy onto the seat with a satisfied nod.

He crawled up beside Wes and clicked to the donkey. "Now, tell me about your life, son."

Taken back by this request, Wes sat silent for a moment. He shrugged, fumbling with the stack of books under his arm.

The preacher glanced at his hesitant passenger. "Start with your name, age, grade, and position in family."

"My . . . my name is Wesley," he said slowly, wondering how he was going to declare his "position in family" once he got to that part. "I'm ten years old and in fourth grade."

"And are you the youngest or oldest in your family, son?"

"Oldest."

Mr. Bowtie pulled out his pocket watch, which was held in place by a red ribbon, and clicked it open. "And all of your problems in life? Tell me them."

Wes swallowed hard, staring at the sad-looking donkey ahead, thinking that he very much disliked this prying preacher. "I had a sister named Ashley, who we adopted, but she ran away in July and went back to the orphanage." He slumped, and his lopsided hat fell over his eyes.

"Ah, now that *is* a problem." Thomas Harris snapped his pocket watch shut and shoved it into his shirt pocket.

Wes shook his head, almost succumbing to tears. "After Ashley got taken back, the sheriff put my dad in jail, so now Mom and I have to take care of the house and my baby sister by ourselves. My dad doesn't get out of jail till November fourteenth."

"Those are tragic circumstances."

Wes looked at Mr. Bowtie and felt his cheeks blush. Then he turned back to the donkey, wishing he hadn't told his troubles.

"But they certainly aren't unsolvable problems. The good Lord will see that justice is done. Now, tell me why Ashley went back."

"I don't know." Wesley wanted to cry. "She never liked my dad. Mrs. Harms won't give Ashley back 'cause she thinks my dad abused her. He really wasn't mean. My dad was always good to her. But she was scared of him when we first got her, and she wouldn't let him help her."

"Not at all?"

Wes shook his head. "I tried to tell her that Dad was gentle and good, but she wouldn't believe me."

Mr. Bowtie banged his feet on the footboard. "I'm glad to hear the reports I've read in the paper aren't true. And I'm thankful I took the time to drive down this road today so I could meet you, Mr. Wesley. I'll be right pleased to have a chance to meet your pop. Think I'll go to the jail first thing in the morning."

"He doesn't like visitors," Wes said.

Mr. Bowtie laughed. "I reckon most people don't like seeing my face at first, but he'll come around soon enough. I've heard a little bit about your daddy from Mr. Sulka; do you know him?"

"He came over once. I go to school with his son."

The preacher nodded. "Jimmy Sulka is a fine young man—you'd do yourself a favor to make friends with him."

"Yes, sir," Wes replied timidly. He had a knot in his stomach.

When the preacher dropped Wesley off at home and turned his cart around with a tip of his hat, Wes shook his head and sighed, wondering how things would turn out when the preacher showed up at the jail.

"It sure was a sight to see," said Sheriff Bilt, sucking on a cigar. "Barry, you would've loved the look on Luke's face. Pure dread."

"Bowtie needs to learn his place," said Barry Lee. "Luke Tanner's already got Sulka on his tail; he doesn't need a preacher too."

"Sulka probably encouraged Bowtie," Patrick said. "I suppose Tanner has some confessing to do, anyway."

"I almost didn't let that preacher in." The sheriff crossed his feet on a low end table. "Luke's gone through enough already. Bowtie will just push him over the edge."

"To insanity," Judge Baker added. "I've seen it before. Prisoners never come out of that jailhouse the same as they went in."

Jonathan Hendricks fisted his cane. "Luke Tanner has more endurance than a mule. If anything, he'll come out of that jail more stubborn than he went in. Bowtie won't make a difference—no, sir."

"I think Tanner will come out kicking and screaming, same as he went in," said Barry Lee. "He'll have a mean ol' grudge on Baker and Bilt, and anyone else who helped convict him. I don't think Bowtie will get him to confess."

Sheriff Bilt blew out a puff of smoke and his keys swung on his belt when he shifted his legs. "Sixty days is a long time. 'Specially since I haven't had a single other rebel in that jail since Tanner got there. There hasn't been a wink of company 'cept for Dan Sulka. Luke wouldn't even let his own wife and son visit him till last week. Then they sat there for two full hours talking. Little Wesley was plumb bawling by the time they left."

"Wesley's a sensitive child," said Mr. Hendricks. "He used to put crazy ideas into Galen's head."

"A penny parcel," Patrick said with a shrug. "I've said it from the beginning: Orphans don't belong in regular homes. Society can never fully accept them. Tanner does all those children disfavors by trying to rescue them . . . ."

"I guess that's a matter of opinion," Bilt said.

"Do you suppose that little orphan girl will ever get over her past?" Barry Lee asked.

"Not likely," said Patrick. "Not after living with Tanner's anger for three months."

"I'm not sure it was Tanner's anger that drove the little girl away," the sheriff said. The men looked at him with surprised stares. "He's incarcerated for snooping around the orphanage; I never proved abuse."

Jonathan Hendricks tapped his cane on the floor. "Of course you did! It was written all over that little girl's face the day we found her in the orphanage. If you say that penny parcel is unharmed, you can't recognize abuse when it's staring you in the face."

Sheriff Bilt cocked his head. "I never said she hadn't been abused, Hendricks. You're putting words in my mouth."

"There! Then I say Tanner gets another trial after his sixty days are over, this time for victimizing an innocent child."

The apothecary fell quiet. While Dale Gildey brewed another pot of coffee on the potbelly stove, the sheriff debated whether he wanted to stick up for Luke Tanner. "I guess it'd take a lot of work to prove that accusation in court."

"I think you're defending a criminal," Patrick Cummings said with a shake of his head. "I'd never expect that from you, Bilt."

"I'm not defending anyone. If you ever find Tanner guilty of abuse, I'll be the first one to lock him up and throw away the key."

"But you don't think he's guilty," Judge Baker said.

The sheriff shrugged. "I'm just saying you're going to spend a lot of time and money proving anything."

The apothecary remained silent for several moments. At length, Judge Baker began a fiery political discussion and the case of Luke Tanner was abandoned.

Luke leaned back on his cot, crossing his leg. He was exhausted after a long, intense conversation with Thomas Harris.

Mr. Bowtie leaned forward on his knees, his eyes squinted. "You don't believe I can help you at all, Mr. Tanner?"

"I appreciate your efforts, but I'm not willing to risk more time in jail because of unwise persuasion and force."

"I'm not considering using any kind of force!" exclaimed the preacher. He tossed his head back and banged it on the cell hall wall. Luke cringed at the hard knock.

Mr. Bowtie's voice lowered. "Look, Tanner, I've got some things to explain to you. I originally came to Galesburg because I wanted a career in acting, with a side job as a jeweler."

Luke bit his cheeks to keep from smirking at the five rings that adorned the preacher's right hand.

"My acting career never took off, and jewelry couldn't support me full time. So I took a job writing for the newspaper. Nasty, competitive work, but I learned the system and survived. I competed against the very men who have written about you and Ashley, and I can tell you more about all of them than you want to know."

Luke couldn't think of anything he wanted to know about those invasive, lying reporters.

"I became quite successful at my job, but only because I did exactly what the other writers did: victimize and ruin lives. So I quit. Decided to become a preacher so I could do as much good in the town as I could."

The preacher began to cough and his face turned tight and red. Just when Luke went to offer him a drink, Mr. Bowtie took out his handkerchief, wiped his face, and continued.

"Now the only writing I do is for the good of decent, Christian mankind," he said. "I haven't had anything published since I quit the newspaper, but I promise you that I have the power and endurance to fight the best of the best. Tanner, if I can get an article about you published in the newspaper, it could change your life. That's the kind of action I plan on taking; not any kind of force.

Luke stared at the man. He tapped his fingers on the wall. "And how are you planning on getting an article accepted, since the entire society hates me? Do you really think the newspaper will print an article pointing out the good about me?"

"It won't be pointing out the good." The preacher smiled broadly. "It'll be pointing out the truth. And I dare say you'd agree there's a great difference between the two."

Luke thought about the vast difference between lies and truth, and wondered if the society of Galesburg could distinguish between the two. "I don't know why you're interested in helping me, or why you, of all people, think it's so important that Ashley come back to my home. But I don't know if I'm interested in taking the step of getting her back just yet. It's true that the papers have told a lot of lies about me, but that's not the reason I'm here."

Mr. Bowtie's brows rose.

Luke tried to ignore the preacher's surprised glare. "I would like nothing more than to have a second chance with Ashley, but there are some things that have to be changed in my life before I'm willing to have Galesburg's attention turned to me. As soon as you print one of those articles, everyone will be watching to see if the good is actually true. Do you understand what I'm saying?"

"You've messed up and you want a chance to fix it," echoed the preacher.

Luke blushed. "Yes."

"And that's the reason you're behind bars? Because you've messed up?"

Luke glanced away and every nerve in his body crawled with annoyance. He could hardly look at the preacher without laughing as he remembered the things the apothecary circle said about him. It was no wonder he despised Mr. Bowtie—he certainly had reason to.

"Anger got me here, not Ashley," Luke said through a clenched jaw. "And I would appreciate it if you would leave that in the past, Mr. Harris."

"It seems to me that it's still in the present, Mr. Tanner. You're still here."

Luke wished he would allow himself to get angry enough to injure the preacher. Instead, he pretended a calm smile. "Mr. Harris, I beg your pardon, but I don't think this is any of your concern."

"Then it's impossible for me to help you." The preacher leaned back, throwing his jeweled hands in the air.

"I reckon I'm not asking for your help."

"You're shooting yourself in the foot."

Luke wanted to tell Mr. Bowtie to go away and never come back. What kind of a criminal did the preacher think he was, anyway? Visiting him in jail was just his way to earn some kind of favor with God—it was nothing short of an insult.

"I really can get that girl back to you," Mr. Harris said at length.

Luke saw something like arrogance that made him even more annoyed.

"I'm not sure I believe you," Luke said.

"You're not giving it a very good try."

"You say you would write true articles about me. How do you even know enough about me to write a single sentence? I've never so much as spent a day with you."

"That's exactly why I'm prepared to commit my time to finding out the truth about you."

"So this isn't just about writing articles." Luke sniffed. "You want to find out about my life so you can exercise some sort of power over me."

"If you want your reputation and your daughter back, you'll have to pay the price."

"What price?"

"You'll have to spend time with me and be willing to convince me of the truth."

"You won't believe me just on my word, 'ey? I have to convince you."

Mr. Bowtie shrugged. "Honesty is reflected in life, Mr. Tanner."

Luke shook his head. "After all I've gone through, you certainly aren't doing me much of a favor, Mr. Harris. You have no idea what's been going on in my life lately, and you're just as bad as the rest of the town—taking me for an insensitive criminal."

"You admitted yourself that your own actions got you behind bars."

"You're using it all against me." Luke forced himself not to explode. "Just because I somehow found my way into Galesburg's jail doesn't mean I need your charitable acts. I would appreciate it if you would leave me alone."

"You're resisting my meddling," said the preacher.

"Meddling is a wounding sin," Luke fired.

"Faithful are the wounds of a friend, sir."

"I don't count you among my friendly circle."

"And I don't reckon you're a person I'm very interested in helping. I'm offering my assistance by the good command of God, and I'm asking very little in return."

"Very little that's not your business."

Mr. Bowtie's eyes narrowed. "Are you that afraid of telling the truth, Mr. Tanner?"

"No. I'm afraid of what you'll do with it."

"I'll write articles! Good, solid articles that will put the people of Galesburg on your side and ultimately bring that little girl back into your arms to give you a second chance."

"Thank you." Luke nodded. "But I'm not interested. I get out of jail in a couple weeks, and I'll be happy to take care of my own problems when I feel like it."

Mr. Bowtie took up his round, black hat. "Very well, then. I have no more to do or say here. I'm afraid I can't help you until you're willing to help yourself, Mr. Tanner."

With a sniff, the old preacher escorted himself out the cell hall and slammed the bars behind him.

Wesley timidly made his way to the jail on Monday afternoon, carrying his book belt and forcing himself to breathe through the anxiousness. School had let out early that day, and he had decided to visit his father.

Sheriff Bilt answered the rap on the jailhouse door with a surprised look on his face. "Afternoon, son," he said with a hint of compassion in his voice.

Wes took off his hat. "I'd like to see my dad."

"Come on in." The sheriff took the key from his belt and unlocked the cell hall door, nodding for his young visitor to go through.

Wes got a lump in his throat when he thought of his father being constrained by those bars and that key. He slowly walked down the row of cells, trying to muster up the courage to face his father.

"Tanner," the sheriff bellowed, "you got a visitor."

The last time Wes had visited the jail, when he came with his mother just over a week ago, his dad had insisted he didn't want any visitors. This time, the hall was quiet.

When Wes approached the cell, he saw his father sitting on a stool in the corner. His weathered face melted when he set eyes on Wes.

"You all right with a visitor?" Sheriff Bilt said gruffly.

Luke nodded and the sheriff left.

"Hey, son," Luke said, his voice thick. He neared the bars and rested his forearms on them.

"I hope you don't mind that I came," said Wes, carefully looking into his father's face.

"Does your mama know where you are?"

"She doesn't know school got out early. I figured I had time to see you for a couple minutes."

"How's Cherish?" Luke asked.

"She's fine." Wes listened for disgust or hatred in his father's voice, but he didn't hear any. "Granddad and Grandma have been staying with us. I've been helping Granddad take care of the farm."

"Good. I'm proud of you."

Wesley tried to fight the tears that threatened to choke him, but they fell anyway.

"You're a good boy, Wes."

Wes rubbed his damp cheeks with the backs of his hands. "I . . . uh . . . I made a new friend at school. Galen doesn't really like me anymore, so I found this boy named Jimmy, and we've kind of become friends. He's really nice, Dad. His dad doesn't let him come to our house, but we get along really well at school."

"Why doesn't his dad let him come over?" Luke asked, swelling with insult.

Wes shrugged. "Jimmy said he didn't think you'd want him coming over."

Luke looked astonished. "Why wouldn't I?"

"I don't know."

"What's Jimmy's last name?"

"Sulka."

Luke closed his eyes and shook his head. He said with an ashamed chuckle, "Tell Jimmy I said it's OK if he comes to visit you."

"Really?" Wes smiled. "Thanks, Dad. You won't be sorry. He's even more responsible than Galen."

"I bet he is. I can't wait to meet him."

"You will soon. Mom counts the days till you come home, and she says there's not many left. Then this whole mess will be over with."

Luke's shoulders slumped. "I still have some work to do, Wes. Getting out of jail isn't going to fix everything."

"What do you mean?"

"I have some things to work on with you and I have to repair some things with your mother. I don't know if the hospital will give me my job back and it's going to take a long time before people in Galesburg trust me again. I don't want you to expect everything to be back to normal right away."

"We have enough money, Dad. Granddad's been working some, and Mom's been sewing a lot, and I've been doing all sorts of stuff to earn money. So you don't have to worry about the bills. It's OK if you don't get your job back right away."

Luke smiled and it warmed Wes to the tip of his toes. "Getting used to being a family of four again is going to be difficult too."

Wes's cheeks stung.

"I know you're lonely without your sister," Luke said gingerly. "When I get home, we're going to have to deal with that."

Wes swallowed hard, wishing he could avoid this subject. "I've been playing with Jimmy, so it's OK." He said that only to remove the guilt from his father's shoulders. He was not OK with Ashley's absence—it haunted him every waking minute of his day.

"Son, Jimmy isn't the same as a sister."

"I don't really want to talk about Ashley."

Luke tossed Wesley's hair and forced himself not to curse at the jail bars that kept him from embracing his son. "That's fine."

"Ashley must be lonely too. Sometimes I have dreams that she's crying in the orphanage, and calling me, but I can't get to her. I don't think she realized when she ran away how much she'd miss us."

"Do you really think she misses us?"

Wes shrugged. "I would if I were her. She doesn't have a family anymore, and that's got to be terrible. Remember how Ashley named our filly Kate, after her best friend?"

Luke nodded.

"Jimmy's little sister is KatieAnne—Ashley's best friend. They adopted her right before we adopted Ashley. If Ashley would've stuck around with us for just a little bit longer, she could've seen her best friend at school every day. We could've had best friends in the same family."

"I can't believe Dan Sulka adopted a penny parcel," Luke said, shaking his head in surprise.

"I don't like it when you call her that."

Luke looked at him. "I don't either."

Wes smiled. Certainly something had changed in order for his father to change his mind about penny parcels.

"We have to keep that situation in prayer," Luke said. "God has a plan for Ashley's life."

Wes swallowed, his throat filled with emotion. "God's not very nice sometimes, you know?" He looked up at Luke.

"It can seem that way sometimes. But Wesley, God isn't the one who put me in jail—you have to understand that."

"I know. It was that good-for-nothing sheriff who wouldn't listen to you."

Luke sniffed. "That's not true. I'm in here because I chose to go to the orphanage after Bilt told me not to."

"You did?" Wes looked up, his eyes searching his father's face.

"Yeah. I made the wrong choice."

Wes turned away, hiding his face from his dad. All this time he had been defending his father at school, assuring everyone there was no way his dad could be guilty.

"But that's all behind us now. My sentence is almost up and then I'll be home to straighten things out. I need you to be the man of the house for just a couple more weeks." He winked at his son. "I can't wait to get home to your mama. I miss her."

Wes took out his pocket watch and checked the time. "I'd better go. School's usually out by now."

"Can't have your mother worrying about you." His father patted his shoulder with a regretful sigh. "Take good care of the place, and I'll see you soon, 'ey?"

"OK."

"Give Mom and Cherish a kiss for me."

"I will."

Luke squeezed his son's hand. "I love you, son."

"I love you too, Dad."

When Wesley stepped onto the street again, he brushed tears from his face, smiling from ear to ear.

The Lord upholdeth all that fall.
—Psalm 145:14

TWENTY NINE

Changes

Tell me the truth, Jolie." Grace bit her lip. "How's Ashley really doing?"

Jolie sighed. "She's sick. She has a terrible cough."

"You should take her to the doctor." *Take her to Luke. Maybe he could fix her real problem.*

"Mrs. Harms says we'll do that if she gets much worse, but I'm not sure there's much the doctors can do about it. She needs you, Gracie."

"Don't say that." Grace's voice broke.

"She talks about you all the time and asks when you can come visit her. She's very sorry she ran away."

"But she still hates Luke. Nothing would be different. If Ashley came back here, she'd end up returning to the orphanage again because she isn't capable of living with my husband."

Jolie took Grace's hand. "You have to forgive Luke."

"I can't." Grace shook her head. "I want to. I've prayed about it. But it's going to take some time."

Jolie's brow creased. "Why is it his fault? What did he do to her?"

"Nothing." Grace sniffed. "That's the problem. He never did anything to her or with her or for her. He demanded that she be perfect in the eyes of the public. He looked for results before he invested any time into her. He didn't love her. That's just it. He did nothing."

Silence came over the sisters.

"Jolie, sometimes I wonder why God smites some people with every plague in the Book, and leaves others alone," Grace said at length. "I'm blind, and barren, and on top of that, the little girl I gave my heart to has been taken away. I can't help but feel totally betrayed. It doesn't seem fair."

"It's not."

Grace closed her eyes and rested her head on the back of the rocker. She realized that her hands were fisted again . . . they always fisted when she talked about Ashley. It was as if her whole being were trying to hold on to an inkling of hope that was trickling through her fingers like water.

"I don't think I'll ever be able to love an orphan again." Grace's voice faltered. "I'm not strong enough."

"I don't think I would be, either." Jolie touched her sister's hand.

"I wish there were some easy solution."

"A magical wave of a wand and Ashley's back at home, 'ey?"

"No." Grace sniffed. "Ashley coming home wouldn't fix anything. Something needs to change in Luke. You know, there are a hundred Scriptures that should mean a lot to me right now, but the only one I've been able to relate to is the one about the man who found a pearl and sold everything he had to buy it. I know that's supposed to be a picture of God's kingdom, but I can't help but think of Luke and Ashley. If only Luke were willing to give more than a penny for the pearl of great price, so much could be different."

Luke awoke to the sound of boots on the floor. He sat up and saw that the sun was just beginning to cast light on the jail cell. He squinted in the shadowy darkness and saw his breakfast tray sitting on the stool in the corner. Strange. Sheriff Bilt always slid meal trays under the bars.

Luke rubbed his face, staring at the breakfast tray, which contained the same thing he had eaten for the past fifty-four days: bacon and corn mush.

As he was reaching for the tray, something caught his attention in the cell hall. He glanced toward the bars. His door stood open. Luke hesitantly neared it and poked his head out. The hall door was also open wide.

Luke heard papers rustling in the office and the sheriff was whistling. He bit his lip. He did still have six days before the end of his sentence, didn't he? Why would Bilt leave both doors unlocked? Surely it wasn't meant as a token of freedom.

Luke stood there for a long moment. A strange feeling came over him and made him want to run. It would be easy to slip away and go home six days early. Nothing was stopping him. For the first time in fifty-four days, there were no bars or locks or keys restraining him from doing what he pleased. He was a free man.

Luke grabbed the cell door and slammed it shut. His heart raced as he sat on the cot and dropped his head in his hands.

He heard Sheriff Bilt come down the hall, his keys tapping briskly against his leg. The man appeared in front of Luke's cell.

"Why did you do that?" Luke said loudly. "Why on earth would you leave the doors open?"

"You shut it yourself?"

"It was a setup, wasn't it? You were trying to keep me here."

"I can't believe you pulled it shut yourself."

"What do you take me for?" Luke rose to his feet and came to the bars. "I haven't so much as threatened to escape from this place. It's been fifty-four days, Bilt!" His head began to pound with anger. "Fifty-four days I've sat on this cot and paid my just sentence. Now you're trying to keep me here longer, and I almost gave in to your scheme. That was a pathetic thing to do."

The sheriff shook his head. "I expected you to run. My office door was shut; you had every chance in the world."

"You take me for a good-for-nothing criminal." Luke took his hands off the bars and they were shaking. "Don't ever do that to me again. That wasn't a fair play." He started toward his cot and then turned back. "Why on earth would you do that?" he yelled.

"I don't know." Bilt's face was smeared with guilt. "I wanted to see if you were going to live up to the upper crusts' predictions."

"Really?" Luke shook his head in disgust. "What do the upper crusts say about me?"

"I thought you'd run, Tanner."

"That's not what I asked!" Luke could feel himself spiraling out of control. "What do the upper crusts say about me?"

"They predict you'll come out of here angrier than ever, and you'll hold grudges against everyone who helped get you here."

"Like you? Are you afraid of me?"

"No." The sheriff looked ashamed. "I just wanted to see if you'd stand the test."

"I can't believe you." Luke raked his hands through his hair. "I could have you put on trial for improper treatment of a prisoner."

Bilt gave a heavy-hearted laugh. "I reckon Baker wouldn't care what kind of accusations you brought against me."

"So Galesburg's sense of justice is distorted by the upper crusts, too? That's disgusting."

Silence came over the jail and Luke dropped his head against the wall and closed his eyes. His body was tense and his hands were sweating.

"Something's changed in you, Tanner," Bilt said at length.

Luke shot his eyes toward him. "I've never been so tempted in all my life."

"But you didn't do it. I thought you'd run."

"And end up back in here? I may have done some things wrong, but I'm not stupid."

"You never gave thought to consequences before." Bilt reached for his keys and stuck them in the door.

"Don't come in here," Luke warned.

The door swung open.

"Bilt, I'm warning you. I'm too angry to deal with you being in here right now."

A rush of vulnerability made Luke's heart pound hard in his chest. Bilt walked in and shut the door behind him. Luke turned away.

"You're not getting out for six days," the sheriff said in an uncharacteristically quiet tone.

Luke raked his hands through his hair. For the last fifty-four days, he had been separated from everyone by a set of bars. Having Bilt so close with nothing in between them was almost too overwhelming to handle.

"I want you to explain to me what's made you a changed man." Bilt took a step closer.

Luke tried to swallow the emotion that choked his throat. "I wish you wouldn't come in here."

"Are my keys getting to you?"

"No." Luke glared at the sheriff. "I'm afraid I'll murder you."

Bilt laughed. "I'm not too worried about it."

Luke stood silently still for a long time.

Tell him what happened to you.

I don't want to. He'll just take it back to the apothecary and smear me some more.

"Did Bowtie make the difference?" Bilt's voice rang deeply.

Luke had to force himself not to cover his ears.

"No." He kept his face toward the wall. "God did it. But why do you want to know? Are you just trying to find something out about me that the public doesn't know so you can gain popularity by reporting the most recent gossip?" His voice was loud and accusing.

Are you afraid of what he can do to you?

Luke breathed deeply. He knew the right answer was no, but he didn't know if he could honestly say it.

Yes.

Son, he can't do anything to you. You're Mine.

"I got right with God," Luke said before the sheriff had the opportunity to answer him. He turned toward the man but couldn't look him in the face. "If you want to know why I changed, read the Bible."

Sheriff Bilt gave Luke a bewildered stare.

Luke shrugged. "I don't know what else to tell you. I didn't change anything on my own."

"But something did change."

"Yeah. My point of view."

"What point of view?" The sheriff's tone was almost mocking.

"My point of view about God. I didn't understand what He wanted from me." *God, I can't believe I'm telling him this.* "My whole life I've been trying to make myself someone I'm not. I didn't understand that God wants me because of who I am, and not what I can do or who I can become."

The sheriff stared at Luke. "You're going to be a different man when you walk out of here, aren't you?"

Luke shrugged.

"Are you gonna try to get that penny parcel back?"

"I don't know." He nodded toward Bilt's handcuffs. "I've had enough of this to last a lifetime."

"I agree—an orphan isn't worth all the pain."

Luke's eyes narrowed. "That's not what I meant. I'm going to do everything in my power to get Ashley back, but I'm going to limit it to my power. I'm not going to overstep my bounds this time."

"You never did hurt her, did you?"

"No. But I did a lot of things wrong."

"You say the Bible brought you to all these conclusions?"

"No. God did. He used the Bible and several other things to give me freedom."

A knock came on the outside door and the sheriff reached for his keys and let himself out of the cell. He smiled at Luke through the bars. "Six more days and I'll have the power to give you your freedom. Wish your sentence weren't so long."

Luke sniffed. "I reckon if you would've let me out in thirty days, you would've been in your grave by now."

Sheriff Bilt laughed heartily as he walked away.

Abide in Me, and I in you. As the branch cannot bear fruit of itself, except it abide in the vine; no more can ye, except ye abide in Me.

—John 15:4

Going Home

When Luke Tanner was released from jail on Monday, November 14, he felt as if he were walking out of a haven into a war zone. A large group of townsfolk had gathered on the boardwalk, and he sensed their contempt the second he set foot outside the jailhouse. Though he tried to enjoy the fresh breeze and the sight of Galesburg's busy streets, his heart was overwhelmed with defeat. The very buildings seemed to sigh with displeasure.

Although deep snow covered the ground, the sun shone on Luke as he rode home. He had borrowed the sheriff's horse, and the saddle creaked with every step the old gelding took.

Wes would be at school when Luke arrived home, and he was almost afraid to face Grace without Wesley's bubbly distraction. His wife had always assured him that she was committed to him, but she had been unusually cold the one time she came to see him in jail. *I can't blame her for hating me.*

Luke passed the church on his way out of town, and for the rest of the ride, he was plagued with a strange feeling of guilt and urgency. He had thought a lot about what Thomas Harris had said about getting Ashley back, and the more he pondered it, the more he realized that he would eventually have to give the preacher a chance.

But that made him incredibly nervous.

Luke had publicly loathed the preacher's strange ways ever since he came to Galesburg. Sitting with that man for any length of time would be something close to torture. But ignoring the prodding he felt inside was equally miserable. And if Mr. Bowtie really could get Ashley back, it would be worth the hours spent with that half-crazy preacher.

The Tanner homestead was brilliantly frosted and utterly quiet when Luke laid eyes on it. Ice clung to the pasture fence and the branches of the trees, creating a glittery wonderland. A lamp burned in the parlor window and Luke wondered if it were lit for him. *Probably not.*

A surge of loneliness swept over Luke as he tied the gelding to the hitching post and trudged to the front door. He had waited two full months to be standing on this porch, but now he felt unsure. For the first time since Ashley had run away four months ago, her absence haunted him.

Luke pushed open the front door and smelled the tantalizing aroma of baking bread. A fire crackled in the hearth and Cherish sat on the sitting room floor, roughly turning the pages of a book. Luke heard Grace working quietly in the kitchen.

He took a deep breath and slowly closed the door. He winked at Cherish as he walked by, and the ten-month-old looked back at him with alarm.

"I'm home, Gracie," Luke called as he approached the kitchen. He stopped at the threshold. Grace turned, her face revealing a dozen mixed emotions.

"I wasn't sure when you'd be here," she said. She cleared her throat. "Is Cherish all right?"

Luke crossed the kitchen and put his hand on Grace's shoulder. She tried not to move away. "I want to know how you are."

"I'm fine." She wiped her hands on her apron. "Dod and Mum left this morning."

"Gracie, I've missed you."

"I've missed you too." Her voice was cool. "How'd you get home?"

"I borrowed Bilt's horse."

"I didn't know if someone needed to pick you up. I didn't have a way of asking you."

"That's all right. I didn't expect you to worry about that on top of everything else." Luke's heart raced with despair. Grace was standing right in front of him, yet she was a thousand miles away.

"Cherish has grown a lot," she said, resisting the temptation to cry. "She's pretty shy with people she doesn't know."

"I suppose I've messed up that whole bonding thing, 'ey?"

Grace faltered. He had taken responsibility.

"I'm not sure I'm going to get my job back, so I'll probably have quite a bit of time at home over the next couple months. I'll have to get to know her again."

"She's started to pull herself up on things."

Luke tried to smile but couldn't.

Grace gripped her apron and leaned against the counter. Luke dropped his hand to his side and studied her.

"Wes made a new friend in school," she said.

"Jimmy Sulka?"

"How'd you know?"

"He told me about him."

"When?"

"He came to see me a couple weeks ago. I had a good talk with him."

Grace paused. "What does that mean?" *He told him everything the sheriff did wrong and he did right,* she thought.

"Grace, things are going to be different," he said boldly. He wanted to touch her but refrained. "I'm going to change."

"What do you mean by that?"

Luke paused, trying to find the right words. "This was all my fault. I thought you knew that."

She softened. "You blamed everyone else."

"I was wrong." He paused. "Do you hear me? I was wrong. I landed in jail because of my own wrongdoing, and the sentence was just. Exactly what I deserved. That's why I served every minute of it without trying to plead my way out. Sixty days, Grace . . . sixty days! You have no idea what kind of misery I've been through."

She was quiet, and the silence rang in his ears. Luke touched her shoulder and saw that her eyes were filling with tears. "I have no idea what kind of misery I've put you through, either."

She brushed her cheeks.

"I'm sorry," Luke said. "What else can I say to you? I'm sorry. I want you to forgive me. I've been a fool, and I've hurt a lot of people. I pushed Ashley away from the beginning, and even though I didn't abuse her physically, I did emotionally. I drove her away." A painful groan escaped from deep inside him. "I know everything I've done wrong."

"I want to forgive you, Luke," Grace said just above a whisper. "But that doesn't mean that I can just forget it all."

"I know."

"And just because you're home, that doesn't mean our life is fixed."

"I realize that too. And I take full blame for everything that's happened. But God has forgiven me, and I need you to forgive me too. I can't live with the guilt if you don't."

She sniffled and brushed her cheeks. "You've hurt me and Wes and Ashley deeply, and that's not going to disappear overnight."

He felt anger surge and pushed it away.

"I want us to be able to move on, but it's a process. Just like when we lost Emma. It took me three years to get past her death. Ashley's only been gone for four months." Grace's voice broke, and she turned away, wiping her tears.

Luke didn't know if his embrace would help or hurt, but he engulfed her in his arms. "It's OK to be sad about it." He kissed her head. "I'm not going to rush you through your grief."

Grace choked on her tears. "Luke, she was my little girl. I loved her so much. I don't know why she ran away."

Because of me, Luke thought, but he wasn't brave enough to say it.

"I want her back," Grace said. She began to relax in Luke's arms. "I've begged God every night for the past four months. I just want my little girl back."

Luke remembered Mr. Bowtie with a heart-throbbing pang.

"Jolie came over the other day. She said that Ashley is very sad and she's beginning to get sick."

"How sick?"

"She has a cough and she's weak. She doesn't play with the children much, just keeps to herself. I think she regrets leaving here. But she didn't know what she was doing."

Luke shook his head. "She knew. She wanted to get away from me."

"But she didn't understand the consequences. She thought she could go back to being an orphan and forget us, but she can't. She loves us too."

"She loves you and Wes and Cherish. I never let her love me." Luke sighed. "I never gave her a reason to want to."

"I feel so bad for her," Grace said, breathing deeply. "She and Wes were like blood siblings, and she clung to me as if I were really her mother."

"You were, Grace." Luke squeezed her gently. "You were a wonderful mother to her."

"It's all so hopeless now."

"God's the only one who can help us."

"But . . ." She paused. "We don't really deserve His help."

"You mean I don't deserve it," Luke said. "You're right, but that's not the point. God forgave me, Grace—fully. I found the truth a few weeks ago and God's told me a dozen times over that He's forgiven me."

"Do you really think He'll give us a second chance?"

"I don't know." Luke's mind danced with thoughts about the preacher's plan. "But I promise you I'll do everything in my power to get one."

"Do you have a plan?"

"I don't know. Maybe."

Grace stood still for a long time. Luke wished she would melt in his arms the way she'd always done before. But she was holding back.

"I'm glad you're home," she said at length.

"Me too," he whispered, then kissed her head. "And I'm glad you're here waiting for me."

Luke stared around the pastor's entryway with raised brows, examining the heads of deer, moose, elk, rabbit, and pheasant mounted on every wall. He sat in a stiff, green chair that was covered with a black bear skin, the bear head dangling very near his neck. He sat cockeyed, trying to avoid the ugly teeth that lurked by his shoulder. Little glass bowls filled with large rings and glazed rock necklaces sat on the dressers and end tables, and a freakish collection of insects in jars lined the dusty baseboards.

Luke was staring at the spiders, caterpillars, snails, fireflies, mosquitoes, and ants when the front door opened, and in stepped Thomas Harris.

"Mr. Harris," Luke exclaimed, standing with a sigh of relief at leaving the bear head behind.

"Mr. Tanner, it's nice to see you!" The old preacher set his hat on the fainting couch and shook Luke's hand. Then he knelt by the insect jars and tapped on each one, laughing. "What do you think of my collection of creatures? I'm guessing you've been here for a while, judging by your sleeping horse. Did you have time to identify my little friends?"

"I've only been waiting a few minutes," Luke said with a rush of regret that he had chosen to visit the preacher in his home.

"Well, you missed a great sight, then. I've been collecting my creatures for two years now. They thrive on entertaining the company." He gave a hearty laugh and stood. "And what have you come for today?"

"To talk."

"Excellent."

Luke followed Mr. Bowtie down a narrow hall.

"I've kept up on the news lately. Newspaper hasn't been this interesting in twenty years."

Luke didn't know what kind of news Mr. Harris was speaking of, but he was too preoccupied with retreating from the inhospitable foyer to ask questions.

The preacher led Luke through a dimly lit sitting room and into a small office which had an orange door. The old man dropped his black gloves onto a littered desk and pulled out a fancy, high-backed chair for his guest. Luke took the seat quickly, his stomach churning with the musty smell of old books and cigar smoke.

"Excuse the cigars," said Mr. Bowtie, brushing a black stub into the wastebasket. "I talked with a man who smoked earlier this morning."

Luke nodded and the old man laughed, dropping his suit coat onto the hat rack. He sat behind his desk and said with a nod, "Now, what is it you've come to discuss, Mr. Tanner? Our meeting didn't end so well last time, but now that you're on the other side of the bars, perhaps things have changed. How can I help you with your troubles today?"

Luke swallowed and said slowly, "I want to get Ashley back."

Mr. Bowtie rubbed his double chin. "Why? Because it'd be good for your name, or because you really want her back?"

Luke was taken back. "You're a bold man, Harris. I think you're condemning me."

"Not at all." The preacher laughed a sort of mocking chuckle. "I just want to know the truth."

"Because I want a second chance."

"At loving her or making her behave?"

"Loving her," Luke responded firmly.

"Very well." The preacher pulled a sheet of paper from his desk drawer and dipped his feather into ink. "Tell me about Ashley."

Luke sat back in his chair. "What do you want to know?"

"How did she become an orphan?"

Luke blinked in surprise. "I have no idea."

"Really? You had her in your home for three months and you never asked?"

"Look, we already know I made some mistakes. I'm not here to have them all pointed out."

"Ah, but that's the way to healing," Mr. Bowtie said. "We must know our mistakes before we can correct them."

Luke's eyes narrowed. "What are you getting at?"

"I want to know everything about Ashley that you know about her. I want to know what kind of a girl she is."

Luke thought quietly for a moment. Just as he took a breath, the preacher interrupted him.

"Leave out personal opinion and behavioral patterns. I only want the facts about the girl."

"Ashley is eight years old," Luke began cautiously.

"When's her birthday?"

He blushed. "I'm not sure."

The preacher wrote on his paper. "Continue."

"She's lived at the orphanage her entire life, and she's in the second grade."

"She's in the second grade this year, or she was last year?"

Luke faltered. "I'm not completely sure. I think it was last year." He continued, "She likes to sew with Grace, and she's good at caring for the baby. She doesn't like to take baths, and for some reason she's deathly afraid of getting strapped."

The preacher looked up. "You don't know why?"

"No."

"I see."

Those words brought fire to Luke's cheeks. "I do know that she has a particular hatred for men."

"And why's that?"

Luke shrugged. "I could never pull that out of her."

"Meaning you tried, but she wouldn't let you?"

"I didn't exactly try. I guess I never really addressed the situation. I just tried to figure it out by watching her."

The preacher's eyes squinted in the dim lighting. He bit his cheek. "But if this is as long of a list as you can come up with, it doesn't appear to me that you watched her very much."

Luke stiffened. "What more do you want?"

Mr. Bowtie looked at the list he had written. "I want to know why she doesn't like to take baths, what grade she's actually in this year, when her birthday is, who her parents were, and why she was orphaned. I want to know what her favorite color is, if she's ever heard about Jesus, and what's her favorite thing to eat. I want to know what she's afraid of and why, what makes her happy or sad, and if she has any pleasant memories." The preacher paused. "I also want to know what forced her to make the decision to escape from your home to the shelter of the orphanage. Answers to those questions would make me happy, sir."

Luke threw his hands in the air. "Well, I'm sorry that I don't have answers to all those questions."

Mr. Bowtie looked back at his paper. "So am I. I'm sorry for your sake."

"Thanks for the sympathy."

The preacher's brow rose. "I'm not sympathetic. Only disgusted."

Luke sniffed. "Well, that makes everything easier."

The preacher laid his feather down and looked at Luke. "I don't know what you're looking for, Mr. Tanner, but if you're trying to make your life easier, you're going to be disappointed. Getting Ashley back will only make your life a lot harder. We might as well give up trying now if all you're interested in is making things easier."

Luke forced himself not to lash back. "I just don't appreciate being made to feel guilty," he said, trying to remain composed.

"I guess only guilty folks would fear that," returned the preacher.

"I am guilty, Mr. Harris." Luke clenched his teeth. "I'm already dealing with a lot of guilt with the town and my family and everyone else."

"Good." Mr. Bowtie leaned back in his chair. "Only the ones who know the bad news will ever understand the good news."

"What good news?" Luke asked.

"The gospel of the grace of Jesus Christ."

"I know all about that."

"Perhaps not. If you still carry guilt, you haven't properly understood. When you've been washed in the blood of Christ, sin is no longer yours to claim. The world will constantly try to get you to accept shame. But shame is not part of God's gospel."

Luke looked at Mr. Bowtie skeptically. "I don't know that I believe that."

"I wish you would. It'd make your burden a lot lighter."

Luke half smiled. "Mr. Harris, I don't think you know what this kind of burden is like."

The preacher chuckled. "Mr. Tanner, I don't think you know much about me."

I know all I want to know, Luke thought.

"You have a big job ahead of you." Mr. Bowtie tapped a massive, red ring on the desk. "Getting Ashley back is going to be difficult, but keeping her once you get her will be harder."

"You really think we can convince Mrs. Harms to let Ashley come back?"

"Oh, your worst enemy isn't Mrs. Harms. It's the people of Galesburg. They'd rather see you hanged than let that girl back into your house."

"Hanged," echoed Luke, almost amused.

"With no trial," added Mr. Harris. "First we must convince Galesburg of your ability to raise Ashley properly. I'd advise you not to approach that woman until you have at least half of the town's sympathies aimed toward you."

"That'll take until next Christmas," Luke moaned.

"I hope not," said the preacher. "We only have five weeks."

"Five weeks?"

"Didn't you read the paper this morning? The Galesburg orphanage is closing in five weeks. And when it does, Ashley will either be given to another family or moved out of state."

Luke's heart began to throb. "Why is it closing?"

"The papers say it's because of financial issues."

"But how can we get Ashley back that quickly?"

"My plan is to write articles telling the truth about you and your family. My guess is that it'll take three or four good, solid articles to get Galesburg's eyes opened to the facts."

"You should start right away, then."

"I'd love to." The preacher smiled. "Unfortunately, I don't know enough about you to write even one paragraph. I have to get to know you."

Luke cringed. "And how are you planning to do that?"

"I suggest you come three times a week: Mondays, Wednesdays, and Saturdays. I accept visitors from eight o'clock until six, so long as I'm not called elsewhere. Be here on those days every week, and we'll see how far we get."

Luke's eyes narrowed. "If you're planning to write three or four articles and the orphanage closes in five weeks, I'm afraid you may have to take my word for some things."

"Just as soon as I trust that your word is truthful, I'd rather do it that way."

Luke stared at him. "You're calling me a liar."

"No." The preacher cocked his head. "But I can't give you the name 'truthful' until I'm sure it belongs to you."

Mr. Tanner felt his frustration rise again. "What makes you doubt me?"

"I can see that your life has changed over the past two months. But that doesn't mean you've gripped the full truth of the gospel enough to live it out to a performance-based, love-starved orphan."

Luke's heart skipped a beat. "How'd you know about performance?"

"I reckon any man who's lived the performance lie himself can recognize someone else in the same situation."

Luke squinted. "So you saw it all along?"

"I've been watching Ashley ever since the first Sunday she sat in your pew."

"And you didn't warn me?"

Mr. Bowtie threw his head back in laughter. "You?" He looked at Luke as if it were a joke. "You're the man who's mocked me ever since you started attending my church. You've spoken against me in the apothecary and warned others not to take my advice. Do you honestly expect me to have approached you and told you what you'd gotten yourself into by adopting Ashley?"

"I expect, as a man of God, that you would 'warn the wicked of his way to turn from it,'" Luke replied, humiliated.

"I seem to remember attempting that in my sermons, Mr. Tanner. I don't know that you ever heard much, except the one message about reputation that foolish Joseph Plain preached. You aren't very good at hiding your disapproval of me."

Luke stared at the coffee-stained calendar on the preacher's desk. He wished Mr. Bowtie would continue to rebuke him so he could get everything off his chest. Instead, the preacher lowered his voice.

"Every man deserves a second chance," he said. "You've hurt my ministry and my name over the past eight years. But that was because you've been deceived. That's why I'm willing to help you."

Luke glanced away.

"I believe you're capable of raising Ashley because of what I've heard from one of my close friends."

Luke's eyes shot toward him. "Who?"

"Dan Sulka." Mr. Bowtie nodded. "He thinks very highly of you."

"Pathetic." Luke grit his teeth. "I can't believe he talked to you about me."

"Why?" the preacher smiled. "Dan may be an upper crust, but he's only concerned for your good. He told me you were set free well before you left that jail cell."

Luke eyed the man with suspicion. "And that's enough for you to think I'm capable of raising Ashley?"

"I reckon any man who's been set free from his own prison is capable of helping someone else find freedom."

"Ashley will be an entirely different kind of challenge."

"But one that God will make you capable of handling if it's His will." Mr. Bowtie tapped his fingers on the desk. "I've been praying about you apothecary men, but I didn't expect you to be the answer to my prayers."

The idea that he could be an answer to anyone's prayers made Luke squirm.

"Freddy came to my office once. He's a fine young man with a lot of potential. But he hasn't been back since that first time, and pursuing him proved to be futile." The preacher shrugged. "All in God's timing, I suppose. Now that you're here, perhaps the others will learn to trust me."

"I'm not an experimental subject for some kind of method of yours," Luke said with distaste.

Mr. Bowtie smiled. "Quite the contrary."

"And I'm not interested in being listed in some reference paper as a lost soul you saved from the pit of destruction, or whatever you call it in your sermons."

"I wouldn't dream of listing you on my résumé," Mr. Harris said with a boisterous laugh. "I assure you I'm interested in your welfare, not how much I can build my reputation by knowing you. I gave up on that quest a long time ago."

As the clock struck nine, Luke reached for his hat. "I appreciate your time, Mr. Harris," he said, his skin prickling with discomfort.

"I'll see you again this week?" asked the preacher.

Luke nodded hesitantly.

Mr. Bowtie smiled. "I'll be looking forward to your visit."

Luke set his hat on his head and stepped out into the chilly autumn air. He straightened his coat, feeling conspicuous as he walked down the preacher's front stairs.

And the loftiness of man shall be bowed down, and the haughtiness of men shall be made low: and the Lord alone shall be exalted in that day.

—Isaiah 2:17

THIRTY ONE

Christian Men

Wesley sat on a bench outside the schoolhouse door, books settled on his lap. His feet were cold in the November chill, but his hands were sweaty. He felt like crying, but held back his tears for the greater drive of manliness and clenched his jaw in anger instead.

The big carved door swung open, and out stepped Mr. Minden. He glanced at his slumping student. "Into the carriage, Master Wesley."

Wes boarded the fringe-swaying coach and sat with a rebellious bang on the leather seat. Mr. Minden stepped up next to him, and his full beard brushed against his green overcoat. His big hands grasped the sharp leather reins as he clicked to the jumpy mare. "Trot on!" came the gruff command, and Wes's books sprawled on the floor with the initial jerk.

Not a word was spoken between the schoolmaster and the student all the way home. It was unnecessary for Mr. Minden to scold, and futile for Wes to beg mercy, and both of them knew it.

Wesley was ready to give the world a brutal tongue-lashing. He decided that he would be undaunted by discipline when he arrived home. But his stomach still churned as they neared the Tanner property.

"Is your father at home?" asked Mr. Minden as he headed down the lane.

"No." Wes purposefully left out the "sir."

"Then I'll trust you to explain your situation to him when he returns."

Wes's heart leapt.

"You're an honest boy. I trust you to tell every detail fairly."

The wheels jerked to a stop in front of the hitching post. "If your father thinks it's necessary to talk to me," Mr. Minden said gravely, "I'll be at home this evening."

Wes slid off the seat and stepped onto the porch. Mr. Minden turned his carriage around and the horse trotted away. Wes paused for a moment before reaching for the door handle. Then he bravely stepped inside. The smell of hot candle wax permeated the house.

"Is that you, Luke?" Grace called from the kitchen.

Wes swallowed hard. "It's me, Mom."

"Wesley? My goodness, have I lost track of time?"

The lad set his bag on the floor without offering the correct time.

"Did you have a good day at school? Are you cold from walking home?"

"Not really," mumbled the lad, answering both questions. "Is Dad working?"

"No. As far as I know he's still visiting with Mr. Harris."

"Again?"

"Take care of your sister for a while, would you, Wes? She wants someone to play with."

"I don't want to," he replied, setting his lunch box on the table.

Before Grace had the chance to rebuke her son, the back door clicked open and Luke stepped into the kitchen.

"Did you have a good time with Mr. Harris?" asked Grace.

Luke chuckled. "As good a time as anyone can have sitting for four hours with that crazy preacher. I wish I didn't believe him when he says he can get Ashley back."

"He can get Ashley back?" Wes blurted.

Luke plucked a baby potato from a pot on the stove. "'Course, every undertaking comes with conditions. I have to meet with this man three times a week till he decides I'm capable of raising Ashley."

The lad gasped. "He doesn't think you are?"

Luke quickly redeemed himself. "He just wants to get to know me better, that's all."

"But he really can get Ashley back?"

"No promises."

There was a pause, and as if it suddenly occurred to Luke that school wasn't supposed to be out yet, he said seriously, "Wes, why are you home at quarter past twelve? Didn't you have a full day at school?"

Wes shrugged. "Mr. Minden brought me home."

Grace stopped scraping at the wax on the counter.

Luke stared at his son. "Do we need to talk about something?"

"Not really." Wes remembered Mr. Minden's trust in his honesty and he panged with guilt.

"What happened?" Grace prodded.

"I got angry with someone at school."

"Did he get sent home, too?"

"No."

Luke nodded toward the sitting room. "Let's talk, Wesley."

"We don't need to, Dad."

"If you got escorted home from school, we most certainly do need to. Did you get in a fight?"

"Sort of."

"Did you hurt someone?"

"I don't think so."

Luke squinted. "Wes, you're not telling me everything."

Wes sighed. "We boys were having a snowball fight at break, and Jimmy Sulka threw a really hard snowball and hit me in the face. Then we both got mad and went at each other. When Mr. Minden came out, he told us to stop, but . . . I didn't." He looked straight into his father's dark eyes. "Jimmy deserved a lot more than he got, Dad."

Luke took off his coat and hung it on a cupboard handle, nodding toward the sitting room again. This time, Wes went straight to the brick seat in front of the fireplace.

"I want to know why Mr. Minden didn't tan your hide at school instead of sending you home to me," Luke said as he settled into his rocker in front of the fire.

"'Cause I'm in fourth grade!" exclaimed Wesley.

"If you're too old to be strapped, then you're too old to be fighting. Wes, did you hit Jimmy?"

"He had no right to throw that snowball."

"Answer my question."

"Yeah."

"And that's why Mr. Minden sent you home? Why didn't Jimmy get sent home if he fought, too?"

Wesley's cheeks burned and he wrung his hand against his trousers. "I was yelling at him."

Luke looked at him seriously. "What were you yelling?"

Wes stiffened and looked away.

"Answer me, son."

"Nothing." Wes bit his lip.

"I see. Well, I have a feeling this fight was more intense than you're admitting. Mr. Minden hasn't sent anyone home for at least a year." Luke leaned forward on his knees. "Wesley, are you sorry for the way you treated Jimmy?"

"No."

"Son, now don't be unreasonable. Jimmy is your friend. It was wrong of you to cause trouble for him."

Luke waited for a reply, but Wes didn't even flinch.

At length, Luke clenched his jaw. "If you don't start showing some signs of remorse, we're going to take a trip upstairs, Wesley."

Again, Wes made no response.

"All right, then." Luke leaned back in his rocker. "If you won't talk to me, we'll set things straight without words. Go upstairs; I'll be right there."

"That's not fair," Wes said quickly.

Luke cocked his head. "I gave you plenty of chances. Don't argue."

The boy opened his mouth again, but his father shook his head. Wes bounded up the stairs, slamming the door on his way.

Luke went to the kitchen and sat on the tall stool beside the stove. Cherish was slung with a quilt over her mother's shoulder, sucking her fingers and babbling to herself.

"Is everything settled?" Grace asked.

"No." Luke watched his wife move busily from the stove to the sink. "Gracie, sometimes I don't know what to do with him. He's such a good boy nine out of ten days, but sometimes he's downright rebellious."

"Did he tell you the rest of the story?"

"I think I heard about half." Luke shook his head. "I can't believe he hit Jimmy Sulka, of all people. I would expect him to hit Galen or one of the other boys who have been so cruel to him, but not Jimmy. I wanted to just talk to him about it and see what was going on in his heart, but he won't even let me do that. What do I do when he won't respond to words?"

Silence fell.

Luke pushed his hand through his ruddy hair. He was searching to express the ache of guilt he felt. At length, he said bluntly, "Gracie, I can hardly justify disciplining a son who is often more Christlike than I am."

Grace stopped peeling a carrot.

Luke swallowed hard. "How does that work? My son is always more humble and ready to change than I've ever been, yet I'm strapping him for one display of anger. At least Wes tells Jimmy Sulka what he thinks. I used to talk behind people's backs until everyone believed the worst about them. Which does more damage?"

The kitchen was quiet.

Grace finished peeling the carrot, then said, "Luke, Wes needs you to be consistent. You can't fail him because of your own guilt."

"It still doesn't seem right." He took the strap from its place by the back door and started out of the kitchen with a heavy sigh. "I just don't understand how my situation turned out like this."

Entering Wes's bedroom, Luke found his son lying on his back on the bed with his hands under his head, gazing absently at the buckling pinstripe wallpaper under the window. When Luke shut the door behind him, Wes didn't turn.

Luke set the strap on the dresser and sat next to his son. A wave of regret swept over him as he glanced at the ten-year-old sprawled on the bed. Luke wished a father's role could always be painless.

"Wesley, you're a remarkable son," he said quietly.

The boy pressed against the wallpaper with his thumb.

"I never thought I'd have a boy with such good character."

The defiant stiffness seemed to soften.

"The way you took care of Mom and kept the farm running while I was in jail was really impressive. And you kept up your grades at school. I know this has been a hard few months for you, but I'm really proud of you."

Wes's eyes shifted to his father and his brow creased.

"I'm especially proud of how well you obey, and how much hope you have that Ashley will come back someday. You give me so much hope."

Wes's heart pounded with guilt and regret.

Luke felt color coming to his cheeks. "Wes, I don't feel like I can make you apologize to me until I've apologized to you. I've let myself do some things that aren't what God wants in a Christian man's life. I haven't done my part in chasing after God for many years, and I've let my friends and my job get in the way of our relationship. I know you feel pressured to perform when I have company in our house, and that's not the way I want it to be anymore. You should be able to make mistakes, no matter who's watching."

Wes breathed slowly.

"I did the same thing you did today when I handled Ashley forcefully and chose not to have compassion. I need you to forgive me, so you and I can learn how to be Christian men together."

Wes was quiet for a moment. His eyes searched his father's earnest brow wildly, and he finally stumbled, "I forgive you, Dad." He felt particularly sinful when the tables were turned.

A relieved smile creased Luke's face. "The last two weeks I was in jail, I did a lot of Bible reading and talking things over with God." He stared at his son and suddenly wondered how many times his pride had hurt Wes before. "I want you to know that I love you because you're my son, and I'll always be proud of who you are. I don't want you to ever be afraid of disappointing me, 'ey?"

Wes's eyes dropped to the blue-and-white quilt on the bed. He said hesitantly, "Dad, Jimmy hit me with that snowball 'cause I called his sister a penny parcel."

"You used that term?" Luke said with surprise.

"That's what everyone else calls them. That's what I am. Jimmy says KatieAnne isn't a penny parcel 'cause she's adopted, but that's not true. Nobody can ever outlive that name."

Wes put his arm over his head to hide his face from his dad.

"Wes," Luke said slowly, "you're not a penny parcel."

A tear came to the boy's eye.

"Did someone call you that?"

"Everyone calls me that." His eyes burned. "Galen does it almost every day. It's true, Dad; it's true for me and KatieAnne and Ashley. There's nothing anyone can do about it."

"That's a cruel thing for anyone to say. The reason orphans were given that name is because people said that they were only worth a penny. That's not true. Not for you or KatieAnne or Ashley. You and Ashley are worth the world to me. I couldn't make enough money in my entire life to pay what you're worth."

"But that's not true in society," Wes answered quickly. He looked at his father. "That may be true for you, but that's just 'cause you're my dad. Nobody else cares."

"Sometimes what the world thinks of you isn't what's important."

Wes wiped his cheeks.

"People will call you names for the rest of your life, Wes, but the only names that really matter are the ones God's given you."

"God hasn't given me any names."

Luke touched his son's leg. "There's a long list of names God's given you, son. He talks about you in the Bible all the time."

Wes looked at his father with surprise. "Me?"

"Yeah. He calls you the apple of His eye and His delight. He calls you truthful and righteous and full of honor. God loves it when you keep Him company."

"Keep Him company?"

Luke winked at him. "He likes to watch you and be with you every day. When a Person like that is so committed to you, it doesn't really matter what everyone else thinks, does it?"

Wes was trying to understand. "I've never heard God call me one of those names."

"I reckon He wants you to hear, then. Just like you hear Galen calling you a penny parcel, God wants you to hear Him call you a beloved son. Galen's telling lies, Wes; do you understand that?"

The boy timidly shrugged.

"God only ever tells truth. It's your choice who you believe."

Wes brushed tears from his cheeks. "Did God tell you all that about me?"

"He sure did." Luke smiled.

"That's pretty nice." Wesley's smile slowly began to show. "Do you really believe it?"

"I've always believed that about you."

Silence came over the bedroom and Wesley thought for a long while about God's opinion of him. Then his eyes drifted toward the strap leaning against the dresser. "What should I do about Jimmy?" he asked.

"I reckon he deserves an apology," Luke replied. "Don't you think so?"

"I guess."

Luke saw his son's eyes on the strap and he asked seriously, "Do you think I need to use that, son?"

"Yeah," Wes answered without pause.

"Good. Then it's already done its work. As long as you know that you deserve it, it's as good as over with."

Luke stood and winked at the boy as he reached for the door handle.

"I wish I hadn't gotten into that fight," Wes said with a regretful sigh.

Luke smiled. "'Forgiven' is also a name God gave you, Wesley."

Luke stormed out of Mr. Harris's small house and slammed the door. Muttering under his breath, he shoved his hat onto his head and boarded his buggy, slapping the horse's back with unusual roughness.

"Break the third commandment," he grumbled. "That preacher is more insane than I thought."

Driving home in the brisk November weather, he had a chance to think about what Mr. Bowtie had said, and he become angrier by the minute.

"How did it go?" asked Grace when Luke stepped into the house.

He tossed his coat aside. "Even if that man were able to get Ashley back, I would be a lunatic by the time I made it through these meetings. I'm not going back."

She dropped her scissors onto the table. "You have to. It's our only chance."

"Well, it's not a feasible one! Mr. Harris is plum crazy, and he's going to drive me mad if I have to sit in his office again. That man may be a preacher, but that doesn't mean he has the right to tack extreme sins on my head."

"What did he say?"

"He said I broke the third commandment by bearing the name of Jesus and acting falsely. He said my prideful actions have contradicted Christ."

"That's breaking the third commandment?"

"The third commandment says, 'Thou shalt not take the name of the Lord thy God in vain.' Bowtie says *take* actually means *bear,* and when you become a Christian, you bear the name of Jesus. He says I've borne that name in vain."

Grace was quiet. At length, she said quietly, "So maybe you don't agree with him on that. Did you think about what he said before you got angry?"

"Think about it! There's nothing to think about."

"Luke, we all do things wrong."

"So you think I'm that much of a sinner too?"

Grace smiled. "I think it's worth considering—for all of us. I think you should give Mr. Harris another chance."

He threw his hat onto the table. "I won't. No amount of hopeful promises of getting Ashley back could make me subject myself to that man again."

"It's only the third time you've seen him."

"And that's three times too many."

Grace lapsed to silence, and Luke slumped into his rocker in the sitting room, fuming.

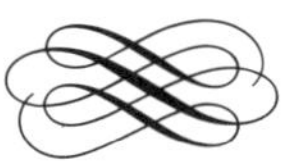

The Sulka family met the Tanners as they were going into church the next morning, and they exchanged friendly greetings. Luke tried to disguise his annoyance as they entered the church, but when he laid eyes on Mr. Bowtie, his anger bristled again.

"Morning, Tanner," the preacher greeted at the doorway, offering his hand to Luke.

"Mr. Harris." Luke nodded, keeping his hands on Cherish and ignoring the invitation to shake. He couldn't look the man in the eye, so he stepped into the little white building uneasily, hoping his rejection was not obvious to the general public.

Although Luke attended church that morning strictly out of duty, he hadn't managed to harden his heart so well that the message didn't sink in. Mr. Bowtie gave a quiet sermon, contrary to his customarily fiery speech and hard challenges. He appeared to be grieved. He didn't stumble over the words in the hymnal or go off on aimless tangents in the middle of his sermon. He was calm and direct. Focused and quiet. His words were deliberate, and his stories were sweet.

When he finally closed the sermon, the congregation hesitated before departing, as if they were not completely satisfied. Somehow, every word he'd said still hung in the air and many found themselves taking the sermon to heart.

Including Luke.

Although Luke fought to ignore the way the preacher's words pricked at his spirit, he couldn't stand before God when conviction bombarded.

In spite of previous resolutions, Monday morning found Luke at Mr. Harris's house. When he stepped onto the porch, he wasn't sure why he was there or what had forced him to arrive again, but he knew he had to go. He had to sit through another session, to search himself again, to be prepared to admit what he saw in himself.

Mr. Bowtie seemed just as surprised to see Luke as Luke was to have come. The old preacher welcomed him with a hearty hug and eyes that almost shimmered with tears.

Although Luke began this meeting with new resolve and a relatively light heart, it turned out to be the most difficult session thus far. Mr. Harris asked questions that made even his own cheeks blush and tore Luke's heart out of his chest.

Five hours of scrutiny resulted in mingled panic, awkwardness, and tears. Luke broke under the hand of the Almighty as contempt and lies and bitter pain was brought to light by the gospel of truth.

That evening, after the children were asleep and the house was quiet, Luke and Grace sat in the sitting room. Except for the blazing fire in the hearth, the house was dark. The two of them busied themselves with handwork and newspaper, silence weighing heavily between them.

"Mr. Harris will start writing those articles soon," Luke said.

"What makes you think that?" Her glassy eyes seemed to stare right through him.

He chuckled with embarrassment. "He has to—that old preacher knows more about me than I knew about myself a month ago."

"Is that what he's waiting for?"

"I don't know." Something told Luke that Mr. Bowtie wanted more than just to know enough about him to write about. He seemed to understand the hidden parts of Luke that needed to be redeemed.

"He sounds like a genuine person," she said.

Luke tapped his foot on the floor. "He's sincerely devoted to helping people in need. On top of everything else, he's trying to find me a job."

"What kind of job?" Grace asked.

"I don't know. But our savings are going to run out soon; I have to find something."

"I can sew more this month."

Luke shook his head. "You've done enough work over the past two months. I'll earn the money."

"But I need you around the house."

That was the first time since his incarceration that Grace had expressed a desire for his company. Luke's heart melted.

"I won't be gone a lot. Hopefully I can get a job with flexible hours, like I had at the hospital."

Her voice sounded lonely. "We can live off of savings for at least two more months."

"What if Ashley comes back home? If I don't work now, I'll have to work when I could be here, with her."

"I need you here now." Grace set her jaw, but tears arrived in her eyes.

Luke's tone softened. "I'm here for you. I'm not leaving again."

"I don't want you to get a job. Cherish is becoming so mobile I can't watch her by myself. Mum's been helping for the past two months, and Ashley was here before that. If you go back to work, I'm going to have to hire a nanny."

"Do you really think so?" Luke always knew it would come to that, but Grace had been capable of handling the baby so far.

"Unless she's on my hip, I worry about her constantly. She's ten months old already; she's going to walk soon. Already she crawls faster than I can keep up with. I want you to stick around so you can train her to stay close to me. I can't do it myself."

"I'm not asking you to do it yourself," Luke said tenderly.

Grace tried to hold back her tears, but they came without permission. Luke went to her and pulled her onto the couch, where he wrapped his arms around her. She melted into his embrace.

"I don't want to hire a nanny," Grace said, her voice faltering. "I want to raise her myself, like I would've raised Emma."

Her words stung Luke's heart.

For a long time the couple sat silently, listening to the crackling fire and the howling wind. When Grace mentioned Emma, memories of the tiny grave and the lifeless little girl burned into Luke's mind, filling him with the intense desire to grieve.

"Do you remember our baby?" Grace asked in a whisper. "Do you remember what she looked like?"

"She had brown hair." He could hardly hold back the tears. "And a face exactly like yours. She had perfect hands and feet, and skinny legs."

"Tell me why she died."

"I don't know." He swallowed a lump of emotion.

"I never saw her."

Luke closed his eyes and the memories flooded. He remembered the day he lost the heartbeat, but argued with Dr. Gere when he said the baby was dead. Luke had brought Grace home, expecting her to carry the child for the last two months, but she became sicker and sicker. Her sight began to weaken and before they realized what was happening, Grace was blind and Emma was stillborn. Luke had held Emma's tiny, lifeless body for only a moment and then he had given her to Dr. Gere, who wrapped her in a blanket and took her away. Grace was sobbing on the hospital bed. Luke had walked away.

At the funeral, Luke let Granddad Jackson bury his baby, refusing to look inside the casket. For two full years he distanced himself emotionally while his wife grieved. It was easier to forget than to face it all.

"She was the same age as Ashley," Grace said. "The day we buried our baby, Ashley was three days old. That was the day her parents died."

Luke looked at her, confused. "How do you know that?"

"Jolie knows Ashley's story. She told me Ashley was orphaned on the second of February, 1903. Ashley's parents died in a fire when she was three days old. If we could've known about Ashley then, she would still be our little girl today."

"We can't regret the past," Luke said with heart-throbbing disappointment.

She clung to his arm. "No. But I don't think it's coincidence that God gave us another chance."

With a little girl, he thought. *A second chance so this time I won't walk away and leave Grace to grieve alone. Another chance so this time I'll fight for her life instead of denying that she's dying.*

"I don't know if I can do it," Luke said, feeling the weight of extreme expectation.

"No, but you can try your hardest and let God do the rest."

"Gracie, if I could take back the last seven years and start over with you pregnant with Emma—"

"Then we would never have adopted Wes or Cherish or Ashley," she interrupted. "I don't regret it, but I want to finally move past it all."

He rubbed his forehead and said with a pang of helplessness, "I don't know how."

Grace squeezed his hand. "You can start by telling the preacher everything so he'll write those articles and we'll have a chance of getting Ashley back before the orphanage closes. Just get real with yourself, so God can work it all out."

Get real, he thought. *By knowing truth. Ye shall know the truth, and the truth shall make you free.*

Luke thought about the man he'd been when Emma was born: selfish, unhappy, and wounded. Then, his only hope to survive was to run from the loss. Now, seven years later, he had the opportunity to be that same man, building his walls higher in an attempt to run from the emptiness Ashley left in his heart.

Instead, Luke felt the incredible sensation that he had finally climbed every stair to the top of his castle, and for the first time in his life, he was staring the prisoner in the face.

For the Lord heareth the poor, and despiseth not His prisoners.

—Psalm 69:33

THIRTY TWO

Courage & Resolution

As articles about the closing orphanage bombarded the newspapers, the weeks seemed to fly and yet drag on. In spite of Luke's hope that Mr. Bowtie would soon begin his own articles, the old preacher showed no desire to hurry. Luke was forced to exercise extreme patience as he counted down the days before the orphanage closed.

In the meantime, Mr. Harris suggested Luke set up an office on his property and build a business as a country doctor to those who couldn't make it to Galesburg for medical care. Glad to put his mind to something constructive, Luke converted the old shed into a small sickroom. He had very few patients at first, but he was glad for the distraction, even more than the hope of income.

Surrounded by early-morning fog on the corner of Fifth and Main Streets, Thomas Harris walked up to a tall, dark wooden door. Tapping on the knocker, he straightened his tie. A black-capped gentleman peeked through the mail slot.

"I'm Mr. Harris," the preacher said. "I met with the editor last week concerning a submission that was promised to be published in tomorrow morning's paper." He thrust a small stack of papers through the slot. "Please see to it that the promise is kept."

The mail slot clicked shut and Harris turned away, then boarded the carriage that waited for him on the street. He slapped Luke Tanner's knee and gave a resounding laugh as they drove away.

"Well, what do you think of that?" exclaimed Jonathan Hendricks as he entered the apothecary on Monday morning, December 12. He slapped a newspaper on Barry Lee's knee and tossed it into the old man's hands. "Another article about Tanner. The media must've found out a lot more about him."

Barry looked at the front page of the crinkled paper and read a small headline tucked into a sidebar: "More on the Tanners."

The article took up the entire sidebar of the front page. As the banker read the first few sentences to himself, he shook his head. "Whoever's discovering all this, he sure is convinced of it. He claims Tanner never abused that little girl. This guy seems to think she came to Luke that way."

"Whoever this writer is, I agree with him," said Sheriff Bilt. "I've said for months that you'd have a hard time proving an abuse accusation against Tanner."

Patrick Cummings looked at Dr. Gere with narrowed eyes. "Gere, you've worked with Tanner for years. What's your opinion of his claim to innocence?"

The doctor shrugged. "I can't say that he ever abused a patient. And he had to have some kind of devotion to those penny parcels to keep adopting them."

"It's got to be an upper crust who's writing the articles," Barry Lee said.

"What makes you think that?" asked Patrick.

"Tanner wouldn't claim his innocence to anyone but an upper crust. And nobody else would try to defend him. Men of our class are the only ones willing to stand up to the community. It's probably one of those *Reporter* editors who show up here occasionally. Most of them don't have time to come to the apothecary every day, but they're upper crusts nonetheless."

"I knew the truth would eventually come out," Mr. Hendricks said, tapping his cane on the floor. "But I still can't say I appreciate Tanner landing himself in jail."

Barry Lee raised his hand and Dale threw him a cigar. "Luke Tanner deserves to fall from the upper crust, but at least he's not an abusive criminal."

"Of course she can go!" exclaimed Mrs. Harms as she hurried down the stairs, sweeping her long nightgown behind her. "For goodness sake, Elizabeth, she hasn't been out of the orphanage since she's been back. It's the last Sunday she'll be in Galesburg. You might as well let her be seen in public one more time."

She hollered for Hattie, who appeared instantly. "Get my Sunday dress, and tell the cook to have tea in my office in ten minutes. Elizabeth, don't stay long after church, and be sure you keep her next to you."

The orphanage was in a state of utter disarray, and Mrs. Harms was in a panic. She fluttered about the old building, up and down the stairs, through the hall, behind the kitchen doors, and in and out of her office like a worried hen, barking out commands and scolding any child who happened to be in her path. It was December 18, the day that had been looming in the distance for three weeks. It was the day all the older orphans were leaving.

Gretchen, Melissa, Ashley and Della sat in their bedroom, all slumped on their beds. Melissa was crying and Gretchen sat in silence, listening to the sobs and trying to hold her own tears back. Ashley turned away from both of them and looked out the window at the misty morning, and she felt her heart chill inside of her.

"Well, it's settled." Elizabeth bolted through the bedroom door and went to Ashley's bed. "Get up and put your shoes on, Ashley. You're going to church."

When the little girl didn't respond, Elizabeth grabbed her arm and pulled her from the bed, straightening her like a wrinkled quilt. "Gretchen and Melissa, you must pack yourselves. The train leaves in an hour, and you have to walk to the depot. Hattie's coming to get you directly, so get your clothes and put on your shoes. Ashley and Della, I'll be back for you in five minutes. Be ready or we'll be late!"

When Miss Elizabeth left the room, silence fell again.

Gretchen stood slowly and picked up the small cloth bag that was beside her bed. She dropped a pair of stockings and her pinafore into the bag and tied it shut. "Come on, Melissa," she said, nodding at her sobbing friend. "Whatever isn't packed we'll have to leave behind."

"I don't care. I don't want to leave."

Ashley stuffed her foot into her boot and glanced at Melissa. "It'll be OK," she said. "At least you get to go with Gretchen."

Melissa's head popped up. "How do you know we won't get to the orphanage and immediately be taken away by strange families who only want someone to help with their work? We may not even live together for a week!"

Ashley sat beside her friend as Della started toward the door. Before another word of comfort could be spoken between the girls, they heard Miss Elizabeth tapping up the stairs. Ashley quickly tied her shoes.

"Come down, girls," said Elizabeth, taking Melissa's hand and pulling her off the bed. "Hattie's ready to leave, and the boys are waiting. Ashley, take your coat or you'll be cold on the walk. Melissa, get your bag and come quickly."

The girls hurried down the stairs to the foyer. Ashley watched from the bottom step of the staircase as her friends were wrapped in coats and mittens and set in line for the depot. Gretchen held her head high and scolded the boys for looking so sad. Melissa briskly wiped her wet cheeks.

Miss Hattie opened the door and a gust of cold air made the orphans step back in surprise. Melissa moved out of line and threw her arms around Ashley's neck, sobbing. "Goodbye, Ashley. I hope everything works out for you."

Before Ashley could return the hug, the orphans marched away.

The younger five orphans left for church as soon as the older ones had been sent to the depot. There was no hint of tear or trace of hurt on any of their faces, for everyone was too hurried to cry.

When they arrived at church, Ashley, Della, and the four little boys were taken to a bench in the back and told to be quiet. But none of them could sit still. Elizabeth struggled with whispers and fights until the last prayer had been said. Then she commanded six-year-old Walter to "take hold of my dress, and mind you don't let go." She grabbed Ashley's hand and marched out, with all the little orphans sulking behind her.

Miss Elizabeth executed her departure with speed, obviously eager to get Ashley far from the church and the Tanner family. But when she stopped in the sanctuary to scold the littlest boy for his wiggles, Ashley fixed her eyes on Wes.

He was sitting at the opposite side of the church, on a bench by the wall, holding Cherish. When Ashley looked at him, he caught her eye.

"Are you leaving?" he mouthed.

She nodded.

"When?"

"Saturday."

Wes looked away. He seemed to be trying to hold back tears. Ashley hadn't seen her brother since she went away, and the sight of him put a deep ache in her heart.

When he looked back at Ashley she was being pulled away by Miss Elizabeth. He nodded at her in farewell.

As he disappeared from her sight, Ashley's heart sank in her chest. She was caught without breath for the excruciating loneliness.

Back at the orphanage, Mrs. Harms was in just as serious a state of disorder as she had been when they left. Miss Elizabeth sent all the children to their rooms for the afternoon.

"Don't you want to play tea?" asked Della.

Ashley shook her head and lay silently on her pillow.

"Please, Ashley? You can use my doll."

"I don't want to."

"It might be our last time," said Della, who was completely poker-faced, even on such a heart-wrenching day. "We have to leave next Saturday, and Sundays are the only days we get to play tea."

A tear slipped down Ashley's cheek. She stared out the window at the pretty winter scene of a misty mid-morning in Galesburg. The trees were robbed of all their leaves and light snowflakes fell on the fancy-topped buildings and brick streets. The fence that bordered the orphanage was highlighted with frost that clung to its rail pickets, and the bare rose stems and sage sticks in the garden bobbed with a chilly breeze.

Ashley gasped when she saw the steam of a train puffing behind a row of buildings. Courage and resolution finally played their last, and before she could stop herself, she broke into sobs.

I was not in safety, neither had I rest, neither was I quiet: yet trouble came.

—Job 3:26

THIRTY THREE

Miracle

Sunday afternoon passed slowly for the Tanners. Luke and Grace talked most of it away, and Wes buried his nose in his latest reading assignment, *Robinson Crusoe*. But no matter how many times he read chapter four, he neither understood nor was interested in its content. He was too busy thinking about Ashley.

When Grace put Cherish to sleep around three o'clock, Luke went to the barn, saddled his horse, and went for a ride. That day's article was the last to be published before Ashley left, and the thought of it left him in a sour mood. Human power had done its best, and Ashley was now at the mercy of a miracle.

Dusk fell early that evening, and the nighttime chill crept over Galesburg before Luke realized that a storm was coming on. He returned home near seven o'clock and put his horse away, settling the animals in the barn in preparation for a cold night. He did Wes's chores and locked the vacant chicken house door before going to the house.

As he walked up the path from the barn to the farmhouse, he was surprised to see a horse with a pretty sidesaddle tied to the post by the porch. *A woman riding alone at this hour?* He hurried to the back door.

"Gracie, who's here?" Luke asked as he entered the kitchen.

His wife stood at the stove. "Oh, Luke, I'm so glad you're here. Jolie came from the orphanage about an hour ago. We have to leave right away."

"Why?"

"It's Ashley."

Her tone chilled his heart.

"She took sick right after church this morning, and she's been vomiting for hours. Jolie said Mrs. Harms won't let any of the other children into her room; she's afraid Ashley has typhoid or measles."

"Typhoid or measles . . . fiddlesticks. There hasn't been a case of either of those diseases in Galesburg for five years, and Ashley hasn't been outside the orphanage long enough to catch anything." His thoughts raced. *Ashley can't handle another burden.* "How did she start getting sick?" he asked.

"I don't know," said Grace. "Jolie's in the parlor; you can ask her everything. But we need to go right away. Ashley needs to see a doctor."

"Grace, unless I've been specifically summoned by Mrs. Harms, there's no way I can go to that orphanage and try to treat the girl."

"Luke, Ashley needs us. Just go talk to Jolie, please?"

Luke stepped into the parlor and nodded at the dark-haired woman who sat with Cherish on the couch. "How are you, Jolie?"

"Fine." Strands of hair were scattered about her face. "Did Grace tell you about Ashley?"

"A little bit. Tell me exactly what's wrong."

"She got sick after church this morning, and by the time I arrived for dinner, she was vomiting. I sat with her all afternoon, but she wouldn't respond to me. Mrs. Harms is at a loss for what to do."

"Why doesn't she take her to the hospital?"

"She's bankrupt as it is."

"Did she ask you to come get me?"

Jolie shook her head. "But I really believe you're the only one who can help her. If you and Gracie come to the orphanage, I'll take care of Wes and Cherish."

Luke sat in a chair across from her and laughed sarcastically. "I'm not going to spend two more months in jail, Jolie. I can't go unless Mrs. Harms calls for me."

"But she won't," Jolie said.

"Then she'll have to find some other way to treat Ashley. I'd no sooner set foot inside that fence and Bilt would have me cuffed. I'm sorry."

"We could go to the sheriff and explain the situation," she persisted. "I'm sure he'd let you go."

Jolie set Cherish down and the baby crawled to her daddy. He lifted her onto his lap. "I'm not willing to embarrass myself by begging. If Mrs. Harms wants me, she knows where I live."

"Mrs. Harms would rather let Ashley die than come to you for help."

"Exactly my point."

"But that doesn't mean she wouldn't accept it if you were there. I think you should try."

Grace stepped into the room carrying a tray of coffee cups. She set it on the ottoman and offered a cup to Luke. He sipped from it, holding Cherish's hand back.

"Are we going?" Grace asked.

"No," Luke said.

She sat on the couch. "Why?"

"Because I don't want to sit behind bars for the next two months! Am I the only one who's concerned about that?"

"I don't think the sheriff would throw you in jail."

"I do." Luke poured a splash of icy milk into his cup. Then he let Cherish drink. "Besides, our going there might make Ashley worse. She'd probably go into hysterics at the sight of me."

"At least she wouldn't be alone," Grace said with desperation in her voice. "She needs to see us doing everything we can for her."

Memories of Emma sent a painful rush to Luke. He closed his eyes and sighed heavily, thinking about Ashley suffering alone in the orphanage, then pondering the consequences of going to her.

The words *penny parcel* danced in his brain and he pushed them away. He had decided weeks ago that he would give his life for Ashley.

"I'll go to the sheriff's," Luke said, then he sucked in his breath, wondering if he would regret that decision. If nothing else, the embarrassment of seeking another man's permission was part of the price he was willing to pay. *To fight for her life instead of denying that she's dying,* he thought. He would do it for Grace as much as Ashley.

By the time Wesley was summoned and Cherish was dressed, Luke had the sleigh piled with blankets and waiting outside the front door. He tied Jolie's horse to the back and made a wool-blanket cocoon for the baby on the front seat. When Jolie, Grace, and Wesley came out, they quickly boarded and Luke clicked to the gelding.

The late-evening air was cold and the wind blew sharply from the east. The bells tied to the lantern post on the sleigh jingled merrily, and the blankets radiated heat on everyone's laps, but the atmosphere was as cold as the wind. Suspense hung over the sleigh like the thick clouds that brought the storm, and no one said a word.

When Luke stopped the horse in front of the jailhouse, the temptation to retreat almost overtook him. He tied the reins on the scroll and jumped down, kicking the mud off his boots as he reached for the door handle.

As he stepped inside, the smell of burnt coffee made his stomach churn. He had awakened to that smell every morning for sixty days.

Luke heard the sound of a key turning the moment he set foot in the foyer, and he forced himself to remain calm.

"Evenin', Tanner," Sheriff Bilt said with surprise, dropping the keys onto his belt loop as he came out of the cell hall. "Can I help you with something?"

Luke stood frozen for a moment, and the speech he had rehearsed during the drive vanished from his brain. "I need to work something out with you," he said after an awkward pause.

Bilt nodded toward the office.

"I'd just as soon be quick with it," Luke said with a shake of his head.

The sheriff stood with his legs spread, as he had done every time he stood outside of Luke's cell.

"Ashley's sick."

"The orphan?"

Luke was glad he hadn't called her a penny parcel.

"Yeah. My sister-in-law told us she's been vomiting ever since church this morning. She wants me to go to the orphanage and see if I can help."

The sheriff looked at Luke with a raised brow. "Did Mrs. Harms call for you?"

"No, and that's why I came here." Luke nodded toward the handcuffs on Bilt's belt. "I'm not interested in coming back here. I refused to go unless you and I could make some kind of a sidebar to our agreement."

"You want to strike a deal?" said the sheriff, looking amused.

Luke nodded.

"All right." Bilt's lips curled into a smile. "You make sure Mrs. Harms doesn't lose her head, and you can do whatever you want. I'd just as soon have you treat the girl than see her land in the hospital with Gere. Do it civilized, though, with Mrs. Harms's approval."

As Luke left the jailhouse and boarded the sleigh again, he felt as excited as a four-year-old at Christmas.

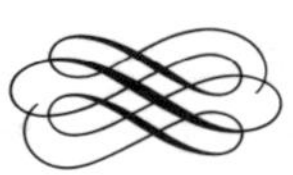

When the Tanner family arrived at the orphanage, Luke jumped from the carriage and tied the horse to the post. His hands were trembling more from nervousness than from cold.

Jolie banged through the iron gate and into the building, leaving Luke to take care of her horse. Luke took Cherish from his wife. Wes hurried to the front door and waited there for his parents, then knocked on it loudly when they arrived.

Miss Hattie answered. With surprise in her eyes, she directed the guests to the library.

Just as Luke sat in a wooden rocker, he saw Mrs. Harms through the glass doors. He stood as she entered the room.

"I have no idea what the child is doing," said the old mistress, her hair in long, ugly shambles about her face. She stepped up to Luke and said firmly, "Sir, I'm shocked that Jolie asked you to come here, but I'm forced to allow it. Ashley's been vomiting the entire afternoon, and she won't mutter a word to explain herself. Imagine! An eight-year-old utterly ruining an otherwise peaceful Sunday with hysterics! I can't tell if she's truly sick or simply rebellious, but I've done everything I can to calm her."

"Can I see her?" Luke asked.

"No. I believe that you showing your face in that room will cause the death of the child."

Wes's eyes grew wide, and he sat stiffly silent on the fainting couch.

Mrs. Harms nodded toward Grace. "However, I will allow Mrs. Tanner to visit the girl and see if she can be quieted. Mind you, Mr. Tanner, do not set foot out of this library."

In a sweep of skirts, Mrs. Harms commanded Hattie to escort Grace to "the girl," and she retired to her office.

Luke and Wes sat silently for a long while after Grace was escorted out. It took every ounce of self-control Luke had to stay within in the confines of the library doors. The orphanage was strangely quiet, and he wondered where the other children were. He could hear Mrs. Harms talking in her office, and then the door slammed and shoes clicked on the wood floor.

Cherish squiggled and Luke put her on his shoulder and patted her back. She sucked her thumb and fell asleep.

The large pendulum of the clock on the wall swung back and forth as the dusty hands slowly turned.

"Luke," Jolie's voice suddenly called from the doorway. "Grace needs you."

He stood and gave Cherish to Wes. "What about Mrs. Harms?"

"I got her permission. Hurry."

Luke forced himself to remain calm as he followed Jolie up the large staircase. She opened the door to a room at the end of a dark hall and he cautiously stepped in.

The bedroom was filled with the sound of sobbing and the crushing weight of dark sorrow. Luke felt a blow to his confidence and a strong desire to retreat. But when he saw Grace sitting on the bed next to a heap of blankets, he slowly proceeded.

"It's me, Gracie," Luke said, and his wife turned toward him.

"She's really sick."

All Luke could see was a string of blonde hair on a white pillow. The blankets moved and Ashley's tear-stained face stared out at him.

"Hey, baby," Luke said calmly, though his heart raced. He faltered at the sheer dread and devastating grief he saw behind her eyes. He wondered if the pain in her eyes was new or if it had always been there but he hadn't cared to notice.

Ashley whimpered, turning back into her pillow. "Mama, tell him to go away."

Grace rubbed her back. "Daddy wants to help, darlin'."

"No." Her voice was coated with tears. "Make him leave."

All she could see was Mr. Berk. The shadows in the bedroom reminded Ashley of nights in the woodshed, and when Luke's voice filled the darkness with the overwhelming presence of power, Ashley cowered.

"Please?" She squiggled. "Make him go."

"Can I just see if you're sick, Ashley?" Luke persisted, sitting in a hard-backed chair beside the bed. He didn't look in her eyes. He couldn't. They were hollow, like dark caves. "I won't hurt you. I just need to see if we should take you to the hospital."

"No!" Ashley shrieked, shoving herself against the wall so forcefully that the window banged. She imagined Mr. Tanner pulling her from the bed and forcing her to sit still while he examined her. She wondered if her mother would protect her from him. Probably not, because she hadn't ever protected Wes.

Ashley held her stomach, begging her mother to take the pain away. She squirmed under the thin sheet and wheezed heavily.

Luke's mind screamed in desperation. *God, I'm helpless! You know I'm willing to go through this with her. Show me how.*

"There's no reason to be afraid," Luke heard himself saying. The horror in her eyes gave him strength. "Ashley, honey, can I just ask you some questions?"

Ashley pressed her cheek against the wall and lay perfectly still. Maybe he wouldn't notice her if she were perfectly motionless. Maybe he would leave her alone if she didn't attract attention, like Mr. Berk used to do.

"Does your stomach hurt?" he asked softly.

She put her shaking hand over her ear.

"Do you know why you're sick?"

"Please don't."

Luke struggled to control the urge to pull her out of this miserable establishment and take her home, where she belonged.

Grace continued to rub Ashley's back, and in the dim lamplight, Luke saw that his wife's cheeks were tearstained. He would've cried, too, if he thought it would do any good.

"Ashley, can you tell me what hurts?"

"Her stomach and her head," Grace answered for the girl. "Isn't that right, Ashley?"

She nodded so slightly that Luke wondered if that was her answer. Before he could ask the next question, Ashley burst into a fit of heavy coughing. Luke closed his eyes as he listened to the painful sound. As she gasped for breath, Grace bent near her face and whispered comfort.

"My throat," Ashley said loud enough for Luke to hear.

"It hurts?" he asked tenderly.

She didn't answer.

"Can you tell me why you got sick?"

Ashley cowered into the sheet, her entire body trembling. She remembered seeing Wesley in church that morning. When she had returned to the orphanage, somewhere during her helpless groping to think of a way to go back to the Tanners, she had fallen asleep and dreamt about Jack. It wasn't a nightmare, like every other dream had been. She hadn't awakened in terror. She hadn't even seen Mr. Berk's face or heard Bonnie cry. She had only seen Jack standing outside the orphanage, saying goodbye on a cold, snowy night. Ashley had seen herself running inside and then Jack had walked away. She saw herself looking out the window and in the darkness, Ashley had seen Jack crying.

"Why did you get sick?" Luke's voice pierced through her daydream.

"Tell him," Ashley said in a squeaky voice. "Mama, tell him why!"

Grace squeezed her hand. "I don't know, Ashley."

Ashley sobbed so hard she could barely breathe. Grace tried to calm her by giving her a drink of water, but seconds later, she vomited.

That was all Luke could handle. He left the bedroom to keep from bursting into a fit of protective wrath, slamming the door behind him.

What a pathetic case of injustice! He leaned against the wall, seething. "She's dying, God. Even if she lives through this, she'll be a hollow shell the rest of her life. Can You see her eyes? The light's going out. Why don't You rescue her?"

Wait quietly, Luke.

You expect me to be quiet while she suffers like that?

I'm rescuing her. Help Me.

Luke paused. *How?*

Talk to Mrs. Harms.

Luke scrambled down the stairs. He flew past the library, where Wes watched him, his eyes wide with panic.

Quietly, Luke, he heard as he reached up to knock on the office door. He breathed out slowly and rapped a soft knock. When a sharp voice answered, he entered.

A sense of pity settled on Luke when he saw Mrs. Harms's disorderly desk and felt the tension of her stress.

The woman's eyes bulged when she saw Luke. "I was right, wasn't I? The girl went into hysterics when she saw you."

"Quite the contrary," he responded with unusual gentleness. "My wife is taking care of her, and I've come to give you my report on her condition."

The old woman crossed her hands on her desk. "Take a seat, Mr. Tanner."

Luke sat in the chair in front of the desk and paused, feeling like a schoolboy about to get sent home. He searched for a medical term to relate to Ashley's condition, but after several moments of silence, he said simply, "Mrs. Harms, Ashley isn't sick with any medical condition."

Her brows rose. "For heaven's sake, what's her problem, then?"

"She's had an emotional breakdown."

Mrs. Harms stared at Luke with disbelief. Her wrinkled face dropped and she said with a stuttering murmur of surprise, "I'm sure I don't know what you mean."

I don't either, he thought. There was so much about Ashley that he couldn't hope to understand; how could he explain it to Mrs. Harms?

"Ashley needs a home with a proper family and a regular routine," he said. "She's obviously been wounded in the past, and she needs someone to invest in her healing."

The old mistress looked at him suspiciously. "And I suppose you haven't contributed to her problems?"

Luke clenched his jaw.

Quietly, Luke.

"I made some mistakes with Ashley. But I swear, with God as my witness, that I never physically abused her."

Mrs. Harms sat back in her chair and crossed one leg over the other, revealing a poky-toed, high-heeled boot under her dress. "Tell me, Mr. Tanner—as a doctor—what do you think should be done with Ashley?"

"She must be placed in a good home immediately."

"She's scheduled to transfer to an orphanage in Maryland on Saturday!"

"Mrs. Harms," Luke said quietly, "I believe that Ashley is too weak to survive that move. She can't even keep down a glass of water. She won't be ready to move on Saturday unless she can be helped out of her grief immediately. If you're not willing to place her in a home directly, I'll escort her to the hospital tonight. You have no other choice." The authority with which he spoke surprised him.

"There's no way I could pay hospital bills. This institution is financially devastated as it is. Besides, you said she has no medical condition."

"She has a very serious condition. Her health has been affected because of something from her past. Until she can be healed from the inside, she's going to need proper medical care. Mrs. Harms, Ashley has obviously seen a great amount of emotional devastation in her life."

Mrs. Harms straightened. "I pride myself in running a well-managed, reputable institution. My orphans receive the best care in Vermont; there's no question about that."

"You're right." Luke swallowed. "But children were meant to be raised in families, not institutions."

Silence struck the room like a crack of thunder, and Luke felt his palms sweat.

Mrs. Harms stared at him for a long while, then pulled open her squeaky desk drawer and slapped a piece of paper in front of him. "I'm going to cancel Ashley's tickets and put her in your care for one week, and that's simply because you have the advantage of being a doctor, and I'm crippled by lack of money to place her in the hospital. I expect that girl to be in your pew next Sunday, or she'll be taken away immediately. If Ashley is in any worse state, or if she reports to me the slightest hint of abuse when I visit in one week, she'll be sent to Maryland immediately. Is that understood?"

He almost smiled. "Completely."

Mrs. Harms looked at the calendar on her desk and put her finger on a square in the month of December. "One week from now is Sunday, December twenty-fifth. Expect a visit from me."

Luke swallowed a protest at having the assessment on Christmas.

Mrs. Harms gave him her pen and he scribbled his signature at the bottom of a form. "I guarantee Ashley will be safe in our home."

"Yes, well, time will prove that." She stood and opened her office door. "We'll see you at church next Sunday."

Luke heaved a sigh of relief as he trotted up the stairs. *It's a miracle,* he thought. *She's coming home sick out of her wits, but it's a miracle all the same.*

To every thing there is a season, and a time to every purpose under the heaven: . . . a time to keep silence, and a time to speak.

—Ecclesiastes 3:1, 7

THIRTY FOUR

Wesley's Reservations

Grace heard the whimpering, and then the painful sound of heavy coughing, and she threw off the bedcovers again.

"What's the matter?" asked Luke groggily.

"Ashley's coughing again. Don't you have anything you can give her?"

"No." He sat up and reached for his robe. "I'm out of medicine. Bring her in here and I'll make a bed on the floor so you don't have to run all night."

Grace sighed and left the room.

"Ashley, honey," she said when she entered the little girl's bedroom, "are you OK?"

"It hurts, Mama." Ashley began coughing again.

"Come sleep in my room so I can help you. Daddy's making a bed on the floor."

Ashley rolled over in her bed. "I wanna stay here."

"Darlin', I can't help you if you stay in here. Come on; I'll rub your back so you feel better."

"I don't want to."

Grace pulled the girl's blankets up to her chin and kissed her forehead. "I'll listen for you then. If you need anything, just call, and I'll be here right away."

Ashley tucked her chin into her pillow.

"She won't sleep in here," said Grace when she returned to her bedroom.

Luke had just dropped a pillow onto the bed on the floor. "Really? Is she sick to her stomach?"

"No. She hasn't vomited since she came home, but if she keeps coughing like that, I'm afraid she's going to hurt herself."

"I wish I had more supplies from the hospital," Luke said as they climbed back in bed. "I didn't think about stocking up before I left."

"Can't you get medicine from somewhere else?"

"The drug store would have it. If her coughing continues, I'll ride in and get something."

Grace leaned against his arm. "One week, Luke," she said thickly.

"Don't think about it." He had spent most of the night thinking about the deadline, and it made him desperate.

"But do you really think we can uncover it all in only a week?"

"No. All I want is for her to see a difference in me."

"My family's coming for Christmas in three days."

"How long are they staying?" Luke groaned.

"Until Christmas."

"Four days?" he blurted. "We'll never accomplish anything with Ashley if we have a houseful of people."

"I can't change the plans." She felt as upset as he sounded. "I couldn't get a letter to Ruth soon enough."

The coughing began again, and the parents were silent as they listened to see how long it would continue. Grace cringed.

Luke sat up and threw off the quilt. "I'll go to town for medicine. You might as well stake out in Ashley's room. She doesn't need another lonely night by herself when she's finally made it home."

The Vermont sky was dancing with stars and the air was sharp as Luke saddled his gelding outside the barn. He pulled his driving gloves out of his long coat pocket and slipped them on. Light reflected off the deep snow, making the world sparkle. The horse breathed heavily. Luke mounted and the gelding broke into a trot, puffing steam against the briskness of the early-morning sky.

The streets of Galesburg were quiet, and light from the windows of a few buildings highlighted the boardwalk. The barbershop pillars were wrapped with Christmas greenery and the big window at the fabric store was outlined in red and green silk. Luke passed by a tiny toy store, where the window was crowded with porcelain dolls and a large rocking horse. It reminded him of the winter mornings when he used to go to work at the hospital. Sometimes he wished he could go back to regular hours at the hospital . . . back to the days before Ashley. At least he would be one of the men welcome in the overcrowded apothecary this morning.

Luke turned his horse down Tenth Street and stopped at the tiny drug store on the corner. *Podunk*, he thought. This was the drug store Dale Gildey loathed. Luke dismounted and swung his reins over the post.

A loud bell above the door welcomed him. The strong smell of herbal soaps made his eyes water. No clerk stood at the counter and Luke felt as if he were intruding, though the sign in the window read OPEN. He searched the short shelves for a potion that would soothe Ashley's throat, but after several minutes, he approached the counter. An uncomfortable silence filled the little store. He tapped his fingers on the counter, but no one came. He scanned the shelves one more time and left.

Luke's pocket watch read 7:16. He sat in his saddle and wondered if Dale Gildey would sell him something for Ashley. He knew the apothecary had what Ashley needed. But walking through that door at this hour with the sole intention of purchasing medicine was almost too much for Luke to consider.

Luke turned his horse toward Main Street. He became more tense the closer he got to the apothecary. He wished he could just ride past. But with each step the gelding took, Luke felt more certain that he had to conquer the intimidation of the apothecary . . . for his own sake as much as Ashley's.

More than ten horses were tied at the apothecary hitching post. Soft light glowed inside the building, but it looked cold and harsh to Luke. The gentle rolling of men's voices drifted into the street. Luke tied his horse to the post, whispered a prayer, and approached the familiar white door. The OPEN sign that hung in the window danced in mockery.

Silence struck the apothecary the second the bell announced Luke's arrival. He entered with a courageous smile. When he saw the dozens of eyes staring at him, it almost made him laugh.

"Morning, gentlemen," he said with a nod.

Dale Gildey stood behind the counter. When Luke began to scan the shelves, he said with bewilderment, "You need something, Tanner?"

"I'm looking for some medicine," he said without looking up. "You got anything strong enough to knock out a heavy cough?"

"For your penny parcel?" Patrick Cummings asked, accusation coating his voice.

Luke didn't respond.

Jonathan Hendricks took out his pocket watch and snapped it open loudly. "Do you have any idea what time it is?"

Luke looked over the shelf, fired with determination. "Twenty minutes past seven. That OPEN sign has been flipped almost as long as I've been up."

"That OPEN sign doesn't mean what it says till eight o'clock," Barry Lee said.

"I reckon Gildey won't refuse medicine to a sick child."

Mr. Cummings banged his feet on the floor. "Tanner, have you honestly lost your mind?"

"Not quite." Luke looked up firmly. The only friendly face in the crowd was Sheriff Bilt, who watched him with surprise but not disdain. Luke looked at Mr. Gildey, forcing himself to remain calm. "Do you have anything for me?"

Mr. Gildey took a bottle off the shelf behind him and set it on the counter. He announced the price and Luke dug the money out of his pocket. When he had dropped the bottle into his coat pocket, he turned back to the men. "Good morning, gentlemen. I hope you all have an excellent day."

As he walked out, Luke's heart was filled with such an intense sense of victory it captivated him for the entire ride home.

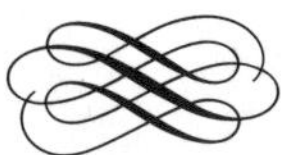

When he returned from the apothecary, Luke was in a triumphant mood. Then he looked into Ashley's hauntingly silent eyes—eyes that begged to be rescued from some dark world, and he lost all sense of triumph. He had seen the expression before, and it always made him feel like he'd received a blow to the gut. Before she ran back to the orphanage, that crushing emptiness only showed itself when Ashley was especially terrified. Now it was a constant presence.

Luke tried to reach out to Ashley, but she was stone cold. When he looked at her, she looked away; when he neared, she cowered; when he talked, she withdrew. Dreams of victory quickly left him, and by the time mid-morning had fallen on the countryside, he had escaped, leaving Grace to try to pull Ashley out of the shadows.

When Wes arrived home from school that afternoon, he found Ashley lying on the couch, covered with a blanket and drinking a cup of hot water. Grace sat near the fire with Cherish on her lap, and as soon as she heard Wes come in, she retired to the kitchen to start supper.

Wes approached Ashley and smiled at her.

"How're you feeling?" he asked as Cherish crawled after him.

Ashley avoided his eyes. "Fine."

"I heard you coughing last night."

"Yeah."

He bit his lip. "Did you sleep in this morning? I tried to be really quiet so I wouldn't wake you."

Ashley tapped her finger against the pattern on the teacup. "I didn't really sleep much."

Wes sat on the ottoman. "Dad said you were pretty sick, but you should be feeling better in a couple days."

She glanced at him for a split second, then her eyes darted away.

"It's really cold outside," Wes continued. "Mr. Sulka gave me a ride home 'cause the snow makes it hard to walk. Have you played in the snow much this year?"

"No."

"I do at school every day. I've been training Kate so she'll be ready to ride in the spring."

Ashley nodded.

"Dad says he's going to break her come April. I think I'll be riding her by June."

"Oh."

Wes faked a smile. "Maybe you could ride her, too."

"I don't want to." Ashley absently sipped her water.

Wes watched Cherish poke her skinny fingers into the rug. "Were you surprised at how big Cherish is?"

Ashley shrugged.

"She grew a lot while you were gone. She's ten months old now. I think she's going to be walking pretty soon. She already pulls herself up on the couch."

Ashley stared blankly.

Wes watched her, but it didn't seem like she was looking at him. "What's wrong? Why won't you talk to me?"

Ashley coughed. "I'm sick," she said, as if suddenly overcome by weariness.

"But that's not why. Aren't you happy to be here?"

Ashley's eyes brimmed with tears. "I don't know."

He looked at her with confusion. Ashley couldn't stand to see him frown on her, so she turned her head into the couch. "Go away, Wes. Don't look at me like that."

"We all went to a lot of work to get you here," Wes said. "Did you know that Dad spent sixty days in jail for you?"

Ashley stared at him in utter shock. Wes felt a pang of guilt for disobeying his mother's request never to tell Ashley of their father's jail sentence.

He kicked the chair leg. "You don't even care. After all the stuff we've been through to get you back here, you act like you would've been happier at the orphanage." He stood. "Fine! Go back there while you still have a chance. Mrs. Harms is coming to talk to you on Christmas. Tell her how unhappy you are here. Then you can go with her and end up in some dirty, smelly orphanage in Maryland. I don't care!"

Wes stormed out the door.

Wes opened the door to his father's little office and leaned against the wall. Luke was pounding a nail into a shelf bracket on the far wall.

"I think I'm going to be a doctor when I grow up," Wes said when the pounding stopped.

Luke turned around with surprise. "Oh, hey, son. I didn't see you come in. Did you make it home from school all right?"

Wes nodded, crossing his arms in his chest.

"A doctor, 'ey?" Luke chuckled, tapping another nail into the whitewashed wall. "How'd you come to that decision?"

"It seems like a good thing to do. Jimmy says we could start a practice together, and maybe you could be our senior doctor."

"Me?" Luke smiled. "Well, I guess I'd be old enough by then."

"Well, if you don't have any more children, it'd be a nice thing for you to do, since there won't be much at home anymore."

Luke stopped pounding and turned to his son. "And why don't you think I'll have any more children?"

Wes shrugged. "After Ashley goes back to the orphanage, you'll never get to adopt more children. Cherish and I will be the only ones."

Luke set his hammer down and leaned against his workbench. "Where'd you get the idea that Ashley's going back to the orphanage?"

"She's just so bad!" Wes suddenly burst. "Everything's changed since she went back. I don't even like her anymore. I don't know if I want her for a sister."

"Wes, we have to help Ashley."

He sniffed and turned away. "I don't want to."

"God gave us Ashley to help her for the rest of her life, not just when we feel like it. She has to know that we're all committed to her."

Wes bit his lip to avoid tears. "No one else at school has a sister like Ashley. Jimmy has two sisters exactly Ashley's age, and he plays with them and talks to them, and doesn't ever have to worry if they're going to cry for no reason, or start screaming all of a sudden." Wes rubbed his eyes harshly. "Ashley cries at night, and she fights with me, and she doesn't even like you. Who knows—she might get taken away just as soon as she gets better."

"Well, son, I guess God's given you a different way of getting brothers and sisters," Luke said tenderly. "But if we give up on Ashley, the orphanage system won't let us adopt again, and you and Cherish really will be the only children forever. I understand that you're frustrated with Ashley. I am too. It's hard to be a good friend when Ashley doesn't really respond. But Wes, we have to understand that Ashley's been homesick ever since she left our place. She needs time to get rid of those feelings. She hasn't even been here for a full day, and she's still pretty sick. Give her another chance."

Wes shook his head. "I thought she was going to be good someday. But she's still bad." He tapped on the table leg with his heavy boot. "Is she ever gonna be normal?"

"I don't know." Luke crossed his arms. "All we can do is teach her good things and pray for her, and hopefully she'll come around."

"Not for a long time, though."

"She's only eight. We have to take one day at a time."

Wes stared at the floor.

"You're a great big brother," Luke said softly. "And if we keep loving Ashley, you won't be able to ask for a better sister. I need you to help me work toward that goal."

"How?"

"Your cousins are coming in just a few days. While they're here, you won't have much time to spend with Ashley, just the two of you. Why don't you do all you can with her before they get here?"

"I don't think she wants to talk to me."

Luke shrugged. "I don't reckon she really wants to be alone, either. Give it a try, 'ey?"

Wes's eyes looked far away. "Mr. Sulka says that God loves Ashley a whole lot. I wish I were a good enough Christian to do that too."

Luke smiled. "It's not a matter of being good enough, son. It's a matter of keeping close to God so He can work through you to make a difference in Ashley's life. That's the secret."

A thought popped into Wesley's head and he grinned. "Wouldn't it be something if we really did get to keep Ashley for good?" His eyes sparkled when he looked up. "What would the apothecary circle think of that?"

Luke winked at him and then burst into laughter.

And let us not be weary in well doing: for in due season we shall reap, if we faint not.

—Galatians 6:9

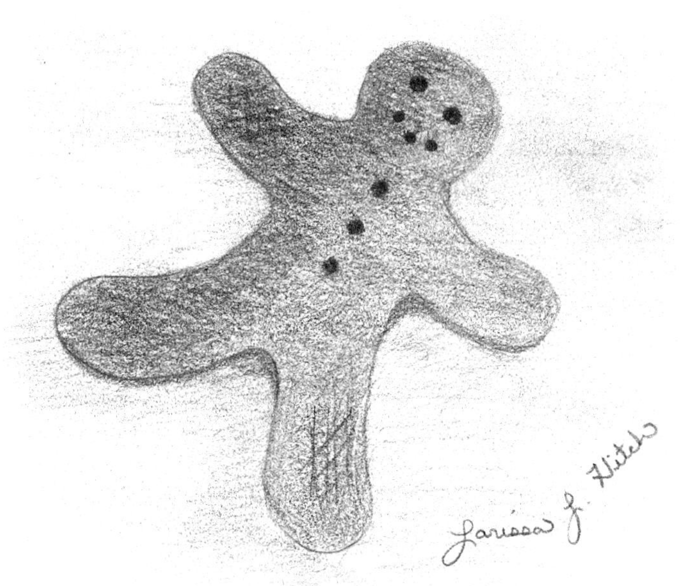

THIRTY FIVE

A Game

Luke awoke early on Tuesday morning, his mind filled with thoughts of Ashley. He remembered the questions Mr. Bowtie had asked him the first time he met with the preacher, and he was determined that he was going to answer every one of them.

"I want to know why she doesn't like to take baths, what grade she's actually in this year, when her birthday is, who her parents were, and why she was orphaned."

The man sighed with defeat. *How am I supposed to find all of this out when she won't even let me get near her? Lord, how am I supposed to make this work when I don't have enough time to teach her to trust me?*

He lay for a long time and heard no answers. Finally, he got up and dressed. On his way out to do chores, he stopped at Ashley's bedroom door and quietly peeked inside. The little girl looked angelic with her eyes closed and her scraggly blonde hair scattered on the pillow. A surge of regret came over Luke. If he hadn't been such a fool, he could've owned Ashley's heart by now. Instead, she was a thousand miles away—living under his roof but completely detached from everything in the present.

Luke shook his head and walked away. He realized how helpless he was to accomplish his goals on his own, so for the hour that he spent in the barn doing chores, he fervently cried out to the only One who knew how to solve his problems.

When Luke returned to the house shortly after seven o'clock, he was surprised that Grace and the children weren't downstairs. He left his boots at the back door and climbed the stairs. He heard quiet voices in Wesley's room and stood outside the closed door for a few moments.

Wes's voice rang in laughter. "Jimmy and I started playing a new game at school. We sorta made it up. Do you like games?"

Luke pressed his ear against the door.

"Yeah," Ashley said. Her light giggle made Luke's heart soar. "We used to play games at the orphanage."

Luke stepped back from the door with a huge grin on his face. He went to his bedroom and found Grace sitting on the bed, still in her nightdress. Cherish was snuggled on her lap, clapping her hands as Grace sang a nursery rhyme. When Luke walked in, Cherish squealed and laughed, and her baby curls bobbed on her mama's chest.

"Good morning, Cherish," Luke said with a chuckle.

"Are you done with chores already?" Grace asked.

"Yeah; I just got in."

"Wes and Ashley have been laughing in the bedroom ever since I woke up."

"I know. I listened to them through the door." Luke sat on the bed, winking at Cherish.

Grace smiled. "I don't know what they're talking about, but they sure are having fun."

"I think Wes is teaching Ashley a game, which gave me an idea that I think may help me reach her."

"Really?" Grace leaned forward and Cherish crawled off her lap, gleefully throwing herself at her daddy's chest.

"We're gonna play a game at breakfast," Luke said, kissing the baby.

Grace laughed. "A game?"

"Yeah."

As Luke began reciting a nursery rhyme with Cherish, Grace stood. "I suppose you're wanting me to make breakfast, then."

Luke chuckled between patty-cakes. "I guess that would be helpful."

By the time Grace had made breakfast and the children were dressed and ready for the day, Luke was so excited about his plan he could hardly wait for his wife to serve the food. He sat at the head of the table with Cherish beside him in the high chair and tried not to let Ashley see that he was watching her. She seemed particularly cheerful this morning, while Wes was bubbling with excitement.

"Before we pray, we're going to play a game," Luke said once the plates were set on the table and Cherish was contentedly sucking on an apple slice.

Wes's eyes lit up. "What kind of game?"

"From now on, before we eat our meals, we're going to take turns asking a question. I'll ask the question this morning, and we'll go around the table and everyone will answer it. Does that sound like fun?"

"Why are we doing that?" Wes asked with a giggle.

Luke winked at him. "Because I like to play games. You answer first, Wes. Here's the question: What's your favorite color?"

"That's a funny question," Wes said, glancing at Ashley. "My favorite color is dark blue."

"Mine's purple," Grace echoed.

"Your turn, Ashley," Luke said.

Ashley smiled slightly and squeezed her hands in her lap. "Mine's red," she said with a blush to her cheeks.

"I knew that," Wes piped up.

Luke peered at him. "You did?"

"Yup. What's your favorite color, Dad?"

Luke paused. He couldn't remember having a favorite color since boyhood. "I guess it would be the color of the dress I bought for your mama last Christmas."

"Green," Wes hollered out.

Luke nodded.

The table became quiet, and Luke suggested they pray and eat.

"Can we ask one more question first?" Wes begged. His sister smiled at him.

"You want to keep playing?" Luke asked with a chuckle. "All right."

"What's your favorite thing to eat?" Wes asked quickly.

"Gingerbread," Ashley piped up.

"Chocolate," Grace said.

"Peach pie," Luke added.

Wes laughed in delight. "Peppermints."

Luke suggested prayer after that question, too, but the game was so much fun that they continued. Grace asked the next question, then Ashley, and then Luke. They played for so long that when they finally decided it was time to eat, the food was cold, it was past eight-thirty, and Luke knew more about Ashley than he had hoped to learn in an entire week.

Ashley stood as straight as a sewing form, puffing out her chest to imitate the canvas models she had seen in the fabric store. She was giddy with excitement.

"Do you like your dress?" Grace asked as she pinned the hem.

"It's my favorite color," she said bashfully. It was as red as Christmas.

Ashley pinched the silky fabric between her fingers and noticed how it shone in the dim light of the spare bedroom. She remembered talking with Bonnie about someday getting a red dress, and she closed her eyes to seal out the memory.

"Grandma's coming this afternoon, and she's going to help me with your petticoat so you'll be all ready for Christmas," Grace said. "If you take care of Cherish for me, I'll try to finish everything else before Grandma comes."

"All right." Ashley looked at the lace-trimmed sleeves and bit her lip with excitement.

Grace put in the last pin and patted Ashley's arm. "All done," she said. Ashley spun in a full circle, shivering when the delightfully cool silk brushed against her skin.

"It's really pretty, Mama," she said. "Can I wear it for everyday?"

"Not quite every day." Grace pulled Ashley toward herself and unbuttoned the dress. Ashley leaned against her mother's chest and Grace held her there for a moment, kissing her cheek. "Get dressed and take care of Cherish so I can finish, darlin'. You're a good girl."

Ashley smiled as she threw her old brown dress over her head and scooped Cherish into her arms on her way to the sitting room. The baby struggled against her arms and threw her head back in a fit, but Ashley smiled at her. "Don't fuss, Cherry. I'm good at taking care of you, remember?" But Cherish wasn't convinced, and Ashley barely made it to the sitting room before the baby started wailing.

"Don't cry. I have you." Ashley set her on the floor near the sofa. "Look, here's your dolly. Should we play?"

Cherish crawled away and Ashley ran after her and scooped her onto the couch. "Please stop crying," the eight-year-old begged. Cherish stared back and shrieked loudly.

Ashley heard the back door open and Mr. Tanner stepped into the kitchen. She shoved the dolly into Cherish's arms and tried to persuade her to play, but when Luke came into the sitting room, the baby was still crying.

"What's the matter, Ashley?" he asked.

As soon as Cherish saw him she threw herself off the couch and crawled to his feet.

Ashley timidly looked at him. "I was trying to take care of her."

"She's still shy, 'ey?" Luke picked up the baby and kissed her curls. "Cherry, you're a silly one. It's your sister; see? She likes to play with you."

Cherish buried her face in Luke's shoulder and gripped his shirt, finally silent. "I can watch her for a bit if you like," Luke said. "I'm just going to do some paperwork at the table." He smiled at Ashley, and she retreated to the spare bedroom.

Ashley sat on the bed and watched Grace work for a long while. She stared at the red fabric that glided along the machine. Excitement thrilled her every time she laid eyes on the delicate lace. Her mother's fingers moved along the hem and felt the pins she had placed along the bottom to keep a straight stitch. Suddenly, the machine came to a thumping halt, and Ashley gasped.

"What's wrong, Mama?" she asked.

"Goodness, Ashley, you startled me! I didn't know you were in here. Where's Cherish?"

"In the dining room."

"Does Daddy have her?"

"Yeah."

"Honey, you need to tell me when you're here so you don't frighten me." Grace thumped the wheel up and down.

"Why did the machine stop?" asked Ashley.

"There's a knot on this hem. I wish Grandma were here to help untangle it. Do you see my scissors, darlin'?"

Ashley stood and handed her mother the brown scissors. While Grace rethreaded the machine, Ashley used her little fingers to pick at the knot on the hem.

"Christmas is in five days, Ashley," Grace said as she pumped the treadle. "Our company is coming in only two days. I'm going to need you to help me clean the house and do a lot of baking. Grandma will be here to help us, but I'll need you to work with us so we'll be ready."

Ashley began coughing.

Luke came into the room, cradling sleepy Cherish in his arm and carrying a big book in his hand.

"Do you need more medicine, Ashley?" he asked.

She shook her head and held back her choking.

"You can cough. I'm not going to force anything down your throat."

Ashley still tried to hold back but eventually gave in. As she coughed deeply, Luke watched her and she shied from his compassion. She had never seen that kind of look from a man before, not even when Mr. Berk told her stories or called her pet names.

"Can I read to you while you work, Gracie?" Luke asked.

"Please. Is Cherish here?"

"She's almost asleep."

Ashley leaned against the wall and continued to pick at the thick knot in the hem of her dress. She relaxed as Mr. Tanner's voice rolled smoothly over the words he read from a book he called Psalms. His brow creased, and every so often, he would stop and reread something.

Grace listened in perfect silence and Cherish quickly fell asleep. Ashley didn't understand all the words she heard, but she found herself wondering about several things Luke read.

When he closed the Bible nearly an hour after he had started reading, Luke and Grace began a deep conversation about truth. Ashley didn't understand why truth was so important, but as she sleepily leaned against the wall, she came to understand one thing: Luke Tanner was passionate about truth.

He talked about lies, and Ashley heard him say that he still believed a lot of lies. Then he talked about the power of truth as if it were a weapon of war. He admitted that he was wrestling against the lie that told him he would always be a broken man. Ashley didn't know what a broken man was, but Mr. Tanner obviously didn't want to be one.

"I feel like my past is going to keep me a prisoner all my life," Luke said, looking intently at his wife. "It's hard for me to fight that lie with truth because I've believed it so long, it's become truth to me."

"God is a redeemer," Grace said thoughtfully.

"I know He can redeem me from everything I've gone through, and He wants to restore what I've lost. I just wish . . ." He chuckled to himself. "I wish this lie would speak to me in an audible voice, but it talks to me so quietly I end up believing it before I even realize it's speaking."

As her parents continued to discuss lies versus truth, Ashley felt slightly disturbed, though she wasn't sure why.

By the time Wes returned from school and darkness fell on the countryside, Ashley had forgotten about the heavy discussion. However, just before the children were sent to bed, Mr. Tanner read to the family from that book again. He also prayed for Ashley. The little girl was so astonished she didn't hear what he prayed for; she only heard her name four times. Ashley quickly decided that something was either terribly wrong or incredibly right for so much to have changed in Luke Tanner. It made her especially wary of him.

The next day, while Grace and Ashley were sewing, Luke came into the room again and read a single verse, then discussed it with his wife for nearly two hours. Ashley still didn't understand all the words, but the more she heard from that book and the more Mr. Tanner talked about lies and truth, the more disturbed Ashley felt. She didn't know why, but every time the word *lie* was spoken, she thought of Mr. Berk or Jack or Henry or Bonnie. For the first time, something told her there was something incredibly wrong with what had happened at their house.

A deep and powerful stirring began in Ashley's heart, and she began to recognize that there was a tremendous difference between the Berk family and most other families. Deep down, a light went on in Ashley's dying spirit and she realized there was an intense amount of pain attached to her bleeding soul. More important, she began to understand that something called truth had the power to set her free.

And ye shall know the truth, and the truth shall make you free.
—John 8:32

THIRTY SIX

Mama's Little Angels

"I don't really want to be on the city council when I grow up," said Wes. He stuck his hands in the soapy dishwater and stared out the window above the sink. He was in a particularly pessimistic mood that morning because school was over for Christmas break and he wouldn't see Jimmy for at least three days.

"Why not?" Ashley asked, scratching a china plate with her dry towel.

Wes shrugged. "Galesburg is messed up, Ashley. A lot of the men on the council aren't Christians, and majority rules. So I'd probably be in the minority."

"What's that?"

"It means I'd usually lose the vote."

Ashley set the plate on the counter and reached for another.

"The only really good people in Galesburg are the preacher and the Sulkas," Wes continued.

"Who are the Sulkas?"

Wesley's heart danced with glee. "They're KatieAnne's parents."

"KatieAnne?" Ashley's brow creased. Surely not the KatieAnne she knew.

Wes looked at her blankly. "The girl from the orphanage—you know, your best friend?"

Ashley's eyes grew wide. "The Sulkas are her parents?"

"KatieAnne's brother Jimmy is my best friend."

"Do they live around here?"

"About fifteen minutes away."

Wes thought Ashley would be excited, but she silently dried another plate, her brow creased in thought.

"I don't really remember her," she said coolly. It seemed like a lifetime ago that she was at the orphanage with KatieAnne. She looked up at her brother. "Are Krissa and Deborah coming for Christmas?"

"Yeah." He scrubbed the inside of a cup. "They'll be here this afternoon, same as everyone else."

"Good."

Wes looked at her. "Good? Last time they were here, you were glad when they were gone."

"I want to talk to Krissa." She wanted to talk about the dead chickens and the picture she'd drawn. She wanted to know if Krissa understood what it meant.

Wes took a handful of suds and threw them against the window, then watched them slide down onto the sill. When he noticed Ashley staring at him in shock, he explained, "We have to clean the windows today anyway."

"Why?" asked Ashley. "I thought Miss Maggie did that."

Wes frowned. "Miss Maggie doesn't clean here anymore. Not since Dad's no longer an upper crust."

When Wes threw another suds ball at the window, Ashley said, "That's not a very good thing to do."

Wes glared at her. "If I said that to you, you'd yell at me."

Her brow creased.

"You do a lot of things that aren't very good things to do, Ashley."

Ashley looked away. "That doesn't mean you should."

Wes sniffed. "Yeah, but I get strapped when I do stuff wrong. You just cry your way out."

Ashley looked at him with confusion. "Stop. Don't talk about that."

"Why?"

The pictures danced in her brain. "I don't want to."

"Just because you don't want to talk about it doesn't mean it's going to go away." Wes rinsed his hands in the cold water and dried them on his pants.

"The chickens are dead, Wes," Ashley said in a rush. "So we don't have to talk about that."

He looked at her, baffled. "This has nothing to do with chickens."

"Just let them all be dead. It's over." Her eyes filled with tears.

Wes stared at her. "Ashley, you have problems."

"Wesley!" a deep voice called from the sitting room.

"What?" Wes answered harshly.

"Come here. And bring Ashley."

"Me?" Ashley whispered in panic.

Wes walked away without answering, and Ashley hesitantly followed.

"What were you two talking about?" Luke asked when Wes dropped into a chair. Ashley stood timidly behind the couch.

"Nothing," Wes answered, slumping.

Luke looked at Ashley and saw grief in her eyes. He turned back to Wes. "Why are you upset with her?"

Wes shrugged.

"What did you say to her about having problems?"

"She was saying all sorts of weird stuff."

Luke crossed his leg in the rocker. "Saying that she has problems isn't going to help anything, Son. Did you try to listen to what she was saying?"

"Yeah." Wes sniffed and glanced at her. "She was talking about dead chickens."

Ashley's cheeks reddened. She looked as if she wanted to melt into the carpet.

Luke saw the change in Ashley and tried to keep his eyes off of her. It suddenly occurred to him that the dead chickens related to Ashley in some way. He was strangely unsurprised. "What were you talking about before?" he asked Wes.

"Strappings."

From the corner of his eye, Luke watched the color disappear from Ashley's face. *"I want to know what she's afraid of and why,"* he remembered Mr. Bowtie saying. "Well," he said slowly, "I would appreciate it if you wouldn't discuss that with Ashley anymore."

Wes looked at his father with surprise. "That's ridiculous."

"Wesley," Luke said, "I want you to obey me without arguing. You don't understand everything."

Luke looked at Ashley and his eyes were quiet. "It's all right, darlin'. Don't worry about the chickens." He didn't know what there was to worry about, but it was obviously a great disturbance to the little girl.

Ashley's heart raced. *"Don't worry."* Bonnie had told her not to fret over Mr. Berk strapping her, but he still did it. No matter how much she tried not to worry, it never helped anything; he always came after her. Mr. Tanner knew about the chickens. And he was wearing his belt. He'd told her not to worry, but that was just because he didn't want her to throw a tantrum before he could get his hands on her.

"Ashley," Luke's tender voice drew her out of her thoughts. "Baby, did you hear me?" He wanted to play another game and ask her why she was afraid of being strapped, and what about chickens made her hate them. But he held back. It wasn't time for that yet.

Ashley gave him a blank stare.

Luke searched her countenance and forced himself not to scoop her into his arms and dig to the very depths of her soul and erase everything like marks on a chalkboard. He leaned forward on his knees. "Wes isn't going to talk to you about the chickens anymore. We're going to forget all about it. It's over."

It's over. In the past. Gone. Buried under two feet of dirt, just like Ronny and Katie. Ashley didn't believe it. She bit her cheek and tried not to cry.

"Wesley, go finish the dishes before Granddad and Grandma get here," Luke said with a nod toward the kitchen.

Wes left, and Ashley stood perfectly still and stiff.

Mr. Tanner sat for a long moment before he spoke quietly. "You don't need to worry about it, Ashley. You're not going to get strapped."

Her pulse quickened. Jack had told her not to worry about it 'cause she'd lose sleep.

Luke watched her for a long moment and could almost see memory streaking her eyes. "Do you want to talk about something, darlin'?"

She shook her head quickly.

Luke leaned back in the chair. "You don't have to finish the dishes," he said. "You can do whatever you want."

Ashley fled from Luke and retreated to the kitchen.

"I'm going outside to sled," Wes called to his mother, flipping his hat onto his head. "I gotta make sure my runners are real slick for when the boys come."

"Wes, Dad needs your help in the barn," Grace said.

"Why can't Ashley help?"

"I have her doing other important things."

Wes breathed deeply, trying to curb his annoyance. He had spent the last two days cleaning the house until it was so fresh he could feel the floor squeak under his stockings. Now the anticipation of spending the holiday with his cousins was almost too much to handle.

"Well," he said with a sigh, "Norm's gonna be really disappointed if my runners are all rusty when he tries to sled."

Grace patted Cherish, who was settled in the sling on her hip. "Then he'll just have to be disappointed. I can't spare you this morning, son."

Wes shoved his arms into his coat and meandered outside, the door slamming behind him. As he was about to kick at a small stone, a familiar voice called to him. He looked up to see Granddad nearing, his arms full of pots and pans and his white beard dusted with frost.

"Nathan, my boy!" the old man hollered. "Come help me with all this stuff in the wagon, would you? Grandma's got a load of things to carry in."

Wes smiled broadly. "What'd she bring?"

"Just baking things," replied Grandma, though her eyes twinkled with Christmas surprises. She put a large basket in Wesley's arms, and the smell of chocolate candy made the boy's mouth water. "Now, be especially careful with this one. I'll get the door for you."

"Mom, Grandma brought her whole kitchen," Wes said as he set a box on the counter. He glanced in the box and smiled. "She even brought chocolate."

Grandma came in and set a basket onto the floor. "There's one more load for you, Nate," she said. She hugged Grace and kissed Cherish's forehead. "Where's Ashley?"

"She's sorting candles in the cellar," said Grace. "I thought I'd already used all the colored ones, but we went down this morning and she said there were candles of every color down there, so I asked her to sort them. She's been waiting for you to come so we can finish her pantaloons. She wants to wear her new dress, but I told her she had to wait until you were here to make sure everything's right on it."

"Did you finish her petticoat?"

"Yes, and I'm sure she must look gorgeous in it."

"Did you manage to get Cherish's dress finished too?"

"Yes." Grace gave Cherish to her mother and began emptying the boxes and baskets Grandma had brought. "But I wouldn't let Wes put it on her until Ashley's was done. I really regret not taking the time to make Ashley's dress before. She's so excited about it."

"Is she doing OK?" Grandma asked.

"Fair," Grace replied. "In a way, I wish we didn't have to have company this year. I feel like we're going to lose a lot of time with her."

"What did Mrs. Harms say has to be different in order for her to stay?"

Grace leaned against the counter with a heavy sigh. "She didn't exactly say it this way, but basically she's looking for Ashley to change in the way she responds to Luke."

"And that hasn't happened yet?"

"Not at all."

Ashley peeked into the kitchen just then, and Grandma said quickly, "There's my girl. I was just asking about you, Ashley."

"Did you finish sorting the candles?" Grace asked.

Ashley leaned against her mother's skirt. "You have mostly red ones."

"Speaking of red," Grandma said mischievously, "Your mama says your dress is done."

"Except my pantaloons."

"Should we try them on?" Grace asked as she patted Ashley's back. "Run and get everything from your wardrobe and you can put it on in the spare bedroom. We'll have Grandma check it all, and if it all looks OK, you can wear it now."

Ten minutes later, Ashley stood in the spare bedroom, fully garbed in red silk, with lace poking out under her dress and her petticoat making her skirt dance on her hips. Cherish had also been dressed and was impatiently tugging at the silk bow in her hair.

"Do you think this pantaloon waist needs to be smaller?" asked Grace after Grandma had thoroughly praised the dresses.

Grandma knelt beside Ashley, but when she reached to feel the waist, Ashley pushed her hand aside.

"I want Mama to do it," she said. She was suddenly overcome with fear that Grandma would see the scars on her legs.

"Grandma's just feeling the waist, darlin'," said Grace.

"No, you do it. You can tell, Mama."

"I think it looks all right," said Grandma, rolling back on her feet. "If you want Ashley to keep the pantaloons for a while, she'll need them just a little bit big. As long as they aren't annoying her or falling down when she plays, I think they're fine."

"They're good," said Ashley quickly, and she smoothed her red dress over her pantaloons and petticoat.

Grandma pulled Cherish into her arms and admired the little pantaloons she wore under her dress, complimenting her daughter's careful stitches and straight seams. Cherish momentarily forgot about the red bow and poked at the lace she found around her hem, kicking her bare toes in wild excitement.

"I've been thinking about something since last time we came, Gracie," Grandma said. "Since Ashley's hair is so unmanageable when it's long, perhaps you should cut it."

Ashley's eyes bulged.

"Just to shoulder length or so. Grace, feel here, where it starts getting thin." Grandma stroked her daughter's hand through Ashley's tangled hair.

Ashley glanced in the mirror and tried to imagine herself without the burden of tangly hair.

"Her hair is so straight, but if you curled it, I think she'd look adorable," Grandma said.

"What do you think, Ashley?" asked Grace.

Ashley stared at the reflection and slowly stroked her hair. It really was thin and scraggly, especially at the ends. "I don't know."

"Should we ask Daddy?"

Ashley shrugged.

"I'll go find him." Grandma took Cherish and left the room.

In a matter of minutes, Ashley found herself sitting on a stool in the kitchen with everyone surrounding her, a brush slowly going through her thin hair. Grandma held a pair of scissors in her hand, and Luke glanced at the hair with a knit brow.

"Cut it really short so it'll curl real good," suggested Wesley with a glance at Cherish's short baby curls.

"We don't want it much above the shoulder," Luke said.

"How about here?" suggested Grandma, placing her scissors against Ashley's shoulder bone.

"I like it there," said Grace, touching the scissors. "What do you think, Ashley?"

She shrugged timidly, staring at Mr. Tanner, who had settled his gaze upon her with a happy smile.

"Is that too short for you?" he asked. She shook her head. He glanced at the scissors once more, then nodded. "That's about right for me, I guess. What do you think, Granddad? Is that gonna be too short after it's curled?"

"Not a bit," said the agreeable man with a wink at the wide-eyed victim. "Cut away, Marjorie."

And so she did. The first cut sent shivers up Ashley's back as she watched nearly ten inches of hair fall to the kitchen floor. But as her father held the mirror up for her, a smile slowly creased Ashley's lips, and her cheeks turned rosy with delight. Everyone was utterly silent as the scissors chopped, but after Grandma had brushed through the short hair several times, the kitchen lit up with praises.

"You look so much better," said Wes, and Cherish squealed in his arms.

"One hundred percent improved," agreed Granddad.

"Oh, darlin', it even feels better," added Mama, and Daddy winked at her.

"Imagine what curls will do now," said Grandma, raking her fingers through the smooth, shiny tresses. "Do you have rag curlers, Grace?"

"Just a few, but Mrs. Sulka gave me a new kind of curlers last week. They're supposed to take a lot less time than rags."

"I'll get 'em, Mom," offered Wes, shoving Cherish onto Ashley's hair-sprinkled lap, then racing up the stairs.

Ashley glanced into the mirror and said softly, "It's as short as Cherish's, Mama."

Grace laughed and hugged her daughter, patting her head. "You two are so pretty together," she whispered. "Both of you have curly hair and red dresses. You're Mama's little angels."

A time to weep, and a time to laugh.
—Ecclesiastes 3:4

THIRTY SEVEN

Company

The rest of the company seemed to arrive in a single sweep that afternoon, and within an hour, the Tanner household was bursting at the seams with guests. Every family member was welcomed with great shouts and half a dozen hugs, and they were invited into the sitting room, where a fire burned in the fireplace and the sweet, spicy smell of gingerbread and green tomato pie permeated the air.

Grace's best candelabras had been set on the hearth, and six red candles burned in each, surrounded by piney greenery and strings of cranberries and holly. Dried pinecones were set in baskets about the house, and paper Christmas trees that Wes and Ashley had made were hung on the doorways, and they swished every time one of the men ducked through. The toy box had been brought out and set in a corner of the sitting room, awaiting the expected raid by the little ones. Cups of hot cider and cocoa surrounded a large bowl of maple taffy on the table.

As the company arrived, Granddad and Grandma rushed about, exclaiming over little ones (who grew up much too quickly), complimenting new dresses, fancy bowties, and the prettily wrapped packages that came for all the cousins. Luke and Grace each kept a daughter by their side as they shook hands, gave hugs, and assured everyone that they were doing just fine.

Ashley clung to Grace, and Cherish threw herself into her daddy's shoulder a hundred times, while the aunties raved over the matching dresses that both little girls wore. Wesley responded to the myriad of questions and comments aimed at him with boyish ease, escaping to lead his cousins in a sledding party before even half of them had arrived.

"My goodness, Ashley, your hair is so pretty," said Jolie when the little girl had found her place on her favorite auntie's lap, her curls bobbing about her face.

"Grandma cut it today," said Ashley.

"And you finally got your red dress. Your parents must think you're pretty special."

The little girl shrugged bashfully and smoothed her dress. Then she leaned back, and Jolie kissed her forehead. "I'm so happy that you're home for Christmas. Are you feeling better?"

Ashley nodded, then coughed hoarsely. "I have to nap every day," she said with a disappointed sigh.

"That's good. Sleep will help you get completely well." Jolie stroked Ashley's hair. "Cherish certainly has grown. She's probably a handful for you now, isn't she?"

Ashley shrugged. "Cherish doesn't like me."

"Oh, nonsense."

"She doesn't. Every time I try to take care of her, she cries. I can't hold her at all."

"I'm sure she just doesn't know you yet."

"I don't know."

"You two look so pretty with your matching dresses. It makes it even more special to have a brand-new dress when your baby sister has one exactly the same, doesn't it?"

"I guess." Ashley thought about Bonnie. She said she had waited all her life for a little sister to do her chores. Ashley couldn't imagine ever making Cherish do her chores.

"Tell me," Jolie whispered, "what did you ask for for Christmas?"

"Nothing." Ashley's brow creased.

"Nothing?"

Ashley squiggled when she thought about the gifts that surrounded the little Christmas tree Luke and Wes had brought in from the forest. Wes had peeked under the tree and told Ashley that he had two gifts under there, but Ashley refused to look for her name on any of the packages. Mr. Berk once brought her a package wrapped in brown paper, like the ones under the tree. He had brought a bottle home that night, too, and soon after she had opened the package, he accused her of stealing and strapped her. She hadn't touched brown paper since that day.

"I'm sure someone brought you something," Jolie said.

Ashley stiffened. "They didn't."

"Did you look already?"

"No. But there's nothing there for me. Wes has something, but I don't."

"I'm sure you have something." Jolie patted her tenderly. "We'll just have to wait until Christmas to see what it is."

Ashley remembered Christmas too. It was the only day of the year that Mr. Berk had spent the entire day at home, yelling angrily because he was trapped in the house by a snowstorm. Jack and Henry had taken the girls to the barn and wrapped them in wool blankets and covered them with straw so they wouldn't have to hear Mr. Berk yelling anymore. That night, Jack barricaded the barn door and stayed awake all night.

"I'm going to find Krissa," Ashley said. She slid off her aunt's lap and left.

Six-year-old Deborah clicked another button on her string and said gloomily, "It isn't right that three good mothers only have one baby a piece."

"Don't worry about it, Dee!" exclaimed nine-year-old Krissa. "What does it matter, anyway?"

"I want to have at least two babies. One is boring." She glanced at her raggedy doll, who had barely survived being mothered by a toddler, and now slumped in the corner decrepitly.

Ashley, who found this business of dolls and playing house to be quite difficult (for she was not "a natural," as Krissa claimed to be), shook down her string of buttons. "Why do you want two babies, Deborah? That's a lot."

"I think babies are fun," the child responded. "Cherish is sweet, and if I were a mother, I'd like to have two just like her."

Ashley smiled at the lace that peeked out from under her dress. "I don't like playing house."

"Didn't you ever have dolls?" asked Krissa with a pitying glance at her younger cousin.

"Just one." She nodded at the button-eyed doll in the rickety baby rocker the cousins had brought.

"And you only have two dresses for her?" asked Dee, glancing at the lacy dolly frock on the dresser.

"Why would I need any more than that?" Ashley looked at her with surprise. "I never change her clothes, anyway."

"You mean your dolly wears the same clothes to bed?" shrieked Deborah.

Ashley picked up a pink china button and slid it onto her thread. "Most of the time." She glanced at her cousin. "Deborah, I don't always have time to change her."

Little Dee glanced at her sister with wide eyes. "We always change our dolls before bed."

"What's your doll's name?" Krissa asked Ashley.

Ashley shrugged.

Deborah's eyes grew wider. "You don't even have a name for her?"

"What do you think I should name her?"

"Bonnie," Krissa said. "That's the name of my kitten."

"I don't like that name." Ashley clicked another button onto her string, wondering why anyone would ever name someone Bonnie.

"I don't think it's fair that we have to leave in just three nights," Deborah said, changing the subject before Ashley had the chance to decide on a name for her doll.

Krissa shrugged. "At least we get to spend Christmas together."

"Do you think my string is long enough now?" asked Ashley, holding it out at arm's length.

Krissa glanced at it. "You're already done? How'd you go so fast?"

Ashley gazed at the pastel decoration. "I'm going to have Mama tie it," she announced, standing up. "When you're done, you can come down."

"Aren't you going to take your dolly?" Deborah asked.

"No." Ashley darted out the door.

Ashley scurried down the stairs, but stopped at the bottom and peeked into the sitting room, looking for any hint of male appearance. Finding none, she crept to the dining room, where she was greeted by kind welcomes from the aunties.

"What have you made?" asked Aunt Susie. "Oh, Gracie, she made a button stringer!"

"I need you to tie it, Mama," said Ashley as she leaned on her mother's shoulder.

Grace took the string and began tying the end. "You did a good job, and you worked so quickly. Are the other girls done?"

"No. Where's Wes?"

"I think all the boys are playing baseball," Aunt Susie said.

Ashley looked out the window at the cold dusk of the winter evening and wondered how the boys got to be brave enough to play in the creepy shadows outdoors.

"Are you getting tired, Ashley?" Grace asked.

Ashley shrugged. "I guess so."

"We should probably make supper before it gets too late," suggested Grandma, glancing at the clock on the wall. "We're just going to do something simple tonight, right, Grace?"

"I have ham and biscuits. I figured we'd eat better tomorrow and the next day."

The women went to the kitchen, leaving Ashley sitting on a hard-backed chair in the dining room. She rested her head in her hands and smiled to herself when her petticoat tapped her leg when she swung her feet. She remembered her scars and felt her cheeks get hot as she pulled her pantaloons as far down as they would go.

"I finished mine," Deborah announced loudly as she paraded into the dining room with her button stringer draped around her shoulders and her doll under arm.

Ashley nodded. "Good."

Deborah plopped onto a chair. "What're you doing?"

"Nothing."

"What do you think I should name my doll?"

"I thought she already had a name."

"She does, but she needs two."

"Why does she need two names?" Ashley glanced at the yarn-haired doll and wondered why Deborah was so devoted to her. She was missing an eye and her arm was half ripped off.

"Everyone has two names," Deborah said matter-of-factly.

"Not everyone," Ashley said with a firm shake of her head. She remembered baby Mary Rose, and her cheeks stung with jealousy.

"My name is Deborah Jane." Dee bounced her doll on the edge of the table. "What's your other name?"

"I don't have one."

Deborah looked at her with pity. "Oh. I think I'm going to name my doll Jenny Lou. Isn't that pretty?"

Ashley shrugged.

"I think you should name yours Jenny Sue. Then we could rhyme."

"I don't much like the name Jenny," Ashley said.

"You don't much like any name. If you named your doll Jenny Sue, you could call her Sue or Jen."

Ashley stood and started toward the kitchen. "I'm gonna help with supper. You should hang your button stringer somewhere."

"I'll put it on the Christmas tree."

Ashley looked at Deborah through narrowed eyes. "No, put it somewhere else."

"Why? Don't you want the tree to look good?"

"It already has enough stuff on it. Why don't you hang it on the mantel?"

"Won't it light on fire?"

"No."

Ashley followed Deborah into the sitting room, where the six-year-old laid the stringer on the mantel and then turned to the presents under the tree. "Do you know how many are for you?" she asked softly.

"None," Ashley said, glaring at Deborah in hopes of silencing her.

"Not a single one? Are you sure?" She bent down in front of the presents.

"Don't read the names," Ashley demanded.

"This one's mine," Deborah whispered with delight. "It's one of the biggest ones. Krissa doesn't have one this big." She looked at Ashley and giggled. "I bet you have a big one too."

Ashley watched Deborah with suspense. The girl slightly moved one package, trying not to let the paper rustle so the parents wouldn't hear.

"I don't have one," Ashley insisted, her heart racing. "Stop looking." Dee ignored her cousin. "Stop it!" Ashley suddenly burst. "Go away, Dee! Stop looking!" She rushed forward, and in her attempt to silence Deborah, she stepped on the cherished doll. With a sickly tearing, poor Jenny Lou lost her good arm.

"Ashley!" Deborah screamed. She stared at the doll for an astonished moment and then lunged at her cousin, sending her to the floor. Ashley shrieked and pulled Deborah down with her, and in a matter of seconds, the girls received scratch marks on their arms and Deborah got a bruising blow to her cheek.

When the mothers came rushing in from the kitchen, Aunt Susie pulled Ashley away and Aunt Ruth grabbed Deborah, and both little girls were harshly set on the sofa and stool. Deborah was bawling and hugging her dolly to her chest. Ashley was on the brink of tears, but managed to hold hers back.

The second Luke Tanner stepped into the room, with the rest of the uncles, Ashley began trembling with terror. Aunt Susie stood near her, staring at her with disappointed surprise, but Ashley didn't care. She tried to dash away, but Luke was one step ahead of her. He caught her arm as she was fleeing toward the stairs.

"What's the problem?" he asked roughly.

Ashley wilted. Her legs lost all strength, and the only thing she could see was his belt. His hand gripped her arm tightly and before she had even shed a tear, Ashley was sobbing.

"She broke my doll!" Deborah shrieked. "She stepped on her!" She held the doll in the air so everyone could see. All the uncles and aunts stared at the two girls.

Luke felt Ashley becoming weaker, and two tears fell down her cheeks. He loosened his grip on her arm. "Why'd you do that?" he asked in a quiet voice. "Did you mean to break it?"

She didn't answer.

"Who started the fight?" Aunt Ruth asked, still holding her daughter's arm.

"She broke my doll!" Deborah screamed.

"Answer your mother, Dee," Uncle Mark insisted. "Did you start the fight?"

"Yeah." She glared at Ashley. "But she broke my doll on purpose."

"Did you mean to break it, Ashley?" Ruth asked.

She tried to answer but only stuttered.

"Dee, why'd she break your doll?" Uncle Mark prodded.

"'Cause I was trying to find her present under the tree," Deborah wailed.

Everyone looked between the girls in confusion.

"Ashley, did you break the doll on purpose?" Luke asked again. She still didn't answer. He panged with embarrassment and forced himself not to lash out at her.

"I don't know about you," Uncle Mark said to Luke, "but I think this fight was entirely inappropriate." He turned to his daughter.

"Dee, you hurt Ashley. Look, her arm is bleeding. I'm gonna have to discipline you for hurting your cousin."

Ashley winced and Luke felt it. He let go of her arm and rested his hand on her shoulder, sighing heavily. She would never open up to him if he responded to Mark's pressure to discipline her.

Mark took the doll from Deborah's arms and set it on the mantel. The little girl cried when her daddy ordered her to go outside, but she went, and he followed her.

The house fell silent, and the rest of the adults watched Luke as if waiting to see what action he would take. Grace knitted her hands together in nervousness.

Luke became tense with the pressure he felt from his in-laws, but he clenched his jaw and said firmly, "I'll take care of Ashley."

Ashley started to cough because she was choking on her sobs. When her father crossed the room and set her on the couch, she curled into a ball and covered her face with a pillow. All the adults left the room.

Ashley broke into a cold sweat as she imagined Mr. Tanner taking off his belt and beating her right there.

"Ashley, I need to talk to you," he said gently, squatting in front of the couch. She didn't respond. "Can you put the pillow down, please?"

"I'm sorry," Ashley groaned, pressing the pillow harder on her face. "I didn't mean to hurt her. Please don't, Mr. Tanner. Please just leave me alone." Ashley knew that begging and crying would only make him angrier, but she couldn't help herself. She trembled under the pillow, and when Luke put his big hand on her arm, she winced.

"I'm not going to hurt you." He took the pillow from her and set it on the floor. "I know you wouldn't break Deborah's doll on purpose." He patted Ashley's back gently. "Did she hurt your arm very badly?"

She held her breath, trying to put the images of Mr. Berk out of her mind. Every time Luke's voice rang, they pierced her sight.

"I have salve for your arm; do you want it?" he asked.

She shook her head slightly.

"All right, then, dry your tears now. Mama can fix Dee's doll and you can help her." He paused, feeling a rebuke on the tip of his tongue. When he saw the tears on her cheeks, he found himself saying, "You're a good girl, Ashley." Then, very reluctantly, he stood and left her on the couch.

"I can't imagine why he was so cowardly about it," Aunt Ruth said to Uncle Mark that night.

"I was completely insulted," he replied. "After I set the standard and did what should've been done to both girls, I couldn't believe he just left her alone."

"He didn't even correct her," Ruth continued. "Not one word of admonishment! He just talked to her kindly and told her she was a good girl. Never in my life have I seen such poor parenting."

"It's no wonder she's so distant from him; he never demands anything from her."

Ruth shook her head. "I just hope Dee doesn't find out; poor thing. After all, she's the one who got her doll ripped."

Luke slumped on the bed. "Grace, she didn't even respond to me except to shake her head one time. If that would've been Wesley, I would've given him the strapping of his life."

"But if you strapped her, that would've been the end of everything." Grace sighed as she brushed her hair. "It's unfortunate that it happened, but you needed a chance to prove yourself to Ashley. I was praying for you the whole time."

Luke raked his hand through his hair. "I don't know that it made any difference. She avoided me like the plague all night."

"At least she wasn't avoiding you because you hurt her."

Luke sighed. "Still, it would've been nice if Mark wouldn't have crucified me with his stare all the way through supper."

Through God we shall do valiantly.

—Psalm 108:13

THIRTY EIGHT

To Choose Love

The morning of Friday, December 23 started early for the Tanner household. By five o'clock, the mothers were rocking their bright-eyed babies and the fathers were traipsing through the forest on their annual deer hunt. The children began tossing just after the clock chimed six, and they were ready for breakfast by half past.

Shortly after the boys had been sent outside and the girls were settled in Ashley's room with more buttons for stringers, the men returned with two deer. They kissed their wives and poked at each other, ecstatic at their hunting success.

"There was only one other year when we got two deer on a single hunt," said Uncle Paul, grabbing a biscuit from the counter in the kitchen. "I reckon our luck is in your forest, Luke."

"Naw, it was my aim," replied Uncle Mark, laughing.

Luke hung his gun on the rack above the back door and chuckled. "I think Providence knew you two don't have enough food for the winter." A general burst of laughter erupted. Granddad Jackson laughed so hard his face turned red.

"Do you suppose that buck was watchin' out for a regular herd?" asked Mark as his wife put his youngest son, Neal, into his arms.

Luke shrugged. "I wouldn't doubt it. He was nervous, that's for sure."

"We would've gotten a lot more out o' that draw on the east side if we'd had us a dog." Paul shook his head as his red hair danced about.

"A dog?" Susie laughed. "Since when did deer hunting have any use for dogs?"

"Since I had to walk chest deep in a thicket."

Grandma picked up baby Mary, who was batting a crumb across the kitchen floor, and nodded at her three sons-in-law. "If the girls come down from their play and see those deer lying dead in the front yard, I can guarantee you'll all have your hands full."

All heads turned to the corpses lying on the snow-covered lawn. Grandma laughed when she saw five boys poking at the deer with sticks and popgun barrels.

"Is your barn floor clear enough to give us room to work, Luke?" asked Uncle Mark.

"I think we can make room." He peeked into the dining room and smiled at his wife, who was talking with Jolie. "Gracie, where's my butchering knife?"

"Just above the sink," she replied. "Luke, watch the boys so they don't cut themselves trying to help."

He winked at his sister-in-law and said to Grace, "I'll be sure of it, darlin'."

The men donned coats and gloves again and went outside, laughing like schoolboys.

"It's amazing how quickly they reconcile," Jolie said after the men left and the other aunts started washing dishes in the kitchen.

"I'm sorry the situation last night turned out like it did," Grace said. "I don't think Mark and Ruth understand that Luke can't respond to Ashley like a normal parent would. It's a big struggle with her right now."

"But a little incident like that isn't enough to separate our family. Ashley and Deborah are playing today like nothing's ever been between them."

Grace sighed. "I think we still have some big battles ahead of us."

Granddad walked in, wiping tears of laughter off his cheeks. “You two look like you’re talking about sad things, and that’s not allowed so close to Christmas,” he said loudly.

Jolie smiled. “Redemption is why Jesus came to the world, Dod. It’s a perfect time to talk about it.”

“Redemption, ’ey?” The old man sat beside Grace. “I reckon redemption never makes a soul sad.”

“Unless you’re talking about the one who still needs to be redeemed,” Jolie said.

Granddad nodded, his white beard brushing against his blue shirt. “And which soul were you talking about that still needs to be redeemed?”

“A little blonde-headed girl,” Jolie said.

“Ashley doesn’t need to be redeemed,” Granddad said with a chuckle. He looked at Jolie and his eyes sparkled under white eyebrows. “She just needs to be healed, and Luke is the perfect person to do the job.”

“Do you think so?” Grace asked.

“Of course.” He patted her hand. “The day Luke found redemption in the jail cell, God was saving Ashley, too. This situation can’t fail. Ashley will be a lot better off, even if she does get moved out of your home, and maybe that’s what God wants.”

“I wish you wouldn’t say that,” Grace said. “It was difficult enough for me to lose Emma, and going without Ashley from July until the middle of December was heart wrenching.”

“But it was the turning point for Luke,” Granddad said. “And it might have been the key to success with Ashley.”

“I don’t know if she’ll ever be completely healed,” Grace said. “Do you think she’ll ever function normally? She’s had to deal with so much already.”

Granddad shook his head. “Normal for Ashley may be different than it has been for Wes and Cherish. She’s always going to have scars.”

“Do you think you’ll adopt again?” Jolie asked, resting her elbows on the table.

Grace sniffed. "If Ashley gets taken away, the orphanage system will throw our name out of their file. But if we end up keeping her, I'm not afraid of adopting again."

"Another baby would do you good," Granddad suggested. "A person who hasn't been scarred so much by life."

The little girls came pounding down the steps and Ashley fell into her mother's lap, her curls bouncing on her shoulders.

"I don't know." Grace pressed her cheek against Ashley's head. "I think I'd take another one of these any day."

Ashley looked at her mother. "Another what, Mama?"

Grace kissed her. "I'd take another one of you if I ever found one. But I'm pretty sure there's not another little girl in the world as special as you."

Ashley's cheeks glowed.

"I think she's a keeper," Granddad said with an ebullient laugh.

Jolie winked at her and Ashley giggled.

"Should we go fix Dee's doll, Ashley?" Grace asked.

"I already did."

"You did?" Grace was surprised.

"That's what I was doing up there. She's just like new."

"Deborah, where's your doll?" Jolie called into the kitchen. The six-year-old peeked into the dining room with the doll clutched under her arm. "Did Ashley fix Jenny Lou for you?"

"Yeah." With a big smile Deborah handed the doll to Grace. Grace felt the repaired arm as Ashley and Deborah watched intently.

"Deborah didn't want me to poke Jenny with a needle," Ashley said, "but I told her I had to, else she wouldn't get fixed."

The doll's arm was slightly crooked and the stitches were large and uneven, but Grace smiled. "You did a wonderful job," she said. "Look, Dod, Ashley healed Jenny Lou. She'll probably always have a scar, but Ashley did her work well."

"Your turn Ashley!" exclaimed Wes, tossing the wooden bat toward his little sister.

She stepped up to the flour-sack home plate and timidly picked up the bat. The sun glared in her face. "I can't see the ball."

Wes shrugged. "You just have to watch closely."

"Can't I bat the other way?"

"Dad said we couldn't bat toward the shed."

"But I can't see. I'll miss the ball and get out. I'll hit really lightly the other way."

Wes glanced at Len, who was playing umpire, then turned back to his sister. "I guess that's OK. Krissa, switch places; second base is going to be home plate now."

"Why?" asked Norman, the pitcher.

"'Cause Ashley can't see the ball. Just scoot closer; it'll work."

The children switched places, and Ashley was soon stepping on the pile of acorns that was the new home plate, staring at the pitcher with the sun at her back.

Wes stood behind her and whispered, "Just watch the ball. You can do it."

Norman pitched the baseball. Ashley swung and missed.

"Strike one!" hollered Len.

Ashley glared at him, then put the bat up to her shoulder again. The ball came slowly. She swung exactly when Wes told her and hit it softly.

"Run, Ashley!" Wes hollered. "Go to first base!"

She darted toward the acorn pile that was lumped on the snow and stepped on it just as Gerald touched her back.

"You're out!" yelled Len, waving his arms wildly.

"Is she really?" Wes asked the umpire.

"Yeah; I touched her," Gerald called.

"Give her another try then," suggested Kenny.

Wes nodded his approval, and Ashley shuffled back to home plate. She took up the bat and squeezed it in her hands.

"I'll tell you when to swing again," said Wes softly.

The ball came before Ashley was ready for it. But Wesley timed the swing perfectly, and Ashley swung her fastest, hitting the ball with a hard crack that made all the little ones wince and duck. Ashley threw the bat and ran for base.

"Go to second!" shrieked Krissa, who was supposed to be on the opposing team. "Gerald, catch the ball! Catch it!"

The big boys backed farther toward the shed, but stopped abruptly when the ball crashed through the window.

"Wes!" screamed Len.

Ashley stopped halfway between first and second base, staring at the broken window in horror. Wes gasped, and all the children ran to the shed, abandoning homemade gloves and wooden helmets on the dirty snow.

Wes stopped in front of the window and his rosy-cold cheeks turned pale. The other children gathered around him, shaking their heads and whispering.

"What should we do?" exclaimed Ashley. She tugged on the long sleeves that covered her hands, ignoring the frightened whispers of her girl cousins.

The lad shook his head and glanced at Norman. "You think we could fix that?"

"Do you have glass?"

Wes sighed. "No."

"Can we keep playing?" asked little Dee.

Gerald poked his sister. "Hush, Deborah."

Kenny glanced at Wes. "Maybe we should've played in the meadow."

"In the deep snow?" said Len, shaking his head. "We couldn't run in that if we tried. Besides, we were fine until Ashley couldn't see."

Ashley felt a pang of guilt, and her eyes widened in fear.

The children stood silently for a while, staring at the shattered window. Ashley put the coat collar up to her chapped cheeks. She glanced repeatedly at Wes, waiting for his direction.

Wes sighed. "Do you think we can get the ball out, Norm?"

The oldest cousin stood on tiptoe and looked through the window. "It's right by the stove. If the door isn't locked, we can get it out for sure."

"But your dad said we couldn't go in there 'cause of that real expensive shipment," Kenny said.

"What shipment?" Len asked.

Wes peered through the window and saw a stack of boxes by the door. "Medicine," he replied. "You think those boxes are too close to the door, Norm?"

Norman shrugged. "Not too close."

"I guess we can try, then."

"But we're not supposed to," Ashley said quietly.

Wes glared at her. "What do you expect us to do? We have to get the ball out."

The little party moved toward the door. Wes clicked the handle and found it unlocked. The boys ordered their sisters to stay back, and watched intently as Wesley slowly opened the door and peeked inside.

"I see it," he said, poking his head through the crack. He opened the door a little bit farther and squeezed partly through. Wes reached for the ball while still halfway squished by the door. The three medicine boxes tottered, then crashed to the floor.

"No!" Wes shrieked, his heart leaping in his chest. He barreled through the door and stepped on a pile of broken glass and seeping medicine.

"You broke them!" cried Ashley, shoving her way through the crowd of boys. "What are you going to do?"

"What am *I* going to do?" he scolded. "What are *you* going to do? You're the one who broke the window!"

"Pick it up, quick!" said Len, kneeling on the floor and shoving the broken bottles back into the boxes. He stopped with a painful shout and stared at his bleeding finger.

"Get away from it." Norman picked Len up and pushed past the gaping crowd out the door. "Just leave it for Uncle Luke."

Ashley clung to Wes's arm. "What are we gonna do?" she whispered. "He's gonna find out."

"Of course he is," said Wes, shoving his sister's hand away. "Everyone just stay out of the shed now. I'm going to the house."

The children stood in silence as Wesley walked away, shaking his head in disgust.

Ashley slipped on her old boots and stepped onto the porch. She wrapped herself in her coat and sat next to Wes, who was slumping on the swing.

For a long moment, the siblings watched an intense snowball fight taking place in the yard as they rocked slowly in the chilly, winter wind.

"What are you gonna do?" asked Ashley.

"Wait for Dad to get home."

"Where is he?"

"In town."

Ashley shivered. "Then what are you gonna do?"

"Tell him."

"You can't!" she shrieked. "We'll get in trouble."

"We'll be in even bigger trouble if we don't tell. He'll find out as soon as he sees it."

"But Wes, you can't."

"Why not?" He glared at her.

"I don't want him to know."

"He has to know."

Ashley sank onto the swing and tears sprang to her eyes. She imagined every sort of discipline that could possibly befall her, and panic came over her. Luke had already been merciful and chosen not to strap her yesterday; surely this would push him over the edge.

"When is he coming back?" she asked.

"Around three."

"What time is it now?"

Wes pulled out his pocket watch. "Ten till."

"Is that close to three?"

The lad nodded.

Ashley's cheeks flushed when she saw the wagon coming down the lane, and her heart raced when she laid eyes on Luke Tanner.

Wes stood. "I have to help unload the wagon." He shoved his hands into his pockets and stepped off the porch. Ashley quickly retreated to the house and the warm company of the womenfolk.

It took Wes less than ten minutes to confess to his father after the wagon was unloaded. The lad's face was so smeared with guilt that Luke knew something was wrong before Wes admitted it. When the boy did come out with the story, Luke was so surprised and so angry, he threatened to strap both Wes and Ashley and left the boy in the parlor while he talked with Grace.

"How much more can I handle?" Luke exploded the moment the couple reached the privacy of their bedroom. "After everything that went on with Ashley yesterday, when I was utterly humiliated in front of all my company, this has to happen. Wes and Ashley both need a good dose of heavy discipline so they'll think about the consequences next time."

"You can't do anything to Ashley," Grace said quickly.

"No?" He threw his hands in the air. "So I should just let her bury me in the dirt of frustration, walk all over me, and fake fear whenever consequences catch up to her? This is a pathetic case of manipulation, and it has to stop."

Grace sat in silence.

"Any parent would agree that Ashley needs to be disciplined. And I should make Wes work off every penny it's going to take to replace that medicine. Do you realize what's happening? Wes is going to make up for what he's done, but Ashley will be let go again. I spent two months worth of paychecks for that medicine. That little girl is costing me a fortune."

A penny parcel.

Luke stopped, and his face stung. He pushed the thought aside. *I've already paid more than a penny for her; that term is history.*

You gave some, but not all.

"She cannot run my life!" he answered the voice aloud, pulling roughly at his hair. "Grace, if I don't strap Ashley for what happened, Mark will criticize me. If I do strap her, she'll never forgive me. I'm in a trap, and there's no way out."

With the temptation I'll also make a way of escape.

What escape? I'm surrounded on every side!

Love her.

I have.

Love her again.

Luke dropped onto the bed. "I hate being controlled by an eight-year-old."

The love of Christ controls you.

The Bible says he who spares the rod hateth his son.

Love is patient.

I know.

Love doesn't seek its own.

What's that supposed to mean? I already gave up striving for my reputation, remember? This is all about Ashley now.

Not Mark?

Luke got off the bed and went for the door, shaking his head.

"What're you going to do?" Grace asked.

"Nothing." He swung the door open. "I'm going to see this thing out to the end, that's what I'm going to do. Nothing!" He marched down the stairs.

It took every ounce of self-control Luke had to walk into the kitchen and approach Ashley gently. She was standing on a stool, helping Aunt Susie peel potatoes. When his shadow fell on her, she winced.

Luke stepped up behind her and wrapped his arms around her shoulders. "Ashley, honey, I love you," he said in a deep, quiet voice. He pressed his cheek next to hers and she could smell his spicy cologne. "Wes told me what happened in the shed. He and I are going to clean up the glass, but I want you to bat away from the shed next time, OK?"

She couldn't breathe or squeak an answer. She could feel his breath on her face, and his arms could've wrapped around her twice.

"You're a good girl." He patted her arm and walked away.

As Ashley heard his big boots pound out of the kitchen, she felt a layer of her wall come crashing to the ground.

Charity shall cover the multitude of sins.

—1 Peter 4:8

Larissa L. Hitch

THIRTY NINE

Holiday Traditions

The children sprawled out on the sitting room floor, giggling and chatting while wiggling their toes in front of the fire and letting the heat sting warmth into their rosy cheeks. Ashley sat in the corner of the sofa, separate from the cozy party on the floor.

"You all ought to come to our place next Christmas," said ten-year-old Len with a dreamy grin. He crossed his hands under his head and lay on a tiny sofa pillow. "We've got the best sledding hill in the country."

"Really?" Wes looked over several bodies to see his cousin. "But don't you live in the city?"

"We have to walk to the hill, but it's great after that."

"I hate living in the city," grumbled Norman.

"Me too," agreed Gerald.

"I've lived in the city," Wes said.

"You have?" Len leaned up on his elbow.

"Yeah, when I was an orphan."

"Orphans misbehave a lot," said Krissa from where she lay against the brick hearth, wool stockings pulled up to her knees.

Wes scowled at her. "That's because they don't have fathers. Once they aren't orphans anymore, most of them turn out really good. That's not a very nice generalization."

"What's a *gen-ral-setion?*" Deborah asked.

Wes searched his mind for the definition he had learned at school. "'It's a statement presented as a general truth, but based on limited or incomplete evidence.'"

"You're too smart," said Norman. "You should stop reading so much."

"I like to read."

"Too much reading is bad for you," Len said, turning over on his stomach.

Kenny glanced at Wesley through the flickering firelight. "I like it that Wes reads so much. He's probably a lot smarter than you, Len." He poked his younger brother's ribs.

"Can you believe tomorrow's Christmas Eve?" Krissa said, and all the boys turned their heads to her.

"That means we have to leave in two days," said Gerald gloomily.

"You're leaving on Christmas?" Wes asked.

Norman sighed. "Yup. Dad has to be back to work on Monday."

"There is one good thing," Wes said. "Since Christmas is on Sunday, we won't have time to open our presents on Christmas morning, so Dad said we get to have our Christmas one day early."

Len smiled. "I think I got what I really wanted for Christmas. That one package with the blue string is just the right size."

Gerald leaned up on his elbow excitedly. "What did you want?"

"I'm not telling."

"I didn't get what I wanted," Deborah said with a heavy sigh. "I wanted my own pony, and none of those boxes would fit a pony."

"Dad and Mum wouldn't bring a pony here anyway." Norman laughed. "If they did get you a pony, it'd be at home."

Deborah's face lit up.

"What do you want for Christmas, Ashley?" asked Wes, smiling at what he could see of her shadow.

Ashley's heart leapt into her throat. "Nothing."

Len grinned at her. "Awe, come on. You gotta want something."

"I don't. Nothing under the tree is mine."

Deborah began to argue, but Norman put his hand over her mouth and she fell silent.

"I'm sure you'll get something, Ashley," Norman said. "Your dad will make sure you get at least one gift for Christmas."

Luke stepped into the room, his towering frame spreading an impressive shadow on the floor. The children turned their heads to him. "Are you children ready to hear the Christmas story?" he asked as the other adults came in behind him.

"We're going to listen to it tonight?" asked Krissa sleepily.

Uncle Mark dropped onto the floor beside her. "I'm going to sit here so I can pinch you if you fall asleep," he said with a smile.

"Wes, would you get my Bible from my bedroom?" Luke asked as the adults squished onto the couches or joined the children on the floor. Ashley shoved herself against the arm of the sofa so she wouldn't touch Uncle Paul, who sat beside her with baby Mary in between.

Wes darted up the stairs and came back with the large Bible, setting it in his father's lap.

Luke lifted Cherish onto his lap, then turned the torn and stained pages of the book. He nodded at Granddad Jackson. "Would you like to read it?"

The old man smiled, and the wrinkles around his eyes deepened. "I'd love to." He took the Bible, and as the children quieted and the fire roared, Granddad read in his deep, gruff voice: "The gospel according to Saint Matthew. Chapter one, verse eighteen. Now the birth of Jesus Christ was on this wise: When as his mother Mary was espoused to Joseph, before they came together, she was found with child of the Holy Ghost. Then Joseph, her husband, being a just man, and not willing to make her a public example, was minded to put her away privily. But while he thought on these things, behold, the angel of the Lord appeared unto him in a dream."

A knock came on the front door and Granddad stopped reading. Luke went to the door and as soon as he opened it, Mr. Bowtie shouted, "Merry Christmas! I see you have the whole family here, Tanner. Well, congratulations—I'm glad you have a party! I came to spread a little Christmas cheer."

Luke chuckled and swung the door open further. "Welcome, Harris. Come in. We were just reading the Christmas story. Would you like to join us?"

The preacher smiled and thrust a large flour sack toward Luke. "I brought presents for the children. It'd do my soul good to hear the Christmas story. I'd be honored to join you . . . if you have a seat."

The children scrambled about the floor, squishing each other against couches and walls to make room for the preacher near the fire.

When all were settled, Granddad continued reading. "And an angel of the Lord appeared unto him in a dream, saying, 'Joseph, thou son of David, fear not to take unto thee Mary thy wife, for that which is conceived in her is of the Holy Ghost.'" Granddad's face lit with a smile, and his pale eyes searched the faces of his grandchildren as he read with passion, as if this were the most exciting story he knew. "'And she shall bring forth a Son, and thou shalt call his name Jesus: for He shall save His people from their sins.'"

Ashley's eyes wandered to the preacher and she examined every part of him that she could see—from his stiff, white collar to the pointy shoes on his feet and all the jewels on his fingers and the chain around his neck. Mr. Bowtie had the same, gruff voice that Ashley remembered Mr. Berk having, and the bag the preacher had brought was perfectly haunting. Ashley couldn't get her eyes off of it. If he offered her one of those gifts, she would firmly refuse it.

"Would you like to read some for us, Mr. Harris?" offered Granddad when he reached the end of chapter one.

The preacher's cheeks blushed in pleasure. Like a rosy-painted clown, he laughed heartily and reached for the Bible, showing his shiny head to the curious children.

Mr. Bowtie cleared his voice and Norman tweaked his own collar in mocking gesture of the teal bowtie. The boys stifled their laughter.

"Now when Jesus was born in Bethlehem of Judea in the days of Herod the king, behold, there came wise men from the east to Jerusalem, saying, Where is He that is born King of the Jews? for we have seen His star in the east, and are come to worship Him. When Herod the king had heard these things, he was troubled, and all Jerusalem with him."

Luke caught Ashley's gaze. He studied her, forgetting the reading and the other children and the draft that made Cherish shiver on his lap. He wanted to rescue Ashley from the deep pain he saw behind those eyes, but she nervously shoved herself against the couch as he watched her.

Lord, what should I do?

Love her.

I have.

Do it again. Love her no matter what.

Luke saw the way Ashley eyed Mr. Bowtie's bag on the floor, and he smiled to himself. He had bought her the prettiest pair of black shoes he could find, and they were wrapped and under the tree, ready to be opened in the morning. She may have doubted it tonight, but once morning came, Ashley would have to realize that Luke loved her.

Be not afraid nor dismayed . . . for the battle is not yours, but God's.

—2 Chronicles 20:15

FORTY

A Christmas Present

Ashley heard whispering before she opened her eyes. She peeked over the side of the bed and saw that Krissa and Deborah had their heads under the bed on either side of her, and they were giggling to each other. "What are you doing?" she asked.

"She's awake!" Deborah shrieked, sitting up into the wooden sideboard. She squealed in pain and lay holding her head for a moment, then giggled as she looked at Ashley. "We've been waiting for you to wake up. Let's go downstairs and open our presents."

"I don't want to." Ashley fell back on the bed with a sickly knot in her stomach.

Krissa jumped to her feet. "Whyever not? You *did* get something, Ashley; I saw your name on a package with a red bow."

"I don't want it." Ashley rolled over and covered her face with the pillow. She heard her cousins open the wardrobe and pull out their ruffled dresses and put them on.

Ashley sighed. Her hair was wrapped tightly in rags and she fooled with the raveled end of one and tried to think of anything but Christmas presents. She'd been Dee's age when she got the first Christmas present she actually liked. She had always received schoolbooks or mittens at the orphanage, but Mr. Berk had given her a bright pink bow for her hair and a piece of chocolate candy. Soon after she opened them, Bonnie had done her hair with the bow while Ashley licked the creamy candy. Then Mr. Berk called for her. Bonnie told Ashley he was angry and that she shouldn't go, but Ashley thought he wanted to see her with her hair done. When she showed her face downstairs, Mr. Berk took the candy from her hand, ripped the bow from her hair, and dragged her through the snow to the woodshed, blaming her for stealing.

Ever since then, Ashley had hated Christmas presents.

Krissa and Deborah left Ashley alone. Shortly after they left, Grace came into the bedroom.

"Are you ready for Christmas?" she asked excitedly. She unbuttoned Ashley's nightdress and gave her her red silk.

"I don't want to open presents," Ashley said gloomily.

"Why not?"

Ashley pulled the dress over her rag curlers.

Grace buttoned her dress and said gently, "You should be grateful for the gifts people give you."

That's exactly what Mrs. Berk said when Ashley refused to keep the pink bow.

Ashley began to untie her curlers in front of the mirror, just to busy her hands with something. "I don't think I got anything, anyway."

"Of course you did." Grace helped with the curlers. "I know Daddy got you a gift."

Ashley's heart throbbed. "I don't want it."

"Your daddy is very good at picking out gifts, Ashley. I'm sure you'll love what he bought you."

Ashley watched her mother pick at a tangle in one of the rags. "I don't want him to buy me anything."

"Darlin', people give gifts because they love you," Grace said. "Daddy won't ask for anything in return."

Ashley forced herself not to cover her ears. "I don't like it when people love me." Her mind burned with the memory of Mr. Berk's gruff voice telling her over and over that he loved her. Every time he brought something home for her, Mr. Berk told her he loved her. Whenever he brought a bottle home, he said he loved everyone.

Grace pulled at Ashley's springy curls. "Why don't you like it when people love you?"

"Just because." Ashley tried to move away from her mother, but Grace held her back.

"I'm not done with your hair."

Ashley bit her lip as she stared into the mirror and watched her mother's hands work through her curls until they swayed gracefully about her face. She heard Mr. Tanner go into the parents' bedroom and talk to Cherish. As he took the baby downstairs, Ashley's heart leapt.

Grace had to do a lot of persuading before she convinced Ashley to show her face in the sitting room.

Luke had awakened with something powerful nagging at him. He wasn't sure what it was, but as he did chores that morning, he felt uneasy. By the time he came back to the house and found the adults up and the children beginning to stir, he was completely disturbed. On his way upstairs to get Cherish from her cradle in the bedroom, he walked by the Christmas tree, and a bizarre thought popped into his head. It was so forceful, it was almost a command.

That's ridiculous, he thought as he lifted Cherish from her cradle and kissed her. *You told me to love her, God. I'm giving the gift out of love.*

But Luke had the strange feeling that something about that gift was not love. Ignoring the unthinkable urge to put Ashley's gift away, Luke poured himself a cup of coffee in hopes of quieting the inner voices that screamed at him.

It took the children less than ten minutes to eat the large breakfast the women had prepared, and they gathered in the sitting room, staring at all the packages under the tree and whispering and giggling among themselves. Ashley stayed by Grace's side in the dining room and Luke felt uncomfortable every time he looked at her.

At last, the adults finished their meal and told the children to sit still while Grandma passed out the gifts. The sitting room was tense with anticipation as packages were passed from one hand to another.

Ashley sat next to her mother on the couch, pinching her dress between her fingers as she watched the gifts being passed around. Krissa and Deborah squealed every time another package was placed in their laps, and Mary and Cherish watched wide eyed and smiling. The boys poked at one another and tried to guess what was under the brown paper.

When Grandma announced Ashley's name, the girl stiffened. Grace set a package on her lap, and Ashley saw that it was from the cousins.

Luke saw his package with the red bow sitting under the tree, and he smiled when Grandma picked it up and gave it to Ashley. But her face turned white when she read the tag, and her eyes filled with tears. Luke watched her as she dropped the present onto the floor and brushed tears from her cheeks.

"You can open now," Granddad announced when the floor under the tree was bare. The sound of brown paper ripping filled the sitting room, and Granddad's laugh boomed over all the noise as he exclaimed over every box the children opened. Krissa and Deborah shouted with glee when they each received a new doll, and the boys excitedly exclaimed over pocketknives. Aunt Susie helped Mary wrap her tiny doll in a crocheted baby blanket, and little Neal threw a ball at Granddad's face.

"What'd you get, Ashley?" Jolie asked, turning from where she was sitting on the floor to look at the little girl. Ashley looked back at her, and the hollowness of her eyes was almost unbearable. "Didn't you open yours yet?"

Ashley shook her head.

"Come on, Ashley," Grace prodded, "open your gifts. Who are they from?"

Ashley nervously looked at the labels of the two packages in her lap. "Granddad and Grandma and the cousins."

"Let's see what's inside."

Ashley hesitantly took off the brown paper and smiled slightly when she found a doll dress from Granddad and Grandma that matched her red silk. Krissa and Deborah beamed from across the room when Ashley opened the tiny china tea set they'd bought for her.

"Didn't you get one from Daddy?" Grace asked with surprise.

"No." Ashley anxiously clicked a teacup on the serving tray.

Grace felt her lap. "I'm sure he got one for you. Is it on the floor, Jolie?"

Jolie picked up the package with the red bow. "It's right here." She set it in Ashley's lap, but the little girl pushed it away.

"Open it," Grace said.

"I don't want to."

The mother picked at the knot on the package and Ashley watched tensely as the brown paper came off. When the lid of the box was open and Ashley saw a pair of shiny, black shoes, she pushed the gifts off her lap and scooted off the sofa, tripping over wrapping and bows and feet as she scrambled out of the sitting room.

"Where are you going, Ashley?" Luke called after her.

She fled up the stairs.

"Is she all right?" asked Grandma.

Mark shook his head, sniffing in disgust.

Luke picked up the shoebox, set Cherish in Jolie's lap, and went toward the stairs.

When he found Ashley's bedroom door locked, Luke almost exploded with frustrated. He wasn't about to beg her to let him in. He strutted to his bedroom and slammed the door, dropping the shoebox onto the dresser.

She's impossible, God! I do everything I can for that little girl, and she turns me away without a second thought. You told me to love her, and here I am, spending my good money on gifts for her, showering her with every form of love I can think of. And what do I get? A locked bedroom door and a rude refusal of my gift. I don't know what else to do! This child is too much for me to handle; she doesn't accept love in any form.

Luke sank onto the bed and covered his face with his hands. "I don't know what else to do, God," he whispered. "Ashley doesn't want me for a father; that's all there is to it."

A lie pierced Luke's thoughts, sending a pang of rejection. *It was stupid for you to try to reach out to Ashley. She hates you because of who you are.*

"No," he said quickly. "'O send out Thy light and Thy truth, let them lead me.'"

Luke sat quietly for a long while with thoughts of Ashley dancing in his brain. Slowly and gradually, he began to receive some insight. He started to understand that Ashley was filled with memories that had the power of distorting the beauty of wonderful things.

He thought about bathing, and it occurred to him that she probably hated it for good reason. He thought about chickens and schoolwork and strappings and Christmas presents. Somehow, they were all intertwined in Ashley's mind, and somehow, at the root of each of them, there was no doubt some excruciating memory.

"So what can I give her, God?" he whispered with a heavy sigh. "You want me to love her, but I don't know how."

Luke remembered hearing Ashley and Deborah talk about names, and he paused. Deborah said her middle name was Jane, and Ashley said she didn't have a middle name.

She said it sadly, he thought. *She wants a second name.*

Luke glanced at the box with torn paper and the red bow hanging off the edge of the dresser. "So I'm just supposed to give her a name, 'ey? That's really what she wants for Christmas?" He shook his head as he reached for the door. "I don't think I'll ever figure that girl out."

When the staircase door opened, everyone in the sitting room looked toward it. "You left her up there?" Mark's voice piped.

Luke resisted the temptation to be ashamed. "I reckon forcing myself on her won't do any good."

Mark shook his head with a heavy sigh, and Luke blushed under the disapproval.

He looked at Grace. "Honey, would you come talk to me in the parlor for a minute?"

The children slid out of the way to make a path for Grace, and Luke took her hand and led her out of the room.

"I want to give Ashley a middle name," he said as he shut the door.

"Why?"

"Because I know she wants one. I heard her and Dee talking about it."

"Did you talk to her just now?"

"No. She locked her door and I didn't even try to open it. I should've known she wouldn't accept a Christmas gift."

"You couldn't have known that," Grace said firmly.

He sniffed. "If I would've been listening to God, I could've known it. I just hope I didn't do damage by trying to give it to her."

"Why didn't she take it?"

"I don't know. But I know that she'd like to have a middle name, and I want to give it to her."

"Do you think she'll accept it?"

Luke tapped at the edge of the rug with his foot. "It may take a little time and a few tears, but I think she can go to bed tonight knowing she's loved." He paused, fighting a deep sense of grief. "That girl has an awful memory for every normal life activity and every holiday on the calendar. I want to give her one good memory this year."

"I'm sure I'll love whatever name you pick," Grace said with a little smile. "Are you going to talk to her about it now?"

"First I have to persuade her to open her door."

"And if she doesn't?"

"Then I'm going to unlock it and hope she doesn't go into hysterics. I'll take my normal position, ten feet away, and try to talk to her. I hate constantly keeping a distance, but I'm afraid if I don't, I'll lose the little ground I've gained."

"Do you want me to come with you?"

"Not yet." Luke reached for the door handle. "What do you think of the name Elise? Ashley Elise Tanner."

"After Emma Elise?"

"Yeah. This time I'm going to give my life before I give up on that little girl."

Ashley sat in the corner of her room, hugging her knees to her chest and watching the door as if it would burst off its hinges. A cold draft leaked in through the window and seemed to chill her heart. When she heard footsteps on the stairs, she held her breath. The steps came to her door and then she heard a soft knock. Her sweaty hands gripped her knees and she forced herself to breathe.

"Ashley, it's Daddy," Mr. Tanner's voice rang through the door. "I want to talk to you; can you open the door?"

She didn't move.

"I'm not going to discipline you; I just want to tell you something."

Ashley heard him stick the key in the door and twist it. When the latch popped and the door swung open, Ashley crouched down as far as she could.

"I put the gifts away," he said.

She held her breath.

"I want to give you something else instead." He paused, lingering in the threshold. "I want to give you a name."

Ashley's heart pounded, but she kept her eyes on the floor.

"Would you like a second name, Ashley?"

She glanced at him for a split second and barely nodded.

"Good. I was thinking we could call you Ashley Elise Tanner; how's that?"

Ashley bit her lip and tried to keep the smile from taking over her face. She felt herself relax. "Good," she squeaked.

Luke winked at her. "I'm glad. Now you can have something to be happy about on Christmas." He backed out, pulling the door after him.

Ashley went to her desk and pulled out a piece of paper. She wrote "Ashley Elise Tanner" in big letters. Then she stood on her bed and hung the paper where the picture of the rocking chair used to be.

Thou shalt be called by a new name, which the mouth of the Lord shall name.

—Isaiah 62:2

FORTY ONE

Luke's Promise

The house was cold and dark, and the only noise that could be heard was the deep breathing of slumber. The winter sky was lit with bright stars, and the wind tapped at the window and rustled the curtain. Luke felt the heat of the stove downstairs swelling through the vent in the floor, and he turned over in his bed.

He felt the open-faced clock in the dark. Three thirty-seven. Even after hours of prayer, he was unable to rid himself of the great disturbance in his spirit, and sleep refused to comfort him. A burning knot stuck in his stomach.

God, I have to sleep. Tomorrow was Christmas, but Luke didn't think he could celebrate. Mrs. Harms's evaluation of Ashley was getting closer with every tick of the clock.

It's over, God. I have no more time for effort. It's all up to You now.

Luke pondered how much painful exertion it had taken him to break through to Ashley enough that she wouldn't cower in his presence. He had made it no further than that. Even though he had played the question game consistently for five full days, he hadn't discovered anything about Ashley that he considered worthwhile. He still didn't know why she hated so many things and what made her respond to him the way she did. He was clueless as to where she had come from or why she was orphaned. He didn't know why she hated chickens or why she could hardly stand to even talk about strappings.

I failed, God. I ruined too much the first time she was here, and I can't make up for it in a week. I'm up against a brick wall, and there's no way to make it to the other side. I've done my best—You saw me! I tried to love her with everything I was worth, but there's too much to dig up and not enough time.

The darkness of the night seemed to seal hopelessness into Luke's heart. He thought about the way it could've been if company hadn't come that week—he could've had more time to spend directly impacting Ashley. Maybe he shouldn't have let them come. Maybe that was one of those mistakes he would regret for the rest of his life.

Grace stirred in her sleep beside Luke, and he panged with desperation. She had held Ashley all evening and clung to her at bedtime. She'd done exactly what Luke had wanted to do, but instead he'd forced himself to entertain the uncles.

Before Grace had taken Ashley to bed, Luke had locked the window in the little girl's bedroom. He wasn't really afraid of Ashley running away again, nor of anyone coming in the window and stealing her, yet he felt compelled to do anything he could to keep Ashley under his roof. The window had nothing to do with his fear; he only had to seal out the lurking threats outside the four walls of his home and try to protect Ashley from the pain that Christmas Day could bring.

Luke couldn't get the frantic thoughts to stop antagonizing his brain. He felt the clock at three fifty, and again at four twenty-two. By then, the wind had quieted and left nighttime noises to creep about the house. He heard the fire crackling faintly in the stove, but it soon died down. Trees cracked outside from the weight of the snow, and the moon shone through the window, leaving freckled shadows on the wood floor.

Exhausted and weary, Luke stood, dressed, and kissed his sleeping wife. "I'm going for a walk," he whispered.

Grace grabbed his arm. "What time is it?"

"About four-thirty."

"Can't you sleep?"

"I'm tired of trying. I'll be back in a while—don't worry."

Luke kissed her again and left.

Outside, a vast spread of stars scattered sparkles on the snow. Luke's boots crunched on the icy blanket, and his warm breath sent puffs of steam in the cozy nighttime air. He stuffed his hands in his pockets and strolled toward the pasture, staring at the limitless expanse of sky. He heard snow fall from the trees in the deep forest, and as he pushed down the fence and stepped over, Luke felt the twinge of barbed wire brush against his leg. The horses in the barn perked their ears and watched him disappear over the rolling pasture—beyond the creek and along the far fence line. Like a snowflake encircled by the storm, Luke was soon a speck engulfed by a sea of winter blackness.

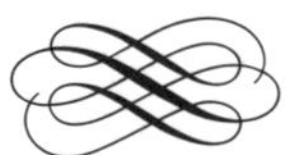

Wesley rolled over and bumped heads with Len for the third time. He opened his eyes and snuggled farther under the heavy quilt, glancing at the fire, which smoldered and glowed in the hearth. He heard the clock chime five.

Wes glanced out the window at the dark sky. Dad wouldn't be up for another hour to do chores. He gave Len a shove and settled back on his pillow.

Suddenly, like a lightning flash in the darkness, a shriek pierced the night. It was a shriek of horror, a sound almost too awful to be human—like the death cry of an animal or the wail of extreme pain.

Wes scrambled to his knees as a shiver snaked down his back.

"What was that?" Norman asked, sitting up with a start. Wes heard doors opening upstairs and Uncle Mark came rushing from the spare bedroom.

"It's Ashley," Wes answered the panicked stares of the boys in the sitting room.

"Ashley?" Norm's eyes grew wide with alarm. "That was too awful to be a person."

Wes felt his heart pounding in his throat. "She's having a nightmare."

Light flickered from the candle that Uncle Mark lit, and Kenny stoked the fire until it roared in a futile attempt to drown out the horrible sound of the cries.

"Wes!" Aunt Susie yelled down the stairs, and all the boys banged up the staircase. Wes shivered with eerie fear in the dark hallway. He heard sobbing and begging inside Ashley's room, and he rushed for the door.

"Find your dad," Susie commanded, poking her head into the hall. "Go quickly; your mother needs him."

"Where is he?" Wes bit his lip with concern. He saw Krissa and Deborah crying on the bedroom floor and his mother was kneeling beside a heap of blankets.

"I don't know," Susie said. "Your mother said he went for a walk. Look in the barn, and holler until you find him. Hurry."

Wes darted away and passed Grandma, who lifted her long gown and pranced up the stairs, muttering, "The poor child."

"What's happened?" asked Aunt Ruth as she carried Neal out of the spare bedroom and grabbed Wesley on his way by.

"Ashley had a nightmare."

Ruth darted up the stairs. Wes stuck his feet into his boots and crashed out the back door.

Grace knelt beside Ashley on the bedroom floor and pulled away the tangle of blankets that kept the screaming child trapped. Ashley fought and scratched against the cocoon of quilts on top of her as if she were struggling against human strength that was trying to strangle her very life.

"Ashley, Mama has you," Grace cooed.

"Don't touch me! Don't hurt me!" Ashley screamed. She pushed away from her mother and buried herself in the quilts, kicking and tearing and shrieking. Her cheeks were wet with tears. Grace knew Ashley was fighting a real battle against power and brutality. This wasn't a dream—it was a memory.

As Aunt Ruth rescued her two terrified girls, Grandma entered and lit the lamp on the bedstead. She knelt at Grace's side.

"Wake her up," she pleaded, her old voice trembling. "She's in a nightmare. You have to wake her up."

"I can't, Mum. She won't let me touch her. It must be horrible—listen to her!"

Grandma lifted Ashley into her arms, and the girl shrieked again. Her screaming turned to begging, and her little voice sobbed and pleaded with a hundred apologies and promises, as if her only hope was to try to rouse a tender side that would choose mercy over anger. Grandma tried to bring her out of her dream but Ashley didn't hear the gentle soothing.

Finally, Grandma released her and she fell back on the floor. Her voice became hoarse from screaming and her pillow was wet with tears.

Grace touched Ashley's trembling arm. "Is there light in here?" she asked loudly. "Susie, bring the light here so she can wake up."

Aunt Susie appeared with the lamp, followed by Uncle Paul.

"Where's Luke?" Paul asked gently.

"He went for a walk at four-thirty. What time is it?"

"Just after five," said Grandma. "Where'd he go?"

"I don't know. He said he'd be back soon. Did you send Wes to find him?"

"He's looking now," Susie said.

"Pick her up, or pinch her," Uncle Mark suggested as he entered. He squatted beside the little girl.

Grace put up her hand. "Don't touch her! You'll only make it worse."

"Why is she doing this?"

"It's a nightmare. Oh, sweet Ashley, wake up, baby. I'm here now, darlin'. Wake up for Mama." Grace's lip trembled as she tried to hold back tears. "Paul, put her on the bed, but gently. Don't force her."

Paul lifted Ashley onto the bed. The girl fought him violently, and the more he constrained her, the louder she screamed.

Granddad and Aunt Jolie pushed through the crowd of boys in the doorway.

"Let me hold her," Jolie suggested.

"Don't try," Uncle Paul said, holding up a scratched arm.

Then, just as suddenly as Ashley had broken into the fit, she awoke from it. Her screaming turned to weeping as she sat up and crawled into her mother's arms. "Don't let me go, Mama. Hold me—please hold me. He's going to come again, Mama! Don't let go. Where's Wes? He has to lock the window. Hurry, or he'll come again. Please. I can't see him again; he's gonna do it again!"

A blanket of silence came over the room as everyone listened to Ashley sob. The boys in the doorway whispered amongst themselves and the uncles backed away from the bed, their faces smeared with pity. Jolie retreated down the stairs, and the crowd of boys followed.

"Let's leave these two alone," suggested Granddad. "Let Grace take care of Ashley."

"I need Luke," said Grace, grabbing Susie's arm as she started to leave.

No sooner had the words escaped her mouth than Wes stomped up the stairs, panting. "I can't find Dad."

"You have to find him," Grace demanded. "Did you look in the office and the barn?"

"I looked everywhere. I called to the pasture and I checked in the privy and I searched the barn and the feed room."

"Should I saddle a horse and find him?" offered Uncle Paul.

"No. He'll come back. We can wait."

"I'll be in the bedroom if you need anything," said Susie.

The hall emptied and Grace took Ashley into her bedroom so Krissa and Deborah could return to their beds. She settled Ashley on the big bed and lit a lamp when she begged for light. Cherish was asleep in her cradle, surprisingly undisturbed by the recent chaos.

Ashley buried her face in the pillows and sobbed until her little body shook. Voices screamed in her head and she could do nothing to get away from them. She tried to cover her ears, but they still taunted her. She curled up in a ball and swaddled the quilt around her, sobbing and fighting against the battle that raged inside.

Grace lay beside her and rubbed her arm, but Ashley couldn't respond. She felt a lump in the sheet underneath her and thought it was a spring in Bonnie's bed. She could almost feel cold rags on her legs, and she could hear Jack's voice asking her if she was OK.

Ashley covered her face with her hands. She felt sick to her stomach and her head pounded.

"Are you cold, darlin'?" Grace asked tenderly.

Ashley shook her head and gasped for breath between sobs. She felt pain in her leg when Grace bumped against it. "My leg hurts." Maybe it hadn't been a dream.

Ashley brought her head out of the pillow and looked around the room. She saw the cradle and the pretty quilt and the bright lamp.

"Why does it hurt?" Grace asked.

"I don't know." Ashley pulled back her pantaloons. Her heart sank when she saw blood. "It's cut."

"Your leg?"

"Yeah."

Grace sat up and scooted off the bed. "I'll get Aunt Susie to get a cold rag."

"No!" Ashley whimpered, breathing heavily again. "Not a cold rag. Get something else."

"Don't worry, Ashley. I'll take care of you. Just stay here; I'll be right back."

As soon as Grace left the room, the shadows seemed to come to life. The lamp caused the darkness of the corners to dance, and Ashley closed her eyes, trying to seal out the images. She looked down at her leg and when she saw the scars, she gasped.

The bedroom door opened and Susie stepped through with Grace behind her. "You can't come in here," Ashley yelled, scrambling under the quilts.

"I'm here to help you," Susie said.

Ashley snapped her pantaloons on her ankles. "I don't need help. Go away. Mama, don't let her in here!"

Grace sat on the bed, gently touching Ashley's arm. "Darlin', Susie's very gentle; I want you to let her look."

"No." Ashley sobbed when she saw a torn rag in Susie's hand. She gripped the quilts with all her strength.

A knock came on the door, and Jolie timidly stepped through. Her cheeks were stained with tears and a shadow of grief was over her pretty face. She smiled at Ashley and said sweetly, "What's the matter, honey?"

"She has a cut," said Susie.

Ashley stared at Jolie. "I only want Mama to look at it," she begged.

"Honey, you know your mama can't see," Jolie reminded her. "Will you let me take a look so we can fix it?"

When Jolie neared the bed, Ashley burst into hysterical tears.

Seconds later, Wes knocked on the bedroom door.

"Go get your daddy," Susie commanded. "Search everywhere and don't come back without him. Bundle up so you don't freeze."

"Please leave Ashley alone," Wes begged. "Don't force her." He darted down the stairs and out into the early-morning chill.

By the time Wes returned with his father, Ashley was screaming again. Luke kicked off his boots as he stepped through the back door. The boys stared at him from the sitting room floor, and Grandma sat in the rocker with Cherish, who had done her share of crying with Ashley's recent burst of hysterics.

"Where is she?" Luke asked Grandma, trying to stay calm.

"Grace is with her in your room. She had a nightmare and then she hurt her leg and Susie and Jolie tried to help but gave up. Poor thing; she's been battling for pert near an hour."

Luke told Wes to stay with the boys, then climbed the stairs. His heart throbbed and his mind raced. *Not another nightmare. The evaluation is today! This can't happen now.*

Luke entered the bedroom with a calm authority that seemed to make the cold walls sigh in peace. He glanced at the crumpled mass of quilts and nightgown on his side of the bed, and hesitated. Then he neared.

"What's the problem, Gracie?" His voice sounded surprisingly confident considering he was wilting inside.

Ashley immediately fell silent.

"I heard you hurt your leg, Ashley," he said. He had to force her not to retreat from him.

"I think she hit it on something when she fell out of bed," Grace said. She brushed the tears from her cheeks with trembling hands.

"Does it hurt really bad?" Luke asked as he pulled off his heavy coat.

Ashley lay still and silent as Luke dropped his coat on a nearby chair and approached the bed. She felt his shadow and cringed. Her eyes were so heavy they fought to close, but she forced them open.

Luke didn't know whether to come closer or keep his distance. He cautiously pulled a chair to the side of the bed and sat in it, resting his hands on his knees. "Do you think I could take a look at it?" he asked in as tender a voice as he could muster.

Ashley shook her head.

"It sounds like it may be a pretty bad cut. Be good and let me see, 'ey?"

A vivid memory rushed through Ashley's mind and she winced. As if chasing each other in a game of tag, the words *be good, be good, be good,* streaked and echoed. "I'm trying!" she blurted. "I'll be good now—really."

Luke stared at her as she began to cry again.

"I can't be good," she said. "I don't know how. I was trying."

"You are good, Ashley," Luke stuttered. He saw her eyes under the quilts, and his heart sank in his chest. They were far from empty—that lifeless, barren glare that had once left them hollow was now replaced with dark memory. They were brimming with agonizing pain so intense, Luke had to look away. He felt something very much like a physical blow, and it took his breath away. "Just let me see your leg, 'ey?"

"I can't." Ashley squeezed the blankets close to her face. She heard Jack's words in her memory: *You can't ever tell anyone. Not even if they threaten to kill you, don't ever say a single word. What goes on in that woodshed is nobody else's business.*

"Why not?" Luke asked.

Her eyes flashed at him. "Because it's nobody else's business."

Ashley remembered the lady who had tried to get her to tell on Mr. Berk, and the consequences Jack had paid. She remembered the bruise on his cheek and the belt marks on his arms. Jack said Mr. Berk would've killed her.

Ashley turned away from Luke and squiggled under the sheets. He saw that she was trying to withdraw from him.

"I'm not going to hurt you," he said quickly. "No matter what you tell me, I'll never hurt you. Just don't back away from me, baby."

"I can't tell you!" she suddenly shrieked. She burst into fresh tears, fighting against the overwhelming temptation to spill the whole story.

The bedroom became silent. Grace rubbed Ashley's arm through the quilt, and Luke crossed his arms. Ashley whimpered and then broke into a fit of coughing.

Suddenly, a thought popped into Luke's mind, and before he had considered the vulnerability of it, he looked at Ashley and said calmly, "Darlin', I want to tell you a story."

He stopped. *God, what am I doing? I've never told that story to anyone!*

It's all right. Tell her.

Luke resisted panic. His cheeks burned and his eyes blurred in the shadows of the lamplight.

"When I was a little boy," he began very slowly, "my father didn't like me very much. I had an older brother, Jacob, that my father loved, but he was mean to me. One day, I was doing chores in the barn and Jacob accidentally knocked over a stack of wood that my father had told us not to play on, but Jacob didn't want to get in trouble for it. So while I was milking, Jacob got Pop from the house and told him that I had knocked over the wood. Pop was very angry. He came to the barn and started yelling, and even though I tried to tell him that Jacob had knocked over the wood, he wouldn't believe me. He . . . he beat me with his belt."

Ashley gulped down a sob. Grace sat perfectly still, looking astonished.

"That hurt very badly," Luke said. "I had to stay home from school all week because Dod didn't want people to see my bruises. But you know what?" He fought back tears. "Even though that beating really hurt, what hurt more was the fact that the punishment was unfair."

"It wasn't unfair," Ashley said. Her face was still covered with the quilt and her knees were tightly curled into her chest. "I lost the chickens. I was supposed to watch them. Bonnie said I deserved it. And I did! The chickens got away. I tried to find them, but they were lost in the forest. I should have watched them better."

Ashley suddenly covered her ears and dove into the pillow again. "I can't tell you!" she said as more tears flooded her cheeks. *Not even if they threaten to kill you.*

"Yes, you can." Luke touched her arm and she pulled away. "It hurts bad, doesn't it?" His voice broke. He wanted to pick her up and cradle her in his arms but he was afraid that he'd cry if he felt how much pain was stored in that little body.

"When he beat you, it hurt worse than anything in the world," he continued. "He was a big, cruel man, and he didn't care how much he hurt you. Whoever did that to you was the meanest man on the face of the earth." *How could anyone do such a thing?* "But you didn't deserve it."

"You don't understand," Ashley whimpered.

Luke sat back in his chair and tipped his head back, wishing he could cry.

Ashley shook her head under the blanket. "Jack tried to make him stop," her little voice squeaked.

Jack. Luke gasped inwardly as the image of the boy with the broken wrist crowded his mind. He cringed when he thought about the man who had brought that boy to the hospital. Luke tried to remember what he looked like. He was gruff and whiskery, and he had a beer belly.

"He hurt Jack." Ashley said. "And he was going to kill me."

Ashley squeezed her mother's hand and the tears quieted.

How do I do it, God? Luke's thoughts raced. *How do I tell her who I am? How do I make her see that I'm different?*

Son, fix the cut.

Luke almost argued aloud. He put his head in his hands. *If I force her to let me see it, I'll never gain her trust.*

Let her cry, but fix it.

Luke's mind wrestled against the voice in his spirit until he finally gave in. "Ashley Elise," he said awkwardly, "I need to see your cut."

Grace stiffened.

"I'm not going to hurt you," he said in a soothing voice. "I want you to let me see."

Ashley lay perfectly still, swaddled in the quilts with the sheet against her face.

Luke touched her arm but she didn't flinch. *Why does the physical matter right now, God? Can't I just leave that part alone? She's finally opening up to me! This could ruin everything.*

He slowly moved the quilt off her feet. She squirmed but didn't pull back.

"Did Susie bring anything to wash with?" Luke asked, his voice shaky.

"I think she put water on the bedstead," Grace replied.

Luke felt like he was suffocating. He wanted to retreat but forced himself to go forward. He picked up the water jug and the rag and drops of water splashed on the rug as he wet the cloth.

Ashley winced when Luke pushed the pantaloons over her knee. When he saw the scars on her legs, he began to cry. For a long moment he held the dripping rag in his hand as tears streaked down his cheeks. He felt his insides heaving with pain and compassion.

His shoulders slumped in weakness, and he said between several sniffles, "It's not so bad. Just a little cut, baby." He wiped his tears with the back of his hand, and his eyes blurred and stung.

Luke saw Ashley peering at him from under the quilt. "It's OK," he said, looking into the searching gaze. "I see it, but it's all right."

Ashley knew he wasn't talking about the cut.

Luke bent to rinse his cloth, and Ashley's eyes fell to the belt around his waist. She began to tremble. When Luke reached out to touch her again, she shied away.

He gazed at her with confusion. "What's the matter, darlin'? I'm not hurting you."

Ashley rubbed her swollen eyes. "Please don't touch me," she said, pushing his hands away. She remembered Jack bending over her, stroking her hair and telling her it'd be OK.

Luke dropped his hand into his lap. "Oh, darlin', I won't do anything to hurt you." He saw the girl's eyes land on his belt, and he barely restrained from flying into a fit of righteous wrath against whoever had caused her so much pain.

Ashley covered her face with her hands, trying to ignore the pictures that danced through her mind. "I don't want to hurt again." Her voice broke.

Though she wished she could push memory into a bottomless pit, the deep sound of Luke's voice reminded Ashley of harsh words and strength and anger that couldn't be bridled or stopped. She saw the man as he appeared in her dreams so many times . . . the salt and pepper hair, the tanned face and the brutal expression of fury and hate. She could almost feel his chubby hands on her arms and she remembered his large belly covered with a dirty shirt and held up by a black leather belt.

Ashley tried to bring herself back to reality. She felt the glow of the lamp and wished that it would penetrate her memory. But all she could see was the man in front of her—a real one this time; one much taller than the other, with bigger hands, broader shoulders, and the ability, perhaps, to inflict more pain than Ashley had known.

Luke took Ashley's hand and rubbed his thumb on her knuckles. "Baby, it's Daddy," he said, searching eyes that seemed to be watching the past. "Ashley Elise, I'm your daddy. I'm not the man who hurt you."

Ashley took her hand out of Luke's grip and brushed her cheeks. She gasped from her sobs, trying to hold them back.

"Cry, Ashley," Grace said. "Don't hold back. Just cry."

Ashley turned on her side, buried her head in her daddy's pillow, and wept. Eight years of neglect and two years of physical pain and emotional havoc came forth in a shower of tears. Everything came on her at once: the harshness of Miss Elizabeth and the heartlessness of Mrs. Harms. She cried from the memory of abuse and from a sense of utter devastation at being an orphan in the first place. She sobbed from her very soul as years of fear and devastation threatened to choke out childhood and render her an adult at the age of eight.

When at last the little girl had soaked the pillow in tears and was lying quietly in her pile of quilts, she rubbed her eyes with the crumpled sheet and blinked. The first thing she saw was Luke's buckle, and three more tears fell down her puffy cheeks.

Luke's chair squeaked on the floor as he stood and unbuckled his belt. Ashley watched him as he pulled it from his waist and dropped it behind the overstuffed chair in the corner. Then he returned to his seat. "Ashley Elise, my belt is made only for my waist," he said firmly. "I'll never use it on any person, least of all you. I won't even wear it as long as it makes you cringe. It'll stay behind that chair forever if that's what it takes."

Ashley's eyes shifted to her father's face, and for the first time, a hint of understanding shone in the blue pearls. She glanced at the water and rag on the bedstead. "You can . . . finish with . . . my leg," she said through jerking sobs.

Luke hesitated. *God, I don't care about the cut. I want to know more about her.*

You will. Minister to her physical body for now. Love her again.

Luke picked up the gauze that Susie had left and carefully wrapped the wound, all the while sniffling and trying to blink away the tears. He wanted to use his hands to erase the scars and the memory of how they got there. *That's going to have to be Your job, God. I can't fix her spirit.*

Ashley was overcome by an alarming pang of exposure as Luke tended to the wound on her knee. She thought about Jack and what he had told her, and her cheeks blushed with shame.

Luke saw the change. "It's all right, Ashley," he said calmly. "You'll be fixed up real soon."

The words *it's all right* danced in Ashley's head, and she remembered Luke talking about truth for hours at a time. She wondered whether Jack or Luke were telling the truth. She could almost feel Jack's presence and see his face. "*What goes on in that woodshed is nobody else's business.*"

"What's truth?" Ashley blurted. Her eyes frantically stared at Luke.

He looked at her and his brow creased. "Um . . . truth is something that's right."

Her eyes were filled with fire. "But what's truth?" *What goes on in that woodshed is nobody else's business.*

"Tell me your dream and I'll tell you truth," Luke replied with heavenly gracefulness. His heart pounded and he wondered what had compelled him to say that.

"He hurt me," Ashley whispered. Her face lit up with horror. She heard the helpless cry of her voice in the dream and her glare became so intense that Luke had to look away.

He swallowed hard. "Who?"

"That man. The big man." She saw his face vividly in her mind.

"What was his name?"

Ashley wiped her cheeks and turned away. When Luke dropped the gauze on the floor, she shoved her legs back under the quilt and curled up like an infant. "I don't know."

Grace brushed the curls from Ashley's forehead. Ashley squeezed her hand. "Why did he come back?" she cried. "Mama, he came in my window—how did he get in? I couldn't find you! I tried, but I couldn't. He was yelling at me, but nobody came to help. Not even Jack. Everybody was gone. Why did he hurt me again?"

"He didn't hurt you, Ashley," Luke said softly. "It was just a dream. You've been safe all night, and no one came in your window. Mama and I have been right here, and so have Wes and Cherish and the rest of the family. You're safe."

"But it wasn't a dream," Ashley persisted, looking into her daddy's eyes. "It really happened. I have the scars on my legs." Ashley took her mother's cool hand in her hot one and pushed it against the scars. "You can't see them, Mama, but I have them."

Grace sniffled and Luke turned away.

"I couldn't get away," Ashley continued. "I tried, but he was too strong. Listen to me!" Ashley turned her mother's head toward her when the woman looked away to wipe her tears.

"How did he give you scars?" Luke asked.

"With his belt."

Luke winced.

"I know it was a dream this time but it really did happen before. All the time. He was angry when he came home from work and he took off his belt." Ashley covered her face with her hands. "When I ran away, he found me and was even angrier. I lost the chickens, and that's why. Bonnie said to stay away from him when he had a bottle, but I didn't want to. It was all because I lost the chickens."

Luke thought about his empty henhouse and was glad that every one of Grace's chickens were dead.

Ashley looked at him through her tears. "I don't want him to hurt me again."

"Ashley, who are you afraid is gonna hurt you?" Luke asked.

She closed her eyes and whispered, "Mr. Berk."

Mr. Berk. Luke seemed to recall having heard that name long before Jack came to the hospital. *At the saloon,* he thought. *He was drunk. I took him home because the jailhouse was full.*

Luke remembered the day he had taken Mr. Berk to his home on the doctor's horse. The vile old man had sung the entire time. Luke had escorted him into the house. That's where he first saw Jack. *Jack.* He remembered thinking that Jack was a nasty, unpleasant boy who would someday become exactly like his father.

Luke's brow creased with regret. *If only I would've called Bilt's attention to that place. If only I'd thought more about the children than about how quickly I could get that awful man off my horse.*

"Why didn't Mrs. Berk stop him, Mama?" Ashley said in a pleading whisper.

Luke leaned forward on his knees. "I'm going to tell you the truth now, Ashley. Sometimes when men are angry, they do terrible things." He tried to keep his voice gentle, but he was welling with anger on Ashley's behalf. "It's not right to strap anyone unless they've done something wrong, and it's wrong to hurt someone so badly that they have scars. When daddies discipline their children, it's supposed to be because they love their children *so* much that they can't stand to see them naughty and unhappy." He paused. "Ashley, look at me."

She shot her tearful eyes at him and they tore into his heart.

He gently rubbed her arm. "When I strapped Wes, you were afraid I was hurting him the way Mr. Berk hurt you, weren't you?"

Her softened eyes gave the answer.

"Darlin', I would never do that to your brother. I love him too much. I don't strap my children like Mr. Berk strapped you. I only strap Wesley because God has given him to me to train him in righteousness. I'm telling you the truth. I love my children so much that I would die for any one of you. I would let myself be killed to save you."

He paused, and an inkling of revelation flashed through her tears. "I will never, ever hurt you like that man hurt you because I love you too much. How can I make you understand?" Luke raked his hands through his hair and desperately searched for the words he had wanted to say for months. He rested his elbows on his knees and his voice was gentle. "Ashley, I know you've been afraid of me ever since you came to live here. And I know I've gotten angry with you and been too harsh."

Luke paused, battling against himself. "That's the wrong way for a daddy to be. I had to ask God to forgive me and make up my mind to be better."

He swallowed a lump in his throat. "Now I have to ask you to forgive me. Will you forgive your daddy for what I've done wrong?"

Ashley sobbed deeply and rubbed her stinging cheeks, closing her eyes. She felt as if something suddenly took away the voices and faces echoing in her head, and the pictures that danced, and the words that pounded and yelled and haunted. Suddenly, the wellspring of pain began to dry up. She searched Luke's face and couldn't understand. For the first time, someone had admitted that he had hurt her.

Ashley remembered the day she had broken the shed window, and how Luke had responded. Everything came to her in a rush—she remembered Wes rebuking her about the chickens and Luke telling her that it was OK. She remembered the fight with Deborah, the question game, and the Christmas present. It was as if everything Luke had labored to do finally clicked in her brain, and she stared at him with something close to appreciation.

"Will you forgive me?" Luke asked again, this time in a whisper and with tears in his eyes. He saw a flicker of light in her eyes like he hadn't seen before, and the hollow silence that had haunted him for so long was almost gone. He had made it through her castle wall.

"Yeah," Ashley said almost inaudibly. Her heart pounded and made her head swim. She shivered when she felt her daddy's big hands slide around her back and she could feel his breath on her face.

"I want you to trust me, Ashley Elise," Luke said with a tearful smile. "I want you to know that my hands will never hurt you and that I'll always try to be the best daddy I can be to you. I want so badly to have you as my little girl, and I don't want you to be afraid of me anymore."

Ashley lay speechless on her pillow. A picture of the woodshed jumped into her mind. "I wasn't supposed to tell you."

"That was a lie." He squeezed her tight. "The truth is that no matter what's happened in your life, Mama and I will always love you. It makes no difference about Mr. Berk or Jack or anyone else."

Luke kissed her tear-bathed cheek. His voice faltered as he whispered, "You're more precious to me than anything in this world, Ashley. I'll always protect you from anyone who tries to hurt you. I promise."

For the first time, Ashley believed the promise of a man.

For the Lord God is a sun and shield: the Lord will give grace and glory: no good thing will He withhold from them that walk uprightly. O Lord of hosts, blessed is the man that trusteth in Thee.

—Psalm 84:11–12

FORTY TWO

Violated

Grandma bounced Cherish in the crook of her arm and set a bowl of jelly on the table. She clicked the tray shut on Neal's highchair and patted Deborah's head. Ruth came from the kitchen with a plate of biscuits, and she passed them among the boys, who sleepily demolished half the plate.

Uncle Paul turned to the quiet crowd. "Boys, you need to help Wes with chores this morning since Uncle Luke is busy. We leave for church in two hours."

Granddad chuckled, his white beard bobbing on his green shirt. "And when we get back, we'll have a quiet afternoon listening to stories, since it's Sunday, 'ey?"

The staircase door clicked open, and all eyes watched Luke step through with Ashley behind him. They were both disheveled and appeared to have survived something close to a train wreck. Luke's shirt was untucked in his beltless pants, but his face bore the expression of victory, and every inch of his six-foot-four-inch frame slumped in relief.

Ashley's hair was scattered all about her crunched red dress. Tear stains still streaked her cheeks, and her eyes were swollen, but they had lost the haunting well of sorrow and almost hinted at happiness.

"Good morning," Granddad said.

Luke nodded at the group, his eyes bloodshot. "Morning, everyone."

Ashley shyly loitered behind him.

Grace came down the stairs and tossed her long hair over her shoulder, buttoning the sleeves of her dress. She made her way to the dining room and Ashley sidled next to her and leaned against her.

"Wesley," Grace said, "bring me Cherish, would you?"

Wes took his little sister from Grandma's arms and took her to her mother. Cherish smiled a toothy grin and buried her face in Grace's shoulder.

"Was she all right, Mum?" Grace asked.

"She was fine," Grandma said. "She only cried for a few minutes."

Grace sat in a chair and Cherish snuggled into her lap. "Did everyone sleep all right?" she asked.

Several of the children mumbled a reply and all eyes were staring between Ashley and Luke. Wes's heart melted when he saw Ashley's swollen eyes and heard a little sob come from her throat. His mind danced with curiosity when he saw Luke glance at Ashley and she met his eyes.

Luke pulled a chair away from the table and sat down.

"Are you hungry?" Jolie asked him.

"Not really. Ashley, do you want something to eat?"

She shook her head.

"The boys are going to help Wes in the barn," said Granddad, "so you don't have to leave the house, Luke."

"Thank you, but that's not necessary. I'll be able to do chores and get the sleighs hitched for church." Luke knew that going to church would be the worst thing for Ashley that morning, but he was compelled by the agreement he had made with Mrs. Harms.

"It's time for you girls to get dressed," Aunt Ruth said abruptly. "Krissa and Dee, put on your Sunday dresses and bring Mama the brush."

The girls darted up the stairs, and the boys began a search for their boots and chore clothes. Luke rose from the table with a weary groan and approached his wife.

"I'm going to supervise the boys in the barn," he said with a sigh. He touched Ashley's back and the little girl looked up at him with sleepy eyes. "Help Mama get ready, OK, darlin'?" She nodded. "I'll be back in as soon as I can." Luke patted Ashley once more and left, with a trail of men and eager little lads behind him.

The snow under the runners was slick and wet, and the children hung over the sides of the sleighs to watch it creak and slide under them. Merry chatter lit up the air in both of the family sleighs, and the cousins giggled and joked as they squished together, surrounded by babies and parents. Luke drove the big sleigh and Uncle Paul drove the small one, both full of passengers.

"Look at the deer!" someone shouted. Luke's team of draft horses snorted when the sleigh jolted with movement.

"Do you see it, Ashley?" whispered Grace. "Aunt Jolie says it's a female."

"Where's the father?"

"He's probably just beyond in the forest, where you can't see. The fathers always stay back, where they can watch over their families and protect them. If you look closely, you'll probably see lots more deer before we get to church. They usually come out in the early morning to eat and drink."

"We're going to church?" Ashley rushed with panic.

"Yes, darlin'. Didn't you know that?"

"I thought we were just going for a ride. Mama, what if Mrs. Harms is there?"

Grace patted her daughter. "Mrs. Harms will be there."

"Then—then she'll take me back!" Ashley gasped. Her voice grew loud. "Mama, we can't go to church. What if she takes me to Maryland? We have to turn around."

"Ashley, we have to go," Grace said calmly. "Part of the agreement Daddy made with Mrs. Harms was that you'd be in church this Sunday."

Ashley gripped her mother's sleeve. "I can't go back. I can't!"

"What's the problem?" asked Luke from the driver's seat. He glanced at his wife, who sat backward directly behind him.

"She doesn't want to go to church," Grace said quietly.

"Why not?"

"She's afraid Mrs. Harms will take her back."

"Did you explain to her why we have to go?"

"Yeah."

"Ashley, we're going to do the best we can to make Mrs. Harms understand that you want to stay," Luke said tenderly.

Ashley flashed her eyes up to him. "But we can't go."

"Darlin', we have to go; we told Mrs. Harms that we'd come this Sunday."

Ashley buried her face in her mother's cloak. More tears added to her already swelled cheeks. "Mama, please," she begged in a voice that wrenched Luke's heart. "Don't take me back. I can't see Mrs. Harms!"

Uncle Mark watched from the seat across from Grace, and Luke caught his glance. He clenched his jaw in frustration and waved to Uncle Paul in the other sleigh, pointing for him to pull over. Then he reined the horses to the side of the road and pulled them in.

Uncle Mark stood from his seat. "I'll drive," he offered. Luke looked at him with surprise. "You can take care of Ashley."

"Thanks." Luke jumped from the driver's seat. The children became silent as they watched Ashley choke on the sobs that readily returned.

Luke climbed into the sleigh and sat down beside Ashley. "Honey, don't cry," he said softly.

"What's the matter?" Aunt Susie called from the other sleigh.

"We're fine. Giddyup!" yelled Mark. The runners scratched on the snow, and the children began to giggle again.

"Ashley, listen to me," Luke said, "I'm going to do everything I can to keep you in our family, but if you cry, Mrs. Harms will think I hurt you."

"I can't go back." She leaned into Grace's chest. "We have to turn around. I wanna go home."

Luke lifted Ashley onto his lap and she stiffened. She struggled against him until she felt him stroke through her curls. Then she crumbled in his arms and sat perfectly still.

"If we don't go to church today, Mrs. Harms will take you back," Luke said in her ear. "That's the agreement we made."

"But she'll take me," Ashley whimpered. "I don't wanna go back."

"I know, darlin'. I want you to stay with us, too, and we're going to try our hardest to make that happen. But if you cry, Mrs. Harms will wonder if I hurt you."

Ashley lay back in Luke's arm and choked on her sobs. She brought her hand up to wipe her cheeks and sighed deeply. Luke kissed her forehead and was surprised when she allowed him to run his fingers along her arm.

"Please?" she squeaked.

"Just relax and try to go to sleep."

Grace gripped Luke's arm, and he patted her gently. "Pray, Gracie," he whispered in her ear.

When the Tanner party arrived at the church, the children were so excited, the parents had to give them all a brief talk outside the building before they were allowed to go inside. It was a beautifully crisp morning, and the folks who came from every direction were happy, for it was Christmas Day.

As the children poured out in every direction, Luke lifted Ashley into his arms and laid her on his shoulder.

"I don't want to go in there," Ashley said, stiffening her back.

"We won't talk to Mrs. Harms until after the service. Everything's going to be OK."

Her eyes were wide. "She's gonna take me back. I know she will!"

"Please stop. I need you to stop crying." He gently rubbed her back and hugged her close on his shoulder, and she wilted in exhausted weakness.

Mr. Bowtie stood at the door and greeted the people as they came in, shaking hands and tweaking babies' chins. When he saw Luke approach with Ashley on his shoulder, he stuck out his hand. "Did we have complications this morning?" he asked with a big grin.

"A few," replied Luke. He saw Mrs. Harms sitting on a bench in the church.

"Are we gonna make it through the interview this afternoon?"

Luke patted the old preacher on the shoulder. "We're sure praying that way. Keep jolly on Christmas—that's what we need this morning."

Mr. Bowtie laughed quietly, and as Luke stepped by, the old man set his jaw and glanced at Sara Harms, rehearsing a sermon that was not meant for his Sunday pulpit.

Mrs. Harms watched the Tanner group enter and take up three benches in the middle section. She searched the busy crowd of children for Ashley, but didn't see the blonde head among them. Then she saw Luke standing halfway down the aisle, talking with Dan Sulka. On his shoulder lay a limp little girl.

That's Ashley! Mrs. Harms gasped. With her hair cut and curled, and a new dress and coat on, she hardly recognized the girl. Her cheeks were obviously tearstained.

Mrs. Harms restrained herself, gripping the wooden pew and staring at Ashley. As Luke set the girl on the bench, she noticed the swelled eyes, skinny form, and a frightening bashfulness as the girl snuggled beside her mother and repeatedly wiped her cheeks.

She shook her head in disgust. *He violated the agreement and beat her plum out of her wits.*

Luke whispered something into Ashley's ear, then winked at her. The little girl didn't smile, but she didn't shy away, either. Mrs. Harms's eyes narrowed. Why would Ashley not resist Luke if he had abused her? And if she had been hurt that morning, why would Ashley enter church in Luke's arms?

Mrs. Harms stood and took up her hymnal, singing the morning song as a hundred questions raced through her mind. Her countenance was sharp as she rehearsed the rebuke that was coming to Luke Tanner. Then she set her mind on the preacher, who fired his sermon directly at her pew, entitling it "Believing the Truth on Christmas."

After the service, the Tanner pews emptied, and Luke urged everyone to make a fast exodus. Mr. Bowtie came directly over to Luke and caught his arm.

"Can I have a word, sir?" he said loudly enough for the rest of the party to hear.

Luke gave Cherish to Wes and followed Mr. Bowtie to the back of the sanctuary.

Granddad told the children to sit back down, and as Wes snuggled Cherish into his shoulder, he felt his stomach twist.

"Is he talking to your dad about Ashley?" Gerald whispered to Wes.

Wes shrugged. He watched as Ashley sat down at the end of the bench near where Grace stood. She looked petrified.

Wes stood and scooted past his cousins' feet to the end of the bench. He sat down next to Ashley and she glanced at him bashfully.

For a long moment, the siblings sat silently. Wes sighed heavily and patted Cherish.

"You tired?" he asked at length.

"Yeah," Ashley said barely above a whisper.

Wes was burning with curiosity. "Did you sleep much last night?"

"No. We were talking."

Wes sat Cherish on his lap and she leaned against his chest, staring at Ashley. "Are you all right?" Wes asked.

Ashley looked at him and he saw tears coming to her eyes. "I don't want Mrs. Harms to take me with her," she whispered.

Wes's heart skipped a beat. His sister brought her hand up to brush her already swollen cheeks and he leaned closer so his shoulder touched hers. "Maybe Mr. Bowtie's trying to help some more and that's why he's talking to Dad."

"I think Mrs. Harms is angry," Ashley said.

"Did she leave already?"

Ashley's face paled. "I don't think so. I saw her waiting outside." She scooted so close to her brother that her hair fell on his shirt.

Wes watched as his father leaned against the wall with his hands in his pockets, listening to Mr. Bowtie. Then the preacher reached out his hand and Luke shook it. Luke returned to his family's pew and nodded at Granddad.

"Let's go," he said shortly. Grace moved toward him and he took her hand.

As the family quickly departed and began boarding the sleigh, Ashley hid behind her mother as if she could make Mrs. Harms overlook her. Luke was about to step up to the driver's bench when Mrs. Harms came from the back of the church building, wrapping her cloak around her shoulders.

"Mr. Tanner," she said firmly, "I'll be at your house directly."

Luke nodded. "We have several issues to discuss."

"We certainly do. I'll be stopping at the orphanage first, then coming to your house immediately after."

Luke tipped his hat at the old woman. "We'll be awaiting your arrival."

From the doorway, Thomas Harris winked at Luke as he drove away.

Plead my cause, O Lord, with them that strive with me: fight against them that fight against me.

—Psalm 35:1

FORTY THREE

Mr. Bowtie's Secret Ties

Returning from church, the children burst from the sleigh and quickly traded their stiff church clothes for hole-in-the-knee trousers and play frocks. They bundled in their wraps and darted out the door, where Granddad and the parents—save Luke and Grace—were waiting to go on a walk. This event was purposefully planned to rid the house of little, eavesdropping souls so the Tanner parents and Ashley could have their interview with Mrs. Harms.

Before he left, Wes approached his mother. "What did Mr. Bowtie want to talk to Dad about?" he asked nervously.

"I guess he wanted to know why Ashley looked so upset this morning. Dad told him what happened last night."

Wes slowly nodded. Then he said quickly, "Mom, if Mrs. Harms takes Ashley, don't let her leave until I'm back. I wanna say goodbye."

A pang went through Grace, and she hugged him. "I'll do everything I can to stall her if that happens. Pray while you walk, Wesley—pray that Mrs. Harms will believe what Daddy and I have to say."

"I will, Mom." Wesley darted away with an anxious smile.

Once the house was emptied of company, Luke, Grace, and Ashley sat in the sitting room to wait for Mrs. Harms. Ashley was intensely nervous, though she refused to shed tears. Grace felt just as fidgety, and entertained her shaking hands with crocheting. Luke sat silent in his rocker.

The clock struck the noon hour, and Ashley snuggled into the couch. "Mama, I'm cold."

Grace tossed a blanket at the sofa. "Did you keep your stockings on, darlin'?"

"Yeah."

"Then you should warm up in just a minute."

Silence fell again. They listened to the clock tick and watched the flames in the fire intensify to shades of blue and bright orange.

Twelve-thirty came, then one o'clock. Luke picked up his Bible and started studying. Ashley slept on the couch.

"I wonder if she's coming?" asked Grace.

Luke chuckled. "She's coming."

But two o'clock came, and the sky began to darken with winter clouds. Luke lit a lamp to read by, and Grace retired her project to the basket.

The walking party came home. With a loud burst, they entered the house rosy, wet, and curious. Granddad commanded the group to take off their wraps in the foyer while he "checked on the situation." He stepped into the sitting room with a half-hesitant, half-eager glance.

"How'd it go?" he asked. A large smile creased his face when he saw Ashley sleeping.

"Perfectly." Luke laughed, but his voice reflected disgust. "She never showed up."

"Really? Well, I'll be. She must've decided to let Ashley stay."

Wes stepped in with rapturous excitement on his face. "She's staying?"

Luke shook his head with a sigh. "We don't know. Mrs. Harms hasn't come yet."

Disappointment clouded his eyes. "But she said she'd be right here."

"I know, son."

"Now we have to wait even longer to find out!" Two and a half hours of a sick stomach was not something Wes was willing to face again.

"I don't know what to say," Luke replied with a bewildered shrug. He stood and set the Bible on the mantel. "I guess we just go on with our day."

Darkness fell early on the countryside that Christmas, and with it came a fast supper and the traditional, drawn-out good-byes. Everyone dispersed into the quiet Christmas night by the time the clock chimed the eight o'clock hour. The ones who had a long distance to drive planned to spend the night at Granddad and Grandma's and leave early the next morning. The rest would drive until they arrived home, bundled in blankets from head to toe, with bags of hot potatoes stuffed at their feet.

Although it was sad saying more than a dozen good-byes, when the Tanner home was left quiet, it was a great relief to the entire family. Ashley was put to bed, for she was exhausted from a poor night's rest and a day of emotional anguish, and Cherish fell asleep almost as soon as darkness set in. Luke, Grace, and Wes were alone in the sitting room by the time eight thirty came.

Wes was on the brink of tears. "Dad, do you think Mrs. Harms will ever come?"

A heavy sigh escaped Luke's chest. "Wesley, Mrs. Harms has me baffled. All I know is that Ashley is ours tonight. I have no idea what the morning will bring."

A shiver went through Wes when he thought about the possibility of Ashley being taken away.

"Maybe something happened to her between church and our house," Grace suggested.

Luke rested his chin in his hand. "You'd think we'd know about an accident by now. I suppose it's possible, but I doubt it."

Wes watched the fire blaze in the hearth, and he felt tears stream down his cheeks, in spite of his attempts to stop them. "I want this to be over," said the lad softly.

Luke glanced at his son. "Come here, Wes."

Wes went to his father and Luke put him on his lap, patting him with his big hand. "Son, it's hard for all of us to go another day without knowing what the outcome of this situation will be. But we do have reason to be thankful. At least we aren't shedding tears tonight because Ashley's gone forever."

Grace shifted uneasily.

"Even though this situation seems out of control, God still sits on the throne tonight."

"Maybe He isn't watching." Wes sniffed.

Luke's expression became gravely serious. "Wesley Nathan, God never makes mistakes, nor does He turn His face away from His children. He loves Ashley much more than any of us do—which says a whole lot. No matter what happens, God's going to be just as powerful and just as close. We have to choose to believe that."

"That's really hard."

"Yeah, it is. In fact, choosing to believe the truth when it doesn't seem true is probably the hardest thing any of us will ever do."

The upstairs door clicked open, and little Ashley showed her face; her blonde hair tightly wrapped in rags.

"There's our little girl," Luke said warmly.

"Is it time to wake up?" asked Ashley as she climbed onto her mother's lap and strips of pink, yellow, and purple cloth bobbed in Grace's face.

"No, darlin'." Grace laughed heavy-heartedly. "We just haven't gone to bed yet. Aren't you tired anymore?"

Ashley shook her head.

Ashley watched Luke tenderly stroking her brother's back. "What's wrong, Wes?"

He shrugged.

"I wanna play the question game," Luke said with a small smile.

Wes's eyes lit up. "Tonight?"

"Yeah. I get to ask the first question. What's your favorite Christmas memory?"

Ashley's eyes flashed toward him.

"Not your worst one," Luke said gently.

"Sledding with the boys," Wes said, and happiness began to reflect on his face.

"Mine is from last year," Grace said. "We found out on Christmas Day that we were accepted for adoption at Cherish's orphanage."

Luke looked at Ashley. Her gaze was far away. At length, she glanced up and found his eyes on her.

Luke watched her with confusion. "It's Ashley's turn to ask a question," he said awkwardly.

"But she didn't answer the first one," Wes argued. "And neither did you."

"I will eventually," he said, studying the little girl.

"How come we have to have Christmas?" Ashley asked.

Luke heard Mr. Bowtie's voice: *"I want to know if she's ever heard of Jesus."*

"Get me my Bible, Wes," Luke said with a smile.

Wes jumped off his lap. "Are we gonna do the skit?"

"Yep."

Ashley shifted nervously. "What skit?"

"Daddy reads the Christmas story and we act it out," Grace answered with a large smile. "And we'll have enough people to fill all the parts this year, Luke. Last year we didn't have Ashley or Cherish."

"Get some sheets from the hall and a white blanket for Cherish," Luke directed as Wes climbed the stairs after his Bible. "I'll read, and the children can be Joseph and Mary, and Cherish'll be Jesus. Grace, you can be the angel."

Ashley stared at him and he winked at her. "You can even leave the rags in your hair, Ashley. I'm sure Mary liked curls too."

In the darkness of that cozy winter night, amidst the giggles of the children and the crackling of the fire and the sound of Grace singing like an angel and Luke narrating, the Tanners created Ashley's first pleasant Christmas memory.

Luke arrived at Mr. Harris's house for his Monday meeting bewildered, irritated, and in a hurry. He had hesitantly left his home that morning, hoping to return as soon as possible in case Mrs. Harms should visit.

"So," said Mr. Bowtie, settling behind his desk after tossing a half dozen piles of paper on the floor, "did you have a good Christmas?"

"It was eventful," Luke answered curtly. Mr. Bowtie's unfinished breakfast plate sat on the desk and Luke tried to avoid looking at it. His anxious stomach churned.

"And Ashley's well?"

Mr. Tanner sniffed. "She's still with us. Mrs. Harms never came yesterday."

"She didn't?" The old man looked surprised. "So you don't know if Ashley is yours?"

"No."

"Well, what a shock. I can't believe that woman would be so rude." He shook his head in disgust.

Luke tried not to let the preacher's blunt ways add to his annoyance. "She's certainly made a decision by now."

"I would think so."

"Anyway, let's get on with our appointment. I'd like to return home as soon as possible."

"Of course." The preacher leaned back in his chair and looked thoughtfully at Mr. Tanner. "You and I have gone through a lot together. Since you have Ashley back at home now, do you think all of the counseling and everything we struggled through has made a difference in your life?"

Luke sat back impatiently. He tried to steer his mind away from anxious thoughts of Ashley, but he couldn't help but wonder if Mrs. Harms was at his house at that moment, taking her away.

"Yeah, I think it's helped," Luke said quickly. "You've done a lot for me." Did the preacher want to be thanked?

"That's not the answer I was looking for." Mr. Bowtie put his hands behind his head and swung his feet onto the desk. "I'm wondering how you're feeling about Ashley being in your home. Have you made progress with her?"

Luke slowly nodded. "I explained to you what happened the other night. Ashley made incredible steps toward healing."

Mr. Bowtie sat quietly as if waiting for Luke to continue.

Luke looked at him and said roughly, "What are you wanting me to say?"

The preacher laughed loudly at that, and his face lit up in the lamplight when he threw his head back. "You're not a child," he said through his laughter. "I'm not waiting for you to say the right thing so I can be satisfied."

Luke bit his cheek. "I guess I don't understand the question." He wanted to scold Mr. Bowtie for wasting his time. "Look, I don't know if we're making any significant progress here. Do you mind if we finish this meeting after I know what Mrs. Harms decides about Ashley? I think I need to go home so I'm ready for her when she comes."

Mr. Bowtie shrugged. "Whatever you want to do is fine with me. But I have to tell you that I don't think Mrs. Harms is coming to your house today."

Luke panged with mingled frustration and relief. "Why? Is she sick?"

"No." Mr. Bowtie dropped his feet to the floor and leaned forward on his desk. He began thumbing through a stack of papers and produced a crisp sheet, setting it face down in front of Mr. Tanner.

"I would have preferred this letter remain disclosed only to myself and one other person, but circumstances force me to expose it." He seemed distressed. "After your battle to win that girl, and the integrity you showed in honoring your agreement with Mrs. Harms, I'm disappointed in her for having failed you. However, I believe I know more about the outcome of this situation than you do."

Luke's brow creased with surprise.

Mr. Harris shook his balding head. Then he flipped the paper over and handed it to Luke. "I would appreciate it if the information you'll find in this letter didn't leave this room."

Luke took the paper and read silently.

My dear Tom,

Although I was quite surprised to learn of your dealings with the business I was conducting with Luke Tanner, I am relieved to hear the results of your counseling and time spent with him. I am also glad—though partly angry for the interference—to hear what you have learned about Ashley. I am disappointed to discover that I have been ignorant to many things.

I pray you will continue to attend to business with Ashley and Luke, as we agreed. I have given a signed adoption form to Jolie. Please assure that this makes it into Luke's hands.

I believe we kept our secret well in Galesburg. It was to the benefit of all. I will see you in Virginia, when you come visiting.

A loving farewell,

Sara

Luke looked up from the paper, stared at the preacher for a dumbfounded moment, then stuttered, "Harris, you . . . I . . . What does this mean?"

Mr. Bowtie laughed. "It means that you have yourself a fine new daughter."

Luke's heart skipped a beat. His eyes wildly searched the letter. "This is from Mrs. Harms?"

"Yes."

"But how . . ." Luke stopped and looked at the preacher suspiciously. "Why would she write you a letter about my business?"

The preacher sat back in his chair, whistling through his teeth. "Because I talked to her about you. We talked for three hours yesterday afternoon. She was piping angry when she left church and I barely made it to the orphanage to stop her before she came to your place."

"You stopped her from meeting with us?" Luke shook his head. His voice began rising with anger. "We waited all afternoon for her to come and you stopped her?"

"She was going to take Ashley away the second she set foot in your house."

"I had an explanation ready! And Ashley was going to tell her that she wanted to stay. I can't believe . . ."

Mr. Bowtie held up his hand and Luke stopped short. "You wouldn't have convinced her," he said quietly.

"How do you know? If you can talk about me for three hours with her, surely I could've taken a while to explain. What'd you tell her, anyway?"

"Luke, what are you afraid of?" The preacher's voice was firm. "I was out to help you."

Luke looked away. "I was prepared to help myself."

"No, you weren't. She wouldn't have listened to you."

"Why would she listen to you any better than me?" Luke shot his eyes toward him.

Mr. Bowtie scratched his head. He glanced at Luke and said seriously, "Because she's my sister."

Luke's mouth wanted to drop open but he forced it shut. "Your sister?" His voice quieted. He could hardly believe it. "Why on earth didn't you tell me that?"

"We had to keep our blood relationship private while we both lived in the same town, for the benefit of us and the community. Since the people of Galesburg are so against the orphanage, Sara thought they might ignore my preaching if they knew she was my sister."

"So you've hidden it all this time you've lived in Galesburg?"

Mr. Bowtie shrugged. "It hasn't been incredibly difficult. Sara was always busy with her orphans and I had the church."

Luke felt the anger drain from his face. He rubbed his forehead and looked at the preacher quietly. "So that's why you talked to her yesterday? Because you knew she'd listen to you better than me?"

"She didn't listen to me very well." Mr. Bowtie smiled. "It took all afternoon to convince her that her preconceived thoughts about you were false. Once she has her mind set on something, my sister very rarely changes it."

"But she did change it?"

"That's what the letter says."

Luke shook his head.

Silence came over the musty office and Luke's thoughts turned toward home. Excitement surged through his body and he felt his heartbeat quickening. He thought about Ashley and wondered what her response would be. Grace would probably hardly believe him when he announced the news.

Luke shifted in his chair and his stiff back ached. Suddenly, memories of the sleepless nights, intense frustration and painful suspense he and his family had gone through came back to him. He remembered Wesley's battle with trusting God the night before and the way Grace had exploded with frustration after the children were put to bed.

"Harris," he said slowly, "my family has gone through sheer agony with Ashley for months, and all the while you've had this critically important secret you've been keeping from everyone. Why didn't you talk to Mrs. Harms in the beginning? You could've saved us from everything."

"Aye, but I couldn't." Mr. Bowtie tapped his ring on the desk. "My sister is a woman I don't confront easily. She precedes me by eleven years and she doesn't usually listen to my wisdom. Do you think I would demand so much of you and put you through so much in our meetings if I thought there was an easier way?"

"I just don't understand why you waited so long. You say that you convinced her that what she thought about me wasn't true. Why on earth did you wait so long and let us go through so much before you stood up for me?"

"I was waiting until I was sure about you—certain that my opinion was correct. Until I was completely aware of Ashley's situation, it was impossible for me to approach Sara." Mr. Bowtie shrugged. "I was planning to keep my dealings with you completely private and let Sara discover your integrity on her own accord, but when it looked as if she wasn't going to let you keep Ashley, I had to tell her about what you and I have gone through. I knew she wouldn't understand why Ashley was upset in church yesterday, so I had to find out the truth from you, and then tell her." He leaned forward on his elbows. "You see, Tanner, I've spoken to my sister about the orphans only once in all her years of running the orphanage. My pulpit is the only means by which I keep track of her children—I watch them on Sundays. Occasionally, I hear a report on a special case, but never from Sara. She doesn't speak of my preaching, and I don't consult her on her orphans—except for once, and that was also in the case of Ashley."

"When?" Luke asked.

"When she was living with the Berks. I knew Sara had placed her with them so when I was teaching a one-day catechism study at a country school, I met Jack."

"You know Jack?"

"No. I only met him that once. He had a bruise on his face but when I questioned him about it, he wouldn't tell me anything. When he found out I was from Galesburg, he made me promise that I'd make sure no one hurt Ashley if he returned her to the orphanage. I only vaguely knew who Ashley was, but when she showed up on the orphanage doorstep late one night, I spoke to Sara. I told her not to go to the Berks's and question anyone and she swore she wouldn't. That's the only time I've ever spoken to my sister concerning the orphans. Until yesterday. You have to understand that it wasn't easy for me to approach her, but since my advice is rarely given, she didn't take it lightly. I can tell you one thing for certain: Without the counseling you and I have gone through, you wouldn't have that child in your house right now."

"Why?"

"Because I wouldn't have interfered with Sara's wisdom in the case of Ashley unless I had been convinced that you never abused her. I had to assure Sara that I trusted you completely, and that wasn't an easy task. I tried to tell her that you weren't abusive, but she wouldn't believe me until I told her how you and I have been meeting and that it was me who wrote the newspaper articles. You see, Sara noticed a change in Ashley when she came back from the Berks. Unfortunately, Elizabeth, Sara's right-hand employee, argued that Ashley wasn't any different than she was before she went to live with the Berks. When Sara saw Ashley responding to you in fear, she believed Elizabeth and decided the little girl's fear of you was because you were abusing her."

Luke thoughtfully nodded.

"You should have seen Sara." The preacher's eyes danced. "If she would've made it to your house yesterday, it would've been ugly. She wasn't going to let anyone change her mind."

"But you managed to?"

Mr. Bowtie's face became engulfed in a smile. "Well, I suppose the fact that she rode out of Galesburg on the morning train is a pretty good sign."

"She's gone?" Luke's eyes bulged.

"I took her to the station myself. She moved to Virginia."

"That's it? She's gone, just like that, without saying goodbye or discussing anything?"

"What more is there to discuss?" Mr. Bowtie laughed loudly. "I spent half my day yesterday discussing everything from your marriage to your job to your beliefs in child rearing. Sara couldn't have had a single question to ask you. She said that Ashley was begging her to let her go back with you long before she got sick and you came to the orphanage. She didn't need to hear Ashley's report."

Luke's brows rose. He sat for a quiet moment, scanning over the letter again. He looked at the preacher. "It's unreal. I never would've imagined that Mrs. Harms would leave town with her business unsettled."

"Unsettled, 'ey?" The preacher smiled. "Mr. Tanner, my sister was committed to the orphans because they were her husband's passion before he died twelve years ago. She loved them as much as any person could love a job, but her main goal was only to find them good homes and have the opportunity to retire. I did my job of convincing her that you have a good home for Ashley, and she was happy to do her part in pursuing retirement in Virginia. Besides that, Jolie will be related to Ashley and Sara has been pleased with that arrangement from the beginning."

"I just can hardly believe it." Luke found himself smiling.

"Jolie should be delivering an adoption form to your house any minute," the preacher said.

Luke felt a load of relief fall off his shoulders. He could hardly sit still. "You think we could postpone this morning's meeting? I want to get home with the good news."

Mr. Bowtie stood, waving his hand toward the door. "Absolutely! Go home! Spread the news! Rejoice for the day, and come back and tell me all about it tomorrow."

He shook Luke's hand heartily and threw his coat at him, laughing.

When Luke entered his house through the back door, he heard voices in the kitchen. Pots clanked and Cherish giggled and Ashley and Wes were chatting quietly. The moment his boots pounded into the kitchen, Wes turned from where he dried the dishes his sister washed.

"Oh, Dad!" Wes exclaimed. He threw his towel onto the counter and disappeared into the dining room, returning with an envelope in his hand. "Aunt Jolie was here and she left a letter."

Luke's heart skipped a beat. "Did you read it?" He glanced at Grace.

"No." Grace moved a pot from the stove to the counter. "I wanted to wait for you. Jolie came just a couple minutes after you left and stayed for over an hour, waiting for you to come. Finally, she left the letter and said she'd come back for supper tonight. I couldn't squeak a word out of her."

"That's strange." Luke tried to hide his smile as he took the envelope from Wes and slowly broke the seal.

"What does it say?" Grace asked.

Luke felt his hands trembling as he glanced at Mrs. Harms's signature at the bottom of an adoption form. He dropped the paper onto the counter and swung Cherish from the floor, kissing her before glancing between Wes and Ashley. "It's an adoption form from Mrs. Harms saying that Ashley is officially a Tanner."

Ashley's hands dripped on the counter when she pulled them out of the dishwater. She stared for a silent moment before whispering, "I'm adopted?"

Luke nodded.

Wes hollered and threw his towel in the air. He jumped up and down, shrieking, "We did it! It's for real!"

"But how?" Grace said quickly.

"Mr. Bowtie actually told me this morning," Luke said. "It's a long story; I'll tell you later."

Ashley smiled at her brother, then sidled close to her mother. "Did you hear that, Mama?" she asked, pressing her face against the woman's apron.

"I heard, Ashley," Grace whispered with tears in her eyes. She kissed Ashley's head.

Wes crossed the room and swung Cherish from his father's arms, bouncing across the kitchen floor. "This means you'll never have to go back to the orphanage, Ashley. It's honest to goodness the real thing."

Ashley glanced at Luke and her smile was almost too big for her face.

Luke squatted down in front of her, resting his forearms on his knees. "I'm glad we finally have our little girl," he said, touching her arm. He went to stand again, but Ashley caught his hand, and her little palm disappeared in his grip. She squeezed it once and then tucked her head into her shoulder and leaned against her mother again, giving him a bashful smile.

When Luke stood, something on the cupboard door caught his attention. He stared at a white sheet of paper hanging beside the stove. A young hand had written words above a colorful drawing. They said, "Ashley and Daddy."

Luke felt tears fill his eyes. It was a drawing of a man in a rocking chair holding a little girl.

WP